CAPPED

Making A Billion Was Your First Mistake

A Novel

by Susan Trott

Tagger Press

DEDICATION

In 2025, when this story was conceived, there were over 3,000 individuals on this planet with a personal value in excess of $1,000,000,000.

Some say the accumulation of wealth so significantly beyond anything they can humanly use, is an obsession, like hoarding.

Certainly, as it is said in the story, if you had $1B and spent $500,000 every year of your life, you would have enough money for 2,000 years. Think about that.

Who really needs that kind of money?

So this story is dedicated to all the people who believe they need $1B.

You may not get the happy ending you're counting on.

COPYRIGHT

CHAPTER 1

CONGRATULATIONS MR. KADE

The notification woke him before the alarm.

Kyrel blinked into the half-dark of his bedroom, the pale blue glow from the smartglass window painting the ceiling in lines of dawn. Atlanta's early traffic hummed faintly beyond the double-pane, delivery vans, buses, someone's music thudding under the soundscape. Beside him, D'Andra's side of the bed was already empty. She'd left before five for a complicated case, kissing his forehead on the way out. He remembered that much.

What he didn't remember was setting the implant to priority alerts.

The inside of his left wrist tingled with the steady, insistent buzz of a flagged message. Not the soft pulse of a calendar ping or social feed. This was deeper, a bone-level vibration he'd only felt a handful of times in his life.

He lifted his arm, palm toward his face. The subdermal LinkLife chip, his chip, his invention, warmed in response, projecting a private display only he could see. A single line of text floated in the air above his wrist, crisp and white.

FEDERAL NOTICE: LIFETIME EARNINGS THRESHOLD REACHED

Tap for details.

He frowned, still halfway in fog. The words didn't fit any mental box in his mind. Lifetime earnings threshold.

"System, repeat last notification," he mumbled.

The apartment's soft-voiced AI dutifully obliged, piping it through the bedroom speakers.

"Federal Notice: Lifetime Earnings Threshold Reached. Tap for details."

He sat up slowly.

For a second, he thought tax audit. Maybe some weird new IRS pilot program, or a glitch in the DEI's wealth-tracking algorithms. There were always bugs the first year of a rollout. Madeline Vyre, Valiant's primary compliance counsel, complained about them every quarterly review.

But this didn't look like a bug.

The header at the top of the projection carried the gold-and-slate seal of the Department of Economic Integrity. The same symbol they printed in the background of every Cap Act PSA: a circle with a horizontal bar through it.

The Cap.

"Open," he said, throat dry.

The message expanded, lines of text stacking neatly in front of him.

FROM:	Department of Economic Integrity
TO:	Kade, Kyrel Emmanuel – SSN ending 2049
SUBJECT:	Confirmation of Lifetime Earnings Cap Status

Dear Mr. Kade,

Congratulations. Our records confirm that as of 02:14 EST this morning, your verified lifetime earnings have surpassed $1,000,000,000.00 (one billion US dollars), as defined by the Wealth Equity and Lifetime Earnings Limitation Act ("The Cap Act").

In accordance with Section 3(a) of the Act, you are now designated as Completed.

The following automatic changes have been initiated...

His eyes skimmed down, pulse thudding louder in his ears.

– All active income-generating accounts linked to your SSN are temporarily suspended pending divestment.

– All outstanding equity holdings, including but not limited to: Valiant Systems, *LinkLife* Technologies, and affiliates, are scheduled for mandatory liquidation within 72 hours.

— Proceeds up to $1,000,000,000.00 will be deposited into your designated Lifetime Trust Account at Federal Equity Bank (non-interest-bearing).
— Any proceeds in excess of $1,000,000,000.00 will be transferred to the Public Equity Trust for allocation to approved charitable initiatives.
— Effective immediately, you are prohibited from:

- entering any contract that may result in financial gain
- accepting wages, salary, tips, commissions, or royalties
- acquiring equity, stocks, bonds, derivatives, or digital assets
- acting as owner, partner, director, or executive of any for-profit entity
- applying for or accepting loans or lines of credit

Your current Completed balance is: $1,000,000,000.00

A DEI representative will visit your residence today at 09:00 EST to review your new fiscal rights and obligations and to answer any questions. Attendance is mandatory.

Once again, congratulations on reaching this significant milestone. Your success is a testament to your talent, perseverance, and contribution to our shared economy.

Respectfully,
Thomas J. Weller

Senior Compliance Officer, Department of
Economic Integrity

The message ended with a simple, incongruously cheerful button:

LEARN MORE ABOUT YOUR COMPLETED
STATUS →

Kyrel stared at the figure for a long time, the zeros blurring
together.

A billion.

He'd joked about it. He'd sat in dorm lounges and maker-spaces
while classmates argued loudly about the Cap Act, about socialism,
about tyranny, about fairness. He'd listened quietly while people
said things like, "If I ever hit a billion, Auntie Sam can take the rest,
I'll be on a beach forever," and thought: A billion is not my
problem. My problem is rent.

Even in the last year, as LinkLife saturated the world and the
numbers grew more abstract, the cap had stayed somewhere out on
the horizon. A line on a distant graph.

He checked the timestamp again.

02:14.

He'd been asleep.

The economy had decided he was finished while he was drooling on
his pillow.

"System," he said slowly, "show me current lifetime earnings breakdown."

There was a short pause. Then his personal financial HUD rolled into view, something he'd coded himself before Valiant had an accounting department. It aggregated every source: salary, dividends, stock sales, speaking fees, book royalties, early consulting, even the crappy phone repair shop he'd worked in at Georgia Tech.

At the top, in bold:

Total Verified Earnings (lifetime): $1,200,468,901.72

The number hit him harder than the billion.

He had been tracking, obsessively, for months. Watching the run-up to the IPO, the license deals, the international expansion. Watching Valiant's valuation yo-yo, but always with a mental buffer:

> You're safe. You're under. You're at eight hundred-something. You have time.

He flicked his eyes down to the detailed log. The last entry, flagged with the DEI seal, read:

> 02:14 EST – Automatic exercise of performance warrants – Valiant Systems Class A.
> + $222,637,514.09

He hadn't authorized that. There hadn't been any vote. Warrants like that were supposed to be scheduled, negotiated, fought over in boardrooms.

"System, source of last transaction," he said.

A hyperlink blinked underneath the line.

> Initiated by: Board Compensation Committee
> Executed by: GlobalTrust Securities (auto-trigger)
> Basis: Pre-approved performance warrant package, activated when Valiant Systems crossed market cap threshold of $450B.

He swore under his breath.

Rhett had been pushing for months to "stop being precious" about the board comp triggers. "If we hit those targets, man, we deserve to cash in. The law's the law, but we can dance on the line."

Looks like someone had danced hard.

A hollow feeling opened up under his ribs.

"System," he whispered, "where should my total be without that last transaction?"

Numbers flickered, recalculated.

> Projected Total Without Warrant Exercise:
> $977,831,387.63

His throat went dry.

He'd been under. Safe. Barely, but enough.

Someone, or some combination of someones, had decided to bundle the warrants and push them through anyway, kicking him cleanly over the edge.

The Cap Act didn't care whether you had spent the money, or even wanted it.

It only cared that you'd earned it.

He sat very still, letting the information settle like silt.

Completed.

Life over at twenty-five. Economically, anyway.

Outside the window, a MARTA train rattled by on elevated tracks, the faint shimmer of its advertising wrap catching the morning light. He thought absurdly of the small boy he'd been on those trains, forehead pressed to the glass, watching downtown towers slide by and thinking, One day, I'll work in one of those buildings.

Not: One day I'll be capped out of them.

The wrist-tingle shifted, a new notification sliding in.

> REMINDER: DEI Representative Arrival – 09:00 EST
> Location: Home Residence
> Attire: Business casual acceptable.
> Note: Non-compliance is a federal offense.

He checked the time. 07:11.

Enough time to shower, put on a clean shirt, maybe call Rhett, call Madeline, call… somebody.

His LinkLife display flashed another small icon in the corner, media alerts piling up. He hesitated, then blinked it open.

TRENDING: LinkLife FOUNDER OFFICIALLY COMPLETED AT 25

"From East Atlanta to the Earnings Ceiling: The Kyrel Kade Story" – morning segments scheduled on four networks.

#CompletedAt25
#CapAct
#BillionaireGame

They knew already.

Of course they did. The DEI's systems talked to the markets, and the markets talked to the newsfeeds. Somebody had leaked the alert or built an AI crawler to sniff them out. There were probably cameras warming up on the sidewalk already.

He closed the feeds before the first pundit could say his name.

For a long moment he sat there on the edge of the bed, bare feet on the scuffed plank floor, wrist display hovering in the air like a ghost of everything he'd built.

He tried on a few sentences in his head, stupidly:

It's fine, you knew this might happen.
It's enough. A billion is more than enough. You're set.

You can still make a difference without money.

None of them fit.

He got up, showered, shaved. Put on dark jeans, a white button-down, the navy blazer his mother liked because it made him look "respectable on TV." By the time he stepped into the small kitchen, the sun was pushing a weak strip of light across the counter, glancing off the stainless-steel kettle D'Andra had found at a thrift store.

A note waited under a magnet on the fridge, scrawled in her looping handwriting:

> 4:45 – long case this morning – might be late
> Love you. Don't forget to eat.
> – D

He stared at the word case for a second too long. She didn't know yet. She'd turn on a hospital TV in the staff lounge between surgeries and see some over-coiffed anchor telling the world about her husband's "milestone."

He poured coffee he didn't want and drank half of it anyway.

At 08:52, the apartment's front-facing camera chimed.

"External motion detected," the system said. "One vehicle. Three individuals."

"Show me," he said.

The wall screen blinked from a nature screensaver to the view from the small camera over the front door. A dark, nondescript sedan idled at the curb. Two people stepped out: a woman in a slate-gray skirt suit, tablet in hand; a man in a darker suit with that government-straight spine and an expression like a locked filing cabinet. Behind them, another man stayed in the car, eyes scanning the street.

As the pair approached his front walk, Kyrel caught a flash of the pin on the man's lapel. A small metal circle, split by a horizontal bar.

The Cap, gleaming in the pale morning light.

"Front door," he said. "Unlock."

The bolt clicked just as they reached the porch.

He opened the door before they could knock.

"Mr. Kade?" the man said.

He was shorter than Kyrel by an inch or two, mid-forties maybe, with close-cropped sandy hair and the kind of face you forgot as soon as you looked away. His voice was perfectly neutral. Not warm. Not cold.

"Yes," Kyrel said.

The man extended a hand. His grip was dry, precise, exactly two seconds long.

"Thomas Weller," he said. "Department of Economic Integrity. This is Ms. Han, administrative liaison."

The woman nodded and offered a quick, professional smile. "Thank you for seeing us, Mr. Kade."

"Did I have a choice?" he asked, before he could stop himself.

Weller's mouth twitched in something that might, in a different world, have been humor.

"Not legally, no," he said. "May we come in?"

Kyrel stepped back and let them enter. Ms. Han's eyes flicked briefly over the space: the narrow hallway, the worn runner rug, the framed photo of his parents and siblings at his Georgia Tech graduation. Weller seemed to see none of it. He moved as though every house he visited existed only as a temporary container for a table and chairs.

"Kitchen's through here," Kyrel said. "We can sit at the table."

"Perfect," Weller said.

By the time they reached the small four-seat table by the window, Ms. Han had already placed a sleek, matte-black folio on the surface and opened it. Inside were printed documents, actual paper, which somehow felt more serious than any digital form.

Weller took the head of the table without asking, setting a small, government-issue tablet beside the folio. Ms. Han sat to his right. Kyrel took the chair opposite, the sunlight landing in a bright rectangle across his hands.

For a moment, no one spoke. The faint hum of the fridge filled the silence.

"First," Weller said, folding his hands, "allow me to officially congratulate you, Mr. Kade."

Kyrel watched him, waiting for a trace of sarcasm.

None came.

"You have achieved what a vanishingly small fraction of citizens ever will," Weller continued. "The Cap Act was designed with the understanding that such success is… profoundly rare. You have joined a very small cohort of Completed Individuals. Your contributions to the economy are, in a sense, exemplary."

"That is why you froze my life at two in the morning?" Kyrel asked.

Ms. Han shifted faintly. Weller didn't.

"The timing is automated," he said. "The moment your verified earnings cross the threshold, the system responds. It's not personal."

Weller tapped the tablet. His gaze unfocused briefly, reading something only he could see via his own implant.

"As of 02:14 this morning, your lifetime earnings totaled one billion, two hundred million, four hundred sixty-eight thousand, nine hundred one dollars and seventy-two cents," he recited, as though reading a weather report. "Pursuant to Section 3(a), your status is now Completed. Our purpose here today is to ensure you understand what that entails and to answer any questions you may have."

He nodded to Ms. Han.

She slid a stapled packet across the table toward Kyrel. The title on the cover, in clean federal type, read:

YOUR NEW FISCAL LIFE: A GUIDE FOR
COMPLETED-CITIZENS

He stared at it.

"This is real," he said quietly. "You're not here to tell me there's been a mistake."

"No, sir," Weller said. "It's quite real."

Kyrel flipped the packet open.

Page one: an overview of rights and restrictions. Page two: an explanation of the Lifetime Trust Account. Page three: prohibited activities, enumerated in careful bullets. The words blurred halfway down the list.

"No wages, no consulting, no equity, no interest," he said. "No loans, no credit, no… anything."

"You retain full access to your existing funds up to the cap," Weller said. "You may spend that money as you see fit, within standard legal constraints. You may own property, personal vehicles, personal belongings. You may travel, donate, volunteer, and participate in civic life. You simply cannot generate additional income."

"And the extra two hundred million?" Kyrel asked. "That I didn't authorize?"

Weller blinked once. "All proceeds beyond the cap are redirected to the Public Equity Trust," he said. "That transfer has already been initiated."

"So someone pushes an auto-trigger at GlobalTrust in the middle of the night," Kyrel said slowly, "and you get an extra two hundred million to sprinkle over the charities of your choice. That about right?"

"Allocation is determined by an independent committee," Weller said. "I don't have authority over distribution."

"That wasn't the point," Kyrel muttered.

He set the packet down, resisting the urge to tear it in half.

"What about my family?" he asked.

"Immediate household members cannot legally earn income while residing with you," Weller said. "Children, spouse, dependents. That provision exists to prevent laundering and circumvention."

"So my wife loses her salary because she married me."

"She retains her credentials," Weller said. "She may provide services on a volunteer basis. Many spouses of Completed Individuals choose to direct their efforts toward pro bono work."

"You make it sound like a lifestyle brand," Kyrel said.

"This system ensures that the benefits of enormous success do not concentrate indefinitely," Weller said. "It keeps the game fair."

There it was, the phrase he'd heard pundits use a hundred times. The game. As if eating, housing, and caring for people were a kind of playoff bracket.

Kyrel flexed his fingers once, then forced them to relax.

"What happens if I try?" he asked. "Hypothetically. If I accept a consulting fee. Sign onto a startup. Put my name on some kid's cap table. What do you do?"

Weller's tone didn't change.

"First offense," he said. "Administrative penalty, seizure of illicit earnings, formal warning. Second offense, criminal charges. If patterns suggest deliberate evasion or conspiracy, we refer the case to federal prosecutors. Some Completed Individuals are currently serving custodial sentences."

"Prison," Kyrel said.

"Yes," said Weller.

He studied Weller's face, looking for any sign of discomfort. There was none. Only a kind of patient certainty.

"You believe in this law," Kyrel said.

Weller held his gaze. "I do."

"You think no one should ever have more than a billion dollars."

"I think," Weller said, "that no one should control more wealth than they can responsibly steward. The cap is generous. It provides for lifetimes of comfort, even extravagance. Beyond that, accumulation tends to distort the system. You know this as well as anyone, Mr. Kade."

The annoying part was that, on some level, Kyrel did agree. He'd read the papers, watched the hearings. He'd seen what the pre-cap billionaires had done to politics, to housing, to entire countries.

He'd just never planned to be the example in the brochure.

"What about my company?" he asked. "Valiant. LinkLife. I founded it. I built the tech. Do I get any say in what happens to them now?"

"Your equity holdings are being liquidated as we speak," Weller said. "Control will transfer to remaining shareholders, boards, and market forces. The law does not allow Completed Individuals to retain ownership stakes."

"So I lose my life's work and get a pamphlet," Kyrel said.

"You receive a billion dollars," Weller said. "And the freedom to live without the burden of further accumulation."

Kyrel laughed then, a short, sharp sound that made Ms. Han flinch.

"Right," he said. "Freedom."

A faint buzz at his wrist told him his implant had caught the spike in his heart rate and was considering whether to suggest a breathing exercise. He dismissed it.

Outside, a car slowed in front of the house. A second later, another notification hovered at the edge of his vision.

WNN LIVE: "KYREL KADE OFFICIALLY CAPPED –
WHAT IT MEANS FOR LinkLife"

He clenched his jaw.

"Mr. Kade," Weller said gently, as if aware of the drifting attention,
"I understand this is… disorienting. Many Completed citizens report
a sense of loss at first. Identity restructuring, as the psychologists
put it."

"You make it sound like a midlife crisis," Kyrel said. "I'm
twenty-five."

"That is… earlier than most," Weller admitted. "But the principles
remain consistent."

He slid another document out of the folio and turned it toward
Kyrel. It was a printed summary of his Lifetime Trust Account,
already initialized.

    LIFETIME BALANCE: $1,000,000,000.00
    INTEREST RATE: 0.00%
    INSTITUTION: FEDERAL EQUITY BANK
    AUTHORIZED ACCESS: Kade, Kyrel Emmanuel

"This is yours," Weller said. "Untouchable by creditors, immune
from market volatility. No one can take it from you, not even the
government. That is the trade you have made, whether consciously
or not. You are done with the earning side of life. Now you get to
focus on how you wish to live it."

Kyrel stared at the neat black digits.

A billion dollars.

If he spent half a million a year, Madeline had once joked, he could live two thousand years. He wasn't sure he'd make it through this week.

He swallowed.

"I have a question," he said.

"Of course," Weller replied.

"Who authorized the warrant trigger," Kyrel asked, "that pushed me over?"

For the first time, Weller hesitated.

"That level of detail is outside the scope of my access," he said carefully. "If you wish to contest specific transactions, you may file a petition with our audit board. However, the designation itself is not reversible. Once Completed, always Completed."

"So even if someone gamed the system," Kyrel said, "I stay in the cage."

"The law cannot account for every interpersonal dynamic," Weller said. "It can only apply the rules consistently."

On the street, a small cluster of people had begun to gather on the sidewalk opposite his house. Neighbors, maybe, or early risers drawn by the sedan, the half-visible camera crews down the block. One of them lifted a phone to snap a picture of the unremarkable front door

where "the youngest Completed in history" now sat being told his
life was over, politely.

The game.

He'd told himself he believed in the cap. In theory. That it was a
necessary brake on madness. That nobody needed more than enough
to live comfortably for five thousand years.

It was easier to believe in brakes when you weren't the one being
thrown through them.

"Is there anything else you'd like to ask right now?" Weller said.
"We'll leave written material, and Ms. Han will be your point of
contact for future administrative questions."

Kyrel looked down at the packet again. Your New Fiscal Life.

He thought of his father, Darrin, coming home with aching knees
from a twelve-hour maintenance shift and still fixing broken lamps
for neighbors. Of his mother, Ellen, falling asleep at the kitchen
table over their bills. Of his little sister Kaiya, text-bombing him
last year with jokes about, "don't you dare get capped before you
pay off my student loans, big bro, I swear to God."

He thought of Rhett, laughing at a whiteboard scribbled with Cap
Act provisions: "We'll back right off at nine hundred ninety-nine
million nine hundred ninety-nine thousand, okay? Leave a little air
gap. It'll be fine."

"Just one," he said softly.

Weller waited.

Kyrel tapped the packet with his index finger.

"How did I earn the last two hundred million," he asked, "if I never approved the trigger?"

Weller's jaw tightened almost imperceptibly.

"As I said," he replied, "those details would be best directed to our audit board. Or to your company's compensation committee."

"Right," Kyrel said. "My company."

He sat back, suddenly very calm.

Outside, a news van pulled up, the logo bright on its side. A camera operator stepped out, shouldering gear. On his wrist display, another headline rolled up:

"CAP ACT CLAIMS TECH PRODIGY – IS THE LAW KILLING INNOVATION?"

Weller followed his glance toward the window. His expression remained unreadable.

"We can arrange for you to exit through a side entrance," he said. "If the presence of media is distressing."

"It's my house," Kyrel said. "They'll get their shot either way."

For a moment, the three of them sat in a small island of silence while the outside world aligned its lenses.

"Mr. Kade," Weller said at last, his tone almost gentle, "I know this feels like an ending."

Kyrel looked up at him.

"It is an ending," he said.

Weller inclined his head, conceding the point.

"Perhaps," he said. "But endings and beginnings often share a doorway."

He rose, gathering the folio. Ms. Han closed her tablet with a soft click.

"Please read the packet thoroughly," Weller said. "Ms. Han will follow up this afternoon with your Lifetime Trust access credentials and a schedule for mandatory financial counseling. If you have questions about permitted uses of your funds, your assigned advisor at Federal Equity Bank will assist you."

He slid a small, embossed card across the table. It bore his name, title, and a bland, toll-free number.

"If any irregularities arise, in your accounts or in your activities, I will be notified."

"Of course you will," Kyrel said.

Weller nodded once more.

"Congratulations again, Mr. Kade," he said.

The word landed differently this time. He wasn't sure if he heard a faint thread of something under it, envy, maybe, or fatigue, or if he was just projecting.

Then they were gone, their footsteps receding down the hall, the door closing softly behind them. The car engine outside purred, then stayed idling.

Kyrel sat alone at the kitchen table with a billion dollars on paper, a packet of rules, and the echo of a life shutting down around him.

His wrist buzzed one more time, insistent.

He lifted his arm.

INCOMING CALL: RHETT COLBURN

He stared at the name, the small looping R logo he and Rhett had joked about in their dorm room a lifetime ago.

He didn't know yet that this call would matter more than any term sheet he'd ever signed.

He just knew his heart rate jumped ten beats and his hands felt suddenly cold.

"Answer," he said.

The call connected.

CHAPTER 2

SIX YEARS EARLIER

Georgia Tech never slept.

At least, not the parts Kyrel loved.

The Invention Studio, six thousand square feet of humming 3D printers, solder fumes, laser cutters, scattered tools, and half-finished prototypes, was technically supposed to close at midnight. Technically. In practice, the student managers locked the doors, dimmed the overheads, and looked the other way if a few geniuses and insomniacs wanted to court the muse until dawn.

Tonight, the air smelled like melted filament and burnt coffee, which meant midterms were close.

Kyrel Kade sat cross-legged on the concrete floor, laptop open, circuit boards spread around him like the guts of a tiny mechanical animal. The soft whir of a resin printer pulsed nearby. A half-eaten bag of vending machine pretzels rested beside his knee.

His T-shirt read MAYBE I'M DEBUGGING YOU, which was approximately true.

"Come on, come on," he muttered, soldering iron balanced lightly in his fingertips. "Stop being dramatic and work."

The microcontroller board in front of him spat out another angry red blink. Incorrect signal mapping. Again.

"You're supposed to recognize the muscle input," he grumbled. "Not have an existential crisis."

Kyrel wiped his forehead on the back of his wrist, smearing a faint line of solder dust.

Around him, the Studio thrummed in its usual chaos, three robotics teams arguing over servo torque curves, someone calibrating a drone that kept veering left like a drunk pigeon, a girl with pink braids testing a prosthetic hand that could finally grip a cup without crushing it.

It was the kind of chaos that made him feel calm.

Just like in high school, he'd sit in the common area studying while life surged around him—students walking, laughing, arguing about nothing, drifting between classes. The background noise sharpened his focus. Silence never had.

He'd never been able to afford distractions. Getting to Georgia Tech had required every ounce of effort he had. His family's small house in their Atlanta suburb held six people and one shared computer. As the eldest of four, he'd grown up knowing college wasn't something his parents could pay for, no matter how hard they worked.

So he worked harder.

Scholarships, competitions, summer programs—anything that pushed him forward. He'd always been the kid taking things apart, building things no one asked for, testing ideas his parents didn't entirely understand but proudly encouraged. They believed he would make something of himself.

He believed it too. He just hadn't realized how high the cost would be.

"Please tell me you've eaten something that isn't salt in the last twelve hours." The voice came from directly behind him, bright, amused, and unfamiliar.

Kyrel turned.

A blond guy in a Georgia Tech hoodie stood over him holding two cans of caffeine-laced something, like a benevolent frat god of energy drinks.

He had that effortless, comfortable posture of someone raised in nice neighborhoods where sidewalks didn't crack and lawns got professionally edged every Saturday. His face wasn't smug, exactly, just open. Warm. A little too confident in that easy Southern way.

This was Rhett Colburn. Though Kyrel didn't know the name yet. Kyrel blinked at him.

"Did I order a health inspector and forget about it?" he asked.

Rhett laughed, quick, bright, a little loud. "You look like you've been held hostage by a motherboard. Here." He tossed one of the cans. Kyrel caught it with a reflex he didn't know he had anymore.

"I didn't ask for this," Kyrel said.

"I know," Rhett said. "But I've been watching you fight with that thing for an hour, and I figure either you're exhausted or that board has personal beef with your entire bloodline."

Kyrel looked back at the blinking red LED. "It's the second one."

"Mind if I sit?"

Kyrel shrugged.

Rhett dropped onto the floor across from him with the grace of someone who'd been on many, many tennis courts, crossed his long legs, and cracked open his drink.

"So," Rhett said, nodding at the scattered components, "tell me what you're making."

"I'm not making anything," Kyrel said. "I'm trying to get something to work, which is different."

"Fair. What's it supposed to do?"

Kyrel hesitated. He didn't like talking about projects unless they worked. But the board was fried enough that shame didn't matter anymore.

"It's a wearable muscle interface," he said. "Part of a larger idea. Detects micro-voltage patterns in forearm muscles and maps them to authentication signals. Like… instead of typing passwords."

Rhett's eyebrows rose. "So your arm unlocks stuff?"

"If it worked, yeah."

Rhett grinned like he'd just been handed the keys to the Batmobile.

"That's sick."

"It's just signal validation," Kyrel said, uncomfortable under praise. "Biometric patterns are more unique than fingerprints. Harder to fake. But the controller's not cooperating."

"Can I see?"

Normally Kyrel would have said no. But something about the guy, his openness, his lack of pretense, made refusal feel weird.

He handed Rhett the board.

"You built this from scratch?" Rhett asked.

Kyrel nodded.

Rhett whistled softly. "Dude. I thought I was decent at hardware. I'm— Wow. No wonder you look like you haven't moved in hours."

"I haven't," Kyrel admitted.

Rhett set the board down carefully.

"I'm Rhett, by the way. Colburn."

Kyrel raised an eyebrow. "Should I know that name?"

Rhett's grin flickered. "God, I hope not. My dad works for Lockheed. Mom sells houses. Nothing glamorous."

"Oh," Kyrel said. "Engineering legacy kid."

Rhett winced. "Guilty as charged. But I promise I'm not one of the ones who treats their internships like hereditary titles."

Kyrel snorted before he could stop himself. "I'm Kyrel."

"Cool. What year?"

"Freshman. You?"

"Same. Business/CS hybrid. I'm the guy who pretends to code in group projects but is actually keeping the investors happy."

Kyrel frowned. "You have investors?"

"I like pitching," Rhett said. "Always have. I was the kid selling lemonade but also running A/B tests. It's a disease."

Kyrel wasn't sure if that was supposed to be charming or horrifying. He decided on charming.

"So," Rhett said, tapping the board, "you want help?"

Kyrel laughed. "With the embedded controller? No offense, man, but unless you're a microelectronics ninja—"

"I meant in general," Rhett interrupted. "I'm putting together a hackathon team for the Atlanta Open next month. We need a hardware person. And you're... clearly possessed by the right spirits."

Kyrel blinked. "You want me on your hackathon team?"

"Yeah," Rhett said. "Why? You busy inventing the future?"

A flush crept up Kyrel's neck.

He didn't have the words for it yet, but something in Rhett's tone told him the guy wasn't mocking him.

He believed it.

"I mean," Kyrel said, "I guess I could—"

"Great," Rhett said, springing up and clapping his hands once. "Consider yourself conscripted. Team name pending. I'm thinking something like Circuit Saints, but that may be the caffeine talking."

Kyrel shook his head. "That's terrible."

"Perfect," Rhett said. "You're already contributing. Let's get food. My treat."

"Your treat Why?"

"Because," Rhett said, beaming, "I know talent when I see it."

Kyrel groaned, but stood anyway.

As they walked out of the Studio, the failure board blinked sadly behind him, and for a moment Kyrel felt an unfamiliar fizz in his ribs.

Not excitement, exactly.

More like… inevitability.

Like the air had shifted.

CHAPTER 3

SPARK

The Invention Studio always felt different after midnight. The noise softened. The energy sharpened. The people who stayed weren't there for grades or credit, they were there because something inside them refused to stop.

Kyrel was exactly that kind of person.

Tonight, he and Rhett had taken over the back corner table, the one closest to the emergency power outlets and farthest from the vending machines. Rhett said it made them look "mysterious and productive." Kyrel suspected it just kept them from being asked to share their surge protectors.

The table was a chaos altar of wires, solder reels, empty cans, and circuit boards. Rhett's laptop was plastered with stickers: ATL Tech, HackSouth, Move Fast & Don't Break Things (LOL), Ask Me About My Prototype.

Kyrel's laptop was bare. It felt wrong to clutter a workspace.

"Okay," Rhett said, stretching so far his hoodie rode up an inch. "Explain it again. Slowly. For those of us who were not born understanding electromagnetism."

Kyrel rubbed his eyes. "It's not that complicated."

"Buddy," Rhett said gently, "I once misunderstood Ohm's Law so badly my lab instructor sent me outside to 'reconsider my choices'. Pretend I'm a golden retriever with a minor in business."

Kyrel sighed, then couldn't help the faint smile.

"Fine. The idea is, everyone uses biometric authentication, right? Fingerprints. Retina scans. Face unlock. But those can all be spoofed. Copied. Printed. Recreated."

Rhett nodded. "Right. Creepy."

"So I'm thinking… What if your identity isn't something a camera sees? What if it's something your body does? Something you can't fake, and can't force?"

He tapped the small sensor array attached to a thin flexible cuff.

"Micro-voltage patterns," he said. "Your forearm muscles make unique electrical signatures when you move, even tiny movements. Involuntary ones. They're different for everyone. Even identical twins don't match."

Rhett leaned in, brows furrowed. "So this thing records… like, your muscle fingerprint?"

"Sort of. It records your neuromuscular identity. The way your nerves talk to your muscles. It's impossible to copy."

Rhett looked up at him with the slow, dawning expression he got when he saw a business model forming in real time.

"Ky," he said softly. "You realize what you're building, right?"

Kyrel shrugged. "It's just an idea."

"No," Rhett said. "This is— dude! This is security. Banking. Payment systems. Access control. Medical environments. Secure voting. Identity verification. Even cars could—"

Kyrel groaned. "Please don't make it into marketing yet."

"Too late," Rhett said, typing furiously. "I've already named it."

Kyrel froze. "What?"

Rhett spun the laptop toward him.

Two words sat on a pristine mockup slide:

> LinkLife.
> Your identity, seamlessly linked.

Kyrel stared.

"That's stupid," he said.

"Thank you," Rhett said. "It's perfect, then."

Kyrel rolled his eyes, but something warm fluttered in his chest. "You're ridiculous."

"And you're brilliant." Rhett leaned back. "This could be a real company one day. We could run it together."

Kyrel's throat tightened, but he didn't answer. He didn't trust his voice.

Instead, he adjusted the cuff on his wrist, checking the electrode alignment. Tiny gold pads gleamed against his skin.

"Alright," he said. "Moment of truth."

"Oh, hell yes," Rhett whispered. "Do it."

Kyrel took a breath. Then another.

"Controller armed," he murmured. "Signal baseline set." He flexed his fingers.

The LED flickered.

He flexed again.

Nothing.

He tried a different pattern, closing his hand as though gripping a small ball.

The LED blinked red. [Error].

Kyrel slumped. "Still not mapping properly."

Rhett opened his mouth, probably to reassure him, or crack a joke, but Kyrel wasn't ready to hear either.

He adjusted the electrode sensitivity. Shifted the sampling rate. Rewired one connection.

"Just one clean signal," he whispered.

"One," Rhett agreed quietly.

Kyrel flexed his hand again. And everything went wrong. A spark snapped from the controller. The power supply surged. A puff of blue smoke curled upward.

Rhett yelped and jumped back. "Dude! Did it explode?!"

Kyrel coughed, waving the smoke. "No. No. No. No! No, it just burned out a sensor. Damn it."

He peeled the cuff off with shaking fingers, disappointed in a way that hurt deeper than embarrassment.

"It's okay," Rhett said. "We'll rebuild—"

But Kyrel froze.

He was still wearing the cuff.

The controller board was fried.

But his phone, sitting ten inches away, had unlocked itself.

The screen glowed quietly in the dark, waiting for input.

Kyrel didn't breathe.

"Um," Rhett whispered. "Ky?"

Kyrel slowly moved his hand away. The phone locked. He moved it closer, his fingers twitching involuntarily. The phone unlocked.

Neither of them spoke for a long, breathless moment.

Rhett finally exhaled, voice cracking: "Bro,... did you just unlock your phone... with your nerves?"

Kyrel stared at his own hand like it wasn't his. The hair on his arms lifted. The air felt electric. He swallowed.

"No," he said softly. "It unlocked itself with me."

Rhett's eyes went huge. "Kyrel. Holy—holy—do you understand what this means?"

Kyrel did. For the first time, he truly did. "This isn't a wearable," he whispered.

Rhett leaned in, breathless. "It's an identity."

Kyrel nodded slowly, heart pounding. "It's the first device that knows you're you... because it speaks the same language your body does."

Rhett laughed, a wild, unbelieving sound. "Dude. DUDE! We just birthed the future. Right here. In this Styrofoam graveyard of a workspace."

But Kyrel wasn't hearing him. He was staring at his hand. At possibility. At destiny.

At the small, accidental miracle that would one day make him the youngest capped billionaire in history ...and the most hunted man in America.

CHAPTER 4

DIVERGENCE

The next 48 hours were a blur.

Between classes, sleep deprivation, cafeteria food inhaled without chewing, and a half-dozen emergency trips to retrieve replacement parts, Kyrel and Rhett barely touched the ground.

But underneath the manic energy, something heavier grew, an undertow neither of them noticed yet.

The Invention Studio was quieter than usual. It was Sunday morning. Half the campus slept like the dead, and the other half was at brunch pretending they'd slept at all.

Kyrel sat at the same back corner table, wrist cuff reassembled, signal processor rebuilt from the ground up. The prototype looked nothing like the night of the accident; cleaner, sharper, impossible to mistake for a fluke now.

Rhett walked in with two coffees and a grin like he was bringing news of the Second Coming.

"How many hours have you been awake?" he asked, sliding one cup toward Kyrel.

"Two," Kyrel lied.

"Add ten," Rhett said, sitting. "I can see it in the curls. They're in full gremlin mode."

Kyrel shrugged. "It's fine. I'm close."

"Close to what?"

Kyrel turned the controller toward him, displaying a clean reading. "I stabilized the voltage mapping. The sensor bank is reading me consistently."

Rhett leaned in, eyes bright. "Show me."

Kyrel flexed his hand. A perfect green pulse rippled across the screen.

Rhett let out a low whistle. "Dude. That's… beautiful."

Kyrel flushed, unused to praise that wasn't performative.

"It's just consistency," he said. "No outside noise. No false triggers."

"No, Ky." Rhett tapped the screen. "This is the start of a product."

Kyrel stiffened slightly. "It's the start of an idea."

Rhett blinked. "Same thing."

"No." Kyrel unplugged the board gently, as though handling a newborn. "One is creation. The other is monetization. I'm not ready for that."

Rhett's smile faltered.

"Ky," he said carefully, "this thing could change the world. You don't think people are going to want it?"

"I think people are going to misuse it," Kyrel said. "Hack it. Weaponize it. Governments will want back doors. Corporations will want data access. Privacy groups will lose their minds."

"Okay," Rhett said slowly. "And?"

Kyrel frowned. "And we're not building anything for anyone until I'm certain it can't be abused."

Rhett lifted both hands, palms out, the international sign for don't freak, but… "Ky, no product has ever been perfectly safe."

"Yes," Kyrel said, tightening his jaw. "That's the problem."

Rhett blew out a breath. He'd grown up in rooms where ideas were pitched, not protected. Where innovation was a race, not a responsibility. Where the measure of brilliance was how fast you could scale.

Kyrel had grown up fixing neighbors' radios and watching his parents double-check safety valves in the house. He measured brilliance by how little harm it caused.

Two worlds.
    Same room.
        Same table.
            Different gravity.

"Okay," Rhett said, forcing calm. "What if we build it slow? Private testers. Medical angle. Controlled rollout."

Kyrel hesitated. "Medical… maybe."

"Exactly." Rhett leaned forward. "Imagine a kid with epilepsy whose emergency response system activates automatically when their muscles seize. Or older adults who fall, instant alerts. Or surgeons needing sterile authentication. The health implications alone— Ky, this could save lives."

Kyrel stared down at the cuff. Rhett wasn't wrong. He hated that Rhett wasn't wrong.

"…We'd have to make a version with medical-grade sensors," Kyrel said quietly.

Rhett beamed. "Yes. And? That means investors."

Kyrel's stomach tightened. "Slow. Ethical. Thoughtful investors."

Rhett patted his arm. "Buddy. There's no such thing. But we'll get close."

Kyrel winced. "Rhett—"

"We'll pick the good ones," Rhett insisted. "Ones who'll support you. Ones who believe in safety."

Kyrel huffed. "Investors don't care about safety."

"Then we'll find the weird altruistic ones," Rhett said, shrugging. "There's always some idealist who made a fortune selling eco-straws or sustainable toilet paper."

Kyrel cracked a reluctant smile.

"Fine," he said. "We'll test. But on our terms. And no public exposure yet. No demo videos. No bragging online."

"Got it," Rhett said solemnly.

He lasted three hours.

The first time LinkLife went viral, Kyrel didn't even know about it. He walked into the Studio to find a crowd gathered around Rhett's laptop, eyes wide, whispers flying:

> "Holy crap."
> "That's real?"
> "Is he in our year?"
> "Dude, this is like, next-level biometrics."

Kyrel's pulse spiked. He pushed through the crowd. "Rhett."

Rhett looked up from his laptop, eyes bright and a little manic. "Oh, Ky! Hey! So, this is going to sound crazy, but you know the prototype? The muscle mapping bit? So I made a private post on the hackathon Slack, just the tiny closed group, to get early testers and, uh—"

Kyrel's breath stopped. "What did you post?"

Rhett winced. "Just a short clip. Super short. It shows you unlocking your phone with the cuff."

Kyrel closed his eyes for a long, silent moment. The room buzzed behind him. Someone whispered, "He's the guy who made the nerve ID tech."

Someone else: "Bro invented the future for fun."

Kyrel opened his eyes and looked at Rhett, and Rhett suddenly looked like a kid who'd broken a priceless vase.

"Ky," he said softly, "I'm sorry. I just—I wanted feedback. And people needed to see what you made."

"What we made," Kyrel corrected automatically.

Rhett swallowed. "Right. What we made."

Kyrel exhaled through his nose, forcing himself to stay even. "Rhett... I told you to keep it quiet."

"I know," Rhett said. "And I'm sorry. I really am. But listen, look at them."

Kyrel turned. Twenty students were staring at the cuff like it was alien technology. A few were recording discreetly. A couple were whispering excitedly into their phones.

"People want this," Rhett said. "They get it. They feel it. It's real."

Kyrel's throat tightened. He felt exposed. Unprepared. Unprotected. This wasn't invention anymore. This was momentum. A wave forming. A tide pulling them both forward.

-44-

Rhett stepped beside him, voice soft. "Ky… I think we just started something we can't stop."

Kyrel closed his eyes again. Because he knew Rhett was right. And for the first time in his life, the future scared him.

CHAPTER 5

THE FIRST STILLNESS

The Georgia Tech library at 2 a.m. was a strange, holy place.

Rows of desks lit by lonely pools of lamplight. The soft rustle of pages for the few who still believed in paper. The occasional, exhausted moan from someone wrestling a physics problem like it owed them money.

Kyrel liked it here.

Not because he studied better in silence. But because it was one of the only places on campus where his brain didn't try to sprint ahead of itself.

He'd retreated here after the "accidental" mini-viral incident.

Rhett had apologized three times, then gotten swept up by the attention. Everyone suddenly wanted to talk to Kyrel. Ask him questions. Pitch ideas. Push him toward incubators. Show him "just one thing" they'd built that LinkLife could plug into.

His nerves felt like frayed wires sparking at both ends.

He needed quiet.

So he'd slipped into the library, found a corner seat far from the center, and buried himself in rebuilding the sensor algorithms. At least code didn't want something from him.

He was so deep into debugging that he didn't notice the soft thump of a backpack on the table across from him until a voice said: "You're in my seat."

He blinked up, startled. A woman stood across from him, hair wrapped into a loose, practical bun, dark eyes steady and unimpressed. She wore scrubs, blue-gray, with the badge clipped to the neckline reading: D'Andra Mitchell – EMT Trainee.

Kyrel opened his mouth, then closed it. "Sorry," he said. "I didn't see anyone here."

"That's because you were six layers deep in whatever that is," she said, gesturing vaguely at the cuff on the table. "But yes. You're in my seat."

He half-stood. "I can move."

She waved him down. "Relax. I'm not a tyrant. Just… if you're taking my spot, you owe me the courtesy of not blowing anything up while I'm here."

Kyrel blinked. "I've never blown anything up in a library."

Her eyebrow lifted. "So you have blown things up elsewhere."

Kyrel's ears went hot. "It was one time."

D'Andra laughed under her breath and slid into the seat opposite him, cracking open a massive paramedicine text.

He forced his attention back to the code, but he could feel her presence—still, steady, like a weight that kept his thoughts from drifting off the table.

After ten minutes she said, without looking up:

"You're tapping your foot."

"What?"

She flipped a page. "It's loud."

He froze. He hadn't realized he was doing it.

"Sorry," he murmured.

"You're anxious," she said simply. Not a question.

Kyrel stiffened. "I'm fine."

"You're vibrating like a tuning fork," she replied, still reading. "So no. You're not fine."

He stared at her.

Most people on campus treated nervous energy as a sign of brilliance. She treated it like a vital sign.

D'Andra finally looked up, meeting his gaze with that same calm steadiness.

"Whatever you're working on," she said, "it's not going to get better if you fry your brain doing it."

"It's important," he said quietly.

D'Andra studied him for a beat. Not the device. Not the code. Him.

"Everything important still needs sleep," she said. "That's biology. Not opinion."

He huffed. "You sound like my mother."

"She sounds like a smart woman."

Kyrel let out a breath he hadn't realized he'd been holding. "She is," he admitted. "And she'd tell me to stop torturing myself."

"Well, I'm telling you the same," D'Andra said, tapping her book. "If you collapse, who's going to keep working on... whatever Frankenstein cuff project this is?"

Kyrel hesitated. Then, very quietly: "It's an identity system."

D'Andra leaned back, studying him. Not mocking. Not impressed. Just curious. "Show me."

Kyrel felt a flutter in his stomach—an odd mixture of pride and fear. He slipped the cuff onto his wrist.

"Okay," he said softly. "So it maps neuromuscular patterns, electrical signals in the muscles that I can't control consciously. It recognizes me by how my nerves behave."

He brought his phone closer.

Unlocked.

D'Andra's eyes widened. Just a fraction. But for a woman that controlled, it was like shouting in surprise. "That's…" she whispered, "real."

"Yeah."

She reached forward, then paused. "Can I…?"

He extended his arm. She touched the edge of the cuff with careful fingertips, medical-gentle, respectful of anything delicate or alive.

"It feels like nothing," she said. "Like hospital sensors."

"That's the idea."

She looked up at him, eyes more serious now. "This could be used for medicine."

Kyrel nodded. "I know."

"You could build fall alerts… seizure warnings… authentication for sterile environments…"

"Yes."

"What do you want to use it for?"

Kyrel hesitated.

No one had asked him that yet. Everyone else asked: What can it do? How fast can you build it? How much can you scale? How much can you sell?

But D'Andra had asked: What do you want?

He swallowed. "I want it to help people," he said. "Not be taken. Or misused. Or turned into surveillance."

D'Andra nodded slowly, as though that answer told her everything she needed to know.

"Good," she said. "Then keep control of it."

Kyrel blinked. "It's not that simple."

"Yes, it is." She held his gaze. "If you don't protect it, someone else will own it. Someone bigger. Someone who doesn't care about people. You know that."

Kyrel felt the warning under her tone, the exact fear he'd had since the viral incident. He whispered, "Yeah. I know."

She closed her book gently, her tone softening.

"You need someone in your life who keeps you tethered," she said. "Someone who makes you stop and think before you give your life's work to the wrong hands."

He stared at her. She said it like she wasn't volunteering. But the universe clearly was. Kyrel exhaled slowly. "What's your name?" he asked.

"D'Andra Mitchell," she said. "You?"

"Kyrel Kade."

She raised an eyebrow. "Kyrel Kade. You sound like someone important."

He laughed under his breath. "I'm not."

"Not yet," she said. Then she smiled, small, steady, quiet.

A smile that calmed him without trying.

And somehow, in that fluorescent-lit corner of the library, surrounded by textbooks and coffee cups and the faint hum of air vents, Kyrel felt something he hadn't felt in weeks.

Stillness.
No pressure.
No hunger.
No fear.
No momentum rushing him downstream.
Just… stillness.

And he didn't know yet, not truly, that this woman would one day save him from the worst decisions of his life, stand at his side during the rise of LinkLife, kiss him in the hall of a rented apartment with a cheap kettle, and refuse, absolutely refuse, to let the world hollow him out.

He only knew that when he looked at her, the future felt less sharp.

Less dangerous. Less lonely.

"Kyrel," D'Andra said softly.

"Yeah?"

"Go home and sleep."

He smiled.

"Only if you do too."

She smirked. "Deal."

They packed their bags in silence. An easy silence. A trusting one. They walked out through the library doors as the sky began to lighten.

Neither of them realized the world had just shifted again.

CHAPTER 6
THE ACCIDENTAL AUDITION

Georgia Tech's annual HackForward Expo wasn't a competition. Not officially.

The Administration insisted it was a "celebration of student innovation," a friendly showcase of prototypes, research demos, maker experiments, and projects too weird for traditional academic lanes. But students knew better.

HackForward was a battlefield wrapped in poster boards and folding tables. It was where faculty scouted lab talent. Where startup incubators prowled. Where venture clubs sniffed around for "the next big thing." Where one lucky idea, every few years, exploded into something iconic.

Kyrel, of course, was not thinking about any of that. He was thinking about whether his cuff's neuromuscular readouts would stay stable without the lab's insulated testing rig… and whether the wristband cover he'd 3D-printed at 3 a.m. would hide the exposed components long enough to count as "presentable."

Rhett, meanwhile, was in peak Rhett-mode; adjusting their table banner, straightening the display stand, checking that their stickers were aligned "for visual impact," and practicing his pitch under his breath like a caffeinated televangelist.

"Rhett," Kyrel murmured, "it's just a demo."

"Everything is a demo," Rhett corrected, smoothing the LinkLife prototype logo on the banner. "Life is a demo. First impressions are demos. Breathing in public is a demo."

Kyrel snorted. "You're ridiculous."

"And you," Rhett said, pointing at him with a display pamphlet he'd hastily printed at FedEx, "are about to undersell yourself into oblivion if I don't talk pretty on your behalf."

He wasn't wrong.

Kyrel's instinct in crowds was to shrink, not shine. But today… Today felt different. D'Andra's words from the night before still echoed faintly in his head:

> "If you don't protect it, someone else will own it."

He didn't have a plan for protection yet. But he could at least present the thing properly.

Students and faculty milled through the hall as the expo officially opened, vibrant and chaotic. Machines whirred, robots skittered, drones buzzed overhead, and someone's solar desalination prototype made small "blorp" sounds every few seconds.

Rhett bounced on his toes.

"Okay, okay," he muttered, rubbing his hands together. "We've got three goals today: one, don't break your own tech. Two, don't pass out. And three, if anyone with a lanyard that looks expensive comes by, let me do the talking."

Kyrel smirked. "Define expensive."

"You'll know."

Their first hour was slow—students curious, a few engineering professors intrigued, someone trying to sell them a startup bootcamp membership.

Then, midway through the afternoon… The crowd shifted. Kyrel didn't notice at first. But Rhett did—he went still, which was saying something.

A group of people entered together. Not loud. Not flashy. But unmistakably out of place among the student chaos: crisp suits, polished shoes, ID badges that said "Campus Partner" but in fonts no one had ever seen before.

Rhett leaned toward Kyrel, whispering through unmoving lips: "Do. Not. Panic."

"I'm not panicking."

"You're about to. That's the Venture Bridge delegation."

Kyrel blinked. Venture Bridge. The university's elite early-stage fund. The one that occasionally gave a student startup a five-figure runway and a dedicated workspace.

"They don't come to undergrad expos," he whispered.

"They're here for someone," Rhett said. "And, God willing, it's us."

The delegation split, greeting faculty, scanning tables, evaluating with that eerie silence of professionals trying to look casual. Then one of them, a tall woman with silver-streaked braids and a sleek black jacket, stopped dead in front of the LinkLife booth.

She read the banner. Then the spec sheet. Then she looked directly at the cuff on Kyrel's wrist. "Is it functional?" she asked.

Kyrel swallowed. "Yes."

"Show me."

Rhett inhaled sharply, this was the moment he lived for, but Kyrel beat him to the punch. He lifted his wrist. The cuff hummed softly, just a whisper, a stabilizing flicker of LEDs. He held his phone near it.

Unlock.

The phone chimed.

The woman raised an eyebrow. Not impressed. Not surprised. Just... calculating.

"What's the false acceptance rate?" she asked.

"Zero so far," Kyrel said quietly.

"What about false rejection?"

"0.02 percent when the user is extremely cold or dehydrated."

"What's your power source?"

"Bioelectric. Supplemental induction charging if necessary."

She nodded slowly. "How many prototypes?"

"Four."

"What stage are you at?"

"Proof of concept moving toward integrated board design."

She tilted her head. "And the encryption?"

Kyrel hesitated. Then, slowly, he turned his laptop around. The console displayed the algorithm he and Rhett had been refining for months. Not the full code, never the full code, but enough of the architecture to show he wasn't bluffing.

The woman's eyebrows lifted a fraction, a reaction so small it nearly qualified as an emotional outburst.

Rhett whispered, "Is that good?"

Kyrel had no idea.

She straightened, then addressed him with crisp authority: "What's your name, son?"

"Kyrel Kade."

She gestured toward Rhett. "And you?"

"Rhett Colburn," he said, chest out just slightly.

"Colburn," she repeated, recognizing the surname with a flicker of interest. "Lockheed Colburns?"

"Yes, ma'am."

She nodded once.

Then she turned back to Kyrel.

"This," she said, tapping the cuff lightly with one finger, "is going to ignite a war."

Kyrel's stomach flipped. "A what?"

"A war," she said casually, as though discussing the weather. "Between cybersecurity firms. Between medical technology companies. Between federal agencies. Between ideologues. Your technology intersects with too many domains for there not to be a fight."

Kyrel stared at her. "I didn't design it for war."

"No one ever does."

She reached into her jacket and handed him a card.

"Come to Venture Bridge on Monday," she said. "9 a.m. Your idea needs protection. And we need to know if you're the right person to lead it."

Kyrel's pulse spiked.

Rhett made a soft noise that sounded like a prayer, a laugh, and a suppressed scream all at once.

The woman began walking away. Then paused. Turned. And with a gaze that seemed to pin Kyrel to the floor, she said: "And son… keep your prototype close."

Kyrel blinked. "…Why?"

"Because after today, you'll have competitors." She smiled, a razor-thin, knowing arc. "Some of them will play fair." She started walking. "Some won't."

CHAPTER 7
BEFORE THE WORLD TILTS

The Venture Bridge card stayed in Kyrel's pocket all the way back to his apartment. He didn't look at it. Didn't let himself.

He and Rhett had walked out of HackForward like two people who'd accidentally pulled a sword from a stone and weren't sure whether to celebrate or run.

Rhett tried for celebration.

"Dude. BRO. Do you understand what just happened? Venture Bridge doesn't show up for graduated startups. They don't show up for faculty inventions. They show up for companies with Series A money on the table. We're nobodies. We're two dudes with a folding table and a 3D printer."

Kyrel kept walking.

"Ky?"

"Mm?"

"Tell me you're excited."

"I'm… thinking."

"You've been thinking for two hours."

Kyrel exhaled. "Rhett… she said this could start a war."

Rhett waved that off like it was seasonal allergies. "People in tech always say that. 'Revolutionize the world.' 'Disrupt systems.' 'Ignite a war.' It's hype language. She wants us to take the meeting."

But Kyrel wasn't convinced. It wasn't the words the Venture Bridge woman used. It was the way she said them. Clinical. Certain. Like someone who had seen innovation spark conflict before.

That night, Kyrel didn't sleep much. He sat at his desk, the prototype cuff glowing faintly beside him. Watching it pulse like a heartbeat.

At 2:17 a.m., he sent a text. Kyrel: Are you awake? A response came almost instantly.

D'Andra: I'm an EMT trainee. I'm always awake. What's going on?

Kyrel: Something happened at the expo.

D'Andra: Bad something or good something?

He hesitated. Kyrel: Both. Can I talk to you? A moment. Then:

D'Andra: Edgewood Waffle House. Booth by the window. 20 minutes.

He arrived early. She arrived precisely on time.

D'Andra slid into the booth across from him, still in partial scrubs, hair tied back, face alert despite the hour.

"So," she said, "tell me."

He told her everything. About the demo. About the questions. About the card. About the warning. D'Andra listened without interruption, sipping a terrible cup of coffee like it was part of the assessment. When he finally finished, she steepled her fingers.

"Okay," she said. "So now you're scared."

Kyrel blinked. "I'm not—"

"You're scared," she repeated, gently but firmly. "Not of failing. Of succeeding too fast."

He swallowed hard. That hit too close. "You're not wrong," he admitted.

D'Andra leaned in.

"Kyrel… when you have something powerful, two things happen. People try to take it, and people try to use you. You need to go into Monday knowing which category that woman belongs to."

He nodded slowly.

"And more importantly," she said, tapping the table for emphasis, "you need to know what you want out of all this."

He stared at her. "I don't know yet."

"Then find out. Or someone else will decide for you."

Kyrel felt that land like a stone in his stomach. They talked for another hour. About medicine. About ethics. About systems that chew up people and innovations alike. By the time they parted ways, Kyrel wasn't less afraid. But he was more anchored.

Rhett, in contrast, was vibrating with pure momentum.

"You HAVE to go," he declared when Kyrel found him Saturday afternoon. "This is our moment. Our once-in-a-generation door. You don't walk past a door like that."

Kyrel rubbed the bridge of his nose. "It feels fast."

"Fast is good," Rhett said. "Fast means we're ahead."

"What if it's too big?"

Rhett laughed. "Ky… every founding story starts like this: someone shows up, sees the potential, gives you your shot. That's what this is. Don't overthink it."

Kyrel didn't answer. Because Rhett wasn't wrong. But neither was D'Andra. He was being pulled in two directions: the world that wanted LinkLife and the world that wanted him to stay whole.

The Venture Bridge card sat on his desk like an object that didn't belong to this timeline. Matte black. Weighty. Too polished. Too serious. It felt like something meant to be handed to an older version of him, someone with confidence, swagger, experience. Not a college kid with student loans, a mismatched thrift-store couch, and a fridge with one sad yogurt inside.

He stared at it for hours. Not touching it. Just trying to understand what had happened to his life.

By 10 p.m., his room was dim except for the glow of his laptop. The cuff prototype pulsed faintly beside it, that soft green halo reflecting in the metal. Kyrel exhaled and finally did the thing D'Andra had urged him to do. He started digging.

He looked up Venture Bridge first. It wasn't just a campus fund. It was a gateway tied to Atlanta tech giants, government contracts, and companies whose valuations made no sense for their size. It had helped birth three AI unicorns, two cybersecurity firms, and a medical wearable corporation that practically owned half the patent space in the Southeast.

Their board listed CEOs, former defense analysts, the retired CFO of Delta, and two people whose LinkedIns simply said: "Federal Consultant – Strategic Programs".

His stomach tightened. Then he searched for the woman. Her badge gave only initials: L. O. Haider. Kyrel cross-checked conferences, faculty collaborations, obscure tech journals, old listings from defense symposiums. He found her.

Dr. Leona O. Haider: A ghost disguised as a resume; MIT undergrad; Stanford PhD in embedded systems; Ten years in an unspecified federal research "unit" (red flag). Three years consulting with the Department of Homeland Security (bigger red flag). Now a "strategic liaison" for Venture Bridge (giant, screaming red flag).

He sat back. D'Andra had been right. Something like LinkLife doesn't slip quietly into the world. Someone wants to own it. Someone wants to weaponize it. Someone wants to chain it.

And Dr. Haider? She wasn't scouting for "innovation." She was scouting for leverage.

Kyrel rubbed the back of his neck, feeling the weight settle on him like a yoke.

He closed his laptop and stared at the cuff. When he first built it, it felt like a miracle, a bridge between human and machine, but subtle, humane, elegant.

Now he looked at it and saw tracking, surveillance, identity control, military applications, government systems, corporate ownership, dark markets, exploitation, and his own name stamped on every one of those nightmares. His throat tightened.

What if he'd invented something that could ruin people? What if he lost control before he even understood what he had done? He rested his hands on the desk, head bowed, the cuff's pulse reflected in his eyes.

"I didn't want this," he whispered. The room didn't answer.

The Waffle House smelled like coffee and fried batter and a thousand bad decisions, but somehow walking inside calmed him. D'Andra was exactly as she had been the night before: steady, centered, sane.

She listened as he walked her through what he'd found. When he finished, she didn't gasp or panic or wave her hands like Rhett would have.

She simply said, "Good. Now you're finally seeing the scale."

He swallowed. "D'Andra… what if I'm not ready?"

She leaned forward, elbows on the table.

"No one is ready for the thing that changes their life. You grow into it. But you have to start by making choices instead of letting other people make them for you."

She didn't reach for his hand. Didn't soften her tone to soothe him. That was the grounding. The steadiness. The truth. And it worked. Because Kyrel didn't need comforting. He needed clarity.

Rhett's reaction the next afternoon was the exact opposite.

"You RESEARCHED her?" Rhett cried. "Ky, nobody researches the people who hand them a golden ticket. You grab the ticket. You don't check who printed it!"

Kyrel half-laughed despite himself. "That's exactly why I looked."

Rhett clapped him on the shoulder.

"Look, man. You're brilliant. But you overthink. I know Dr. Haider sounds scary on paper, but come on. Every big tech executive has spooky-sounding credentials. It's part of the aesthetic."

"It's not the aesthetic I'm worried about," Kyrel murmured.

"It should be the opportunity you're excited about!" Rhett insisted. "This is our moment. Don't slow down."

And Kyrel felt the contrast sharp inside himself: D'Andra, anchor. Rhett, acceleration.

Two gravity wells. Both honest. Both right in their own ways. The decision was still his. And it terrified him.

Sunday night, he sat on the floor of his room with the prototype cuff in his hands. He turned it over slowly, feeling the curve of its casing, the tiny screws, the warmth left behind from his skin.

He remembered: the first time he got the sensor to read; the beam of pride when Rhett called it "world-changing"; the flicker in D'Andra's eyes when she said, "This could help people."

He remembered his father once telling him: "Your gifts are never just for you."

And suddenly, the question D'Andra had asked came back sharply: "What do you want this to become?"

The answer rose like a quiet truth from somewhere deep inside him. "I want it to be mine," he whispered. "My invention. My rules. My responsibility."

He looked at the Venture Bridge card. And this time, he didn't feel like a kid holding something too big. He felt like someone about to make a choice that mattered.

Kyrel placed the cuff down next to the card. Two symbols. Two paths. He drew a slow breath.

"Okay," he whispered. "Monday." But now the word felt different. Not fearful. Not passive. It felt like someone taking one measured step into the unknown, with both caution and resolve.

Because he understood what was at stake. He understood who might want to control him. And he understood who he wanted to be. The weekend hadn't calmed him. It had clarified him.

CHAPTER 8
A DOOR WITH NO RETURN

The Venture Bridge headquarters didn't look like a building where lives changed. That was the first thing Kyrel noticed. It wasn't tall and glassy. It wasn't covered in logos or investor banners. It wasn't buzzing with staff or crowds or screens. It was… understated.

A converted textile mill near the BeltLine, red brick, wide windows, a courtyard filled with native plants and quiet paths. It looked like a retreat center, not a launchpad. Kyrel hesitated outside the entrance. Rhett was practically vibrating beside him, straightening his blazer for the fourth time.

"Ky," he whispered, "they're going to LOVE us."

Kyrel didn't answer. He was staring at the door, a door that felt like a threshold not just into a meeting, but into a different version of his life.

"Ready?" Rhett said.

No, thought Kyrel. "Yes," he replied softly. They stepped inside.

The lobby was quiet. Uncomfortably quiet. No receptionist. No staff bustling around. Just a small sign on a podium that read:

"Kade / Colburn — Conference Room B. Welcome."

Rhett's eyes widened. "Oh damn, they were expecting us."

Kyrel's pulse quickened. The second surprise came fifteen feet later: Madeline Vyre.

She stood at the end of the hallway in a charcoal-gray suit, holding a tablet close to her chest. Her expression was unreadable, polite, professional, clinical.

"Mr. Kade. Mr. Colburn. Welcome."

Rhett perked up. "Uh, hi! Are you our—"

"Escort," she said. "And today, also your compliance officer."

Kyrel stiffened. "Compliance for what?"

Madeline opened a door. "You'll understand in a moment."

The three of them entered Conference Room B. It was nothing like a startup pitch environment. A long table. A wall of screens. And waiting at the head… Dr. Leona Haider herself.

She looked exactly the same as at HackForward: efficient posture, cool gaze, braids coiled neatly behind one shoulder. Like a person who'd already analyzed every possible outcome of this meeting.

"Mr. Kade," she said. "Mr. Colburn."

They sat. No small talk. No pleasantries. Madeline closed the door, took a seat at the side of the table, and folded her hands. Haider pressed a button. The screens on the wall lit up. Kyrel froze. Because the screens weren't showing numbers or projections or feasibility models.

They showed him. Photos from his childhood: Competition records, his scholarship files, his research submissions, his family's public data, Rhett's academic profile, LinkLife's entire development timeline, the viral video from the hackathon, the prototype schematics, his maker-space access logs, his late-night lab reservations, and even footnotes from the Georgia Tech equipment checkout forms.

Kyrel's stomach bottomed out.

Rhett whispered, "Uh… shouldn't we have signed something before you collected all that?"

Haider didn't flinch. "This is public, semi-public, or institution-accessible information." She tapped the screen. "Nothing here required a subpoena."

Kyrel felt sick. "Why do you have all this?" he asked quietly.

Haider didn't answer immediately. Instead, she gestured at the cuff on his wrist. "That device represents a disruption in three sectors simultaneously: identity, security, and medical interfacing. When something intersects that many domains, we have an obligation to evaluate the creator… before the creation is allowed further into the world."

Kyrel swallowed hard. "Allowed?"

Madeline spoke for the first time. "Innovations that threaten systemic stability trigger an automatic preliminary review by our Strategic Oversight division."

Rhett blinked. "So… we're being vetted?"

"Evaluated," Haider corrected.

 "Not for capability. Not for scalability. For risk."

Kyrel felt heat rising behind his ears. "Risk to who?"

Haider's eyes sharpened. "To everyone." Haider turned to him directly. "What is LinkLife's intended purpose?"

Kyrel steadied himself. "To make identity secure and seamless. To give people more control over their digital and physical access."

"And the unintended purpose?"

He hesitated. "To track people," he admitted quietly. "To surveil them. To restrict access instead of granting it."

Haider nodded once, approving. "So you are aware of the danger."

"Yes."

"Good. Because your awareness will determine whether you leave here today with an accelerator proposal… or an injunction."

Rhett choked. "An— INJUNCTION?"

Madeline slid a document onto the table. "A federal-level pause order," she explained. "If necessary. For technologies with systemic implications."

Kyrel stared. They were telling him, in plain language, that they were legally capable of stopping LinkLife before it ever entered the market. But they were also telling him they didn't want to. Not yet.

Haider leaned back.

"What we need to know," she said, "is whether you intend to build a tool... or an empire."

Kyrel exhaled. "I intend to build something ethical."

"And can you control it?"

That question hit with the weight of an anvil. He thought of: D'Andra's warning, Rhett's ambition, his research late at night, and the way LinkLife had already slipped out of his hands, just a little. He forced himself to answer honestly.

"I don't know," he said.

Haider's lips curved, not into a smile, but into something close to respect. "Good," she said. "Men who say 'yes' to that question are the ones we're afraid of." She folded her hands.

"We don't want to stop LinkLife, Mr. Kade. We want to protect it. And you. And the public. If you're willing to work with us, we can help you navigate this without losing yourself."

Kyrel exchanged a look with Rhett. Rhett was glowing with possibility. Kyrel was vibrating with caution.

Haider's voice softened slightly. "You need to decide what kind of founder you're going to be."

Madeline slid a second document forward. "This," she said, "is your official evaluation period agreement. It outlines what you may and may not do while your technology is under review."

Kyrel scanned it quickly. It allowed development, prototyping, limited testing, advisory and consultation. It prohibited investment offers, outside partnerships, international communications, commercial rollout, and any attempt to profit from LinkLife before review was complete.

Kyrel looked up. "You're telling me," he said slowly, "that I can't take money from anyone yet."

Haider nodded. "Correct."

Rhett was stunned. "But that's the whole point—!"

Haider raised one eyebrow. "We are not blocking you, Mr. Colburn. We are containing the blast radius." Then Haider pressed a final button. The screens shifted to display all kinds of documents: Encrypted documents, blacked-out memos, and internal risk assessments; as well as a list of government agencies with early interest in LinkLife: DHS, NSA, HHS, DoD, Transportation Security Administration, Interpol, and even Europol.

Kyrel's blood ran cold. He should have expected this. Haider folded her hands.

"Your invention is already on every radar that matters," she said. "The question is whether you walk into that storm prepared... or blind."

Silence. Deep, heavy silence. Kyrel felt the shift. Everything that had happened so far, the viral clip, the expo, the weekend research—was mere foreshadowing. This was the first real threshold. The moment the world revealed its teeth.

Haider slid one final sheet across the table breaking the silence.

"Take the week," she said. "Read the agreement. Talk to your partner. Talk to your moral compass." She didn't say D'Andra's name. But the implication was there.

"If you want to work with us, be here next Tuesday morning at nine."

Rhett started to speak. Haider held up a hand. "And Mr. Kade..."

Kyrel looked up.

Her gaze locked onto him with laser precision. "If you walk away now, others will try to take this from you."

A beat.

"Protect your creation. Protect yourself."

The meeting was over.

CHAPTER 9
DECISION WEEK

The Venture Bridge elevator closed behind him with a soft hydraulic sigh, and the city swallowed him again—Atlanta heat rising off the sidewalks, the faint scent of traffic and barbecue drifting on the air, the busy hum of people living lives far less complicated than his suddenly felt.

Kyrel walked the ten blocks home without hearing half the sounds around him.

Haider's words followed him like ghosts: "Take the week. Talk to your partner. Talk to your moral compass."

He didn't need to talk to his partner. Rhett would push him toward the money. Toward scaling. Toward the path that always felt slightly wrong in Kyrel's bones.

He didn't need to talk to his moral compass either. He already knew what she would say. But Haider had said one more thing—softly, as if it weren't meant for the room: "You don't need to own the future to shape it."

That sentence had stuck deeper than anything else.

D'Andra was sitting on the couch when he arrived, wearing scrubs, hair tied up, reading a medical study on her tablet. She looked up the moment the door clicked.

"What happened?" she asked quietly.

He wasn't sure which part of the day to start with—the flattery, the veiled pressure, the million-dollar smiles, or the moment Haider gently pressed her finger against the contract without ever having touched it. Kyrel sat beside her, hands clasped. "When people see LinkLife, they don't see what I see."

"And what do you see?" she asked.

"A responsibility," he said. "A living thing. A line between freedom and exploitation."

D'Andra set her tablet aside and took his hands in hers. "So what did they want from you?"

"They want LinkLife. They want me attached to it. They want to lock me into something I'm not sure I believe in yet."

"And what do you want?"

He took a long breath. "I want to control how the technology is used—without controlling the company."

D'Andra blinked once, slowly. "That sounds… impossible."

"Not impossible," he said. "Just unlikely."

She studied him, searching his face the way she would examine a complex fracture. "Kyrel… are you choosing the hard path on purpose?"

"No," he murmured. "The hard path is choosing me."

She reached up and touched his jaw, thumb tracing the stress line that always appeared when he was building something too fast for his own good. "Then let me ask you the thing my attending tells our interns: What decision lets you sleep at night?"

He didn't hesitate. "The one where LinkLife can't be weaponized."

She smiled softly. "That sounds like you."

They sat together in silence. Her presence steadied him—the anchor he never asked for but always needed.

By mid-week, most of Atlanta was enjoying its midweek rhythm. Kyrel, on the other hand, spent the day quietly rewriting what control meant. He opened the LinkLife architecture. Not the commercial modules—those would belong to the board. Not the derivatives—the engineers could build those without him. No. He opened the root. The ethical core. The place no one else knew existed. Lines of code scrolled past, elegant and terrifying in their implications: Identity encryption, Biometric handshake protocols, Access restrictions, Emergency override controls, Blacklisted functions, Government-request flags, and Consent enforcement.

There was the real weapon. Here was the real salvation. Here was what no investor should ever control. Kyrel added a new safeguard— one that required a triple-key cryptographic signature for any modification of the ethical core. One key for the company.

One key for regulatory oversight. One key for him. He encrypted it so deeply that even the engineers building LinkLife wouldn't know it existed. It wasn't ownership. It wasn't control of the business. It was guardianship.

He sat back, heart pounding.

For the first time since the meeting, he felt the weight lift slightly.

By midday the next day, Rhett had called twice. Then five more times. Then once more at midnight. Kyrel didn't answer yet. He wasn't ready for Rhett's enthusiasm, his hunger for scaling, his obsession with valuation. He needed to be standing firmly on both feet before he walked into that storm.

On Friday, D'Andra brought home takeout—Ethiopian from a spot they both loved. They ate quietly, legs intertwined on the couch. "You look calmer," she said.

"I know what I'm going to do."

"And?"

"I'll sign with Venture Bridge next Tuesday. But I'm only giving them what they need to scale. Not what they need to compromise safety."

"And no one will know you built a gatekeeper into the ethics layer?"

"No one," Kyrel said.

She leaned her head on his shoulder. "You're doing the right thing."

He felt her warmth, her certainty, her fierce belief. Kyrel drew strength from her, the way a circuit draws stability from a grounding wire.

Saturday and Sunday arrived and the world was still spinning normally.

Kyrel updated the firmware, drafted a development protocol, wrote a clear ethical stance, prepared to face Rhett, prepared to face Haider, and prepared to walk into a future where he owned nothing but protected everything that mattered.

This was the first week in his life where he realized a truth he'd been circling for years. He didn't want power. He wanted integrity and, sometimes, integrity required more bravery than power ever did.

By Monday, Rhett was becoming apoplectic. A text buzzed on Kyrel's phone.

> BRO YOU AREN'T GHOSTING ME RIGHT
> CALL ME. WE'RE ABOUT TO BE HUGE.

Kyrel breathed out slowly. Tomorrow, the decision becomes real.

CHAPTER 10

RELUCTANT STEWARD

Venture Bridge's conference room felt different this time. Not hostile. Not welcoming. Just... assessing.

Kyrel walked in quietly, purposefully, looking like a man who had spent a week sharpening himself against a future he didn't ask for.

Rhett burst through the door two minutes later, all charisma and caffeine and bright-eyed ambition.

"Ky, buddy!" Rhett clapped him on the back. "We are about to own Atlanta."

Kyrel didn't say anything. He was still learning how to hold the decisions he'd made without announcing them. Haider entered last.

She looked at the two young men as if she were seeing the structures of two futures in front of her: The one that saves the world; that one that destroys it. And she knew which one depended on Kyrel staying upright.

Motioning Kyle through the door, she followed, then sat quietly in the same chair as the previous time they faced her. A bundle of papers in a folder under her hands, neatly clasped over them. The room fell into a hush.

"Mr. Kade, Mr. Colburn, we've completed preliminary oversight. We are prepared to admit LinkLife into the Venture Bridge accelerator."

Rhett exhaled explosively, shooting Kyrel a grin. But Kyrel watched Haider's expression carefully. She wasn't finished. "There are two non-negotiable conditions." Rhett leaned forward eagerly. Kyrel sat back, wary. Haider turned to Kyrel.

"Condition one: For LinkLife to be ethically viable, you must own at least 51% of it."

Rhett blinked. Kyrel didn't. He had seen this coming.

"Why?" Rhett demanded. "We could split—40/40, give equity to—"

"Because," Haider interrupted sharply, "Mr. Colburn is driven by growth. Mr. Kade is driven by caution. A technology of this magnitude must be governed by someone who will not weaponize it."

Rhett flushed. Kyrel felt the words settle over him like iron links. He met Haider's eyes.

"Heavily diluted shares? Or full decision authority?" Kyrel asked.

"Authority," she said. "You must be the CEO. The company must be ethically anchored."

Rhett coughed. "Wait, CEO? Ky?"

Kyrel didn't answer. His mind was already moving. He didn't want the title. Or the authority. Or the attention. Or the burden. But he had spent a week understanding one painful truth: If he didn't lead, LinkLife would fall to the person who did.

And Rhett, for all his genius with people and markets, for all his loyalty and charm—Rhett would build the empire.

Kyrel would build the safety. Only one of those kept the world intact. He looked at Rhett. "If I don't do this, someone else will."

Rhett's frustration wavered into confusion. "Ky, you don't even want the title."

"No," Kyrel said softly. "But I want control of the ethics. And that means I have to take it."

Haider's eyes flickered—approval, relief, and something like respect.

"Excellent. Condition two," Haider continued, turning toward Rhett. "You," she said, "become CFO." Rhett's eyebrows shot up. "CFO? Finance?"

"You're better suited to scale than governance," Haider said. "The roles fit your natural inclinations."

It was polite. It was accurate. It was also a subtle warning. Rhett puffed out his chest. "Yeah, I can run the money. Build the partnerships. Push the—"

Kyrel interrupted very quietly: "Rhett."

Rhett looked at him. His eyes bright. Hungry. So sure they were about to launch a revolution. Kyrel swallowed. "If we do this, it has to be done carefully. No shortcuts. No black-box deals. No backdoor partnerships."

Rhett stared.

"Ky, come on. This is us. We're gonna build something HUGE."

Kyrel felt D'Andra's voice in his head: "What decision lets you sleep at night?"

He turned back to Haider. "I'll accept the role," he said. "As long as I have final veto power on safety and ethics."

Haider nodded. "We expected that."

Kyrel exhaled. The decision solidified. The die cast. The future sealed. The papers were slid across the table. A single line for CEO. A single line for CFO. Rhett signed so fast the pen squeaked.

Kyrel signed slowly. Deliberately. This wasn't ambition. This wasn't ego. This was acceptance of the thing he had spent a week resisting: To protect what you create, sometimes you have to lead it.

Rhett practically danced down the hall and out the door after all was signed.

"KYREL KADE — CEO!" he shouted, arms wide.

Kyrel stood still. He felt none of the exhilaration. He felt the weight. The future rushing toward him. The responsibility settling deep. Rhett slung an arm over his shoulder.

"Man, this is gonna be epic."

Kyrel nodded without smiling. "Yeah," he said quietly. "It is. Just not the way you think."

And with that—Kyrel Kade became CEO of LinkLife.

Reluctantly. Wisely. And in exactly the way the world needed him to be.

CHAPTER 11

THREE YEARS LATER

Graduation robes were not built for Atlanta heat. The fabric stuck to the back of Kyrel's neck as he shuffled along with thousands of other Georgia Tech students toward the stage, the air thick with sweat, perfume, and the humid roar of proud families.

Somewhere up in the stands, his father's voice cut across the din. "Kyrel! Over here!"

He spotted them in the sea of faces—Darrin waving both arms like he was flagging down aircraft, Ellen beside him with a camera raised and tears already on her cheeks. His siblings were clustered around them, each holding a cheap blue-and-gold pennant they'd bought from a vendor outside.

On his left, Rhett bumped his shoulder. "Smile, Kade. This is the last time we're nobodies."

Kyrel snorted. "We've been 'nobodies' for twenty-two years. You'll survive another ten minutes."

Rhett grinned and adjusted his own gown, tassel swinging. "Ten minutes is all it takes to flip a switch, my friend."

Across the stadium, D'Andra was in the medical track line, her cap tilted slightly to one side, expression composed and focused even from a distance. When she caught Kyrel's eye, her mouth curved into a small smile that steadied him more than any speech could.

The ceremony was a blur. Names. Applause. Shuffling students. Booming microphones.

Then he heard his name announced. "…Kyrel Darrin Kade, Bachelor of Science, Computer Engineering." The sound of his family's cheers hit him like a wave. He walked across the stage, shook the dean's hand, accepted the diploma, and thought: This is the smallest thing I will build.

He looked out into the stands again, not at the crowd, but at one person: D'Andra. Her gaze met his and didn't waver.

They found each other afterward in the chaos of the courtyard—gowns and flowers and photo backdrops and folding chairs everywhere.

"Mr. Kade," she said, coming up to him with a mock formality that fit oddly well. "Congratulations."

He caught her around the waist and pulled her in, ignoring the crush of people around them. "Not 'Mr.' yet. I still owe the world something first."

"You already do," she said softly.

His heart kicked against his ribs.

He'd been planning to do this later, after dinner, after family, after the exhaustion had worn off, but standing there, with his diploma still warm in his hand and her eyes shining in the summer light, waiting felt wrong.

He fumbled in the pocket of his gown until his fingers closed around the small box he'd been carrying all day like a spare heart.

"D'Andra." His voice came out too serious. He tried again. "D'Andra Crost."

Her brows drew together. "Kyrel, what are you—"

He dropped to one knee on the uneven concrete, ignoring the gasps and the chorus of "oh my God!" coming from nearby families.

Her hand flew to her mouth.

"This world is about to get…weird." His throat tightened. "LinkLife, whatever it becomes, whatever I become—none of it makes sense without you. I don't know what the next ten years will look like, but I know who I want in all of them."

He opened the box.

The ring was simple. Modest. A slim band with a small stone he'd saved for in increments, month after month, from tutoring and phone repair shifts.

"Will you marry me?" he asked. "Before the world decides who I am?"

For a second, the noise around them melted away.

Then she laughed a soft, incredulous sound that turned into tears.

"Yes," she said, voice shaking. "Of course yes."

He slid the ring on her finger, hands trembling, and stood as she pulled him in.

From somewhere behind them, Rhett shouted, "Finally!" and started a clap that his siblings eagerly joined, but Kyrel only heard her.

"You're sure?" she whispered into his shoulder. "You know this road isn't going to be easy."

"I'm sure," he said. "The hard road never scared me. Doing it alone did."

Three months later they bought their first house. It wasn't much by anyone's Instagram standards—a narrow two-story brick place on a quiet street in East Atlanta, with a patchy front lawn and a few struggling azaleas. The porch railing needed sanding. The roof would need work within five years. The kitchen cabinets were a strange off-white that had once been fashionable but now just looked tired.

To Kyrel, it was a palace. To D'Andra, it was something rarer: theirs. He stood with her on the front step, keys in hand, facing a door that stuck slightly when you pushed it.

"You ready?" he asked.

"Always," she said.

He swept her up into his arms without warning.

"Kyrel!" She burst into laughter, clutching his shoulders. "You're going to break your back before your first mortgage payment."

He tightened his grip and shouldered the door open. "Tradition. I'm protecting you from evil spirits."

"In East Atlanta?" she teased. "I think the evil spirits are raccoons in the garbage and property taxes."

"Then I'm carrying you over both," he said, and stepped into the house with her in his arms.

The entryway smelled faintly of dust and someone else's life. Sunlight spilled across scuffed hardwood floors. The living room held nothing but echoes.

He set her down gently. "We'll fix it," he said. "Bit by bit. Like everything else."

She took his hand and laced their fingers together. "I don't need it perfect. I just need you here."

He exhaled, the last of his doubts about the house dissolving. "You're stuck with me, Dr.-Almost-Crost."

She smirked. "Ask me again when the boards are over."

LinkLife's Launch Day barreled in sooner than he felt ready for. The auditorium at Georgia Tech smelled of stale coffee and fresh anxiety. Rows of folding chairs were filled with faculty, students, a scattering of local tech journalists, and a small ethics committee who'd come expressly to be skeptical.

On the stage, a slim table held a tray with the sterile implant and a small surgical kit. A projector showed the LinkLife logo—two interlocking arcs forming an abstract loop.

Rhett paced at the edge of the stage, checking his notes and the time and his hair in equal measure. "Are we sure the live demo is a good idea?" he asked for the tenth time.

"No," Kyrel said. "That's the point."

D'Andra pulled on her gloves, movements efficient. "You can still bail, you know. We can run the demonstration with a volunteer next week. Or a synthetic arm."

Kyrel shook his head. "If I'm asking people to put this under their skin, I'm not doing it without doing it first."

She studied him, eyes searching. "This isn't bravado?"

"No," he said. "This is responsibility."

She softened. "Okay, Kade. Let's show them."

When they went on stage, the room quieted. Rhett did his part first—he talked about seamless authentication, lost keys eliminated, frictionless security, the end of the twenty-first-century password circus. His charisma filled the room.

Then came the part that wasn't charisma.

D'Andra swabbed the inside of Kyrel's left wrist with antiseptic as he sat on the chair under the stage lights, his pulse a steady hammer in his ears.

She leaned close, voice quiet enough only he could hear.

"You don't have to prove anything to me," she murmured. "You're not less brave if you decide not to do this."

He met her eyes. "I know." He swallowed. "But they need to see that I believe in it enough to stake my own body."

She nodded once. "Then hold still."

The incision was small, precise. He watched her slip the tiny chip that was barely larger than a grain of rice, into the pocket she'd made under his skin. A soft pressure, a sting, then a bandage.

He flexed his hand. The LinkLife reader on the table beside him lit up, recognizing his new internal signature.

The auditorium exhaled as one.

On the screen behind him, his encrypted ID appeared:

    USER: K.KADE
    AUTHENTICATION: VERIFIED

No password. No fingerprint. Just a presence.

Applause started in pockets, then swelled, the space erupting into thunderous noise. Kyrel looked at the glowing confirmation and felt a strange combination of triumph and dread. They had just crossed a threshold. There would be no going back.

The first medical adaptation came three months later.

It wasn't part of any investor pitch. It wasn't in the original roadmap. It started with a late-night email flagged URGENT from an ER physician at Grady Memorial, who'd heard about LinkLife through a colleague of D'Andra's.

The patient was sixteen, epileptic, and had a history of wandering off and seizing without warning. His mother lived in a constant state of preemptive grief.

They met in a quiet hospital consult room that smelled faintly of disinfectant and fear.

The boy sat on the edge of the bed, thin shoulders hunched, wearing a hoodie two sizes too big. His mother's hands never left his arm.

"You're sure it's safe?" she asked, eyes darting between D'Andra and Kyrel.

"As safe as any minor outpatient procedure," D'Andra said calmly. "We've used the implant in healthy volunteers. The difference here is how the software will handle your son's data. It won't change his brain. It will just tell us when his body is about to misfire."

Kyrel added, "The chip will carry his medical profile. If he seizes in public, first responders can access what they need immediately. No guessing. No lost time."

The mother closed her eyes briefly. When she opened them, they were wet. "Do it," she whispered. "Please."

They implanted the device that afternoon.

Two weeks later, the boy wandered downtown and collapsed. The seizure hit, but the system did exactly what it was built to do—the LinkLife gave off an emergency ping when his muscles spasmed in the telltale pattern. An ambulance was dispatched in seconds with his entire profile already loaded.

He survived with no complications. The mother sent a video to the LinkLife office—her son back home, holding up his LinkLife-implanted wrist, grinning shyly at the camera.

"Thank you," she said, voice breaking. "You didn't just make something cool. You gave me my child back."

Kyrel watched it in the small hours of the morning, the office lit only by his monitor's glow. His vision blurred. He wiped at his face, surprised to find tears. D'Andra came up behind him and rested her chin on his shoulder.

"This," she said quietly, "is why I don't worry about you turning into one of them."

"One of who?" he asked, voice rough.

"The ones who forget that people exist on the other side of the balance sheets."

He swallowed hard. "I'm scared of what this can be used for."

"So use it right," she said. "That's all any of us can do."

The protestors showed up not long after the surgery. There were people protesting LinkLife existed and there were some complaining it wasn't wide spread enough.

Kyrel arrived one Tuesday to find a cluster of people outside the LinkLife office holding signs and singing hymns. Someone had set up a portable speaker; a man with a preacher's cadence was warning the small crowd about "the mark of the machine" and "technology in the body meant only for the Almighty."

Across the street, a less religious group held placards reading HUMANS ARE NOT PASSWORDS and NO TO BIO-CORPORATE CONTROL.

Rhett watched from the window, coffee in hand, a smirk tugging at his mouth. "Free advertising," he said. "Nothing sells like controversy."

Kyrel didn't answer. His stomach knotted. D'Andra came up beside him and slid her hand into his. "They're scared of the wrong thing," she said softly.

"What do you mean?"

"They're scared of the fact that this exists." She squeezed. "They should be scared of what would happen if someone else had built it. Someone who doesn't care what it does to people."

He kept watching the signs, the strained faces, the fear.

"Maybe," he said. "Or maybe they're right to be scared of anyone having this much leverage."

She tilted her head. "That's why you're the one who should."

He didn't find that comforting.

D'Andra became "Dr. Crost" on a sweltering May afternoon two years later.

The hospital auditorium was smaller than the Tech stadium but somehow more intense. The graduates in white coats stood ramrod straight as their names were called, the weight of residency and responsibility visibly etched into the lines of their faces.

When it was her turn, Kyrel's hands hurt from clapping.

"D'Andra Eileen Crost, Doctor of Medicine."

She walked across the stage with her chin high and her shoulders squared, the very definition of competent. When they draped the coat on her shoulders, he felt something tight in his chest loosen.

Afterward, outside near the loading dock where their families had drifted to escape the crush, he waited until her siblings had finished shrieking and hugging her and her parents had cried their fill.

Then he stepped in, grabbed her around the waist, and spun her once, unstoppably giddy.

"Careful," she laughed. "I need my spinal alignment intact if I'm going to stand in surgery for eight hours."

He set her down, smiling so hard his cheeks hurt. "The world does not deserve you."

"Maybe not," she said. "But you do."

He kissed her forehead, then her mouth, ignoring the camera phones and the teasing whoops from his brothers.

On the ride home, her coat lay folded carefully on her lap like something sacred.

The first million crept up quietly. Kyrel was in a meeting with the dev team when Rhett burst into the glass-walled huddle room, waving a printed report like a victory flag.

"Stop everything," he said. "You—" he pointed at Kyrel, "—are officially a millionaire."

The devs cheered and clapped. Someone grabbed their phone and played a triumphant trumpet sound.

Kyrel blinked. "What?"

Rhett slapped the report down in front of him. Revenue charts, subscriber growth curves, licensing deals. The number at the bottom sat at seven digits.

"Seven figures, baby," Rhett said, hands on his hips like a victorious superhero. "We did it. We've made our first million in revenue."

The room buzzed with excitement. Someone suggested champagne. Someone else started a Slack channel to collect ideas for how "Boss Man Kade" should celebrate.

Kyrel's first impulse was not champagne. It was to reach for his phone. He stepped out into the hallway, away from the noise, and dialed D'Andra. She picked up on the second ring. "Hey. You alive?"

"We hit our first million," he said, still a little stunned. "Rhett's declaring an early national holiday."

She whistled softly. "That's a lot of zeroes, Kade."

"It doesn't feel like anything," he admitted. "Not yet."

"It will when the first check clears," she said dryly. "So what are you going to do to celebrate?"

He leaned against the wall and closed his eyes, conjuring her in his mind—the way she chewed on pen caps when she read, the way she scrubbed her hands before surgery like she was preparing for battle, the way that coat had settled on her shoulders like something she'd been born to wear.

"Marry you," he said. There was a beat of silence.

"You already asked me that," she pointed out softly. "And I already said yes."

"I mean now," he said. "Not 'someday when things quiet down.' They're not going to quiet down. This is just the beginning. So let's do it while I still remember how to breathe."

On the other end, he could practically hear her smile.

"Okay," she said. "Let's do it. Just don't let Rhett plan it or we'll end up with pyrotechnics."

The wedding was small and impossibly beautiful.

They held it in her grandmother's backyard in Decatur, under strings of warm lights and the wide arms of an old pecan tree: Mismatched chairs, borrowed tables, bouquets of flowers arranged in thrift-store glass jars; The smell of barbecue and jasmine.

His parents dressed in their best, which meant Darrin in the suit he reserved for weddings and funerals and Ellen in a navy dress she'd altered at least three times to keep up with the decades.

Rhett stood beside Kyrel as best man in a tailored suit, his natural polish toned down for the sake of the setting but not entirely suppressed.

When the officiant pronounced them married, D'Andra's voice caught.

"I promise," she said, looking up into his eyes, "that when the world starts asking more of you than is fair, I will remind you who you are."

His throat thickened. "I promise," he said, "that no number in any account, no headline, no valuation will matter more to me than you walking through the door of our imperfect little house at the end of the day."

The crowd laughed softly. Some sniffled. Someone's baby cried in the back.

They kissed to cheers and clinking glasses and the sound of someone's Bluetooth speaker misfiring before landing on the right song.

Later, when the sun slid down and the lights glowed against the deepening blue of the sky, Kyrel and D'Andra stole a moment at the edge of the yard.

The noise of the reception blurred into a gentle roar. He watched the way the lights reflected in her ring, the golden band catching every glint.

"You realize you married a man who spends more nights talking to servers than to people," he said.

She bumped his shoulder. "You realize you married a woman who will sometimes stumble in at three in the morning smelling like antiseptic and blood."

"Romantic," he said dryly.

"Real," she corrected.

He threaded their fingers together, feeling the weight of the ring there. "Real is good."

Behind them, Rhett raised a glass and called for attention.

"To the Kades!" he shouted when the yard quieted. "To the man who's going to put a chip under every wrist on this planet, and to the woman brave enough to keep him from going insane in the process."

Laughter.

Rhett went on, warmth bleeding into something sharper.

"And to the future," he said, eyes gleaming. "The world we're going to own together."

The crowd cheered again.

Kyrel smiled, but something in his stomach tightened.

D'Andra's hand squeezed his under the tablecloth.

Life was not without it's challenges; the night the servers melted, he almost forgot to go home.

LinkLife had opened its first public pilot for everyday users that morning—limited regions, strict controls, vetted early adopters. Kyrel had expected a few thousand sign-ups.

They got over a million in twenty-four hours.

The dashboards turned into fireworks displays. Lines of red error messages began marching across the engineering team's monitors. Data centers strained.

By midnight, the open-plan office looked like a war room. Pizza boxes, energy drink cans, half-zipped hoodies, people muttering into headsets.

Kyrel's hands flew across his keyboard, rewriting allocation logic on the fly. Someone on the Ops team shouted something about throttling. Someone else yelled back about SLAs. The air hummed with caffeine and panic.

"Ky, you need to breathe," one of the devs said.

"I'll breathe when the failover works," he shot back, more harshly than he meant.

Two hours later, the worst of the fire was under control. The graphs stopped spiking. The shouting quieted to exhausted murmurs.

Kyrel stepped away from his desk only when his eyes started losing focus. He found the balcony door and pushed it open. The night air hit him like a gentler wave—cooler, quieter, smelling faintly of rain and asphalt. He put his hands on the rail and let his head drop, muscles trembling from a stress he couldn't code around.

"You're burning yourself alive for this."

He turned. D'Andra stood in the doorway, holding a paper bag that smelled like actual food. Her hair was pulled back in a messy bun, her scrubs wrinkled. She should have been asleep.

"What are you doing here?" he asked.

"Your brother texted me a picture of your face," she said, stepping onto the balcony. "It looked like a server error."

He huffed a breath that was almost a laugh. She set the bag down, came to stand in front of him, and placed both hands flat against his chest. His heart slammed under her palms.

"You don't have to hold all of this alone," she said. "You know that, right?"

"I'm the only one who can fix it," he said, hating how desperate it sounded. "If this breaks, people lose access, hospitals lose access, emergency services—"

"Kyrel." Her voice sharpened just enough to cut through the panic. "Listen to me. Nothing works if you don't."

He closed his eyes.

"I don't know if I can handle where this is going," he admitted, the words tumbling out before he could stop them. "It's too much. Too fast. Every time I think I see the edge of what this could change, the edge moves."

She rose on her toes and rested her forehead against his. The city lights turned her irises into dark mirrors.

"You're not supposed to handle it," she whispered. "You're supposed to lead it. There's a difference."

He let out a shuddering breath. "I'm scared," he said. "Not of failing. Of succeeding so big that I become exactly what I hate."

She held his face in her hands.

"Then remember this," she said. "You have a choice. Every day. You don't have to say yes to everything. You don't have to sell to the highest bidder. You don't have to give the wrong people access."

"Rhett thinks—"

"I know what Rhett thinks," she cut in. "He wants to ride the biggest wave until it breaks. That's who he is. But you—" she searched his face, as if willing him to see what she did "—you want a better world, not just a richer one. That's why you scare them, and that's why you need to be in the room when the decisions are made."

He swallowed hard. She drew back just enough to look him dead in the eye.

"What decision lets you sleep at night?" she asked. "That's the only one worth making."

The question settled into him like a stone finding the bottom of a river.

He didn't answer right away. He didn't have to. She could see it. They stood there in silence, the city breathing around them, the office buzzing faintly beyond the glass.

Finally, he nodded once. "I won't give this to someone who will weaponize it," he said. "I don't care what they offer."

"Good," she said. "Now eat before I admit you as a patient."

It wasn't long before Rhett made his first push for the IPO. It was early morning and the sun was throwing long rectangles of light across the boardroom table.

Kyrel had barely finished his coffee when Rhett walked in with the manic energy of someone who'd slept four hours and listened to a hype playlist on the drive over.

He slapped a stack of documents on the table. "It's time," he said.

Kyrel looked at the header.

INITIAL PUBLIC OFFERING – DRAFT PROPOSAL.

"We talked about this," Kyrel said. "It's too soon."

Rhett dropped into the chair opposite him, eyes blazing. "Too soon for what? We're profitable. The user base is exploding. Hospitals are begging for enterprise licenses. We have governments lining up for secure ID contracts. This is the moment."

"We're still refining the ethics protocols," Kyrel said, keeping his voice even. "We haven't finished the governmental oversight framework. The emergency override system needs external audit. If we go public now, we lose control of the time line."

"We gain capital," Rhett shot back. "And influence. You think we can keep pushing back on government demands without serious leverage? They'll steam roll us if we stay small."

D'Andra, sitting at the end of the table with her tablet and a half-finished night shift in her eyes, watched them both.

"This isn't just about staying small," Kyrel said. "It's about staying sane. The higher the valuation, the harder it will be to say no when someone waves a blank check to use LinkLife for mass surveillance."

Rhett scoffed. "You act like we have to hand them the keys. We'll negotiate. We'll do what every other major tech company does—play ball enough to stay in the game."

"That's exactly what I'm afraid of," Kyrel said. Silence shortened between them.

Rhett looked at D'Andra, seeking backup.

"Doctor," he said with a half-smile that didn't reach his eyes, "you're the resident conscience. Tell him we're idiots if we don't cash in while we're ahead."

She set her tablet down carefully.

"I think," she said slowly, "that if you take this public before you've nailed down the safeguards, you'll spend the rest of your lives answering to shareholders who don't care if this harms people as long as it profits them."

Rhett's jaw tightened. "So that's a no?"

"That's a 'not yet'," she said. "Which is different from 'never'."

Rhett's gaze swung back to Kyrel.

"This is our shot," he said, softer now. "We get to set the terms if we move first. If we wait too long, someone else will come up right behind us with a worse version and no ethics board."

Kyrel hesitated.

He could see Rhett's fear under the bravado—the terror of being outpaced, of losing the first-mover advantage, of waking up in five years to find that LinkLife had been outflanked by something uglier and faster.

He could also see the future D'Andra feared—boardrooms where every discussion began with, "What will this do to our quarterly returns?" instead of, "What will this do to people?"

He closed his eyes, hearing her balcony question again. What decision lets you sleep at night?

"Not yet," he said finally. "We go public when the safeguards are in place. Not before."

Rhett stared at him for a long, long moment. Something subtle shifted in his expression. Not rage. Not betrayal. Just a bruise forming where trust used to be.

"Fine," he said at last, standing abruptly. "But the window won't stay open forever."

He swept up the documents and walked out without looking back like a retreating tornado cloud.

D'Andra blew out a breath.

"You know he's not going to drop it," she said.

"I know," Kyrel said quietly. "But at least now he knows where my line is."

When the IPO finally did happen, it happened like everything else in their lives had lately—suddenly and all at once.

The safeguards were in place. The ethics protocols had been formalized and baked into the architecture. Regulatory oversight frameworks had passed enough muster to satisfy at least the first line of government auditors. And the pressure outside had become relentless. Every analyst blog. Every investor column. Every tech podcast asked the same questions.

WHEN WILL LinkLife GO PUBLIC?
WHAT IS KYREL KADE WAITING FOR?

On the morning of the listing, the financial network anchors were giddy:

"—the most anticipated tech IPO in a decade—"
"—disrupting everything from payments to hospital records—"
"—some calling it 'the new nervous system of the digital world'—"

Behind the frosted glass of the Exchange's VIP lounge, Kyrel adjusted his tie for the third time and wished he were anywhere else.

Rhett looked like he'd been born in a suit, working the room with a perfect blend of charm and adrenaline. Investors, bankers, underwriters—they all orbited him like satellites.

Madeline Vyre, their financial advisor, stood near the monitors with her tablet, assessing the data feed as if she were tracking vital signs in an ICU.

D'Andra slipped her hand into Kyrel's. "You look like someone handed you a live grenade with the pin pulled," she said.

"That's because they did," he replied.

"This doesn't change who you are," she said.

He didn't answer. Because he wasn't sure that was true.

The opening bell was an absurdly ceremonial thing—a polished button, a countdown, a cheer. The numbers on the screens around them flickered and surged, the ticker streaming with their symbol.

LinkLife's initial price jumped within minutes.

"Look at that," one of the bankers crowed. "Look at that climb."

It kept climbing. Rhett watched with something like religious awe. "We're doing it," he whispered. "We're actually doing it."

Kyrel watched the valuation number more than the price. He knew, abstractly, where his equity sat. Knew what percentage he held as CEO, what that meant in theory. But seeing it in real time did something strange to his perception of himself.

The number ticked up again. And again. Forty billion. Forty-two.

Madeline glanced at him, then at her screen, then back.

Her expression changed.

"Kyrel," she said quietly, stepping closer. "I need you to breathe."

He frowned. "I am breathing."

"Not enough," she replied. "And you should know—based on your equity and the current price—"

She turned the tablet so only he and D'Andra could see. The calculation was simple. His holdings had just crossed one billion dollars in value. The number stared up at him:

$$\$1,002,468,901.$$

He felt the floor tilt. It wasn't real, not in any tangible sense—just numbers on screens, valuations that could rise and fall and be argued over by pundits.

And yet.

A line had been crossed. A threshold he had told himself was theoretical—some distant problem for some other version of him—was suddenly under his feet. D'Andra's fingers tightened around his.

"What does that mean?" she asked softly, reading his face as much as the tablet.

He could already hear the echo of a law passed in outrage years earlier. A law most people called symbolic. A law the pundits said no one would ever actually trigger this fast.

The Federal Wealth Equity Act.
The so-called Billionaire Cap.

He swallowed. "I don't know yet," he said. But deep in his chest, something cold took root. He had wanted control so he could protect the world from his invention. Now he was starting to suspect that someone else had been waiting, patiently, to take control from him the second he crossed this line.

The crowd around them erupted into another cheer as the valuation climbed higher.

Rhett clapped him on the back, laughing. "We did it," his friend said. "We just rewrote the future."

Kyrel managed a thin smile. In the glow of the screens, the future looked very bright.

All he could feel was the lengthening shadow behind it.

CHAPTER 12
PRESENT DAY

The morning after the capping, the world looked mostly the same. Same pale rectangle of light creeping up the bedroom wall. Same hum of the old HVAC unit switching on. Same faint smell of coffee drifting up from the kitchen because D'Andra was incapable of facing any kind of crisis without caffeine.

For a few seconds, drifting at the edge of waking, Kyrel let himself believe that last night had been a very vivid, very bureaucratic nightmare. Then his gaze slid to the chair in the corner. The binder sat there where he'd dropped it, its bland gray cover catching the light.

YOUR NEW FISCAL LIFE: A GUIDE

He stared at the words until they blurred.

"Don't," D'Andra said softly from the doorway. "You'll give yourself a stroke before breakfast."

He turned his head. She leaned against the frame, hair twisted into a loose knot, still in sleep shorts and one of his old LinkLife t-shirts. A mug steamed in her hand.

"How long have you been up?" he asked.

"Long enough to discover that the Federal Wealth Equity Bank website is the dullest thing ever inflicted upon the human eye," she said, crossing to the bed. "And that they had your new account pre-generated before Weller even knocked last night."

She held out the mug.

He sat up, back protesting, and took it. "How is that supposed to make me feel better?"

"It isn't," she said. "It's supposed to make you angry enough not to collapse."

He took a cautious sip. The coffee was strong enough to file metal.

"They really had it ready?" he asked.

"Account number, routing, zero-interest terms, the whole package," she said. "Your old bank accounts are already marked 'transition pending.' One of them showed a cute little banner: 'Congratulations on your new status'!"

He made a small, strangled sound. "Of course it did."

She perched on the edge of the bed, watching him the way she watched patients emerge from anesthesia—measuring awareness, stability, the likelihood of unexpected collapse.

"How are you?" she asked.

He stared at the binder again.

"I feel like someone took my name tag off while I was sleeping," he said. "Like I'm still here, but whatever label I had in the system got peeled away and replaced with something… else."

She reached out, brushed her fingers along his jaw.

"You're still you," she said. "The system is what changed."

His phone buzzed on the nightstand, the vibration sharp in the quiet room.

He flinched.

D'Andra glanced at the display. "Rhett."

Kyrel closed his eyes briefly. "Of course."

"You don't have to—"

"I do," he said, and picked up.

"Hey," he said, voice coming out rougher than he'd intended.

"Hey, man." Rhett's voice crackled through, too bright, too fast. "How you holding up? You, uh… you okay?"

Kyrel stared at the binder.

"I had an interesting evening," he said. "How about you?"

"Yeah, no kidding," Rhett said, and laughed in a way that wasn't laughter. "Look, I saw the alert come through from legal and then I sat there for, like, an hour just…staring. They actually did it. They actually capped you."

"It's not a weather notification," Kyrel said quietly. "They didn't do it to a stock symbol. They did it to me."

There was a pause.

"Right," Rhett said. "Yeah. Sorry. Bad phrasing. I just—this law was supposed to be a scarecrow. Nobody thought they'd trigger it this fast."

"Apparently the market disagreed," Kyrel said.

Rhett exhaled. "Look, we'll figure this out. Madeline says there might be timing arguments, valuation challenges, all that boring legalese. Maybe we can make a case that you hadn't actually realized the gains yet. Maybe we can—"

"Rhett."

The word came out flat.

"Yeah?"

"It's done," Kyrel said. "They sent Weller. They had the paperwork waiting. The Bureau's already notified every bank I've ever sneezed near. There's nothing to 'figure out'."

"You don't know that," Rhett said quickly. "You don't know how much leverage we have until we try. Congress didn't intend for this law to gut innovation. If we talk to the right people—"

"Who do you have in mind?" Kyrel asked. " that got grandfathered in and dodged the Cap? The ones this law conveniently doesn't touch?"

Another silence. Longer this time.

"You should come in," Rhett said finally. "We've got a whole team freaking out. The board wants to know what this means for LinkLife's image. There are questions about your role going forward. It would help if you—"

"I can't go in today," Kyrel said.

You can't go in, Weller had said, in that gentle, implacable voice. Not as an executive. Not as an employee. Not as anything that could be interpreted as 'earning.'

"I've got a DEI review at nine," he added. "Mandatory."

"Right. Right." Paper rustled on Rhett's end, like he was shuffling through things just to burn off energy. "Okay, well… keep me posted. And, uh, man—"

He hesitated.

"I'm sorry," Rhett finished. "You know that, right?"

Kyrel wasn't entirely sure what Rhett was sorry for. The law? The timing? The fact that it had happened to Kyrel Kade and not someone more abstract?

"Yeah," Kyrel said, because that was easier. "I know."

They hung up.

D'Andra watched him set the phone down, her mouth tight.

"Well?" she asked.

"He's already thinking about spin," Kyrel said. "And leverage. And people we can talk to."

She snorted softly. "He would be."

The phone buzzed again almost immediately, this time with a calendar alert.

> MANDATORY REVIEW – DEPARTMENT OF
> ECONOMIC INTEGRITY
> 09:00 – 11:00
> ATTENDEES: T. WELLER, M. VYRE, K. KADE

"Efficient," D'Andra muttered. "They didn't waste time."

"They didn't have to," Kyrel said. "They've probably had that template sitting in a drafts folder for years, waiting for someone to cross the line."

He swung his legs over the side of the bed, the room tilting for a second as the weight of the night settled into his muscles.

"You don't have to go alone," she said.

"They made that pretty clear," he replied. "No lawyers, no advisors, no support animals."

"I meant I can wait outside," she said. "In case you someone to watch you punch a wall."

He managed a small smile. "Deal."

The first anomaly hit over something stupid. He needed gas. The world did not pause for macroeconomic reclassification.

On the way to the DEI building, he pulled into a station, slid his card into the reader, punched in his ZIP code on autopilot.

TRANSACTION DECLINED – CONTACT ISSUER

He frowned. Tried again. Same message. Behind him, a silver SUV waited for the pump, its driver already looking mildly irritated. He stepped aside, thumb already swiping over his phone screen to open his banking app. A cheerful banner popped up at the top:

WE'RE UPGRADING YOUR EXPERIENCE!

Some account features may be temporarily unavailable as we transition your profile to your new wealth category. We appreciate your patience.

Below it, a smaller, colder line:

STATUS: RESTRICTED PENDING FEDERAL REVIEW.

He stared at it until the letters stopped making sense.

"Problem?" the SUV driver called, leaning out his window.

Kyrel forced his jaw to unclench. "Card issue. I'm moving." He pulled the car forward, heart hammering, and parked near the convenience store. For a moment he just sat there, hands on the steering wheel.

D'Andra reached over and covered one of them with her own.

"You're not broke," she said quietly. "This is them showing you that they can flick the lights."

He let out a breath through his teeth.

"It's not just about paying for gas," he muttered. "It's the message. 'You move when we say you can move'."

She squeezed his fingers. "Then we treat today as reconnaissance. You're going into the machine's heart. Pay attention to how it ticks."

They went inside and paid in cash.

Cash, at least, still worked.

For now.

———————————

The DEI building looked exactly like the kind of place that would professionally strip the future from you. Not ominous. Not brutalist. Just... aggressively normal. Four stories of glass and beige stone, an American flag out front, a metal detector in the lobby, a row of young security officers in identical navy blazers and polite, watchful eyes.

"Federal Department of Economic Integrity," D'Andra read from the signage as they crossed the polished floor. "Who comes up with these names?"

"The same committee that chooses paint colors for operating rooms," Kyrel said. "So no one feels anything."

At the reception desk, an older woman with reading glasses on a chain took his ID, typed for a few moments, and then looked up at him with a new kind of attentiveness.

"Ah," she said. "Mr. Kade. Yes. You're on the list."

The way she said the list made a muscle in his neck tighten.

She slid a plastic visitor badge across the counter, printed with his name and a barcode. Unlike the other badges in the rack, his had a small red stripe along the bottom.

"What's that mean?" he asked, nodding at it.

"Just indicates you're here for a classified review," she said, as if it were a weather report. "Take the elevators to four. Agent Weller will meet you in Conference C."

D'Andra took the badge and clipped it to his jacket, fingers lingering on his lapel for a second longer than necessary.

"I'll be in the lobby," she said. "If you're not back in two hours, I start a riot."

He gave her a look.

"A very polite, legally non-actionable riot," she amended.

He almost smiled.

Almost.

Exiting the elevator, Kyrel noted the drab interior colors typical of a government building. There were signs on the walls indicating the direction to suite numbers and conference rooms. Turning right he walked past several unoccupied glass-in rooms. Entering Conference C, it smelled faintly of stale coffee and paper.

Thomas Weller was already there when Kyrel walked in, seated at one end of the long table with a neatly stacked folder and a government-issued tablet. Madeline Vyre sat halfway down the side, her own tablet open, her expression a carefully controlled mix of professional and something softer.

"Mr. Kade," Weller said, rising. "Thank you for coming."

His handshake was firm and forgettable. His tie was the exact shade of the carpeting. His eyes were the color of old photocopies.

"Do I have a choice?" Kyrel asked, taking the chair opposite him.

"In attending?" Weller said mildly. "The statute allows for enforcement in absentia, but in-person cooperation makes the process smoother for everyone."

"For everyone," Kyrel repeated.

Madeline gave him the tiniest shake of the head—don't start here—and slid a glass of water toward him.

"We're here to walk through the transition details," she said. "Some of this will repeat what we covered last night, but there are a few new items."

"New items," Kyrel echoed. "You work fast."

"We work within predetermined parameters," Weller said. "When you crossed the threshold, our systems were notified. Automated processes initiated. Our role is to ensure those processes are correctly aligned with your specific financial profile."

"Your systems," Kyrel said. "Meaning the same kind of infrastructure I spent ten years building, except yours is aimed at people instead of passwords."

Weller tilted his head a fraction. "If that helps you conceptualize it."

Madeline cleared her throat softly. "Kyrel, we should start with the basics," she said. "Your total holdings at the time of capping, the portion that has been converted to the Federal Trust account, the assets you may retain, and the restrictions moving forward."

He swallowed annoyance and nodded.

"Fine," he said. "Walk me through my new fenced-in life."

For the next forty minutes, they did.

Madeline did most of the talking, her voice steady and precise. She went over the numbers, the valuations, the liquidations in progress.

Weller spoke only when they hit enforcement triggers.

"Here," Madeline said, pointing to a line item, "is the primary residence. You retain full ownership. Property taxes continue as normal. You may not, however, use the house as collateral against any kind of credit instrument."

"Meaning no second mortgage," Kyrel said.

"Correct," Weller replied.

"And this—" Madeline scrolled "—is your parents' house. Since title transferred prior to your crossing the threshold and you do not hold an equity interest, it is unaffected."

Relief loosened something in his chest he hadn't realized was clenched.

"And my siblings?" he asked. "The trusts?"

"Existing educational and health trusts are grandfathered," she said. "No further funding may be added from your side. Their own earning potential remains intact so long as they do not cohabitate with you as dependents past age twenty-one."

He blinked. "I'm sorry, what?"

Weller folded his hands.

"Section 4C," he said. "To prevent income laundering through dependents, any adult residing in your primary household is subject to derivative cap enforcement. They may not earn income while they are part of your household entity."

Kyrel stared.

"So if my brother ends up crashing on my couch for six months while he looks for work…"

"He would have to choose between his income and remaining in your household," Weller said. "As would you, if you attempted to subsidize him in ways the statute defines as functional income replacement."

Anger flared, hot and clean.

"You do realize what that does to families?" he asked quietly. "To communities where people pile into one apartment just to survive? You realize you've taken the idea of 'making it' and turned it into a contagion that ruins everyone you're close to?"

"Our mandate is to prevent hyper-accumulation and the distortion of democratic and economic processes by individuals wielding disproportionate financial power," Weller said. "Family arrangements are an unfortunate collateral domain."

"Unfortunate," Kyrel repeated, the word ash in his mouth.

Madeline's jaw tightened. "Tom," she said, a warning in her voice. "We're here to inform, not to philosophize."

"I am not philosophizing," Weller said. "I am stating the law as written."

He turned back to Kyrel.

"I understand this is difficult," he said, and sounded like he almost meant it. "You may feel as though something fundamental has been altered overnight. I assure you, the core of your life remains unchanged. Your partner, your parents, your work—"

"My work?" Kyrel said sharply. "I don't have work anymore. You took it."

Weller didn't flinch.

"You still have purpose," he said. "You still have impact. You still have more resources at your disposal than ninety-nine point nine nine percent of citizens on this planet. What you no longer have is leverage. That was always the point of the Cap."

There it was.

Not shouted. Not snarled.

Just calmly placed on the table between them like a loaded, perfectly legal weapon.

Kyrel sat back, the chair creaking softly.

"So that's what I am now," he said. "A cautionary tale with a trust fund."

"If you choose to see it that way," Weller said. "Others might see you as proof that the law works."

Madeline's fingers tightened on her stylus.

"Tom," she said again, more firmly. "We've gone beyond scope."

He blinked and seemed to reset, like a program returning to its default menu.

"Apologies," he said. "In any case, Mr. Kade—we appreciate your cooperation. Ongoing system audits will monitor for any violations. You may, of course, contact our office with questions."

He slid a card across the table.

His name. His title. A generic DEI number.

And in the corner, in small, understated print: WEALTH EQUITY COMPLIANCE DIVISION – HIGH NET-WORTH CATEGORY.

Kyrel picked it up, turned it between his fingers.

"How many names do you have in this category?" he asked.

"I'm not at liberty to discuss other citizens' statuses," Weller said.

"But it's more than zero," Kyrel said.

A beat.

"Yes," Weller said.

Something cold moved through Kyrel's veins.

He slipped the card into his pocket.

Madeline closed her tablet.

"I'll send you a cleaned-up summary," she said softly. "Not the government version. The human one."

"Thank you," he said.

As he stood to leave, Weller rose as well.

"One more thing, Mr. Kade," the agent said. "There will be increased scrutiny on your transactions for the next six to twelve months as the system calibrates. It may manifest as slight delays or additional verification requests. Don't be alarmed. It's routine."

Kyrel thought of the gas pump.

"I'll try to contain my excitement," he said.

Back in the lobby, D'Andra sat in a plastic chair beside a potted plant that looked as depressed as he felt, scrolling through her phone. The moment she saw him, she stood.

"Well?" she asked.

He looked around.

People moved through the space with the same ordinary government-building bustle as before. A suit-jacketed man arguing politely about a parking ticket. A woman in a postal uniform laughing with a friend. A janitor pushing a cart, earbuds in.

The sunlight still slanted in at the same angle through the glass. The world had not tilted. But the line between him and it had.

"Nothing exploded," he said. "That's the good news."

"And the other news?" she asked.

He exhaled, feeling the weight of the card in his pocket, the binder waiting at home, the invisible systems whirring to reclassify his existence.

"The other news," he said, "is that nothing looks different, and somehow that's worse."

As they stepped back out into the daylight, his phone buzzed again.

A new voicemail alert. Unknown number. He tapped it, held the phone to his ear.

"Mr. Kade," a woman's voice said, crisp and low. "My name is Tara Winslow. I'm an investigative journalist with The Ledger. I'm working on a piece about the Wealth Equity Act and its real-world impact. I know you've had the longest twenty-four hours of your life, but when you're ready, I'd like to hear your side of what happened. Off the record at first, if you prefer."

A pause.

"For what it's worth," she added, "I don't think the story they're going to tell about you is the whole one. I'd like to help change that."

The message ended. Kyrel lowered the phone slowly.

"Who was that?" D'Andra asked.

"Someone who wants a story," he said.

"And?"

"And," he said, looking back at the DEI building's bland facade, "it sounds like she already knows the ending they've written for me."

He turned toward the street, the city, the life that was supposedly unchanged.

"I'm not sure I'm ready to accept it."

CHAPTER 13
TERMS AND CONDITIONS

Kyrel woke before the alarm, heart already racing.

For one disorienting moment he expected to see the LinkLife dashboard glowing on his wall, graphs and timelines and rolling adoption curves. Instead there was only the dim wash of Atlanta dawn through the blinds and the soft weight of D'Andra's arm across his chest.

He lay perfectly still and let the previous day replay, frame by frame.

The letter. The visit. Weller's beige smile. The binder on the table, like a brick of law.

And underneath all of that, like a splinter in his brain, two things: the notification he'd seen briefly on his phone before everything went sideways; the sound of Rhett's voice on the call that followed.

He eased his way out from under D'Andra's arm, careful not to wake her, and padded barefoot into the kitchen. The binder sat where he'd left it, beside the cold coffee mug and the plate with the untouched toast.

He didn't touch the binder. He went for his laptop.

The DEI system had already stripped him out of LinkLife's live financial environment, but it hadn't yet caught up to his personal backups. Old habits of his; he made mirrors of anything that mattered, snapshots of databases, exports of logs. Not because he didn't trust his own systems, but because he didn't trust the world around them.

He logged into his offline archive. No two-factor now. The irony stung.

Transaction history. Board resolutions. Licensing agreements. Internal valuation reports.

He opened the financial log export from forty-eight hours before Weller's knock.

Scrolling, his eyes tracked the clean, familiar flow of numbers. Revenue lines. Vendor payouts. Payroll runs. Micro-licensing deals ticking like metronomes.

And there it was.

> 03:14 a.m.
> Transaction ID: LL-AX-77492
> Counterparty: Venture Bridge Holdings (Special Licensing)
> Amount: $224,800,000

He had seen it on his phone in that hazy, stunned blur after reading the Cap notice. A single line in a flood of data, out of place because of its size and timestamp. He'd told himself he'd imagined the number. Or misread it.

But he hadn't.

"Two hundred and twenty-four," he murmured. "At three in the morning. From a shell license that doesn't exist in the primary catalog."

He drilled into the description. The text was weirdly generic for a deal that size:

> Global non-exclusive strategic access to LinkLife infrastructure APIs and protocols.

There was no region listed. No client name beyond Venture Bridge. No board minutes attached. No approval trail under his credentials. And yet the ledger tagged it as founder-attributable earnings. His earnings.

Kyrel leaned back, pulse thudding in his throat.

The letter had listed his lifetime capped total at $1,200,468,901.72. That was before this 3:14 a.m. transfer, his internal estimate had hovered just under $980 million. He and Madeline had run the numbers. There had been room. Breathing space. Time.

That single deal was the difference.

His first thought was: I missed this. I should've seen it coming.

His second was colder: Or someone made sure I didn't see it until it was too late.

He pulled up the metadata. Every internal action left fingerprints—system accounts, device IDs, authentication chains. Even if the DEI had seized live access, the snapshot of what it looked like before they walked in was still his. He found the authorization trail.

> User: R.Colburn
> Device: OFFICE-MARBLE-01
> Authentication: SSO token, elevated admin access.

Rhett's machine. Rhett's credentials. A quarter-billion dollar licensing agreement pushed through in the dead hours before dawn. No email thread. No board vote. No Slack debate. Just a document number and a digital signature.

Kyrel stared at the screen until the text began to blur.

"Ky?" D'Andra's voice was soft behind him. He jumped anyway.

She padded in wearing one of his Georgia Tech hoodies, hair wild from sleep, a faint pillow-crease on her cheek. She stopped when she saw his face.

"That bad?" she asked.

"It's… illuminating," he said.

She came around the table and leaned a hip against it, looking at the laptop. "Is that from yesterday's meeting?"

"Beforehand," he said. He pointed to the line on the screen. "That's the time: 3:14 a.m. Venture Bridge licensing. Two twenty-four eight. No authorization from me, no board minutes, no prior discussion."

Her eyes narrowed. "Who signed it?"

"Rhett."

There was a beat where her features didn't move at all, and then they hardened.

"Did you know anything about this?"

"No."

"And this," she traced the number with her fingertip, "was enough to push you over?"

"Yeah." His mouth felt dry. "It's the difference between 'we have a few years' and 'congratulations, your life is over'."

She slid into the chair beside him. "It could be a mistake."

"It could," he said.

They both knew that in startups of their size, quarter-billion-dollar licensing deals did not accidentally materialize at three in the morning.

"And Rhett called you," she said slowly. "Right after the letter."

"Yeah."

"How did he sound?"

He closed his eyes and replayed it—the way the phone had started buzzing before he'd even processed the whole binder; Rhett's breathless "Ky, man, you okay? I just saw—holy shit, are you capped?"; the tangle of outrage and something sharper under it.

"It didn't sound like a surprise," he said. "It sounded like… panic. But not the kind you get when you didn't see something coming. More like when you did, and it went sideways."

D'Andra folded her arms. "So what do we think? Rhett engineered this? Or someone used his credentials?"

"I don't know yet," Kyrel said. "But this—" he tapped the screen "—this is the last thing that happened before the Cap system tripped. And it's tagged as founder earnings. Which means it landed on my ledger, not his."

"Convenient," she muttered.

He watched the transaction flicker on the display, the numbers impossibly clean.

"I need to talk to him," he said, picking up his phone and turning on the speaker so that D'Andra could hear the conversation.

Rhett answered on the second ring.

"Ky." He answered too fast, too bright. "I was going to call you. How are you holding up, man?"

"I've been better," Kyrel said. "Got a minute?"

"For you? Always. Listen, about yesterday—"

"Did you get capped too?" Kyrel cut in.

There was a silence, sharp and sudden, like a dropped glass.

"What?" Rhett laughed, a little too loudly. "No. Jesus. No. I'm nowhere near your numbers, man. You built the core, remember? I'm just the guy waving my arms at investors."

Kyrel pressed his thumb into the edge of the table until it hurt. "So the DEI didn't call you. No letters. No visits."

"No, Ky." The false cheer peeled a little at the edges. "Why would they? I—look, I've got equity, yeah, but nothing like your stake. You were always the one on the rocket."

"Right," Kyrel said. "The rocket."

He flicked the transaction open again with his free hand, forcing his voice to stay even.

"Tell me about Venture Bridge Holdings," he said.

Another pause. Shorter this time, but heavy.

"Venture Bridge? They're just—one of the licensing vehicles Madeline lined up, I think. Why?"

"I'm looking at a two hundred and twenty-four million dollar 'strategic access' deal that went through at three fourteen a.m. yesterday," Kyrel said. "Signed from your machine. With your credentials. No board vote."

Rhett exhaled slowly. For the first time, his voice lost its manic gloss.

"Okay," he said. "Okay. Look. I was going to bring it up with you today. Everything was moving so fast after the valuation call that

I—yeah, I pushed it through. We had pressure on the cap table, VCs wanting guarantees, governments sniffing around, and Venture Bridge came in with this offer to lock in API access. It was supposed to be a hedge, not a… trigger."

"A hedge," Kyrel repeated with an ever-so-slight rise in his voice. "That credited nearly a quarter-billion to my personal earnings."

"Because the founder allocation was baked into the original structure," Rhett said quickly. "It's pro rata—look, you know this. Our lawyer should've flagged it before—"

"But she didn't."

"It's been chaos," Rhett snapped, then recalibrated. "Ky, I swear, I wasn't trying to screw you. We were getting boxed in by the Cap system anyway, you know that. All the models said you'd cross the line in six months at most. I was trying to give the company some runway before DEI came stomping through the front door."

"You did that part," Kyrel said. "They didn't bother with the door. They just teleported into my living room."

On the other end, he could hear the faint clack of a keyboard, as if Rhett were already pulling up something to defend himself.

"You shouldn't be alone in this," Rhett said. "We should be sitting in the same room, looking at the same numbers. Let me come over, okay? We can—"

"No," Kyrel said.

D'Andra glanced at him, eyes questioning. He shook his head slightly.

"You can send me whatever you think I'm missing," he continued. "Board minutes, external counsel notes, term sheets. For now, I just need to know one thing."

"Anything," Rhett said.

"Were you counting on me being out of the company once the Cap hit?"

The silence this time was a live wire.

"I was counting on you being… limited," Rhett said carefully. "The law is the law, Ky. Founders don't stay in the cockpit when the system declares them a 'completed economic unit' or whatever bullshit term Weller uses. I figured, yeah, DEI would force you to step back, we'd restructure, keep the mission alive. Someone has to."

"And that someone was going to be you."

"Who else?" Rhett said, stung. "I've been in every investor room with you, I know the landscape, the regulators, the—"

"Right," Kyrel said again. This time there was finality in his voice; a definite period at the end. His chest felt strangely cold. "That's what I thought."

"Ky—"

"I've got another meeting this morning," he said. "We'll talk later."

Kyrel hung up before Rhett could form the next word.

D'Andra watched him for a long beat.

"Well," she said quietly. "That was not the voice of a man blindsided by circumstance."

"No," Kyrel said. His hand was still clenched around the phone. He made himself set it down. "He didn't push the button thinking, this will cap Kyrel today. I believe that much."

"But he knew it would happen soon."

"And he was okay with planning for a world where I wasn't in the building," Kyrel said.

He turned the laptop toward her, showing the thin line of text and numbers again.

"This—this is the kind of thing LinkLife was supposed to protect people from," he said. "Invisible access. Unseen decisions. Systems moving unseen under your feet because someone with the right credentials decided they knew best."

She reached over and covered his hand with hers.

"So what do you do, Ky?" she asked. "You can't untrigger the Cap. You can't unsign whatever Rhett signed. You can't go back to not being on that list."

"I can decide what I do with what's left," he said.

He looked down at her hand, at the faint white scars on her knuckles from residency, at the softness that lived beside all the steel.

"I thought about what you said," he added.

Her brow crinkled. "Which part?" she asked. "I say a lot of things when I'm angry at bureaucrats."

"You said I'm more than what the system counts," he said. "That if they take the wealth part away, there's still the part that builds."

He exhaled slowly.

"If I walk away from LinkLife completely, Rhett and whoever else is whispering in his ear will own the code. The board will drift toward whoever promises the best quarterly story. Governments will push for backdoors. Soren Vale and the power-crazed sharks like him will start figuring out how to exploit it in the dark."

"You think you can stop all that by staying?" she asked.

"No," he said. "But I can make it harder."

Kyrel pushed his chair back, the legs scraping softly across the floor.

"They want me economically dead," he said. "Fine. I'll be economically dead. I'll sign whatever they want that says I will not earn another cent. I'll let them hold the billion like a hostage if it makes them feel better."

D'Andra's eyes widened. "Kyrel—"

"But I am not giving up the cockpit," he said. "Not while there's still fuel in the tank. If Rhett thought the Cap Act was going to hand him the captain's chair, he can sue the law, not me."

"You're going to ask to stay on," she said slowly. "As CEO."

"Without salary. Without equity. Without bonuses or perks. No stock, no profit share, no consultancy fees. Just... authority. And accountability."

"And the government is just going to let you do that?" she said.

"That's what I'm going to find out," he said.

This time arriving at the DEI field office, it looked exactly like the kind of building that would administer a law about the end of earning: modern, efficient, and utterly devoid of warmth.

Kyrel sat in a chilled conference room with floor-to-ceiling glass and no view, the binder sitting in front of him like an accusation. D'Andra had wanted to come, but he'd asked her to stay home. There was a part of this he needed to walk into alone.

The door opened at 9:01.

Thomas Weller entered first, his navy suit as unrumpled as if it had been pressed by an algorithm. He carried a slim leather folio under one arm. Behind him came Madeline Vyre in a charcoal dress and sharp-framed glasses, tablet in hand.

"Mr. Kade," Weller said. "Thank you for being punctual."

"Occupational habit," Kyrel said.

If Weller heard the edge, he didn't show it. He sat opposite Kyrel, placed the folio neatly on the table, and folded his hands. Madeline took the chair slightly to the side, positioning herself at an angle that let her see both their faces and her screen.

"I trust you had time to review the Citizen Wealth Transition packet I left with you yesterday," Weller said.

"I skimmed the parts about 'no income, ever, for the rest of your life'," Kyrel said. "The typography was excellent."

Madeline's mouth twitched at the sarcasm, almost a smile. Weller did not deviate.

"The Federal Wealth Equity Act is explicit," Weller said. "Once a citizen surpasses the lifetime threshold, all further earning activity is prohibited. As of this morning, your accounts reflect the transition. Your assets have been consolidated into a non-interest-bearing protected fund. Your name has been removed from all registered earnings-capable positions. We are here to answer questions and finalize any clarifying agreements."

"Good," Kyrel said. "I have one."

Weller waited.

"I want to stay on as CEO of LinkLife," Kyrel said. "With full operational authority. I will accept no salary, no bonus, no equity, no consultancy fees, no honoraria, no speaking fees, no 'in-kind' compensation, no stock, no stock options, no phantom shares, no profit-sharing, no gifts of value from the company. I will not participate in any mechanism by which I benefit financially from LinkLife or any subsidiary."

Madeline blinked.

Weller tilted his head a fraction. "Mr. Kade, the law—"

"I've read the law," Kyrel said. "It prohibits earning. It does not prohibit working. It says nothing about volunteering my time."

"That… is technically correct," Madeline said slowly, eyes flicking over whatever statute she had pulled up. "Prohibited activities are defined as those in which the citizen receives direct or indirect financial benefit. The Act is silent on uncompensated roles."

"Silent is not the same as sanctioned," Weller said. "Mr. Kade, you must understand: the intent of the Cap is to remove the incentive structure that leads to accumulated systemic distortion. Remaining in a position of corporate authority after transition, raises concerns. You would retain significant influence over capital flows."

"I already had significant influence over capital flows," Kyrel said. "The difference now is that I no longer have any personal financial reason to push them in one direction over another."

"That assumes perfect personal integrity," Weller said mildly. "Law is not written on that basis."

Kyrel leaned forward, resting his forearms on the table.

"You need me in that chair more than you need me out of it," he said. "You may not realize that yet, but you will."

Madeline's gaze sharpened. "How so?"

"Because LinkLife isn't just another fintech play," he said. "It's infrastructure: Identity infrastructure. Payment infrastructure. Health infrastructure. Once it's fully deployed, you will have a population that moves, pays, authenticates, and accesses services through a system whose root key I helped design."

He met Weller's pale eyes and held them.

"Who do you want watching that system?" he asked. "The guy who built it and has publicly committed to never taking another dollar from it? Or whoever my board hires next based on how many times they've floated a unicorn in Silicon Valley?"

The air in the room suddenly felt heavier, the hum of the ventilation almost unbearingly loud.

Weller steepled his fingers. "You assume the Department would allow LinkLife to continue operating under purely private governance?"

"You can nationalize it," Kyrel said. "You can regulate it. You can drown it in oversight. I can't stop you. But if you're going to use it at all, someone with a moral stake in how it's used should be in the room. That won't be my successor if you cut me out."

Madeline cleared her throat softly.

"Agent Weller," she said, "there is precedent for uncompensated advisory roles post-Cap. We've permitted capped individuals to serve on non-profit boards, global councils, even certain UN bodies, provided they receive no pay and no material benefits. The law doesn't distinguish between non-profit and for-profit on that axis."

"We are not talking about a neighborhood literacy council," Weller said, maintaining eye contact with Kyrel. "We are talking about executive control of a system that will soon sit beneath a substantial portion of the national economy."

"Which is exactly why you want someone who doesn't need it to make them rich," Kyrel said. "You've seen the papers on concentrated capital, on billionaire capture. You helped write this Act to stop exactly that. Let me help you stop the next wave."

Weller regarded him in silence for several moments.

"Your proposal specifies 'full operational authority,'" he said eventually. "You understand that the Department cannot dictate corporate governance structures to private entities except in cases of criminal conduct."

"I'm not asking you to," Kyrel said. "I'm telling you, under what conditions I'm willing to stay. Whether the board accepts those conditions is their problem. Your problem is whether you consider my unpaid presence in that role a violation of the Cap."

Madeline looked between them, then down at her tablet.

"There is one more thing you should know," she said quietly. "If you take this path, the Department will flag your profile as high-risk."

"Because I'd be near money," Kyrel said.

"Because you'd be near power," she said. "And because if anything goes wrong with LinkLife, a security breach, black-market access, unauthorized forks, the first question every oversight body will ask is, 'Where was Kyrel Kade?' You will be the face of every success and the scapegoat for every failure. With no financial cushion beyond your existing billion."

"Technically," Weller added, "even that cushion is not fully secure if you are found to be in violation of the Act. All assets in your protected fund are subject to seizure upon criminal conviction."

Kyrel nodded slowly.

"I'm aware," he said. "Consider this my collateral."

Madeline's brows lifted. "You're staking your entire remaining wealth on your ability to stay clean in a system that will actively tempt you to cheat?"

"I'm staking it on my ability to say no," he said. "And on your ability"—he nodded at Weller—"to do your job without playing favorites."

For the first time since Kyrel had met him, something like a flicker of emotion passed behind Thomas Weller's eyes. It might have been irritation. It might have been respect.

"You believe yourself incorruptible," Weller said.

"No," Kyrel said. "I believe I know who I am when there's no profit left on the table."

He realized his hands had curled into fists on the tabletop. He made himself relax them.

"Look," he said more quietly. "You called me a 'completed economic unit.' Fine. I'm complete. But I'm not… finished. The work isn't finished. If the Cap Act is supposed to keep people like me from becoming kings, good. I never wanted to be a king. But taking away my crown doesn't mean you have to pluck out my eyes and throw me out of the city forever."

Madeline's jaw tightened. She looked at Weller.

"The law allows what he's asking," she said. "If we deny it, we set a precedent for banning not just earnings, but participation. That's… a different country than the one you and I signed on to protect."

Weller's gaze lingered on her for a heartbeat, then returned to Kyrel.

"Very well," he said. "Here are the conditions under which the Department will not pursue enforcement action regarding your continued involvement with LinkLife."

He opened his folio, withdrew a slim sheaf of paper, and slid it across the table. The top page was already titled:

UNCOMPENSATED EXECUTIVE ROLE
COMPLIANCE ADDENDUM

Madeline's eyebrows shot up. "You had that ready?"

"We have templates for many contingencies," Weller said.

Kyrel scanned the bullet points: no direct or indirect financial compensation of any kind; no personal use of corporate assets beyond strictly defined operational scope; no preferential access to corporate investment opportunities for family, associates, or proxies; full transparency of all personal accounts and transactions; mandatory quarterly audits; immediate resignation required if board or regulators deem his presence a material risk.

At the bottom, a line:

> I, the undersigned, acknowledge that any violation of these terms will be considered a willful breach of the Federal Wealth Equity Act and subject to criminal penalties, including but not limited to asset seizure and imprisonment.

Weller pushed a pen toward him.

"You are placing yourself in a position of profound vulnerability, Mr. Kade," he said. "If your intent is anything other than what you have represented here, I strongly advise you to reconsider."

Kyrel thought of his father patching frayed power cords so the kids wouldn't get shocked. His mother holding an ICU patient's hand on Christmas Eve. The way Atlanta had felt sitting under the glow of a thousand LinkLife launch billboards.

Then he remembered the sound of Rhett's voice on the phone. He signed.

Outside, the air felt too bright.

The DEI building loomed at his back, all mirrored glass and invisible machines. For a strange, suspended moment, he had the sensation of watching himself from above: a man walking away from a vault he had just handed the keys to and voluntarily locked himself out of.

A notification buzzed on his phone. He checked it, expecting another DEI message. It was a news alert instead:

LinkLife FOUNDER TO STAY ON AS UNPAID CEO AFTER HITTING ONE-BILLION CAP
"I'm here to protect the code," says Kade.

Tara Winslow's byline glinted beneath the headline. Of course she'd found out. Of course someone in that building had leaked. Kyrel stared at the words: unpaid CEO. It looked like an oxymoron, like 'bureaucratic efficiency' or 'military intelligence'. It also looked exactly right.

His screen lit again with an incoming call.

Rhett.

Kyrel let it ring out. He slid the phone back into his pocket and started walking toward the street.

Somewhere across the city, in a glass office Kyrel had once helped pick the lighting fixtures for, Rhett Colburn would be seeing the same headline.

Kyrel could imagine the exact moment his partner's expression shifted—from shock, to calculation, to something darker.

You thought the game ended for me, he thought, as the sun cleared the lip of the building and threw his shadow long on the pavement.

But I'm still on the board.

CHAPTER 14

THE SHADOWS CONVENE

By dawn, LinkLife's headquarters rose out of the Atlanta fog like a half-built cathedral, cranes suspended mid-air, glass panels catching the early sun, security badges flashing as employees streamed in.

Kyrel hadn't slept at all.

He stood on the curb for a moment, breathing in cold morning air, feeling the weight of his new reality settle over him. He was the CEO again. But without a cent of ownership. With no income. No legal voice except the authority they begrudgingly gave him. And the entire world was watching.

Kyrel tapped his badge as he approached the front doors. They opened.

He walked past the boardroom where it all happened on that fateful night. It felt unfamiliar now; too large, too polished, too corporate to match the beating heart he'd poured into this company.

Rhett was already there. Standing there, arms crossed and no smile. Not surprising. There were no congratulations either. Just a startled blink that didn't hide the flash of panic in his eyes.

"You're... back?" Rhett said.

Kyrel simply set his binder on the table. "Yes. Pro bono CEO. The board approved it."

Rhett swallowed. Hard. "That wasn't… exactly the plan."

"I know," Kyrel said, meeting his friend's eyes. "That's why I'm here."

Behind Rhett, screens were active on his laptop: spreadsheets, subsidiary ledgers, financial movements that should've been locked away, not on display before the meeting had even started.

Rhett snapped the laptop closed like he'd been caught looking at something indecent. Kyrel didn't comment. He didn't need to. The air said everything.

The door opened again. Madeline Vyre stepped in with a tablet under her arm and a gaze sharp enough to cut granite. She paused when she saw Kyrel in the CEO's chair.

"Good," she said. "This will simplify some things."

Rhett's jaw tightened. "Will it?"

"Oh yes," she replied smoothly. "It's much easier to assess compliance when the subject is in the room."

A faint flush crept up Rhett's neck. She had not said which subject. Kyrel folded his hands.

"Let's begin," she said. "There were irregularities." Madeline projected a financial chart onto the wall.

"Mr. Kade," she said, "you asked to see the data that pushed you over the one-billion mark. I've prepared a summary."

Rhett straightened in his chair. "Wait—he asked who pushed him over?"

Kyrel didn't look at him.

"Yes." Madeline clicked the remote. A series of highlighted entries appeared, small, seemingly harmless payments funneling through two subsidiaries Kyrel didn't recognize: Cascade Media, Vector Crossing, amounts: $480K, $610K, $725K, $1.6M

Rhett went completely still.

"These entities," Madeline said, "do not appear on the original LinkLife corporate map filed at IPO. They were added later."

Kyrel kept his voice neutral. "When?"

"Fourteen months ago."

Kyrel turned his head slowly toward Rhett.

Rhett lifted his hands.

"Don't look at me like that. These were standard expansions, marketing funnels, licensing partnerships—"

"They diverted revenue." Kyrel's voice was quiet. Not angry. Just… certain.

Rhett flushed. "That's how companies grow, Ky! Everyone sets up shells. You think Apple reports every dime directly? These were legal structures, placed by legal counsel."

"Whose counsel?" Madeline asked, her tone clinical.

Rhett hesitated. His silence was a confession.

As if she was sitting next to him, D'Andra's voice floated up from memory, steady, commanding: "If something doesn't make sense, Ky... follow it. Don't assume you're wrong. Assume you're being misled." And for the first time, Kyrel truly followed it. He tapped the table.

"Rhett... the night they capped me, you called. You were upset. Panicked. You said we 'weren't ready.' What did you mean?"

Rhett opened his mouth. Closed it. Opened it again. "That wasn't about this," he said finally. "It was about the IPO fallout. The pressure. Investors wanting—"

"Stop." Kyrel's voice flattened. "Think carefully. You're talking to someone who literally lost everything overnight because of a number I didn't hit alone."

Rhett's jaw worked, but no words came.

Madeline cleared her throat delicately. "For the record," she said, "there is no evidence of criminal activity. Yet. But the irregularities will be investigated. By my department." Which meant, by Weller. Which meant, by the full weight of the United States government.

Rhett finally snapped. "This is insane!" he burst out, half rising. "You think I sabotaged you? You think I wanted you capped? Ky—c'mon. We built this together. Why would I want you gone?"

Kyrel didn't raise his voice. He didn't budge. He simply said, "Because if I was gone… someone else would sit in this chair." The accusation hung there like smoke from a gun.

Rhett's eyes darted to the closed laptop, the one Kyrel had seen open when he walked in. Something electric passed between them. Recognition. Fear. And something darker.

A knock at the conference room door broke the silence. Three soft, precise taps, then the door opened and Thomas Weller stepped in as if summoned by ritual, a lanyard tucked into his jacket. His suit was immaculate of course and his expression was unreadable.

"Good morning," he said mildly. "I understand we are discussing irregularities."

Rhett went pale. Madeline straightened like a soldier. Kyrel said nothing. Weller placed a sealed envelope on the table.

"For you, Mr. Kade," he said. "A record of all transactions attributed to your identity during the earning quarter prior to your capping." He turned to leave, then paused. "And Mr. Colburn…" His gaze shifted, cool and soft as frost. "We'll be reviewing all transactions connected to your digital signatures as well. Merely a formality."

It was not a warning. Not a threat. Just a statement. Which made it a thousand times more terrifying. He left without another word. The door clicked shut.

Rhett stared at the closed envelope like it was a timebomb. "Ky…" he said softly, almost pleading. "You don't think I'd ever hurt you. Right?"

Kyrel didn't answer immediately. He held Rhett's gaze, long enough to make the silence heavy. Finally, he spoke, more quietly than before. "I think you'd protect the company," he said. "At any cost."

Rhett swallowed.

"And I think," Kyrel continued, "that you might not see the difference between protecting the company… and protecting yourself."

Rhett sank back into his chair, chest rising and falling too fast. The fracture between them just became real. Visible. And permanent.

CHAPTER 15

THE APPROACHES

By the time Kyrel left the boardroom, the sky had turned the color of poured molten steel. He stepped out into the wind with the crisp white envelope Weller had left him, its weight feeling unnatural in his hand, as if paper could contain a detonator.

He didn't open it. Not yet. Not with the walls still vibrating from Rhett's panic.

He walked. Past the plaza. Past the construction cranes. Past the glass tower he built and no longer owned. His body knew where it was going before his mind caught up.

LinkLife's campus had a quiet green space tucked behind the research wing where an old willow sheltered a park bench. It was a place he and Rhett used to sit on breaks, mapping out code on napkins. Before the boardrooms, before the lawyers, before the success.

Kyrel dropped onto the wooden bench, elbows on knees, envelope still clenched. The willow branches swayed above him, whispering against each other. You weren't wrong, they seemed to say. You were right to look. You were right to fight. He finally let out the breath he'd been holding since the night of the capping.

That's when he sensed someone watching. A presence, not threatening, but… patient. An observer.

"Mind if I sit?" a voice asked.

Kyrel looked up. A woman stood there with a notebook, a satchel, and hair blowing across her glasses. Tara Winslow: The journalist from the press frenzy. The one who didn't shove microphones in his face. The one who met his eyes with something like understanding. She wasn't holding a recorder. She wasn't holding her phone out. She was just… there.

He nodded.

She sat beside him, leaving a respectful gap, like someone approaching a grieving friend.

"I'm not here for an interview," she said quietly. "Off the record. Entirely."

Kyrel let the envelope rest in his lap. "Then why are you here?"

"Because," she said, "I recognize the look you're wearing."

He turned to her. "What look is that?"

Tara pushed her glasses up her nose. "The look of someone who's been punished for being brilliant."

The sentence sliced into him with the precision of a scalpel. "You think I'm being punished?" he asked.

"I think," she replied, "that your country just told you your worth begins and ends at a number. And that's not sustainable."

Kyrel looked down at the ground.

Tara leaned forward slightly, voice lowered. "I also think," she added, "someone pushed you over the cap. And I think you know it."

His throat tightened. She wasn't guessing. She was reading. "Do you have evidence?" she asked gently.

"Not yet," Kyrel said. She nodded like she'd expected that.

"Then you will. Because someone like you always finds it." She stood.

"Kyrel…" she said, like an afterthought. "When you do find it? Call me. Even if it's just to figure out what it means."

Then she walked away, her hair whipping in the wind, leaving him with the envelope and the soft rustle of willow leaves.

A voice inside him whispered: Open it. But he didn't, he couldn't, not yet. Because another approaching presence made the air shift again, this time with different energy, heavier, slower.

D'Andra was still in her scrubs from the free clinic, a light jacket thrown over her shoulders, hair in a tight bun. The moment she saw him, her face softened.

"Ky," she said quietly, kneeling in front of him. "You look like you're holding a bomb."

He handed her the envelope. She didn't open it either. Instead, she placed it between her palms like she was warming it. "What did they say inside?" she asked, searching his eyes.

"I don't know yet."

"Then what does it feel like?"

Kyrel rubbed a hand over his jaw. "Like Rhett lied to me," he whispered.

Her expression didn't change, just deepened. "Or…" she said softly, "that he lied to himself. And now he's trapped in the lie."

Kyrel swallowed. Because that sounded… true. Painfully true.

D'Andra sat beside him, her shoulder touching his.

"Kyrel…" she said, her voice steady. "You see the world differently. You always have. You don't chase wealth. You don't chase power. You chase meaning. That is why the world will test you."

He let his head fall back against the bench. "I wanted to protect the tech," he said. "I didn't want control. But maybe I was naïve."

"No," she said. Her tone sharpened, not unkindly, but like tempered steel. "You were honest. And honesty terrifies dishonest people."

Kyrel let that sink in. She rested a hand on his.

"And you can still protect it, Ky. Even now. Even without money. Even without owning a cent. You can lead. You can enforce ethics. You can be the one thing they can't calculate."

"What's that?" he whispered.

"Someone who won't break," she said.

He closed his eyes and just for a moment, he let himself breathe. D'Andra leaned her head on his shoulder. After a long minute, she tapped the envelope lightly.

"When you're ready," she said, "Open it. But don't let it define you. Let it direct you."

He traced the edge of the seal with his thumb. Someone had pushed him over. Someone wanted him capped. Someone was afraid of what he could still become. He opened his eyes, and fire settled in his chest. But before he could tear open the envelope—A shadow fell across the grass.

It was smooth, tall, and impeccably dressed. It was Soren Vale, the shark best-known as the Syndicate's recruiter. He was smiling toothily with a politeness that felt like sharpened glass.

"Mr. Kade," Vale said, voice warm with false sincerity. "Apologies for the intrusion. I simply wanted to offer my congratulations... and my condolences."

D'Andra stiffened. Kyrel straightened. Soren's smile widened a fraction. "I represent a network of individuals who believe you should be allowed to earn," he said. "To build. To create freely. Without... restrictions."

Kyrel's pulse kicked. "Not interested," he said.

"Oh," Soren replied, "I'm not here to recruit you, not yet." His eyes gleamed. "I'm here because someone else knocked on our door first."

Kyrel's breath froze. "Who?" he asked.

Soren's smile was slow. "Your partner."

Rhett.

Then Soren tipped his head politely. "We'll speak again, Mr. Kade. When you're ready." He walked away.

The air around Kyrel snapped into clarity. D'Andra closed her hand tight around his. The willow branches above them stilled. Kyrel swallowed hard. The envelope suddenly felt blistering hot in his hand.

CHAPTER 16

THE ENVELOPE

The world felt strangely quiet. As if the willow trees were holding their breath. As if the campus itself sensed that whatever happened next would bend the rails of Kyrel Kade's future.

D'Andra's hand rested lightly on his knee, steady, grounding, present. Kyrel slid a thumb under the edge of the seal.

It didn't tear. It gave way, like it had been waiting for him. Inside were three things: A printed financial report, a small red card stamped URGENT — INTERNAL, and a single sticky note in neat, machine perfect handwriting.

He read the sticky note first: For your clarity and cooperation. — T. Weller

Even D'Andra shivered. Kyrel unfolded the financial report and saw: Numbers, time stamps, routing codes, receipts for payments he'd never approved, Micro-royalties from licensing chains he'd never signed, subsidiaries he'd never touched funneling cash in tiny amounts, so small individually, but in aggregate?

It represented millions, no, tens of millions. It was enough to push him over.

Each entry was tagged with a digital identifier he recognized instantly.

His chest tightened. It wasn't his. It was his partner's. It was Rhett's signature key. Every transaction that pushed him over the one-billion cap had been authenticated not by Kyrel Kade but by Rhett Colburn's authorization chain.

His vision blurred. D'Andra leaned closer. "Ky…" she whispered. "What is it?"

He handed her the sheet. She studied it for maybe four seconds, then inhaled sharply. "That's Rhett's sig," she said. "Every one of these is his."

Kyrel nodded once. No words formed. Not yet. The red card caught D'Andra's attention next. She flipped it over. It wasn't a warning. It was a summary. Printed in unemotional bureaucratic phrasing:

DEI ANALYSIS NOTE — LEVEL 2 REVIEW
*The following earnings were attributed to Mr. Kyrel Kade due to matching project codes and overlapping digital signatures.
Discrepancies detected.
Routing keys inconsistent with K. Kade's standard authorization patterns.
Source signature: R. Colburn (probable).
Note: Attribution to K. Kade remains in effect until formal investigation concluded.*
Case escalated.

Kyrel exhaled through his nose. Escalated. That meant Weller's division was already moving.

D'Andra whispered, "He pushed you."

Kyrel nodded. "Yes."

"Ky…" Her hand found his. "Do you think he did it on purpose?"

Kyrel didn't answer. Because the truth was too complex for yes or no.

He thought of Rhett's face earlier— the panic, the pride, the desperation, the excuses. He remembered the call the night he was capped and the words "we weren't ready." He saw the laptop Rhett slammed shut when Kyrel entered the boardroom. He mused on Soren Vale and the Syndicate; of shadows inside shadows.

Kyrel folded the papers back into the envelope. Then he stood. Not abruptly. Not angrily. Just… with purpose. D'Andra rose beside him, reading the set of his shoulders.

"Ky," she said softly, "you're going to confront him."

He looked at her, really looked, and for a moment the weight pressed into him so deeply he could barely speak. "I have to know," he said. "Why he did it. Whether he meant to. What he thought would happen. If he thought I'd never notice. If he thought it was harmless. If he thought—" His voice cracked. "If he thought I didn't deserve to decide the fate of my own creation."

D'Andra cupped his cheek. "You're not going alone."

He closed his eyes. She kissed his forehead, a subtle, anchoring press of lips infused with quiet fire. When he opened his eyes, they were clear. Resolute.

A man preparing to face a betrayal he wasn't ready for but could no longer look away from. He stepped onto the path leading back toward the main building. Then—

A vibration buzzed in his pocket. His phone. A single message from an unknown number: Rhett is meeting with Vale tonight. If you want answers, go now.   —Madeline Vyre.

The world snapped into motion with crystalline clarity. Kyrel lifted his head, jaw tightening. D'Andra squeezed his hand again with meaning. "I'm coming with you."

"No," he said gently. "Not to this. Not yet."

"Ky—"

"I promise," he said, meeting her eyes, "I'm not walking into danger. I'm walking into truth."

She searched his face for a long moment. Then nodded, reluctantly. "I'll be here," she said. "When you're done."

Kyrel pulled her close, kissed her once, fiercely, gratefully.

Then he turned. And walked toward whatever waited for him. The air smelled like rain. Like a storm gathering. The willow branches rustled behind him as if whispering: Go!

CHAPTER 17

THE ROOFTOP

LinkLife's tower rose thirty floors above Atlanta, a clean spine of glass and steel. Kyrel had always loved the rooftop level. Back before the money, before the fame, before the Cap Act hung over his life like a guillotine, he and Rhett used to come up here to breathe.

There they were: Two kids staring at a skyline they dreamed of conquering together. They would be there late at night, coffee in hand, feet on the railing, imagining the world they would create.

Tonight, the staircase felt colder. He pushed open the heavy access door. It groaned, a long metal exhale, and the humid Atlanta night spilled across his face, warm and heavy with summer rain. Music throbbed faintly from a rooftop bar three blocks away. Neon lights flickered below. The city hummed around him. Near the edge, in the glow of a single rooftop lamp, two silhouettes stood.

One he knew instantly. One his bones recognized like a scar. Rhett. And beside him? That elegant shadow in a charcoal coat, hands tucked casually in his pockets, was Soren Vale.

They both turned when Kyrel stepped forward. For a moment, there was silence. But not empty silence. The kind that follows the moment a fault line finally cracks.

"Ky," Rhett said, again his voice too bright, too thin. "Man, hey, I didn't expect—"

"You did," Kyrel said softly. "You expected me the second Vale showed up at the campus."

Soren's mouth curved with predatory satisfaction. "Good evening, Mr. Kade."

Kyrel ignored him. His eyes stayed locked on Rhett's. "What's going on?"

Rhett ran a hand through his hair, a nervous tic Kyrel remembered from their all-night coding marathons. "It's not what it looks like—"

"It looks," Kyrel said, stepping closer, "like the same digital signature that authenticated your subsidiaries also authenticated the payments that pushed me over the cap."

Rhett froze.

"And it looks," Kyrel continued, "like you're meeting with the man whose Syndicate recruits capped billionaires into illegal earning pipelines."

Soren made a soft, amused sound. "I prefer the term 'unrestricted wealth consultancy'. So much gentler"

Kyrel shot him a look that could cut through glass.

Rhett lifted his palms, stepping forward, desperate. "Ky, listen. I had no idea those subs would route revenue through your signature chain. None. They were expansions, marketing branches, the lawyers approved them—"

"They used your signature, Rhett."

Rhett flinched. "Ky, I swear, I didn't mean to push you over. I didn't even think— I thought you were still… like, a hundred mil shy—"

"I was." Kyrel's voice dropped. "So how did I jump two hundred million in twenty-eight days?"

Rhett's jaw trembled. Soren watched like a cat watching two wounded birds.

"Answer me, Rhett."

Rhett looked down at his shoes, pristine white sneakers he always kept clean. "I—" He swallowed. "They were supposed to stay off your chain. I didn't expect DEI to attribute them to you."

"That is not an answer."

Rhett's voice cracked as he tried again. "I didn't do it to hurt you."

Kyrel nodded slowly. "But you did do it."

Rhett closed his eyes. A confession. Not malicious. Not calculated. Just selfish. Just… careless.

Soren folded his arms, amused by Rhett's unraveling. "Guilt is a fascinating emotion," he murmured. "Some feel it before the fall. Some after. Some not at all."

Rhett's head jerked up. "I didn't sabotage him! I didn't know!"

Kyrel held up the envelope. "This isn't speculation, Rhett. This is your signature. Your authorized accounts. Your subsidiaries. And not one of them was reported to DEI until after the cap."

Rhett's voice rose. "Because DEI is broken, Ky! It's a cage! This whole thing is insane, you know it is—!"

"I live in that cage," Kyrel said.

Rhett went silent.

"And unlike you," Kyrel added, "I didn't put myself there."

Soren let out a soft laugh. "Do you see why I came tonight, Mr. Kade? Your partner has vision. Anger. Resilience. He hates the cage too. And unlike you… he is willing to do what must be done to escape it."

Rhett's eyes widened. "Ky, I didn't— I didn't join him, I swear—"

"Oh, come now," Soren said. "You reached out to us."

Rhett spun toward Soren. "I asked for advice, not to—!"

"Intent," Soren said quietly, "is irrelevant. Action is what matters in my world."

Kyrel took a step forward. "Rhett," he said quietly, "why were you meeting with him?"

Rhett's voice dropped to a hoarse whisper. "I thought he could help me fix the mistake."

Kyrel blinked. "Fix?"

Rhett nodded, desperate. "DEI was never supposed to catch it. You were never supposed to be capped. But once it happened, I thought, maybe Vale's people could reverse it. Hide it. Undo it."

Soren smirked. "I told him the truth. Once capped, always capped. He needed… emotional closure."

Kyrel stared at Rhett. "You went to the Syndicate."

Rhett's throat bobbed. "I was trying to help—"

Kyrel shook his head. "You were trying to help yourself."

Rhett's breath hitched. "Ky, please—"

"Because if I was capped," Kyrel continued, voice low, "then you would be the face of LinkLife."

Rhett looked like a man punched in the stomach. "No," he whispered. "I never wanted—"

"Yes. You did."

Soren stepped closer, hands in his pockets, voice soft as velvet. "Mr. Kade… your friend's ambition is not a crime. It is a clarifier."

Kyrel ignored him. He took another step toward Rhett until they were only a few feet apart. "Tell me the truth," he said. "Were you jealous?"

Rhett's eyes filled. "Yes," he whispered.

It wasn't anger that hit Kyrel then. It was grief. Because jealousy is a wound. And wounds fester when hidden.

"Ky…" Rhett's voice broke. "I didn't mean to push you over. I swear. But when I saw it happening, when I saw those numbers climbing, I didn't stop it."

Kyrel swallowed hard. "And why didn't you?"

Rhett looked at him, really looked, with the hollow honesty of a man stripped to bone. "Because for one second, Ky… one terrible second… I wondered what LinkLife would look like with me in charge."

Kyrel didn't move.

Rhett took a shaking step back from his own words. "I'm sorry," he said. "I'm so sorry."

Kyrel's throat burned.

Meanwhile, Soren Vale smiled like a serpent seeing a very plumb mouse in its. "Well," he said softly, "this is going to be… interesting."

CHAPTER 18

FALLOUT

The next morning, Atlanta woke up already talking about him. Kyrel didn't have to turn on a screen to know it. He could feel it in the way his phone buzzed on the nightstand; in the way D'Andra's colleagues pinged her with "are you seeing this??" texts; in the way the air outside the bedroom window seemed wired, caffeinated, vibrating.

He lay on his back, staring at the ceiling. D'Andra propped herself up on one elbow beside him.

"You're not looking," she said.

"Nope," he replied.

"You're absolutely trending."

"I assumed."

She studied him for a moment.

"Do you want to look?"

"Not yet."

She nodded.

"Good."

They got ready without rushing. A simple meal of coffee and toast. A quiet moment at the kitchen table where D'Andra rested her foot against his under the table.

"This is going to be a long day," she said. "It started long three days ago."

He tried to smile.

She reached across the table and brushed crumbs from his sleeve like a ritual, a small, domestic act trying to anchor something enormous.

The knock came at 8:03 a.m. Exactly on time. It wasn't frantic, it was firm, measured, the rhythm of someone who believed in schedules more than weather.

Kyrel opened the door.

Thomas Weller stood there again, navy suit immaculate, lanyard tucked, expression as politely unreadable as ever.

"Mr. Kade," he said. "May I come in for a moment?"

Kyrel stepped aside. D'Andra watched from the kitchen doorway, arms folded.

Weller acknowledged her with a small nod. "Dr. Crost-Kade. Thank you for your continued volunteer service at Grady South. The Department appreciates your compliance."

"You're welcome," she said, voice thin with controlled dislike.

Weller turned back to Kyrel. "If it's any comfort," he said, "today's developments appear favorable to you."

Kyrel raised an eyebrow. "That's... not a sentence I expected to hear from you."

Weller allowed himself the faintest ghost of a smile. "Please," he said. "Sit."

They all did, Kyrel and D'Andra on one side of the table, Weller on the other, opening a leather folio with reverent precision.

"As you know," Weller began, "Level 2 reviews are initiated when our patterns-detection AI flags inconsistencies in earnings attribution."

Kyrel nodded. "The note in your envelope said as much."

"Yes," Weller replied. "I wanted you aware that DEI considered your case... anomalous." He slid a printed sheet across the table. "This," he said, "is the provisional finding."

Kyrel scanned it. He didn't breathe.

> EARNINGS ATTRIBUTED TO K. KADE:
> $1,200,468,901.72
> PROBABLE MISATTRIBUTION: $219,883,441.06
> SOURCE SIGNATURE DEVIATION: 88.7%
> ORIGIN: COLBURN-AUTHORIZED SUBSIDIARIES.

Underneath, in dense legalese:

Pending a full forensic audit, DEI provisionally concludes that Mr. Kade did not personally initiate, authorize, or benefit from the earnings that caused his breach of the cap threshold.

Kyrel looked up, stunned. "You're... saying I didn't earn it?"

"I am saying our models indicate you did not directly engage in those earnings mechanisms," Weller replied calmly. "However, the law as written is indifferent to internal corporate delegation. You were still the majority owner at the time."

"So I'm still capped," Kyrel said.

"Yes."

"And I still lose the company."

"Yes."

"That doesn't sound favorable."

Weller folded his hands. "Favorable," he corrected, "in comparison to being referred to the Department of Justice for deliberate Cap evasion."

Kyrel exhaled slowly. "Ah."

"Furthermore," Weller added, "the investigation has now expanded to include Mr. Colburn."

D'Andra sat up straighter. "What does that mean?" she asked.

"It means," Weller said, "we are examining whether Mr. Colburn's earnings, including those routed through the subsidiaries he authorized, have approached or exceeded the one billion threshold independently."

Kyrel's heart thumped once, hard. "And have they?" he asked.

"Not yet," Weller said. "But they are... close." He slid another page forward.

> PROJECTED LIFETIME EARNINGS — R. COLBURN: $927,114,308.09
> EST. THRESHOLD BREACH: < 12 MONTHS (if unmitigated).

D'Andra let out a low whistle. "Damn," she murmured.

Kyrel stared at the projection. "Unmitigated?" he repeated.

"This," Weller said, "is where today's developments become relevant."

"The board of LinkLife," Weller continued, "has agreed to a temporary restructuring of corporate leadership in order to stabilize both the company and its compliance posture."

He produced a third sheet, this one printed on LinkLife letterhead. Kyrel recognized the minimalist logo he'd sketched on a coffee sleeve four years ago.

Weller read it aloud in a neutral tone.

"Effective immediately, LinkLife Technologies announces the following leadership update:

— Founder Kyrel Kade returns as Chief Executive Officer, serving on a pro bono basis in accordance with Cap Act compliance.

— Co-founder Rhett Colburn transitions into the role of Chief Operating Officer, under temporary earnings suspension pending completion of DEI review.

— No equity compensation, stock options, or performance-based incentives shall be issued to capped or provisionally constrained executives.

LinkLife reaffirms its commitment to ethical innovation, transparency, and adherence to the Federal Wealth Equity Act."

Weller looked up. "I trust that clarifies the arrangement."

Kyrel blinked. "You're putting me back in charge," he said slowly. "Unpaid. And freezing Rhett's income."

"Correct."

"Who negotiated this?" D'Andra asked.

Weller's gaze didn't flicker. "Ms. Vyre initiated discussions with the board after I forwarded the Level 2 findings," he said. "In my professional opinion, this configuration most effectively safeguards compliance while leveraging Mr. Kade's... stabilizing influence."

D'Andra glanced at Kyrel.

Stabilizing.

Honesty terrifies dishonest people.

"And Rhett?" Kyrel asked quietly. "How is he taking this?"

"Mr. Colburn agreed under protest," Weller said. "His alternative was immediate capping review and potential criminal referral for negligent misattribution."

"So this is his… plea deal," D'Andra said.

"In colloquial terms," Weller replied, "yes."

Silence hummed for a moment. Kyrel stared at the letter.

"So," he said slowly, "let me make sure I understand. I am permanently capped. I cannot earn another dollar. But I am being handed authority over a company I no longer own, to ensure it doesn't break the law again."

"That is an accurate summary," Weller said.

"And Rhett," Kyrel continued, "keeps his earning potential if he works under me for free, under your microscope."

"For the duration of the review," Weller confirmed. "His earnings streams are suspended. His access is curtailed. But he is not yet capped."

D'Andra let out a soft, incredulous laugh.

"So you took the man who worships money," she said, "and made him watch it vanish in slow motion."

Weller's expression didn't shift. "The Cap Act is not designed as punishment," he said. "It is designed as correction."

"Tell that to his ego," D'Andra muttered.

Kyrel looked down at the paper again. Pro bono. Capped. Yet in charge. Exactly what he'd asked for, except now, it wasn't his terms. It was the system's.

"Do I have a choice?" he asked quietly.

Weller considered.

"Yes," he said. "You may decline the CEO position. In which case, the board will appoint an external candidate. One less familiar with the ethical constraints you wish to uphold."

D'Andra's hand found his under the table. "I think you just answered your own question," she murmured.

Kyrel nodded slightly. He had no desire to step back into the fire. But he had even less desire to leave his life's work in the hands of people who saw it as nothing but a printing press. He met Weller's gaze.

"I'll do it."

Weller nodded once.

"Very well. Sign here."

Kyrel signed. His name, neat, practiced, looked oddly naked without the usual trail of stock vesting clauses and incentive notes behind it.

Just Kyrel Kade, next to Chief Executive Officer — $0 compensation.

Weller gathered his papers. "One more thing," he said.

Kyrel waited.

"Mr. Colburn will be receiving a compliance binder similar to yours," Weller said. "He is to adhere to it strictly. Any attempt to circumvent earnings suspension will be treated as attempted cap evasion."

D'Andra's eyes sharpened. "And if he does try?" she asked.

"For his sake," Weller replied, "I hope he does not."

It wasn't a threat. It was something colder, a statement of structural fact. Weller stood.

"Mr. Kade. Dr. Crost-Kade. Thank you for your time. A press release will be issued within the hour."

He paused at the door. "And Mr. Kade...?"

"Yes?"

Weller studied him for a heartbeat longer than usual. "You are not being investigated," he said, as if that mattered somehow. "You are being... observed."

That sounded worse. But surprising no one. Then he left. The door clicked shut behind him.

They didn't see the press release go out, they heard it. D'Andra's phone lit up first, group chats exploding, colleagues sending screenshots, one of her residents simply texting:

YOUR HUSBAND JUST DROPPED BACK INTO HELL

Kyrel finally swiped his own phone awake.

There it was:

BREAKING: LinkLife FOUNDER KYREL KADE
RETURNS AS CEO — PRO BONO
Co-founder Rhett Colburn's compensation frozen under DEI review.

Articles were already popping up:

"Billionaire Back to Work — For Free."
"Cap Act Collides with Tech Royalty."
"Is This the Future of Billionaire Leadership?"

Tara Winslow's byline appeared on one within minutes. Her headline was different:

"The Man Who Can't Earn a Dollar — And the System That Still Needs Him."

D'Andra read over his shoulder. "She gets it," she said.

Kyrel's phone buzzed again. A text from an unknown number. Thank you for not letting them own it without you. —Madeline Vyre

He exhaled. Then another text, this one from Rhett. Just three words:

We need to talk.

If the rooftop had been an earthquake, the offices were the aftershocks. By the time Kyrel walked into the lobby, the staff had already seen the news. Some straightened reflexively when they saw him. Some pretended not to stare. Some whispered. Most just looked… relieved.

Because if there was one thing everybody agreed on, it was this: Whatever else you could say about Kyrel Kade, he wasn't going to sell us out.

The receptionist, Maya, a former intern who'd been there since prototype days, gave him a tremulous smile. "Welcome back, Mr. Kade," she said.

"Just Kyrel," he corrected gently. "Please."

She nodded quickly.

In the elevator, four engineers pretended to check their phones while obviously tracking him in the reflective doors. One finally blurted: "Sir— sorry— Kyrel— is it true? You're not getting paid?"

"Yes," he said. "It's true."

"Why would you do that?" another asked, incredulous.

Kyrel considered. "Because," he said, "the tech matters more than my salary."

Their silence was sharp with astonished respect.

 He stepped out on the executive floor. Rhett was waiting in the glass-walled conference room, pacing. He looked rough, suit jacket on but rumpled, shirt collar open, eyes ringed with exhaustion. The compliance binder sat on the table in front of him, still closed. Kyrel entered. The door hissed shut behind him. They stared at each other through ten years of history.

"I didn't ask for this," Rhett said first, voice raw.

"Neither did I," Kyrel replied.

Rhett gestured angrily at the binder.

"They froze everything," he said. "Salary, bonuses, options, I can't even cash out my vested stock without getting flagged. I'm not capped, but I might as well be. They're treating me like a criminal."

Kyrel's eyes flicked to the untouched binder. "Have you read it yet?"

"No," Rhett snapped. "Have you seen what those things say?"

"Yes," Kyrel said quietly. "I have."

Rhett laughed bitterly. "Easy for you. You're already capped. You've made peace with your golden cage. I'm still getting shoved into mine."

Kyrel's jaw tightened. "Rhett," he said, "I am not at peace with this. I just choose not to break the law to feel better."

Rhett looked away. Silence stretched.

"The Level 2 review cleared you," Rhett muttered. "Did Weller tell you that? You're the martyr now. The one who got pushed over by his reckless cofounder. Very convenient narrative."

"The review didn't clear me," Kyrel said. "It just said I didn't personally initiate the earnings. Legally, I'm still capped. I still lost the company."

"Lost?" Rhett scoffed. "You're CEO again. I'm the one with my neck in the noose."

Kyrel stepped closer to the table. "You're COO," he said. "You still have authority. You still have a future. You still have the ability to earn, if DEI decides not to cap you."

Rhett's hands curled into fists. "And until then?" he demanded. "I'm supposed to just… show up and work for free? Smile while Weller's people audit every breath I take? Wait for some algorithm to decide whether I get to have a life?"

Kyrel's voice dropped. "Welcome," he said softly, "to my last seventy-two hours."

Rhett flinched. He opened his mouth, closed it, swallowed hard. "I didn't mean to push you over, Ky," he whispered. "I swear to God, I didn't. I was stupid. Greedy, maybe, yeah. But I didn't know it would—"

"I believe you," Kyrel said.

Rhett froze. He hadn't expected that. "You... do?"

"Yes," Kyrel said. "I believe you didn't consciously think 'I'm going to cap him.' I believe you thought the law was a joke. That it only happened to other people. That the system wouldn't touch us."

Rhett's shoulders sagged.

"I also believe," Kyrel continued, "that when you saw the numbers climbing, you didn't hit the brakes. Because a part of you wondered what life might look like with me out of the way."

Rhett's eyes filled. He didn't deny it.

"We are where we are now," Kyrel said. "We can't uncap me. We can't unwind the last month. We can decide who we're going to be from here on out."

Rhett laughed, a small, broken sound. "Philosophy," he muttered. "Of course."

Kyrel nodded toward the binder on the table. "Read it," he said. "Learn your cage. Then we can talk about how to work inside it without becoming the monsters this law was designed to stop."

Rhett stared at the binder like it might bite him. "And if I don't?" he asked.

Kyrel held his gaze. "Then Weller will cap you. The Syndicate will own you. And LinkLife will become exactly what you and I swore it would never be."

Rhett swallowed. "You can't stop me from—"

"I'm not threatening you," Kyrel said. "I'm telling you what's waiting at the end of the road you're on."

He stepped back from the table. "If you want to stay my partner," he said quietly, "start by opening the damn book."

He turned to leave.

"Ky…" Rhett's voice cracked behind him. "Do you… hate me?"

Kyrel paused at the door. He didn't turn around. "No," he said. "I don't hate you."

He let out a slow breath.

"I hate what this system brings out in us."

The door whispered shut between them.

Far away, in a cramped Federal office lit by tired fluorescents, Thomas Weller watched the live-feed from the conference room camera. He wasn't supposed to. The system was only meant to flag financial anomalies, not record emotional ones. But someone had authorized internal surveillance on LinkLife's executives the moment the cap event triggered.

He watched Kyrel leave. He watched Rhett slump into a chair, staring at the compliance binder like it contained his obituary. Weller's pen hovered above a blank line on his report. He wrote, in small precise letters:

Subject K. Kade demonstrates high compliance, low evasion risk. Ethical fixation.

Subject R. Colburn demonstrates unstable response to constraint. Elevated evasion risk.

He hesitated.

Then he added one more line:

Recommend continued observation. Potential for <u>systemic</u> stress test.

In another part of the city, Soren Vale stood in a high-rise office with floor-to-ceiling windows, watching the same news crawl Kyrel had ignored that morning. He smiled as the talking heads debated:

"Is the Cap Act working?"
"Are we punishing success?"
"Is Kyrel Kade a hero or a cautionary tale?"

He poured himself a drink, not because he intended to drink it, but because people expected men like him to sip expensive liquor while watching chaos unfold.

An assistant stepped in. "Colburn?" she asked.

"Reading his binder as we speak, I imagine," Soren replied. "Nothing reshapes a man like humiliation."

"How long until he calls?" she asked. Soren's smile widened, slow and confident.

"Oh," he said softly. "Not today. He still thinks he has a choice." He took a sip.

"But then," he added, eyes glinting, "that's what makes watching him so interesting."

CHAPTER 19
THE BALANCE

Three days after Kyrel returned to LinkLife, the mood inside the building had changed in ways no memo could explain. The panicked silence of the capping fallout was gone. In its place was something steadier... quieter... almost hopeful.

He hadn't issued any public announcements. He hadn't rearranged departments or demanded loyalty or overturned decisions. He'd simply walked the floors, asked questions, listened, and stayed late in labs where he'd once slept on beanbags during the earliest prototype nights.

And people noticed.

So when an internal alert went out, Strategic Alignment Meeting | 10:00 a.m. | Executive Conference Room — every department head arrived early.

They didn't look nervous.

They looked ready. Kyrel entered the room at exactly ten. Not with bravado. Not with a "returning hero" posture. Just... grounded. A man who'd lost everything except the thing that mattered.

"Thank you," he said, taking the seat at the head of the table. "Let's begin."

"Today's agenda," Kyrel said, tapping the tablet in front of him, "is alignment. We're going back to core principles. No predatory licensing. No rushed integrations. Medical integrity first, security second, consumer third."

A quiet ripple passed around the table, relief, support, maybe even gratitude.

"Before we move forward," Kyrel continued, "I want updates from each division. What's working. What isn't. What corners were cut."

Priya, lead clinical engineer, spoke first. "We've identified six modules that were fast-tracked under pressure. They need a full audit."

"Approved," Kyrel said immediately. A few more heads nodded, as if they'd been waiting to hear exactly that. Then the strategic lens sharpened, staff leaning toward him with a gravitational pull that made the hierarchy unmistakable:

They trusted him. Not because of the title. Because of the ethos.

Kyrel felt it. Everyone did.

A click dropped into the silence as the conference room door opened.

Rhett stepped inside wearing a brittle smile. Perfect suit. Perfect hair. Perfectly rehearsed casualness that screamed I'm fine. He scanned the room, saw every seat filled except one. His. They'd waited for Kyrel. They hadn't waited for him.

That hit him like shrapnel.

"Morning, team," Rhett said, dropping his bag onto the table with a thud. "Didn't realize we were starting without me."

Madeline cleared her throat. "Mr. Kade requested—"

"It's fine," Kyrel cut in. "Let's sit."

But it wasn't fine. Not for Rhett. Everyone could feel the static rolling off him.

He sat, stiffly, slowly, and forced a grin. "So," Rhett said, gesturing broadly, "what's on the agenda for the new LinkLife?"

Kyrel didn't blink. "Accountability," he said calmly. "Transparency. And a return to the mission we built on Day One."

A few people shifted in their seats. Rhett's smile tightened.

"Well," Rhett said lightly, "we all know missions evolve."

"Not this one," Kyrel replied quietly. That landed. Hard. Rhett's jaw flexed, just once, before the smile snapped back into place.

After the meeting, employees drifted toward Kyrel like iron filings toward a magnet.

Some asked questions. Some thanked him. Some simply wanted to be near the calm, steady presence that had once made the company feel like a family.

A project manager approached him timidly. "Kyrel... is it true you're not being paid?"

"That is correct."

"Then why are you doing this?"

"Because I built this. And I won't let it break."

She nodded, eyes bright. Behind them, Rhett watched. Hands in his pockets. Expression unreadable. But inside? A storm.

Across the street, in a parked electric sedan, Tara Winslow sipped her coffee and watched the building entrance through a telephoto lens. Kyrel had returned. The staff were flocking. Something was shifting. She whispered into her recorder:

> "Day 12 after the Cap.
> They pulled him from his own throne and he's walking back in like he's still king. This is going to get interesting."

On the 42nd floor of a private club a few blocks away, Soren Vale leaned back in a leather chair, swirling a glass of amber liquor.

A Syndicate operative approached. "Kade's back inside LinkLife."

Soren smiled. "Good. Let the government believe he's playing their game…" He lifted the glass to his lips. "…while we prepare ours."

CHAPTER 20

D'ANDRA'S LENS

The hospital always smelled faintly of disinfectant and coffee, a scent D'Andra had long ago woven into the fabric of her sense of purpose. But lately, since LinkLife's meteoric rise, it carried a new undertone as well: the metallic, slightly sweet odor of sterile implant packaging. It was subtle, but once she noticed it, she could not un-notice it.

She hung her coat in her tiny office, tied her surgical cap, and scanned her schedule for the morning. Three surgeries. Two consults. One post-op review. A typical day… except it wasn't. Because each time she saw the small red notation beside certain patient names—LL-verified—she felt a tiny twist in her stomach.

She had asked Kyrel once, jokingly, whether he'd ever meant for her to see those letters more often than his name. He'd smiled, a soft, worried smile she felt in her sternum.

Today, three of her patients carried the implant.

Her first consultation was with a woman in her seventies, brought in by her daughter. The patient, Ruth, had early-stage dementia, and the daughter explained in a trembling voice that the LinkLife implant had stabilized her identity verification system.

"It helps her at the pharmacy," the daughter said, her voice thick with equal parts relief and exhaustion. "It reminds her of her medications when her phone syncs. And she hasn't wandered since we paired it with the door lock."

Ruth sat quietly during the explanation, her hands folded neatly in her lap, her gaze drifting in and out of understanding like a ship at the edge of fog. But when D'Andra said her name, gently, directly, intentionally, Ruth looked up.

"I know you," she said softly. "You're my daughter's friend." It wasn't accurate, but it was coherent, and the daughter's eyes shone with grateful tears.

Some creations brought tenderness into the world. Some innovations genuinely helped. And D'Andra held that truth close, because she needed it. But the next case reminded her that not all uses were benevolent.

Her second patient that day, was a woman in her early thirties with a fractured orbital bone and deep bruising along her ribs. She claimed she had fallen down stairs. The story was thin, evasive. But D'Andra had seen enough domestic violence cases to recognize the signature.

When she scanned the woman's wrist to check for medication interactions, her console blinked:

> LL-Linked Identity: Authorized by Partner.
> Full Access: Household Emergency Override permissions enabled.

D'Andra froze. The patient's eyes flicked away, shame cutting through the room like a draft.

"Did you choose this implant?" D'Andra asked quietly.

The woman hesitated, then whispered, "He said it would keep us safe."

D'Andra's pulse tightened. The chip was meant to empower users, not enable someone to track their partner's movements, open locked doors, or override emergency settings.

"I can refer you to social services," D'Andra said, keeping her voice steady but gentle. "And I can mark the implant for restricted review. You don't have to… go back." The woman looked at her, and for a moment, hope flickered. But it flickered only briefly.

"He'll lose it if he finds out I talked to you," she whispered. "He'd know. He sees everything."

D'Andra felt her stomach knot. LinkLife had given that man a new weapon. She finished the consult with growing fear in her chest.

By the time she reached her third case, D'Andra was already emotionally exhausted. The patient, a young man brought in after a construction accident, looked terrified as she approached.

His arm was shattered. He needed surgery. He also needed reassurance.

"What's your name?" she asked gently.

He hesitated, then answered. His accent was thick, his voice barely audible.

When D'Andra registered him into the surgical queue, the console flashed again:

> Identity Status: Unverified.
> DEI Watch Flag Level 2.
> Cross-referencing economic activity…

"What is that?" he asked, voice trembling.

"Nothing you need to worry about right now," D'Andra lied. She hated lying in her work, but truth could cause real harm. The DEI database had no business reaching into a hospital's triage system. No business cross-referencing economic status or immigration status during a medical emergency. But it was happening anyway. She approved the procedure manually, overriding the alert with her surgeon's authority. She would deal with whatever fallout came later.

At noon, between surgeries, D'Andra stepped into a meeting with the hospital board. It was meant to be a simple briefing, but she saw from the slick pitch deck on the table that it was anything but. The board chair beamed at her.

"Dr. Crost-Kade, we're exploring a full-tech partnership package from LinkLife. Grants for equipment. Subsidies for mandatory implant programs. Subsidized upgrades for staff and patients. They're offering an entire integration suite."

D'Andra stared at the glossy mockup: Images of nurses scanning implants instead of IDs; Doctors using biometric LinkLife streams for triage; Administrators cheering efficiency gains.

It made her skin crawl. "You're proposing mandatory implants for frontline workers?" she asked carefully.

"It's optional," the chair said smoothly, "but highly incentivized. Insurance partners love it. And defense contractors are using similar systems. We'd be ahead of the curve."

"Or part of the problem," she murmured. The room stiffened.

"This is not the direction healthcare should go," D'Andra said, her voice growing firm. "Patients should not fear that identity verification will be used against them. Medical safety doesn't require merging with national security."

The board chair tapped his pen, unimpressed. "You're married to the creator," he said. "Surely you understand the potential."

D'Andra leaned forward. "Yes," she said quietly. "And because I understand the potential, I understand the danger."

That night, she sat beside Kyrel on the couch, both exhausted from different battles fought on different fronts.

She told him everything: The dementia patient who blossomed for a moment; the abused woman trapped under her partner's digital boot; the undocumented man flagged by a system that should never have accessed his data; the board salivating over mandatory implants and defense contracts.

Kyrel listened without interruption, his hands clasped together, his gaze heavy.

"Ky…" she said softly, touching his arm, "your creation is beautiful. It helps people. Really helps them. But the system around it?" She shook her head. "It's leaning toward something monstrous."

He closed his eyes. "Then I'll pull it back," he said finally. "I'll fix what I can from inside."

She exhaled a long breath, one of relief, admiration, and worry.

D'Andra wasn't just his emotional anchor anymore.

She was his window into the real-world consequences of his genius, and the moral compass he leaned on when the world twisted around him.

CHAPTER 21
PRESSURE LINES

Rhett Colburn had always believed he functioned best under pressure, that crises sharpened his instincts, polished his charm, and clarified his path forward. But three days after Kyrel's return to LinkLife, he discovered a more uncomfortable truth:

Pressure didn't sharpen him anymore. It exposed him.

He felt it in the way employees glanced past him to speak to Kyrel. He felt it in the silence that greeted him in hallways where he once commanded applause. He felt it in the meeting room when ten department heads had leaned naturally toward the man who no longer owned a single share.

Kyrel had walked back into the company he founded, stripped of wealth and title, and somehow he carried more authority than ever.

Rhett wasn't sure if it was charisma or martyrdom, but whatever it was, it was suffocating him.

At 8:34 a.m., Rhett entered his office and found a stack of compliance forms on his desk. Madeline Vyre's handwriting was precise, measured, and entirely intolerable.

REQUIRED REVIEW:
All executive transaction histories (past 8 months)
DEI Level-2 Inquiry Triggered
Deadline: 72 hours

He read the note twice, then dropped the packet onto his desk as if it were a dead insect.

A Level-2 Inquiry. Triggered on him. Not a warning. Not a routine check.

This meant someone had flagged unusual financial movement, either the government AI, or worse, a manual review. He felt the floor tilt beneath him. He opened his desktop console and pulled up his encrypted ledger, the one no one was supposed to know existed.

The shell subsidiaries were still intact, masked behind layers of compliance-friendly phrasing and offshore abstractions.

Except one entry, eight days old, had a faint red highlight. He clicked it.

Unverified routing sequence.
Destination Account Flagged for Review.
Do Not alter.
Audit pending.

His breath went thin.

Soren had promised these channels were invisible, untraceable, protected. And now one of them had a glowing DEI beacon attached.

It took a long moment before Rhett realized his hands were shaking.

He didn't call Soren. Couldn't. Shouldn't. But at 10:12 a.m., Soren Vale called him. The name on the screen made Rhett's throat clamp. He let it ring almost to voicemail before answering.

"Rhett," Soren said smoothly, as if they were old friends meeting for brunch. "Is it a bad time?"

"You said it couldn't be traced." The words rushed out of Rhett in a low, strangled whisper. "You guaranteed it."

"There are no guarantees," Soren replied, sounding vaguely amused. "Only tolerances. Something triggered an inquiry. Could be random. Could be the system sniffing for patterns. Could be someone else's mistake. But this is not the moment to panic."

Rhett walked to his office window. Kyrel was visible on the floor below, talking calmly with two engineers, listening, engaged, focused. People gravitated to him like plants seeking sunlight.

"He's taking everything back," Rhett muttered. "Without money. Without stock. Without a single legal lever. He walks in and people treat him like— like—"

"A leader," Soren finished gently.

Rhett's hand tightened around his phone.

"You can't fight gravity, Rhett. But you can change the shape of the world around it."

"I don't need philosophy," Rhett hissed. "I need this inquiry to go away."

"And it will," Soren said. "But it will require something from you."

Rhett closed his eyes. "What?"

"A choice," Soren replied. "One you've been avoiding since the day Kyrel's cap letter arrived."

Before Rhett could respond, the line went dead.

Across town, Tara Winslow sat in the corner booth of a small Midtown coffee shop, her laptop open, earbuds in, eyes narrowed at a cluster of data points she had only just begun to understand.

She hadn't intended to become obsessed with Kyrel Kade. But obsession had a way of choosing its subjects.

She replayed a DEI compliance report she'd obtained through a contact who owed her far too many favors. It was anonymized—technically—but the figures were unmistakable: someone inside LinkLife had triggered a Level-2 review for financial irregularities eight days before Kyrel's capping.

Eight days before the "accidental" spike in valuation. Eight days before Kyrel was forced out. Eight days before someone pocketed a suspiciously timed licensing payment routed through three vendors and a shell company in Bermuda.

She didn't yet have names. But she had something better: Patterns. Corporate betrayal always left fingerprints, not visible to the naked eye, but to someone like Tara? They were as clear as blood on snow. She jotted a note in the margin of her notebook:

> Was Kyrel pushed over on purpose? By someone inside? Or by someone with influence outside?

She looked at the timestamp again. Eight days. Something happened eight days before Kyrel lost everything. Something nobody talked about.

Back inside LinkLife, Kyrel finished reviewing a medical module for compliance and sent a detailed note to Priya. He liked the feeling of working again, not coding, not inventing, but guiding. Steering the mission back toward what he intended.

He didn't need money to do this. He needed will.

As he stepped out of the lab, a few employees straightened, as though unconsciously aligning themselves to his presence. It still surprised him, but he was learning not to apologize for it.

Rhett watched from across the floor; unreadable, calculating, brittle.

Kyrel paused. For a heartbeat, their eyes met. A silent acknowledgment moved between them: Something between us is changing. And whatever it is, it's already begun.

CHAPTER 22
FRICTION AND FAULT LINES

By the end of his first full week back at LinkLife, Kyrel could feel the subtle reshaping of the company's internal weather. Not a dramatic shift, no thunderclaps, no public declarations, but the quiet, powerful rearrangement that happens whenever one gravitational center replaces another.

Departments were slowing their frantic pace. Conversations contained fewer anxious half-truths. Engineers were re-evaluating rushed iterations. Managers were no longer pushing release cycles that had made no ethical or technical sense.

People weren't afraid to tell the truth again.

But the friction was inevitable.

Ethical course corrections were like tectonic adjustments, necessary, but always preceded by a deep, uncomfortable groaning beneath the surface before the faults gave way.

And LinkLife was beginning to groan.

On Monday morning, Kyrel approved a company-wide recalibration:

> Effective immediately: All Medical and Security modules developed in the last 16 months will undergo full audit and respecification.

> Licensing agreements with external parties will be temporarily frozen pending review.

It was a precise, clinical statement, but its meaning reverberated far beyond internal memos.

Medical journals picked it up. Cybersecurity forums exploded. Tech analysts began speculating that LinkLife was preparing to "clean house" after a series of troubling silent rumors. By the afternoon, three reporters were waiting outside the building.

Tara Winslow wasn't one of them. She wasn't wasting time with surface-level coverage. She was digging deeper.

In her apartment, a small, cluttered space filled with notebooks, whiteboards, and old hard drives, Tara spread out two timelines on the floor.

One contained LinkLife's public moves: grant announcements, licensing rounds, fundraising events, product launches.

The other contained financial events she had scraped from a combination of public records, leaked investment summaries, and a few datapoints she probably shouldn't have had access to.

When she aligned the two timelines, the pattern emerged in crisp, unnerving clarity:

A rapid surge in valuation eight days before the capping. A large routing transaction through a subsidiary that didn't exist three months earlier. A licensing contract quietly approved without Kyrel's digital signature. And a second valuation bump two days after Kyrel's shares were liquidated.

Four dots. Four choices. Four fingerprints. She drew a clean, dark line through all four. At the end of it, she wrote one name:

Rhett Colburn?

Not certain. Not confirmed. But the pattern bent toward him like iron to a magnet.

She leaned back against her couch, pulse rising. If Rhett did this, he hadn't just betrayed his partner. He had weaponized the system meant to restrain the wealthy, and turned it against the one person who had tried to use it ethically.

Tara closed her notebook slowly. "This story is bigger than I thought," she said out loud.

Rhett received the message when he least expected it: a private notification blinking on his watch, a coded symbol used only by the Syndicate. He stepped into an empty office and accepted the call.

Soren Vale's face appeared, composed, elegant, predatory in that polished way that made charm feel like a venom-laced kindness.

"We need you to approve a minor adjustment," Soren said blithely, as though they were discussing new drapes for a meeting room. "A licensing expansion. It will route through two intermediaries, nothing risky. It keeps the channels open."

Rhett swallowed hard. "Are you insane? I'm already under inquiry."

"That's exactly why we must act now," Soren replied smoothly. "The best way to hide a signal is inside a cluster of similar signals. A clean ledger stands out more than a dirty one."

Rhett closed his eyes. "I can't authorize anything without it going through Kyrel."

Soren smiled faintly. "I never said it needed to be authorized."

Rhett's pulse thudded in his throat. "You want me to forge it."

"I want you to protect your future," Soren said softly, leaning closer to the camera. "The window is closing. You know it. I know it. Kyrel has the moral high ground. He has the employees. He has the public. Soon he will have the regulators. And where will that leave you?"

Rhett didn't answer.

Soren did not push. He only said, with the quiet confidence of a man who had destroyed better men than Rhett:

"You have a choice. Make it soon." The call ended.

Rhett's hand shook long after.

By the evening on the same day, Kyrel had completed the first review cycle. He sent a detailed list of revisions to the engineering teams, each justified with technical clarity and ethical reasoning.

The responses rolled in quickly:

> "Thank you, we didn't feel comfortable with this module."
> "We flagged this risk months ago."
> "This helps us realign with the mission."
> "Finally, we can do this right."

But not all messages were supportive.

One came from the Legal Integration Team:

> We have concerns about freezing the External Licensing Agreements. Several partners are unhappy. One partner has escalated to an external agency regarding sudden noncompliance.

Kyrel frowned. "Which partner?" There was a long pause before the answer came: A firm called Vale Strategic Holdings.

The name hit Kyrel like a dropped weight, not because he recognized it, but because he didn't. Rhett had handled those negotiations. He made a note to ask about it in the morning.

At home, D'Andra was preparing for bed when her personal console chimed, an unfamiliar tone, one reserved for encrypted medical-legal notifications. She frowned and opened it. The message contained only one line, with no sender metadata:

Dr. Crost-Kade, your access logs have been flagged by a DEI cross-reference engine. Further review pending. Do not discuss patient cases with anyone outside approved channels.

D'Andra's breath caught. Her access logs? For which case? The undocumented patient? The domestic violence victim? Or had DEI simply begun monitoring everyone connected to Kyrel?

She sat down heavily on the edge of the bed, the message still glowing in her hand. When Kyrel entered the room, towel draped over his shoulder, he immediately saw the worry in her eyes.

"What happened?"

She handed the console to him.

His expression darkened, not with fear, but with something harder. Something that looked like resolve turning into armor.

"They're watching you now," he murmured.

D'Andra nodded. "Kyle… this is getting bigger."

He took her hand. "I know."

She squeezed back, hard enough that he understood her meaning without a single spoken word: If he continued down this path, he would not be the only one in danger.

CHAPTER 23

THE TRIGGER POINT

LinkLife was never silent, not even at night. The building hummed a low, constant vibration of servers, filtered air, and thousands of devices quietly syncing with one another like an invisible, living organism.

Tonight, the hum felt different, as if the building itself sensed what was about to happen.

Kyrel stayed late again, reviewing licensing agreements in a quiet corner office that once belonged to him. The table lamp cast a warm circle across the contract files, most from before his capping, many bearing signatures he didn't remember authorizing.

He had read twenty-seven documents before he found it. A single agreement, A modest licensing deal on paper, negligible revenue, small distribution, nothing that should have raised eyebrows.

But the metadata told a different story.

> Signature: Emergency Authorization Override
> Timestamp: 02:16 a.m, Digital Trace: Logged to Kyrel Kade's executive key
> IP Location: Unknown / masked
> Routing: VALE Strategic Holdings

Kyrel stared at the screen.

He never authorized emergency override access. He never signed anything at 2:16 a.m. And his executive key shouldn't have been used. It should have been deactivated the moment DEI stripped him of authority.

Someone forged my authorization. Someone with internal access. Someone who needed that deal pushed through before the cap hit.

His first thought, involuntary, sharp, was Rhett.

His second thought was that someone helped him. Someone on the outside.

Kyrel copied the metadata, encrypted it, and saved it to a secure offline drive. Then he sat back, exhaling slowly.

The system was not just flawed. It had been manipulated. And one question loomed over him like a shadowed doorway: Was this the transaction that pushed me over a billion?

Rhett sat alone in his car in the underground garage, the engine off, the cabin lights dim. His suit jacket hung by a finger on the steering wheel. His tie was loose. His eyes looked like someone who hadn't slept in days.

Soren's warning pulsed in his skull: The window is closing. Make your choice.

He opened the secure virtual ledger, the one he never should have touched again.

All he had to do was approve a routing sequence. Just one. A small one. Barely noticeable. The kind of transaction no one inside LinkLife would see unless they were deliberately looking.

But Kyrel was looking now and Rhett felt it in the pressure of his breath, the tremors in his hands.

The inquiry was already on his doorstep, Soren's quiet voice echoed: A clean ledger stands out more than a dirty one.

Rhett hovered over the approval interface. His finger shook; sweat gathered along his jawline.

If he said yes, there was no turning back. If he said no, Soren would move on, and Rhett would be alone in the storm he created.

He thought of the early days with Kyrel: pizza boxes, 3 a.m. breakthroughs, LinkLife's first spark of genius. He thought of Kyrel calling him "brother."

He remembered how quickly that brotherhood had been eclipsed by Kyrel's effortless gravity.

He remembered the sharp, sour sting that eclipse had left in his soul.

Rhett touched the screen.

APPROVED.

There was no sound, no flash, no cinematic cue. Just a quiet confirmation:

Authorization Logged
Routing Initiated.

And with that, Rhett Colburn crossed the point of no return.

It was 11:43 p.m., and Tara Winslow was packing up her backpack when her encrypted inbox chimed, a channel she reserved for sources who feared for their careers.

The sender was unlisted, The message was one line:

"If you want LinkLife's truth, start with the routing that shouldn't exist."

Attached was an anonymized financial packet, raw numbers, not labeled, not interpreted, but Tara recognized the format.

DEI grade-2 audit.

Someone inside the government had leaked it. Someone who shouldn't have access. Someone who was frightened or furious or both.

Her pulse quickened. She pulled up her timeline chart and inserted the new data. A pattern leaped out like an alarm: Three routing anomalies, all within thirty minutes of each other, eight days before the capping.

One matched the signature she'd already suspected was Rhett's. Another matched Vale Strategic Holdings. And the third…

She zoomed in so quickly her coffee spilled.

The third matched a valuation bump logged under federal emergency authorization, the kind used for national security contracts.

She whispered to herself, barely audible: "Oh my god… someone outside the company pushed him over."

She grabbed her phone. Kyrel needed to know.

D'Andra had just left the hospital when she noticed a man standing near her car: suit neat, posture rigid, hair cut in the nondescript style favored by federal departments that liked to blend in. He didn't approach. Didn't move. Just watched her with an expression that wasn't hostile… but wasn't neutral either.

Her pulse leapt. "Can I help you?" she asked, keeping her voice even.

The man offered a polite, practiced smile. "Dr. Crost-Kade," he said. "I'm Agent Rowan with the Department of Economic Integrity."

Her spine tightened.

"We're reviewing several healthcare access logs that may have crossed into restricted identity data. Nothing concerning at this stage, but we encourage cooperation. It keeps everyone safe."

Everyone safe. A phrase that sounded benign and landed like a threat.

"I protect my patients," D'Andra replied.

"I'm sure you do," Rowan said, smiling faintly. "And we protect the system that protects your husband."

D'Andra felt her blood run cold. He gave a slight nod and walked away. No card, No documents. Just a warning disguised as courtesy.

Kyrel was locking his office when his phone buzzed, Tara's name glowing on the screen. He debated whether to answer. Not because he didn't trust her, he did, more than many journalists, but because every conversation was a risk now.

He answered.

"Kyrel," Tara said without preamble. "I need to meet you. Tonight. Or first thing in the morning. I found something."

"What kind of something?"

"Something you're not supposed to know." Her breath hitched. "And something Rhett is very much not supposed to have done."

Kyrel felt a single, cold pulse of adrenaline. "I'll meet you," he said. "Where?"

She hesitated. "Somewhere public. Somewhere safe."

Kyrel's silence stretched long enough that she could hear the weight of it.

She added, softer: "And bring D'Andra, She needs to hear this too."

Kyrel closed his eyes. The world had shifted beneath him again, not dramatically, but unmistakably. The fault line had moved. The trigger had been pulled.

And the next step would change everything.

CHAPTER 24

CONVERGENCE

Morning sunlight had barely begun to warm the glass facade of the Sequoia Café when Kyrel, D'Andra, and Tara converged on the same small corner table. It was early enough that the shop was still quiet, filled only with the muted clatter of ceramic cups and the low hum of an espresso machine.

The world had not yet woken up. But the world they were about to reshape had.

Tara arrived last, laptop under one arm, messenger bag over the other, hair pulled into a hasty knot that made her look more dangerous than disheveled. She sat, opened her machine, and without small talk, said: "We don't have much time. And you both need to hear this."

Kyrel nodded once. D'Andra's hand tightened around his beneath the table.

Tara turned the laptop so they could see the screen. Rows of data. Digital traces. Metadata trees. The kind of information only someone trained to see connections would recognize as a story.

"I got this from a source inside DEI," she said. "Unofficially. Very unofficially."

Kyrel leaned in, eyes narrowing. "What am I looking at?"

Tara tapped three lines with her finger. "These are the routing anomalies I told you about last night. Three approvals, all within thirty minutes of one another, eight days before your capping."

D'Andra frowned. "Three approvals? Who signed them?"

Tara shook her head. "Not who. What. They were recorded under different authorization keys: one belonging to LinkLife's CFO authorization, one belonging to a shell company connected to Vale Strategic Holdings…"

She hesitated, then tapped the third line.

"And one belonging to you."

Kyrel stared at the signature. "That's not possible," he said quietly.

Tara nodded. "I know. It's forged. But the system doesn't know that, it accepted it as genuine. Which means someone had internal access and the tools to replicate your executive key."

Kyrel felt his breath slow.

"And this," Tara continued, sliding her laptop to the next screen, "is the valuation spike logged immediately afterward. A spike tied directly to those transactions. That spike is what pushed you over the cap threshold."

D'Andra inhaled sharply. "They engineered it," she whispered. "They pushed you over."

Kyrel felt something in his chest break open, not pain, not anger exactly, but an understanding so sharp it cut. "They didn't just betray me," he said. "They broke the system to do it."

Tara nodded once. "And that brings us to the part that scares me."

Tara pulled up the third anomaly, the one routed through federal emergency authorization.

"I matched the encryption header," she said. "The signature sequence isn't corporate. It's government. Someone used a national security authorization shell to bypass valuation scrutiny."

Kyrel's voice was steady but cold. "What department?"

Tara exhaled. "DEI's defense-liaison division."

D'Andra went pale. "That's the same branch that flagged my patient logs."

Kyrel turned sharply to her. "What?"

She explained, quietly, the visit from Agent Rowan. His bland warning. The veiled threat.

Kyrel's hands curled into fists on the tablecloth. "They're not monitoring you," he said. "They're monitoring me through you."

Tara nodded grimly. "Yes. Because DEI didn't just cap you. They wanted you out of the way."

"Why?" D'Andra whispered.

Tara gave the only answer she could: "Because LinkLife technology is too powerful, and someone wanted control."

While the three of them pieced together the truth, Rhett was walking into LinkLife headquarters with a face shaved too closely, eyes sunken from lack of sleep, and a suit jacket that didn't quite hide the tremor in his hands.

Madeline Vyre, the compliance director, was waiting outside his office. She greeted him with a polite, professional nod that carried the weight of a verdict. "Mr. Colburn," she said. "We need to speak."

"What is this about?" Rhett asked, voice tight.

"Your authorization logs," she replied. "And a potential conflict with an external audit."

Rhett's heart jolted. "What audit?"

"DEI Level-2," she said. "They requested copies of your executive actions dating back twelve months. We have found one anomaly that cannot be explained." She placed a folder, actual paper, on his desk. "Please review." And then she left him alone with it.

Rhett stared at the folder as if it were a live explosive. A droplet of sweat rolled down his spine. He opened it. There it was: The forged authorization from last night. Timestamped. Logged. Tracing directly back to him.

He felt his stomach drop out from under him entirely.

Meanwhile, miles away, Soren Vale stepped into a private conference room where three unnamed government representatives waited, their faces calm, professional, unreadable.

Soren smiled. "Everything will unfold as planned," he said. "By week's end, LinkLife will be forced into federal partnership review."

One of the officials nodded. "Good. And Mr. Kade?"

Soren's expression flickered, something between admiration and calculation.

"We will let him do exactly what he believes he excels at," Soren replied.

"What's that?"

"Fixing systems," Soren said. "While the system quietly fixes him."

Back in the café, Tara closed her laptop.

Kyrel sat silent, processing. D'Andra watched him with a surgeon's composure and a wife's fear.

"Tara," Kyrel said finally, "why are you helping me?"

Tara met his gaze without flinching. "Because you're the only one not trying to weaponize this technology. And because someone inside the government wants you silenced. That alone tells me you're dangerous to the wrong people."

Kyrel leaned forward. "What do we do?"

Tara's smile was small and fierce. "We start by pulling the right thread. And we let the whole thing unravel."

D'Andra reached for Kyrel's hand. "I'm with you," she said softly. "Every step."

Kyrel looked at both women, one his compass, one his torchlight, and felt something steady crystallize inside him. "The truth has been buried long enough." He straightened. "It's time to dig."

CHAPTER 25

THE BREAKING POINT

The building was already buzzing when Kyrel returned to LinkLife that morning. Not in the usual way, not productive energy, not innovation, but the tense, compressed hum of an organization bracing for an impact it could feel but not yet name.

Kyrel felt it the moment he stepped through the doors. Eyes flicked toward him, then away. Conversations clipped themselves short as he passed. Even the air seemed tighter, coiled around an unnamed pressure.

The truth was beginning to leak.

Madeline Vyre stood outside the executive conference room reviewing three separate data streams on her tablet. Each represented a different audit request: Internal Compliance; External Licensing; and a DEI Inquiry Request.

Thirty-six hours earlier, these had been routine. Today, they formed an unmistakable triangulation pointing directly at Rhett. She had not yet confronted him, not formally, but she had begun assembling a timeline. And in that timeline, eight days before Kyrel's capping was beginning to glow like a red star.

She tapped her notes and added a new line:

Cross-reference forged executive key with CFO routing.
Investigate correlation with VALE Holdings.

Madeline didn't like corruption, but she hated sloppiness. And Rhett had been sloppy.

"Madeline?" She turned. Kyrel stood in the doorway.

"I need ten minutes of your time," he said.

Madeline studied him. No panic. No anger. No attempt to maneuver her. Just clarity.

"I was about to request the same," she replied, and stepped aside.

They entered the room together.

Rhett was waiting inside the conference room, pacing like a trapped animal. His hair was disheveled, his tie uneven, and his eyes radiated a feverish anxiety he was barely keeping contained.

When he saw Kyrel and Madeline enter together, his expression hardened with something between terror and accusation.

"We need to talk," he snapped.

Madeline raised an eyebrow. "We are talking."

"No," Rhett said sharply. "I need to speak with Kyrel. Alone."

Madeline didn't move.

Kyrel sat calmly. "Whatever you say to me," he said softly, "you can say in front of her."

Rhett's composure cracked. "You're working together now?" he demanded. "Against me?"

Kyrel didn't answer with words, only with silence, which was somehow worse. Rhett slammed a folder onto the table. The same folder Madeline had given him the day before.

"I did not authorize that transaction," he lied, voice trembling. "This is a mistake, someone is setting me up, Kyrel. You have to believe me."

Kyrel opened the folder, glanced once, then closed it gently. "Then you won't object to a full audit."

Rhett's breath stopped. Just a fraction of a second, but enough. Kyrel saw it. Madeline saw it.

Rhett saw that they saw it, and panic rippled across his features.

He jabbed a finger toward Kyrel. "You're doing this to me," he hissed. "You're turning them against me. You come back with your saint act, pro bono CEO, moral high ground, employees worshipping you, and now you're going to ruin my life?"

Kyrel shook his head, expression calm but unyielding. "I'm not trying to ruin your life," he said quietly. "I'm trying to save the company."

Rhett barked a humorless laugh. "You don't care about the company. You never did. You cared about being the hero."

"Rhett," Kyrel said softly, "someone forged my executive key. Someone partnered with Vale Strategic Holdings without my knowledge. Someone pushed me over the cap. I need to know the truth."

Rhett's face twisted. "You're accusing me."

"I'm asking you," Kyrel corrected.

Madeline added, "And we now have reason to suspect coordination with an external actor."

Rhett froze, truly froze this time. Madeline's gaze sharpened. Kyrel noticed. She did too.

Rhett swallowed. "You're making a mistake," he whispered. "A huge mistake."

Kyrel stood. "No," he said gently. "The mistake was trusting the wrong people."

Rhett's hand curled into a fist. Madeline stepped subtly forward.

And that was the moment Rhett broke. He grabbed his folder, spun away, and stormed out of the room. The door slammed with a reverberation that echoed through the office.

Two floors below, Agent Rowan entered LinkLife headquarters with a badge clipped to his belt and a subtle air of ownership in his stride. He approached the front desk.

"Agent Rowan," he said quietly. "Here for the executive compliance review."

The receptionist swallowed. "Which executive?"

Rowan smiled with his eyes, though not with his mouth. "All of them."

In a polished corner office overlooking the city, Soren Vale studied a series of incoming reports on his screen. Rhett's approval had been processed. The forged authorization had been triggered. DEI had moved into active review. Perfect.

A colleague, slim, immaculately dressed, wearing a USB bracelet disguised as jewelry, entered without knocking.

"Rowan's in the building," she said.

Soren nodded, eyes gleaming. "Good. The more pressure DEI applies, the more Kyrel will be forced to seek allies."

"Us?" she asked.

Soren gave a faint, cold smile. "Not at first," he said. "But eventually, yes. Men like Kyrel always think they can fix systems. And the more broken a system becomes, the more they believe they can salvage it."

"What's our goal?"

Soren's smile widened. "Our goal," he said, "is control of the only technology capable of rebuilding the world's identity infrastructure."

Her breath caught softly. "LinkLife."

"No," Soren corrected. "Kyrel."

At 11:14 a.m., Tara pressed "Publish." Her article went live within seconds:

THE IMPOSSIBLE VALUATION:
Evidence Suggests LinkLife Founder Was Pushed Over the Cap Threshold by Outside Influence

The headline wasn't an accusation, not legally, but it was an earthquake. By noon, tech analysts were dissecting the anomalies, business networks were running segments, three senators were calling for a review, and DEI had activated a Level-3 containment.

The world had officially been notified that this story was much bigger than a single billionaire.

Kyrel was halfway across the office when Priya ran up to him, breathless.

"Ky— Kyrel— the article— Tara Winslow— she just— you need to see this—"

Kyrel pulled the notification. Read the headline. His pulse slowed, not with fear, but with certainty. The truth was out. The cage had been cracked. And now the world was rushing in.

He looked toward the conference room where he had confronted Rhett. Then toward the elevators where Agent Rowan had just arrived. Then toward the horizon beyond the glass.

Everything was converging. Everything he had tried to shield was now exposed. And for the first time, he realized: There was no going back.

-231-

CHAPTER 26
THE DAY EVERYTHING BREAKS

The storm didn't arrive with thunder. It arrived with silence. A cold, procedural, government-issued silence that settled over LinkLife headquarters like frost. The kind of silence that precedes a raid, an audit, an intervention, something inevitable and heavy, guided by rules nobody voted on and systems nobody understood.

Kyrel felt it before he saw it. He stood near the glass atrium, reviewing a revised licensing flow with Priya, when every office light in the building flickered. Just once. Subtle. Precise. Intentional.

Priya froze. "…that wasn't an electrical issue," she whispered.

No, it wasn't. Kyrel already knew who it was. DEI was taking control of the system.

At exactly 9:03 a.m., the building's internal network switched into restricted-access protocol. Every workstation displayed the same message:

> DEPARTMENT OF ECONOMIC INTEGRITY
> Level-3 Executive Systems Review
> All internal communications are being logged.
> Do not shut down your device.
> Do not disconnect from the network.

Gasps rippled through the floors. Phones stopped ringing. Keyboards went still. Kyrel felt the weight of every eye turning toward him. This wasn't an audit. This was a takeover.

He turned to Priya. "Find the senior engineers. Quietly. Tell them to freeze all development branches. No updates. No changes. Everything stays exactly as it is."

Priya nodded, mobilizing with practiced calm. Kyrel inhaled once, steadying himself.

Then Agent Rowan appeared on the balcony above, flanked by two officers in neutral gray suits. Their presence was quiet but absolute.

"Mr. Kade," Rowan called down. "We need you in the executive conference room."

It wasn't a request.

The conference room was already occupied by the time Kyrel got there. Rhett sat at one end of the table, pale, sweating, and visibly trembling. Two DEI officers stood behind him. Madeline Vyre stood off to the side, expression unreadable but sharp.

Rowan gestured to an empty chair. "Mr. Kade. If you would."

Kyrel sat.

Rowan folded his hands neatly in front of him. "We are conducting a Level-3 inquiry concerning the anomalous transactions preceding your capping. Several irregularities have come to light."

Rhett's voice cracked before Kyrel could respond. "This isn't what it looks like," he blurted. "I didn't authorize anything illegal. I didn't— I didn't push anything through the system— I didn't—"

Rowan raised a hand, and Rhett fell silent instantly. Kyrel watched him, really watched him, and saw something he hadn't expected: This wasn't guilt alone. This was fear. Fear of something bigger than DEI. Fear of someone behind DEI.

Rowan turned to Kyrel. "We have evidence suggesting your executive authorization key was used illegally eight days before your capping. We also have reason to suspect coordination with an external entity known as Vale Strategic Holdings."

Kyrel's jaw tightened. "And Rhett was part of that coordination?"

Rhett looked at him, broken, pleading. "Ky... you have to believe me... I didn't do it alone."

The word alone detonated across the room. Madeline inhaled sharply. Rowan's eyes flicked with interest. Kyrel felt the air shift.

"Then who did you do it with?" Rowan asked.

Rhett's throat bobbed. He looked toward the door. "You won't protect me if I say it."

"We're not here to protect you," Rowan replied calmly. "We're here to investigate."

Rhett squeezed his eyes shut. And whispered the name: "Vale."

Rowan didn't flinch, which told Kyrel everything. DEI already knew. They just wanted Rhett to say it.

Across the city, Tara Winslow was reviewing social media reaction to her article when her secure line pinged, not the DEI leak channel, not the journalist relay, a different one.

One that she had only given to three people in the world. She opened it. A single message blinked onto her screen:

Stop digging. Or your next story will be your last.

Her skin went cold. No signature. No header. A clean threat, sent through a server sophisticated enough to erase its own trail. Her laptop fan spun up sharply. Someone was watching her. Someone with resources. She closed the laptop slowly, pulse steadying.

"You picked the wrong journalist," she whispered.

Meanwhile, at the hospital, D'Andra was prepping for a surgery when two administrators walked in, both wearing compliance badges.

"Dr. Crost-Kade," one said stiffly. "You've been placed on temporary audit hold due to possible identity access conflicts flagged by DEI."

D'Andra froze. "My patient needs surgery in forty minutes."

"The procedure has been reassigned." Panic flared, she tamped it down. "This is retaliation," she said quietly. "Not protocol."

"We don't make those decisions," the other replied. "We only follow directives."

She removed her gloves. "I'm going to LinkLife."

"You can't leave until the audit—"

D'Andra stepped past them without a backward glance. They didn't follow.

Back at LinkLife, Rowan and his officers pulled Rhett out for formal questioning, leaving Kyrel alone in the conference room. Or so he thought. The door clicked. Kyrel turned.

Soren Vale stepped inside with a smooth walk, poised, wearing a tailored charcoal suit and a smile designed to look sympathetic.

"Mr. Kade," he said warmly, "I suspect this morning has been unpleasant."

Kyrel stiffened.

He had never 'officially' met Soren. He had only seen him once, beside Rhett. But he recognized the voice and knew that Soren's reputation stretched like a shadow behind power.

"How did you get past DEI?" Kyrel asked.

Soren's smile didn't break. "When you work as closely with them as I do," he said, "doors open. Even locked ones."

Kyrel held his gaze. "What do you want?"

Soren stepped closer, hands in his pockets, posture relaxed; too relaxed. "To help," he said. "To steady the company during this… transition."

Kyrel gave a slow, deliberate laugh. "You're the one who destabilized it."

Soren tilted his head, impressed. "You're perceptive. Good. That will serve you."

Kyrel's jaw tightened. "Rhett said your name."

"Of course he did," Soren replied casually. "Fear makes men honest."

Kyrel exhaled through his nose. "So you admit it."

Soren's eyes gleamed with a predatory glint. "Mr. Kade… I don't need to admit anything. I need you to understand something." He leaned in, not threatening, but intimate in a way that made Kyrel feel the trap closing. "The DEI is not your enemy," Soren said. "They are merely… a mechanism."

Kyrel's pulse slowed. "And you?" he asked.

Soren smiled. "I am the man who understands what your technology really is. And what it can become."

"Weaponization," Kyrel said.

"Optimization," Soren corrected.

Kyrel stepped back. "No."

Soren sighed softly, disappointed, not surprised. "That's all right," he murmured. "You'll say yes eventually."

"Why would I?"

"Because," Soren said, "the alternative is letting DEI dismantle your company. And they will. Unless someone with true influence intervenes."

Kyrel stared. "You want me to join you."

"I want you to survive," Soren said simply. "And to build something bigger than the cage that tried to break you." He extended a hand. "Work with me."

Kyrel didn't take it.

Soren smiled smugly, unruffled. "You will. Sooner than you think." And then he left.

As Soren stepped out, the elevator chimed, D'Andra rushing in, breathless, worry etched into every line of her face. She saw Kyrel. He saw her. And in that moment, the morning's events, the DEI raid, Rhett's collapse, Tara's threat, Soren's proposition, it all converged at once. The pressure of the world condensed into a single shared look.

"We're in danger," D'Andra said.

Kyrel took her hands. "I know."

She swallowed. "What do we do now?"

Kyrel's voice was low. Steady. Unshakeable. "We find the truth," he said. "And then we show the world exactly what they did."

And with that, their war truly began.

CHAPTER 27

THE PRICE OF SAYING NO

The room still smelled faintly of Soren's cologne by the time D'Andra reached Kyrel. Not strong. Just there. A cool, expensive scent that didn't belong to anyone who ever had to count shifts or worry about overtime. It clung to the air like an aftertaste.

D'Andra stepped close, palms sliding up his arms, grounding him the way she always did when the world tilted. "You okay?" she asked.

He could've lied. Said yes. Said it was just another DEI circus. Said he'd handle it. Instead, he exhaled slowly. "No. Not really."

She nodded, accepting that. "Who was he?"

Kyrel glanced toward the door Soren had used.

"Vale," he said. "Soren Vale."

Her eyes narrowed. "The Soren Vale? From those hearings last year? The 'we only advise within the law' guy?"

"That's the one."

"What did he want?"

Kyrel almost laughed. It came out closer to a cough.

"To 'help'," he said, using his fingers to make air quotes. "Which is always bad news."

They found a small office that hadn't yet been claimed by DEI or panic. D'Andra shut the door behind them and twisted the lock, more for symbolic privacy than actual security. Kyrel leaned against the table.

"He came in like he owned the place," he said. "Said he works closely with DEI. Said he understands what LinkLife 'really is'."

"Did he use that word?" D'Andra asked. "'Understands'?"

"Yeah."

"That's how they talk to psych patients right before recommending commitment," she muttered. "What did he actually propose?"

"Partnership," Kyrel said. "Influence. 'Saving' the company. He framed DEI as a mechanism. Like they're just a tool and he's the hand using it."

D'Andra tilted her head, studying him. "And you said no."

It wasn't a question.

"I said no," Kyrel confirmed.

"How?"

He thought for a moment, replaying it.

"I told him I don't trust anyone who uses chaos as leverage," he said. "And that if he's willing to destabilize an entire company just to get his hands on its tech, I'd rather watch LinkLife burn than put it in his care."

A slow, fierce smile tugged at the corner of her mouth. "Good."

"It may have been the wrong move strategically," he admitted. "But it was the only move I could live with."

She stepped closer, hands braced on the table on either side of him, caging him in, eyes level with his.

"Kyrel," she said, voice low and steady, "we will pay for that 'no'."

"I know."

"But I would rather pay for that than for you saying yes."

He swallowed.

"I keep thinking about the moment this all started," he said. "The first patient you saw with a chip. The look in that dementia daughter's eyes. The DV case. That man on the edge of deportation. Every time the tech helped, it was beautiful. And every time it hurt, it wasn't the chip—it was everything around it."

"Systems are just systems," she said. "They become what sits on top of them."

"I won't put him on top of this one," Kyrel said. "Whatever our cost is, that's his price."

D'Andra slid one hand to the back of his neck, thumb pressing gently into the tense muscle there. "Alright," she said. "Then we plan for retaliation."

Meanwhile, in a deceptively unmenacing federal building, in a smaller, colder room with worse lighting, Rhett Colburn sat facing a metal table and deeply regretted every decision he'd made for the past eight months.

The DEI interrogation room wasn't theatrical. No two-way mirror. No spotlight. Just a table, two chairs, and a discreet camera eye in the corner. Agent Rowan sat opposite him. No notes. No tablet in front of him. But Rhett had the unnerving sense the man already knew things he hadn't said yet.

"Let's start simple," Rowan said. "Why did you authorize the Vale licensing bridge without informing your CEO?"

Rhett's throat felt dry. "I— it was paperwork," he said. "Routine. Standard expansion clause. We were under time pressure."

Rowan's gaze didn't waver. "Mr. Colburn. We have records of your correspondence with Vale Strategic dating back ten months. That is not 'routine paperwork'."

Rhett clenched his hands together in his lap. "You don't understand the pressure we were under," he burst out. "After the cap—after they took Kyrel out—investors panicked. Governments wanted guarantees. We needed someone who could navigate the Cap Act world. Vale was already in those rooms."

"And you decided to bring them into yours," Rowan observed.

"We needed to survive."

"At what cost?"

Rhett looked away.

Rowan let the silence stretch.

"You cooperated with an external entity with a documented history of regulatory edge-pushing," Rowan said at last. "You allowed them to draft contract language you didn't fully read. You enabled an unauthorized spike in valuation that triggered your partner's capping."

He tapped the table with one finger. "What, precisely," Rowan asked, "did you think they were asking you to pay?"

Rhett's voice dropped to a whisper. "They told me I'd still be here when the dust settled," he said. "They said caps come and go. But people like them, and people like me, we're the ones who rebuild after."

"People like you," Rowan repeated.

Rhett's jaw tightened.

Outside the door, unseen, Soren Vale paused as he walked past, listening to the cadence of voices without needing to hear the words. People like you. That was always the best hook.

Tara Winslow did not go to the police with the threat. She went to work. She sat in her small home office, blinds half-closed, laptop open, coffee untouched and going lukewarm on the desk. The message still sat on her secure line, stark and clean.

Stop digging. Or your next story will be your last.

It didn't read like random trolling. No caps-lock, no slurs, no typos. No cheap dramatics. Someone had taken time to craft a threat that telegraphed capability, not chaos.

She had traced it as far as she could on her own before the trail went muddy, routed through layered servers, bounced through jurisdictions, scrubbed by something that didn't look like an off-the-shelf anonymizer. It was from someone with access to serious tools.

She reopened her notes. Chronologically, the anomaly started eight days before Kyrel's capping. That much she knew. A valuation spike that didn't match public filings. A licensing bridge that introduced an entity that barely existed on paper, then did, and then rebranded.

Vale Strategic. On the surface: consulting. Underneath: it was something undefined.

Tara scrolled through an older folder, one labeled simply: Hearings – Archive. This was where she dumped all the "not quite enough for a story" material. Patterns that itched but didn't yet align.

There. A Senate subcommittee hearing from the year before. Topic: "Advisory Firms and Regulatory Navigation in a Capped Economy." A witness. Soren Vale.

She clicked the transcript. Searched for "Cap Act." Read his answers. He talked about efficiency. He talked about predictability. He talked about helping companies "transition gracefully" when an executive hit the ceiling. He never once used the word "power."

Tara leaned back, staring at the screen. "You're circling the system," she murmured. "Not fighting it. Managing it. Optimizing it."

She pulled up public DEI procurement records. Most were boring. Compliance software. Algorithm audits. Training materials. And then she found it. A line item three months old.

> "Regulatory Transition Modelling — consultative services."
> Vendor: Vanguard Adaptive Legal Engineering, LLC.

The acronym was forgettable. The corporate address was not. Same building. Same floor. As Vale Strategic.

"Well," Tara exhaled, heart ticking up a notch. "Hello, shell." She highlighted the entry and opened a fresh document.

> WORKING HEADLINE:
> 'THE MEN WHO NAVIGATE THE CAP — AND WHY THEY NEVER HIT IT THEMSELVES.'

Her notification bar flickered, an encrypted ping on her leak contact channel. She opened it.

> You don't know how big this is.
> Stop.
> Or at least don't do it alone.

No signature again. Just a location tag she recognized. LinkLife's neighborhood. Someone inside was trying to reach her.

Kyrel and D'Andra spread papers out on the table between them, Kyrel's handwriting mixing with D'Andra's straighter, more precise notes.

"We need three tracks," D'Andra said, slipping easily into triage mode the way she did in an OR. "One: internal. Two: external. Three: personal safety."

Kyrel almost smiled. "You're color-coding my existential crisis?"

"Would you rather I just panic?" she asked mildly.

"No," he admitted.

"Good. Internal first," she said, tapping the top of the page. "Who can we trust inside LinkLife?"

"Priya," he said immediately. "Emilio. A handful of the core engineers from the early days. People who cared more about what we were building than what it could be sold for."

"Anyone in Legal?" she asked.

He hesitated.

"Maybe one," he said. "But I don't want to drag anyone in without cause. If DEI flags them, that's permanent."

"Then start with the engineers," she said. "Lock down forks. Create read-only snapshots of the core. If Vale or anyone like him wants to weaponize this, they'll need to change it first."

"They won't expect the original architect to still have that much informal influence," Kyrel murmured. "They think I'm already neutralized."

"Use that."

He nodded, jotting notes.

"External," she said. "That's Tara. Are you willing to give her more?"

"Yes," he said, without hesitation. "But carefully. I don't have the luxury of an off-the-record mistake."

"Then you give her what you can't prove, just enough to make her dig in the right places," D'Andra said. "Names. Dates. The fact that Vale showed up today."

"She's already in danger," he warned. "There's no way she hasn't been threatened."

"Journalists always are," D'Andra said. "At least give her the dignity of choosing her risks with full information."

He paused on that. Personal safety. He hadn't been thinking in those terms. Not for himself. The Cap Act made you a caged king, not a target. But systems weren't the only danger anymore. "You think they'd—"

"Yes," D'Andra cut in, firm. "If someone is willing to game a national wealth ceiling to own your tech, they're not going to balk at intimidation. Or worse."

He absorbed that, the muscles in his jaw flexing. "And DEI?" he asked. "Rowan. Weller. Are they tools or actors?"

"Does it matter?" she said quietly. "Tools can still smash you if they're pointed in your direction."

He leaned back, rubbed his eyes. "You're awfully calm about all this," he said.

"I'm not calm," she replied. "I'm compartmentalizing. It's what you do when a trauma patient comes in and you don't have enough blood on hand. You don't get to freak out until after the work is done."

"After," he echoed. "You think we'll have an 'after'?"

She reached over and folded her hand over his. "Yes," she said simply. "I didn't marry you for a six-year story arc."

That drew a real laugh out of him. Tired, but real. "Okay," he said. "Internal, external, safety. I'll pull Priya and two others into a 'stability review.' You call your one administrator who still remembers why they went into medicine. See if they've seen DEI's fingerprints on hospital data."

"And Tara?" she asked.

"I'll message her a question nobody but me could send," he said. "And we'll see if she's still willing to pick up the line after the threat she's almost certainly gotten."

"You really think she's been threatened?"

"She's telling the truth about money and power," he replied. "Of course she has."

The DEI agents gave Rhett a ten-minute break. He sat alone in the interrogation room, fingers laced so tightly his knuckles hurt, trying not to see the future. If DEI decided he was a willing collaborator, he wouldn't go to prison for tax evasion or some white-collar penalty that came with minimum-security facilities and polite warden visits.

He would be hit with "Cap Evasion Assistance." The law treated helping capped individuals circumvent restrictions as close to treason. The whole system relied on the illusion that once the scoreboard froze, the game ended. If they made an example of him, there wouldn't be a second act.

The door opened. For a heartbeat, Rhett thought Rowan had come back. Instead, Soren slipped in, closing the door behind him with quiet precision. Rhett shot to his feet.

"You— you can't be in here," he stammered. "This is a DEI—"

Soren raised a hand. "Relax. You're on a break. And I am here as your counsel."

"I didn't ask for counsel," Rhett said.

"No," Soren agreed. "But you need it."

Rhett sank back into the chair. "They're going to bury me," he said.

"Only if we let them," Soren replied.

"We?" Rhett echoed.

Soren smiled, the kind of small, controlled curve that never reached his eyes.

"This is not the first time an overzealous agent has tried to turn a frightened executive into a scapegoat," Soren said. "The narrative is clean: ambitious CFO makes a deal with a shadowy advisor, pushes his saintly founder over the cap, profits from the fallout. It plays well in hearings. It distracts from more interesting questions."

"Like what?" Rhett asked.

"Like who designed the cap modelling algorithms," Soren said lightly. "Who advises DEI on 'transition scenarios.' Who benefits when someone like Kyrel Kade is taken out of circulation and replaced with more… pliable leadership."

Rhett stared.

"You," he said hoarsely.

"Among others," Soren said.

"And you're telling me this… why?"

"Because I would prefer not to lose you," Soren said calmly. "You are reckless, yes. But you are also ambitious, smart, and deeply angry at the right things."

"Angry at the right— are you insane?" Rhett snapped. "I helped you push my friend over the edge."

"You helped accelerate the inevitable," Soren corrected. "Kyrel was always going to be capped. The only question was who controlled the aftermath."

Rhett pressed his palms against his eyes. "What do you want from me?" he whispered.

Soren's answer was simple. "Loyalty."

Rhett laughed, a hollow, broken sound. "Why would I give you that?"

"Because," Soren said, leaning forward, "if you don't, they will hang you, Mr. Colburn. And they will leave the real architecture intact. The law won't change. The advisory firms won't change. The old money won't change. The only thing that will change is your liberty."

He let that sink in.

"I can make this survivable," Soren said. "Not comfortable. Not painless. But survivable. You keep your freedom. You keep a slice of influence. You help me ensure LinkLife's next evolution lands in the right hands."

Rhett looked up. "And Kyrel?" he asked.

Soren's face didn't shift. "Kyrel has already made his choice," he said. "He said no."

Rhett thought of Kyrel's expression in the conference room. Calm. Unyielding. "He won't bend," Rhett said quietly.

"No," Soren agreed. "Which is why we must go around him."

Rhett stared at the blank wall opposite him, jaw working. Then he nodded, once, sharply. "What do I have to say?" he asked.

Soren's smile sharpened by a degree. "Only the truth," he said. "Selective, of course. But truth."

———

Tara's phone buzzed on the desk. She glanced at the screen. Unknown, Encrypted channel. She thought another threat. But it could be a source.

She answered. "Tara Winslow." Static for half a second, then a voice, low, male, measured.

"Ms. Winslow, this is Kyrel Kade."

Every muscle in her body went still. She had interviewed before—once, after his capping, when he'd been brittle and half-stunned. But not on this channel. Not with this tone.

"How did you get this line?" she asked.

"From a hospital administrator who still believes in medicine," he said. "And from a wife who thinks you're our best shot."

"That's flattering," she said. "Also terrifying. You should know I've been threatened."

"I assumed," he said. "That's why I'm calling directly."

"What do you want?"

"To give you three facts," he said. "And one warning."

She sat up straighter, grabbed a pen, even though she'd transcribe later. "Go on."

"Fact one," Kyrel said. "Soren Vale came to my office today. He walked past active DEI officers to get there. That shouldn't be possible unless he has formal or informal standing with them."

Tara scribbled.

"Fact two," he continued. "Rhett has been talking to Vale's people for months. He admits that much. I don't know what he's said in there, but I know he's scared enough now to say anything they want."

Tara's free hand tightened around the arm of her chair.

"Fact three," Kyrel said. "The cap algorithms aren't just reactive. I think they're being modelled. Stress-tested. Used to push certain people over the line at convenient times. You're already sniffing this, but you need to know: the pattern is not accidental."

"Who's controlling the model?" she asked.

"That's your investigation," he said. "Not mine. If I get too close to that answer, DEI can frame it as tampering."

"And the warning?" Tara asked.

Kyrel hesitated.

"You already know you're a target," he said. "What you might not know is that they've started dragging my wife into the net. Hospital audits. Suspended privileges."

"Because of you?" Tara asked.

"Because of the story," he said. "Because of the Cap Act. Because of anyone who refuses to let this become just another normalized cage."

She swallowed. "So what's the warning?"

"If they're willing to go after a surgeon whose only crime is being married to me," he said quietly, "they will absolutely come after a journalist whose only crime is telling the truth."

"I assumed that, yes," she said.

"Assume harder," he said. "And don't trust anything that looks like an easy leak. If someone hands you a clean villain with a bow on their head, look for the person standing in their shadow."

Silence pulsed between them for a beat. "Why are you really calling, Mr. Kade?" she asked softly. "Not the tactical reason. The real one."

He blew out a breath. "Because I said no," he said. "And I need someone outside this machine to know what that cost."

Tara's throat tightened. "You just went from story subject to co-conspirator," she said lightly.

"I know," he replied. "I'm trusting you not to get us both killed."

"No promises," she said. "But if your goal is blowing up the illusion instead of just your own cage? Then yes. I'll dig."

"Good," he said. "Because I think the people who wrote this law never expected someone capped to show up as a witness instead of a cautionary tale."

She smiled, despite herself. "Let's make it their problem, then."

After he hung up, Kyrel stayed in the small conference room a moment longer, listening to the muted chaos outside: phones ringing, footsteps, the murmur of DEI officers shifting between departments.

D'Andra returned, a fresh printout in her hand. "The administrator I called?" she said. "He confirmed something. DEI has been feeding hospital implant data into a 'behavioural compliance module'."

He looked up sharply. "That's not just financial."

"No," she said. "That's tracking where people go. Who they visit. Which clinics they use. LinkLife isn't just identity now. It's geography. Relationship. Routine."

"Surveillance," he said.

"Soft at first," she said. "But yes."

He closed his eyes for a moment. "This is the price," he murmured.

"For what?" she asked.

"For inventing something powerful in a sick system," he said. "For saying no when the system asked to own it. For believing we could build something that stayed clean."

She stepped closer, rested her forehead against his. "You can't fix the whole system," she said. "Not alone."

"I know."

"But you can choose what you refuse to be complicit in," she continued. "That's what 'no' is. It's the smallest unit of revolution we get."

He let out a breath that was halfway between a laugh and a sigh. "Then I guess we just declared one," he said.

She pressed a soft kiss to his mouth. "Congratulations," she murmured. "You're an insurgent now."

Outside, in the hallway, DEI's lights pulsed again as another subsystem came under review.

Somewhere two floors below, Rhett quietly signed something he would not be able to take back.

Across town, Tara opened a new file and labeled it: THE GAME BEHIND THE CAP.

And in a different building entirely, Soren Vale poured himself a drink, watched the city lights flicker, and smiled to himself.

Kyrel Kade had said no.

Which meant the real work could begin.

CHAPTER 28
THE FIRST PUSH BACK

The boardroom wasn't built for tension. It was built for investor charm: glass walls, skyline views, warm-tone lighting, curated tech-art on the walls meant to say innovation without danger.

Today, the room felt smaller.

Kyrel sat at the head of the long table, no titleplate, no name, no CEO badge. Just him. Priya sat two seats away, spine straight, chin raised with something like hope. Emilio typed quietly, already running silent diagnostics on his laptop. Two other early engineers hovered near the far corner. Across from them sat three board members, attempting to appear relaxed. And one empty seat toward the right.

Rhett's.

Kyrel noticed it, and ignored it.

"Thank you for making time," he said. "Today will be short."

Board Member Halden lifted a practiced smile. "Mr. Kade, we weren't expecting such an abrupt 'strategic review.' Is there—"

"Yes," Kyrel said, cutting cleanly. "There's a problem with the LinkLife licensing modules."

Priya's gaze flicked to him, she knew what came next.

"The modules were expanded without sufficient ethics review," Kyrel said. "Three contracts are predatory. Two are exploitative. One is structurally coercive."

Silence flooded the room.

Halden blinked. "Mr. Kade… you don't have the authority to make—"

"I don't need authority to identify a problem," Kyrel said calmly. "And I'm advising you now: these contracts need to be frozen pending internal evaluation."

"That could cause instability," another board member said sharply.

"Yes," Kyrel said. "But instability is the consequence of bad decisions, not of correcting them."

Priya smiled faintly behind her notes.

Halden leaned forward. "We pushed Kyrel Kade past the cap for a reason," he said before catching himself.

The room froze.

Kyrel didn't blink. Priya stopped writing. Emilio looked up sharply.

Halden coughed. "I meant—his valuation grew rapidly. The market was overheated. We—"

"You weren't talking about the market," Priya said quietly.

Halden looked cornered.

Kyrel let the silence work on him.

Then: "Let me be clear," Kyrel said. "No matter who pushed me over, no one will push this technology into coercive use cases while I'm here."

Halden's face tightened. "And how long will you be here, Mr. Kade?"

"As long as LinkLife needs protecting." Kyrel stood. "Priya, Emilio, begin the freeze. Board, expect a detailed report by end of week." He walked out before they could object.

Behind him, Priya whispered a single sentence into the quiet room: "He isn't the one who should be afraid."

———————

D'Andra's day had already been brutal when the email arrived. She opened it with a knot in her stomach.

> SUBJECT: REVIEW OF SURGICAL PRIVILEGES —
> URGENT
> FROM: Hospital Compliance Office
> Dr. Crost-Kade,
> As part of a systemwide audit, your patient logs from the last six months have been flagged for secondary review.

Secondary review was code for: We think you're inconvenient.

She walked straight to the compliance office. The clerk at the window straightened, clearly nervous.

"Dr. Crost-Kade, ah—yes, the review… I'm not really the one—"

"Who initiated it?" D'Andra asked.

"Um… DEI requested access to implant-linked patient entries. Just routine compliance—"

"There is no routine compliance that involves federal agents reviewing my trauma cases," D'Andra said quietly. "Pull up the request."

The clerk fumbled, but did. One name sat on the authorization line. Agent T. Weller. Her blood ran cold. Of course.

She turned away, breathing through her teeth. They're not coming for Kyrel alone.

She walked back to the OR suite, stripping off her coat, mind racing. She needed her own team. Her own support. And she needed to warn him before Weller moved to the next step.

Rhett stood before the camera, throat constricted, palms sweating despite the air-conditioned chill of the room. Rowan sat opposite him again. But now Soren was in the corner, arms folded, expression unreadable.

"Mr. Colburn," Rowan said, "you may begin your clarification statement."

Rhett swallowed. This was it. Say the wrong thing, and he was done. Say the right thing, and he became complicit. He took a breath.

"The Vale licensing bridge," Rhett began, "was initiated because I... I believed LinkLife was at risk. Investors were panicking. Government regulators were looking for stability. I thought—wrongly—that Vale Strategic could provide that."

Rowan raised a brow. "You're suggesting you acted alone?"

Rhett hesitated. He could admit everything. He could tell them Vale had pushed him. He could burn the entire corrupted building to the ground. But then he pictured prison. And Soren's cold promise: I can make this survivable.

"I acted without telling Mr. Kade," Rhett said. "It was my mistake. Mine alone."

Soren's smile flickered like an assassin's blade. Rowan studied him for a long moment.

"This statement will be added to your record," Rowan said.

Rhett nodded, forcing steadiness. "All I want," he said, "is to keep LinkLife stable."

Rowan shut the file. "We'll be in touch."

Soren waited until Rowan left. Then he said, softly: "Good. You've proven you understand consequences."

Rhett felt sick. But also, alive. He'd chosen his side. Even if it killed him.

Tara had reached the café ten minutes early. Kyrel had told her to pick a public place, not too noisy, not too quiet. He was already there, hood up, hands wrapped around a cup of tea he wasn't drinking. Tara slid into the seat opposite him.

"You weren't kidding," she said.

"You got the threat?" he asked.

"Two," she said. "Someone told me not to do this. Someone else told me not to do it alone. The second one… that sounded like someone close to you."

Kyrel didn't blink. "What did it say?"

Tara recited the line.

Kyrel stiffened. "That's D'Andra's administrator," he said. "He's trying to protect her."

"Which means he's seen something," Tara said. "Something they don't want reported."

He slid her a folded list. "Names," he said. "People you should avoid. People you should interview. People who will lie. People who won't."

She opened it. Her eyes widened. "Kyrel," she whispered, "this is… explosive."

"I know," he said. "I'm trusting you to verify it before you print anything."

"And if I verify it?" she asked.

"Then you burn it all down," he said. "Every shell company. Every advisory group. Every modeler who rigged the Cap Act. Every DEI liaison who pushed someone over the edge because they wanted a compliant successor."

Tara exhaled, trembling just a little. "You're asking me to go to war," she said.

He shook his head. "No. I'm asking you to go to work. War comes later."

She looked up at him. "You're different," she said. "You were cracked open when you were capped. But now you're... sharper."

"I know what I'm fighting now," Kyrel said.

"And you think you can win?"

"I think," he said quietly, "that someone has to lose. And it won't be us."

D'Andra found Kyrel outside the café and waited until Tara had left. As she approached, Kyrel could read her face; it told him everything.

"They pulled my privileges," she said. "Pending review."

Kyrel's expression hardened. "They're coming for me through you," he said.

"No," she said. "They're coming for us through me."

He pulled her into his arms.

"We need to get ahead of this," she whispered into his chest.

"We will," he promised. "Just tell me what Rowan signed. What Weller accessed."

She looked up, eyes fierce. "Everything."

Across the street, Tara lifted her phone and snapped a single photo of them, not for publication, but for documentation. Beside her, a man stepped from an idling black sedan.

Soren Vale.

"Ms. Winslow," he said smoothly. "A moment?"

She turned, blood colder than the wind. "Why?" she asked.

"To congratulate you," Soren said. "You're about to uncover something very dangerous. I'd hate for you to misinterpret it."

"That sounds like a warning," she said.

"No," Soren replied, smiling faintly. "Warnings come later." He stepped back into the sedan. It glided away leaving Tara, heart pounding, staring after it. He knows I'm working with Kyrel. And deeper than that: He doesn't care. At least not yet. Something bigger was moving.

She sent Kyrel a two-word message: He's watching.

Kyrel responded instantly: Good. Let him. We're not running.

CHAPTER 29
THE LINE IN THE WARD

By the time D'Andra reached the administrative floor, her badge had already stopped working on half the doors. The elevator door dinged open onto carpet she almost never walked on: muted grey, art prints framed in brushed steel, the smell of burnt coffee and stress. The plaque on the wall read:

EXECUTIVE SUITE – HOPEWELL MEDICAL CENTER

She smoothed her hair back, more out of habit than vanity, and knocked on the frosted-glass door marked:

GABRIEL HSU — HOSPITAL ADMINISTRATOR

"Come in," a voice called.

Gabriel Hsu looked like a man who'd been carved out of long nights: early fifties, tie slightly askew, permanent worry creased between his brows. His desk was a geography of color-coded folders and two monitors, both turned so she couldn't see the screens.

"Dr. Crost-Kade," he said, rising halfway, then gesturing to her to sit. "Thank you for coming up."

"Your email said my surgical privileges are under review," she said, sitting but not relaxing. "I assumed that wasn't a social call."

He watched her for a moment, then crossed to close the door and turned the lock. The soft click sounded much louder than it should have. D'Andra's spine tightened.

"That's… not reassuring," she said.

Hsu exhaled, moved to the window, and twisted the blinds so that the slats tilted shut. The office dimmed.

"Dr. Crost-Kade," he said, "I'm going to ask you a question, and I need you to answer honestly. Not as your administrator, just… as someone who still remembers why he went into healthcare."

She blinked. "All right."

"Have you spoken to a journalist in the last two weeks?"

She held his gaze. "Yes."

His jaw tensed, but not with anger. More like confirmation.

"Tara Winslow," he said. It wasn't a question.

"Yes," D'Andra said. "I didn't give her patient names. I didn't break HIPAA. I talked about systemic issues—LinkLife pressure, grant strings, the way federal systems are leaning on clinicians to push implants for non-medical reasons."

His shoulders sagged in something like relief.

"Good," he said quietly. "For a minute I hoped I hadn't misread you."

She frowned. "Misread me how?"

He walked back to his chair and pulled open a side drawer. When he set the printed email on his desk, she recognized the line of text at once. The warning Tara had read aloud in the café:

> If you keep digging, don't do it alone.
> They won't just come for him.
> — A Friend in the System

Her eyes snapped up. "You?"

Hsu nodded once. "I used an anonymizer, but I suspected she might show it to him. Or to you. That was… sort of the point."

D'Andra felt her pulse in her throat. "Why?"

"Because I've been watching the same storm you have," he said. "And I'm on a very narrow ledge between protecting this hospital and selling my soul wholesale."

He tapped a second folder, thicker, with a red band clipped across it.

"Your 'review' is a formality," he said. "No one up here thinks you're a bad surgeon. You're one of our best. This—" he nudged the folder "—isn't about your medicine. It's about your access."

"Access to what?"

"To data," Hsu said. "To LinkLife implants. To DEI's new favorite toy."

He slid the folder toward her. She opened it. The first page was a summary of her last six months of cases. Someone had circled every patient who'd had a LinkLife implant. Not just trauma cases. Not just neurology consults. Obstetrics. Psychiatry. General surgery. Outpatient clinics.

Dozens of names. Every one with a small notation in the margin:

LL-ID PING RECEIVED – DEI MIRROR

Her stomach turned. "They mirrored my patient logs to DEI? When?"

"Formally?" Hsu said. "Two months ago. Informally? I'd bet at least a year."

"That's illegal," she said.

He gave a humorless half-smile. "Not if they say it's about fraud detection, border control, or national security. You'd be surprised what you can slip through in a fifteen-page addendum no one has time to read."

"So my privileges—"

"Are being 'reviewed' because you're not fitting the compliance pattern," Hsu said. "You override implant-based flags. You treat undocumented patients without routing them through the LinkLife ID system. You've refused to enroll three domestic violence survivors in the 'mandatory continuity program'—"

"The one that lets partners track their location," she said sharply. "I'm a trauma surgeon, not a warden."

"I know," he said. "That's why you're sitting in that chair instead of being walked out with security. You're the line, Dr. Crost-Kade. And they're testing how far they can push it before you break."

She sat back, blood hot with anger, cold with fear. "And you?" she asked. "Where's your line, Mr. Hsu?"

He looked at her for a long moment. Then he turned one monitor so she could see it. An email thread scrolled open.

Subject lines stacked on each other:

> RE: IMPLEMENTATION OF LL-ID MANDATE —
> TRAUMA & ED
> RE: FOLLOW-UP – NONCOMPLIANT STAFF
> RE: RISK ADVISORY – CROST-KADE

Her name appeared in three different fonts, bolded, highlighted. Hsu's replies, clipped and cautious, all said essentially the same thing: We are in the process of education and alignment.

The latest reply from a DEI liaison was short and sharp:

> Hospitals that fail to fully integrate LL-ID will be considered high risk. Future funding decisions will reflect this.
> — R. Weller, DEI Regional Liaison

Not Thomas. Someone else. A net cast wider.

Hsu closed the window.

"My job," he said, "is to keep this place open. If we lose federal funding, Hopewell folds. We're not a prestige center. We're a safety-net hospital wrapped in a budget crisis. We go under, this entire quadrant of the city loses its trauma facility and half its clinics within six months."

He drew a breath. "But there's a point where 'keeping the doors open' becomes complicity," he said. "I think we're drifting past that point."

"So what are you saying?" D'Andra asked. "You want to resist now? After you've already integrated LL-ID?"

"I'm saying I can't tear the system out," Hsu said. "But I can slow it. I can redirect it. And I can make sure the right people see what's actually happening before DEI sanitizes the logs."

He tapped the folder again. "That is a sanitized version," he said. "The raw logs are worse."

"How much worse?" she asked.

His jaw clenched. "They're not just pinging identity versus tax records anymore. They've started cross-referencing LL-ID pings with lifetime earnings files."

She felt the room tilt slightly. "Capped files."

"Yes," he said. "They've turned hospitals into soft checkpoints. Anyone whose implant flags as 'under review' or 'at threshold' gets annotated. No one tells them. No one treats them differently—yet. But the data flows."

"And you're telling me this why?" she asked, even though she already knew.

"Because you're married to the most famous capped individual in the system," he said. "Because you're already on their radar. Because a DEI agent signed off on this audit personally. And because I don't want to be the man who stood by while my hospital became a surveillance node."

He opened another drawer and took out a small, plain USB stick. "This never existed," he said. "Technically. But it contains three months of mirrored audit logs. Redacted enough that it won't blow patient confidentiality if it leaks, detailed enough that a competent investigative journalist can infer the pattern."

He set it in the space between them.

D'Andra stared at it.

"If you give me that," she said, "you're burning your bridge with DEI."

"They already lit the match," he said. "This is just me choosing where the fire goes."

She met his eyes. "Why now?"

He hesitated just a fraction.

"My sister died waiting on a transplant," he said. "Wrong insurance tier. Wrong hospital network. Right diagnosis, wrong spreadsheet. I promised myself I would never let a system use medicine as a weapon again."

He pushed the USB stick closer. "I can't fight them alone," he said. "And I can't be the face of this. But I can be a leak in the right direction."

She picked it up carefully, as if it were fragile. In a way, it was. "Does anyone else know?" she asked.

"Yes," he said. "Quietly. There's a back-channel thread among administrators in the regional network. A few of us are... uneasy. There's talk of coordinated 'technical delays' rolling out mandatory LL-ID in emergency departments. Policy rewrites. Consent forms that take a very long time to approve."

He almost smiled. "For a system obsessed with speed, bureaucracy can have surprisingly sharp teeth."

"And if DEI finds out?" she asked.

"Then they'll call it incompetence," he said. "Audit us. Replace a few of us. But not before someone like Ms. Winslow publishes enough that voters start asking questions."

His gaze settled on her again. "So the question is," he said, "where do you want to stand when that happens, Dr. Crost-Kade?"

There was no hesitation in her answer. "On the record," she said. "And in the OR."

For the first time since she'd walked in, his shoulders eased. "Then go," he said. "Take the logs. Talk to your husband. Talk to your journalist. Work your miracles downstairs. I'll keep the lights on as long as I can."

She stood, tucking the USB stick into the inner pocket of her coat.

"At some point," she said, hand on the doorknob, "they'll ask why you helped."

He nodded. "And I'll say I was just following the data."

She gave him a look that said she knew better, then stepped out into the brighter hallway. The lock clicked softly behind her.

Two nights later, Tara returned to her apartment, picked up her mail, and almost missed the envelope. It was wedged between a credit-card offer and a flyer for discount gym memberships tucked into the little metal box in her apartment lobby. No return address, no sender, just her name block-printed in a careful hand:

WINSLOW

Upstairs, she used a butter knife to slit the top open. The USB slid out into her palm. There was a single sheet of paper folded around it. Four lines, printed in that same plain font:

Hospital audit logs.
LL-ID + DEI + Earnings flags.

Not from him. From us.

— A Friend in the System

She sat down hard at her tiny kitchen table, laptop already waking up with a tap. The first directory on the drive was labeled:

HOPEWELL – 90 DAYS – REDACTED

The second:

REGIONAL – CROSS-CHECK SNAPSHOT

The file names read like bureaucratic sleep aids:

LL_MIRROR_09-A
EARNINGS_FLAG_CORRELATION_12
DEI_QUERY_TREE_TRIAL

The content did not. She scrolled through thousands of lines of timestamps, hashed IDs, status codes. Every LL-ID ping cross-linked to a DEI query. Flags for "lifetime earnings threshold approaching." Tags marking "CAP REVIEW CASES." Hospitals noted not by name, but by region code and funding tier. Tara leaned back, rubbing her eyes.

They've wired the hospitals straight into the cap system. Not just for fraud. Not just for crime. For control. Her fingers shook a little as she opened a blank document and started jotting down subtitles:

How LL-ID had been sold as patient safety
How hospitals had been pressured into adopting it
How DEI had quietly attached a second feed
How lifetime earnings — the cap system itself — had
turned into a hidden triage field

She saved the file under a working title:

CAP_LIFELINE_DRAFT_1

Then she encrypted a copy of the USB contents and stored it in three separate places. Wrote herself a note on paper, old-school, and tucked it into her notebook: If they come, they'll come for the digital trail first. Don't let that be the only trail.

Her phone buzzed. A message from D'Andra: We talked to him. He's in. Hospitals aren't all on their side.

Tara typed back: Got something from "us." Logs, DEI pings, cap flags. It's big.

Three dots appeared. Disappeared. Appeared again.

Then it's time to stop writing human-interest pieces, D'Andra finally replied. Write something that hurts them.

Tara smiled, a sharp, tired thing. Working on it.

When D'Andra slid a copy of the USB across their kitchen table later that night, Kyrel didn't touch it right away. He just looked at her.

D'Andra looked up at the ceiling and walls, then back to Kyrel with a question in her eyes. He nodded a 'yes': He'd swept the room for bugs using a device he'd 'borrowed' from LinkLife's security office and found none.

"Who?" Kyrel then asked.

"Gabriel Hsu," she said. "Hospital administrator. The one who signed off on my 'review.' He's not the enemy, Ky. He's trying to keep the place from collapsing while DEI pulls it apart from the inside."

She told him about the meeting, about the blinds, about his sister and the transplant list. About the admins' hidden thread. About "technical delays" and consent forms that would never quite make it to final approval.

When she finished, he rested his elbows on the table and laced his fingers together, forehead touching them for a moment like a man praying to something he wasn't sure was listening.

"They're using you as map pins," he said finally. "Patients. Staff. Me. The implants aren't just keys; they're sensors. Hospitals are the new border."

"Yes," she said. "But some of the gatekeepers are on our side."

He picked up the USB then, turning it between his fingers.

"This changes strategy," he said. "I'd been thinking of DEI as one monolith. One system. But it's not. It's only as strong as the institutions it rides through."

"And now you know the weakest parts of that ride," D'Andra said. "Hospitals that won't roll over. Administrators who want off the leash."

He nodded slowly. "If we can make this public before they patch it," he said, "the narrative changes. It's not 'billionaire punished for success' anymore. It's 'government using healthcare as a surveillance arm'. People who don't care about me will care about that."

"Exactly," she said. "You're the hook, but this is the story."

He looked up at her, eyes tired but clear. "You realize," he said quietly, "if we pull this thread hard enough, Gabe might lose his job. His license. Worse."

"He knows," she said. "He did it anyway."

Kyrel set the USB down carefully, like a small, dangerous stone.

"Then we owe him more than a thank-you," he said. "We owe him a world where his sister wouldn't have died on the wrong spreadsheet."

He stood, kissed her forehead, and reached for his laptop.

"Who first?" D'Andra asked. "Tara? Priya? Madeline?"

"All of them," he said. "Tara gets the logs. Priya gets the technical implications. Madeline gets to read the fine print and tell us which laws they broke on the way to writing new ones."

"And Rhett?" she asked softly.

He paused at the doorway. "We let him keep choosing his side," Kyrel said. "In full daylight. No more shadows for him to hide in."

"And Soren?" she said.

Kyrel's jaw tightened, but there was no fear in his answer. "We make sure he knows," Kyrel said, "that the hospitals are not neutral ground anymore. If he wants a war, he doesn't get to fight it quietly."

He opened his laptop. Outside, a siren wailed somewhere in the night, fading toward Hopewell Medical. Inside, another siren, smaller, quieter, buried in code and logs and pings, had just begun to sound.

Not an alarm. A signal.

CHAPTER 30

TARA WRITES THE STORY

Tara sat at her desk, legs folded under her, glasses smudged, hair clipped haphazardly on one side. She was accustomed to burning the midnight oil. She was on her third pot of strong coffee, and the cup sitting beside her had already grown cold. The USB drive lay on top of her laptop like a talisman and a threat.

Half a dozen windows glowed on her screen:

> DEI audit logs
> Earnings threshold trees
> LL-ID mirror feeds
> Notes from D'Andra
> Kyrel's list of names
> The anonymized admin thread

And in a blank document titled:

> THE HUMAN BODY AS BORDER — HOW DEI
> TURNED HOSPITALS INTO EARNINGS
> CHECKPOINTS

...was the beginning of the story she might lose her job for. She cracked her knuckles, took a long breath, and wrote the opening line.

> If you go to the hospital today, you'll be treated based on your symptoms. If you go tomorrow, you may be treated based on your lifetime earnings.

She stared at it, feeling the cold along her spine. Too heavy to start? Too alarmist? No. Truth deserved to sound like truth. She continued:

> Over the last three months, hospitals across the Northeast have quietly begun reporting patient data not to insurers, not to state health registries, but directly to the Department of Economic Integrity (DEI).

> This is not public knowledge. It is not disclosed on consent forms. It is not legally mandated. But internal logs obtained by The Ledger reveal something unprecedented:

> DEI is using LinkLife implant pings inside emergency rooms to cross-check patients against lifetime earnings files — the same files used to determine whether a citizen is "capped."

She stopped again. The word "Ledger" felt heavy in her mouth. She could send this to them, but the Ledger ran exposés. The Ledger had lawyers. The Ledger took risks.

Her editor at CityLine… might not. But this wasn't the moment to doubt. She kept going.

She scrolled through the logs again, making sure she wasn't missing something, anything, that would weaken the story.

Line after line of cross-checks:

```
LL-ID_PING: 00481291 → EARNINGS_FLAG:
THRESHOLD-3
LL-ID_PING: 99841277 → DEI_QUERY:
CAP_FILE_REVIEW
LL-ID_PING: 77212004 → ACCESS:
MIRROR-ROUTING
```

The pattern was undeniable: Hospitals weren't just treating patients. They were quietly feeding an economic surveillance pipeline.

She highlighted a section and built out the next paragraph:

> In internal communication threads between hospital administrators obtained by The Ledger, staff warn each other that "LL-ID integration is moving faster than the infrastructure can support," and that "DEI is applying pressure to route all admissions through implant verification."

One administrator writes:

> "We've become soft checkpoints. DEI is using LL-ID scans to map economic risk. We are no longer a hospital. We're a border."

She leaned back. Her heart hammered. This was too big for just healthcare. This was surveillance disguised as triage. This was economics disguised as medicine. This was political control disguised as public safety. She wrote:

"Capped" individuals, people prohibited by law from earning more money after hitting a statutory threshold, appear frequently in these logs.

What is not explained in any policy document is why a trauma patient's lifetime earnings should appear in a field intended for medical clearance.

She paused. This was where the story needed human faces. She opened her notes from D'Andra:

The undocumented man
The DV survivor
The dementia patient
The homeless woman flagged "non-aligned earnings profile"

She knew she couldn't use their names. But she could use their truth. She wrote:

One ER doctor, speaking anonymously, described a case in which a domestic violence victim's implant ping triggered a note in the DEI feed:

"Partner-linked access active."

Her abuser had login credentials tied to her implant.

The hospital was instructed to "maintain continuity."

Meaning: they were expected to preserve the abuser's access.

Her hands shook. She kept typing.

At 2:13 a.m., Tara hit save, encrypted the file, and then, against every instinct, dialed her editor. It rang twice before he answered, groggy.

"Tara… are you dying?" he said. "Is someone dying?"

"I need to show you something," she said. "Tonight."

"No," he said automatically. "Whatever it is, it can wait."

"It can't," she said. "It's big."

"How big? City corruption big, state scandal big—?"

"Federal economic control through medical systems' big."

Silence. She could imagine him sitting up in bed.

"How sure are you?" he asked.

"One hundred percent."

"How many sources?"

"Three direct," she said. "Two technical confirmations. One hospital administrator. One trauma surgeon with access to the logs. And I have the raw data."

"…Jesus," he whispered. "Send me the draft."

"I'm not emailing it," Tara said. "Not even encrypted. This needs to be handed off in person."

Another long pause.

"Tara," he said quietly. "Stuff like this gets people sued. Or worse."

Her throat tightened. "I know."

"And The Ledger… might run it. We might not. Depends how clean it is."

"I know."

"And if you publish this under your name," he said, "you won't go back to human-interest stories. You'll be on every watchlist with three letters."

"I know."

He sighed deeply.

"I'm at the office," he finally said. "Give me thirty minutes."

She swallowed. "Thank you."

"And Tara?" he said, softer. "Bring someone with you. Or at least tell someone where you're going."

She almost laughed. "I already did," she said.

It was a short walk, only four blocks, to the office. Normally she loved walking through the city at night with the empty streets, neon reflections, occasional taxis gliding like fish under streetlights. But tonight the shadows felt too thick. The parked cars, too quiet. The hum of the streetlights, too loud.

She kept her phone in her pocket, her other hand gripping the USB tight enough to leave marks on her palm.

Halfway down the block, a dark SUV slowed as it passed her. Her breath caught. Then it kept going. She exhaled, shakily.

She reached the glass doors of the CityLine newsroom at 2:48 a.m., buzzed through security, and took the elevator up. The newsroom was dim except for the rim of light under her editor's office door. He opened it before she reached it.

He looked… not scared. Concerned. Aging. Weighted by the knowledge that a story like this could make or break a career, and maybe a democracy.

"You weren't kidding," he said.

"No," she said quietly. "I wasn't." She handed him the USB.

He opened the document. Read the first page. Then the second. By the third page, he was standing. By the fifth, he was pacing. By the seventh, he was rubbing his temples. When he reached the end, he closed the laptop gently, as if afraid it would explode.

"You wrote something real," he said. "Something dangerous. Something… Pulitzer-adjacent dangerous."

Tara didn't move.

"But," he said softly, "I can't run this."

Her stomach dropped. He held up a hand. "Not yet. Not here. CityLine doesn't have the lawyers. Or the budget. Or the insulation from federal pressure. If we ran this, we'd be wiped out by morning."

"So what do we do?" she whispered.

He looked her dead in the eyes. "We take it higher."

She blinked. "To The Ledger?"

"No," he said. "Higher than that."

He slid the USB back to her. "You take this," he said, "to someone who isn't afraid of DEI. Someone who can publish at scale with legal firepower behind them. Someone with a platform that can't be quietly strangled."

"Who?" Tara asked.

He leaned in. "You take it," he said, "to The Sentinel."

Her breath stopped. The Sentinel. The national paper that governments feared. The one with a reputation for bringing down entire administrations. The one Soren Vale would absolutely, undeniably hate. She swallowed. "They'll never take me seriously."

"Oh, they will," her editor said. "Because I'm sending them a note telling them to. And because this story is bigger than all of us. And because they love taking down a system that thinks it's untouchable."

Her voice came out thin. "What about you?"

He smiled sadly. "My job is to stay standing long enough to keep running local news. Yours… is bigger now."

He lifted her draft again. "This story," he said, his voice trembling with conviction, "could change the country."

She took the USB back. Her hand was steady now.

On her way out of the newsroom, she texted Kyrel: I'm taking it to The Sentinel. If they run it, everything changes. Stay safe.

His reply arrived immediately: We don't want safe. We want true. Go.

She walked out into the cold night air. This time, when a car slowed at the corner, she didn't flinch. She was done hiding.

CHAPTER 31

THE TAIL

Tara stepped out of the revolving doors with her hood up and her breath turning white in the early-morning dark. The newsroom lights clicked off behind her, her editor staying behind in the building to make it look like she hadn't left with anything sensitive. Smart man. Smart enough to know that people get followed for less than this. The street was silent in that strange pre-dawn way, when the city felt like a held breath.

Her boots clicked on the concrete. At the corner, she felt it before she saw it, that shift in the air, the sense of a large object moving without purpose except to mirror hers. Then she heard the engine. A black sedan idled near the curb, windows tinted, lights off. Not the SUV from before. That almost made it worse.

She didn't break stride. Didn't look over. Didn't speed up or slow down. If they wanted her to know they were there, they already did. Her editor's words replayed in her mind: Take it to someone who isn't afraid of DEI. But she realized something then, she was the one who wasn't afraid. Not anymore. She reached the crosswalk. The sedan rolled forward half a car-length. Not aggressive. Not timid. Just tracking.

She considered her options. Taxi? Too traceable. Bus? Too slow. Train? Cameras everywhere. Walking? Predictable. Then she remembered the old trick a source taught her back in Boston, never run from a tail. Run them into a place they absolutely don't want to be seen. So instead of turning toward the transit station, she turned toward the one place in Midtown still awake at this hour: Memorial General Hospital.

Even at 3:40 a.m., its ER bay glowed bright. Security cameras. Nursing staff. EMTs. Police occasionally. A place where following her would leave a digital footprint. She cut across the street. The sedan didn't signal. Didn't honk. Just moved again, syncing with her steps.

"Alright," she murmured. "Let's see how brave you are."

As she approached the hospital entrance, she made subtle adjustments: a slower walk, a brief stop to tie her bootlace, just enough hesitation to widen the distance so security cameras could catch both her and the car behind. She scanned the lot.

There, top corner. A dome camera. Good. She walked under it, looked up into the lens, lifted the USB in her hand like a witness marking evidence, then walked through the sliding doors.

The sedan didn't follow. Of course it didn't. Inside, warm fluorescent light, antiseptic smell, nurses with clipboards, the soft beep of machines. Safe. For the moment.

Out of nowhere a voice said, "Tara?" She froze.

D'Andra Crost-Kade stood at the check-in counter, in scrubs, tired but upright, having just ended a shift.

Tara blinked. "D'Andra? What are you—"

"Double shift," D'Andra said. "You look— are you okay?"

Tara exhaled shakily. "Honestly? No. I'm being followed."

D'Andra's expression changed instantly, physician focus, wife's protectiveness, warrior's instinct. "Come with me," she said.

She guided Tara through a staff-only corridor. Past curtains, past tired interns, past a nurse who mouthed rough night? and received D'Andra's tiny nod.

Inside a supply room, D'Andra locked the door. "Tara," she said softly. "What did you publish?"

"I haven't published yet," Tara whispered. "But when I do… nothing is going back to normal."

D'Andra stepped closer. "Kyrel told me you were writing something big. He told me to be ready."

A beat. "Tara… DEI does not follow people casually. If you're being tailed, it's not a warning. It's a containment." Tara tightened her grip on the USB in her coat pocket. "I have to get this to The Sentinel."

"Then you need to disappear for the next few hours," D'Andra said. "And you can't leave by the front door."

D'Andra rolled a wheeled hamper to the side, revealing a secondary exit badge-locked from the inside. "This leads to the ambulance bay. No cameras."

"You're letting me out the back?" Tara murmured.

"No." D'Andra reached into her pocket and pulled out her own swipe badge. "I'm going with you."

Tara swallowed. "Won't that cause problems for you?"

"It already has," D'Andra said. "LinkLife is in every corner of this hospital now. Every patient. Every admin memo. Every ethics violation." Her eyes hardened. "And someone has to protect the truth before it disappears." She placed a hand on Tara's shoulder. "Let's get you out."

The two women slipped out the service exit into the cold night. The sky was just beginning to lighten, faint silver over the skyline. The sedan was no longer at the curb. Something worse had replaced it. A different unmarked government-style car idled in the near distance, its parking lights glowing like patient eyes. D'Andra whispered, "They switched vehicles."

Tara nodded. She tucked the USB deeper into her coat. And together, the journalist and the surgeon walked into the shadows of the ambulance bay, toward the one place in the city where truth still had a fighting chance.

CHAPTER 32

THE HAND-OFF

The ambulance bay smelled faintly of diesel and cold metal. Three rigs sat empty, their doors open, their paramedic crews inside restocking supplies.

Perfect cover. Too much movement for anyone tailing to pick out a single face unless they were very close.

D'Andra kept her head down, posture crisp, gait purposeful, the gait of someone who belonged.

"Stay beside me," she murmured.

Tara matched her pace.

The sky was deep indigo now, ripening toward dawn, but the cold kept everything sharp: her breath, her nerves, her sense of the world tightening around her. Behind them, the unmarked sedan rolled forward a few meters. It didn't try to block them. Didn't flash lights. Didn't call out. Which made it infinitely worse.

A paramedic stepped out of the nearest rig, mid-40s, shaved head, deep lines carved around his mouth from too many night shifts. He recognized D'Andra instantly.

"Doc," he said. "Rough night?"

"You have no idea," D'Andra said.

He saw Tara next, saw the tension in her shoulders, the stiffness in her gait.

"Friend of yours?" he asked.

"Yes," D'Andra replied. "She needs a ride."

That threw him. "A ride?" His tone dropped. "To where?"

"Anywhere but here," D'Andra murmured.

He looked past them toward the sedan. His jaw tightened. A beat. Then he opened the passenger-side door of the rig. "Get in," he said to Tara. "No paperwork. No questions."

Tara climbed in, heart pounding.

D'Andra leaned in after her.

"Do not drive her to her home," she said quietly. "Don't go to a station. Don't go to the ER."

"I know how to shake a tail," he replied, offended. "We do it every time the press tries to follow us out of a celebrity call."

Tara almost laughed. He had no idea how different this was.

D'Andra squeezed Tara's hand.

"I'll text Kyrel," she said. "Stay low. Turn off your phone and don't use it unless you're on secure signal."

Tara nodded.

"I'll see you soon," D'Andra whispered.

The paramedic climbed in, started the engine, and hit the lights; not the sirens, just the lights. Enough to create urgency without drawing cops.

The rig peeled out of the bay, tires screeching slightly on cold pavement. In the mirror, Tara saw the unmarked sedan move. Then another one rolled out from behind the parking garage.

"Jesus," she whispered. "There are two."

"Two's amateur hour," the paramedic said, eyes narrowing. "Real trouble starts at four."

Not reassuring. He swung onto 8th Street, then took a sudden left through a yellow light. The sedan followed. So did the second. He muttered, "Alright, you bastards…" He hit the gas hard.

The ambulance roared forward, weaving between early-morning delivery trucks and the occasional commuter car. His hands were steady on the wheel. Too steady.

"This isn't your first time," Tara said.

"Lady, I've worked this job twenty-two years," he said. "You pick up every trick the streets have. But I'll tell you this—" He checked the mirror. "They're not cops. They're not press. They're not vagrants. Tail cars like that? They're either private contractors or federal shadows."

Tara exhaled through her teeth. "Federal."

He nodded once. "Then we're going off-grid."

He turned down a narrow side street she didn't recognize. "You ever done the bridge trick?" he asked.

"No," she said.

"Good," he said. "Because if they know it, they won't expect an ambulance to try it." He made a sharp right that nearly threw her against the door. Ahead, the old industrial bridge over the freight tracks. A dead zone. No cameras. No traffic sensors. No patrols. He killed the lights.

The ambulance thundered onto the bridge in darkness. At the midpoint he cut the engine entirely. Coasted. And the ambulance drifted to a silent, ghostlike stop. The paramedic killed the cabin lights too. They sat in darkness.

Nothing but her heartbeat and the soft clicking of cooling metal. After ten seconds, the first sedan appeared at the far end of the bridge. It slowed. Stopped. And waited.

"They want eyes on you," the driver whispered. "They don't want to lose you."

The second sedan pulled up behind it. Boxing them in. Which meant—

"They think we have no other exit," he murmured.

Then he grinned. "They're wrong." He flicked a switch under the dash Tara hadn't seen before. Hydraulics hissed. A panel on the left side of the bridge, one she'd thought was solid metal, lifted three inches. A maintenance ramp. The paramedic nodded at it.

"Railway access. Restricted. But ambulances use it when the streets are jammed."

"You're kidding," Tara breathed.

"Nope." He restarted the engine quietly, low idle, and the ambulance crept toward the ramp. Behind her, the federal tail realized too late what they'd missed. Headlights flared. Doors opened. Men stepped out. Too far to reach her.

The ambulance dropped off the bridge onto the gravel rail maintenance road and vanished into the industrial district.

Twenty minutes later, after slicing through side streets and slipping under a half-closed warehouse gate, the driver brought the ambulance to a stop beside an old brick building with no signage.

"This is where you get out," he said. "They don't know I brought you here. They'll waste hours sweeping the wrong quadrant. Look, go down this block and you'll be across the street from the Harbourlight Hotel. "

Tara swallowed. "Thank you."

"Don't thank me," he said. "Just stay alive."

She stepped out, the USB warm in her coat pocket.

"The Sentinel building is six blocks east," he said. "Don't go in the front entrance."

"Where should I go?"

"The back. Alley. Loading dock." He paused. "And Tara?"

"Yes?"

"Whatever's on that drive, the country needs it." Then he pulled away, lights off, gone like he'd never been there.

She started walking in the direction of the hotel, staying under awnings, between buildings.

The street was quiet. Too quiet. Then, a clatter. Metal shifting above her. A silhouette on a rooftop. Broad shoulders. Still as a statue. Watching. Not a car tail. Not DEI. Something worse.

Someone who didn't follow on wheels. Someone who followed on foot. Her breath hitched. But she didn't run. She reached into her coat, touched the USB again. And whispered to herself: "Just one more block." Then she moved, not fast, not slow, just steady, toward the loading docks of The Sentinel. Toward the place where her story would become unstoppable.

CHAPTER 33

THE DARK ZONE

When the ambulance pulled away, the red taillights shrank into the warehouse district. Tara checked her watch: 3:20 a.m. Now she had to use her head. What was open? What did she have access to?

The instant the rig vanished, the cold reality hit her: No car. No bag. No prepared evasion kit. Just a coat, a USB, and a mind running too fast. She checked her pockets. Wallet. Keys. Phone.

That damn phone. She looked up. Three stories above, the silhouette on the rooftop still hadn't moved. She needed to cut her digital trail now.

She stepped deeper into the alley behind the loading dock. A cluster of dumpsters lined the brick wall, metal lids rimed with frost.

"Tara…" she whispered to herself. "Think." Phones broadcast location even powered down. She'd learned this from an ex-NSA whistleblower she'd interviewed five years ago. The trick wasn't shutting it off. The trick was shielding the antenna. She flipped open a dumpster lid with her sleeve.

Inside she found cardboard, plastic wrap, a half-broken cafeteria tray, and a foil catering pan,

"Victory!" she said to herself quietly. She grabbed the pan, shook off old rice, snapped a flat section free, and bent it into a crude envelope. She powered down the phone, removed the SIM with a paperclip scavenged from the dumpster's debris, and wrapped both tightly in foil. She then used the cafeteria tray, stainless steel, as a box and folded it around the foil-wrapped package. Double shielding. Her heart steadied. Now she was dark.

She needed unpredictability. If DEI was reading tower pings, she had seconds before her phone went silent on the network and flagged her as "lost."

She started to move. Through the alley. Across a silent intersection. Past a bakery warming its ovens for dawn. She kept her head down but not hunched, normal enough to blend, purposeful enough to avoid looking lost.

At the corner she spotted a city bus idling, driver drinking coffee. Perfect. She boarded without hesitation, fed a dollar into the machine, and sat. Not because she needed the ride. Because she needed noise in her pattern.

The bus pulled away. If anyone was following her on foot, they couldn't keep up now. At the next stop, she stepped off. Two streets later, she boarded a different bus and repeated a similar move getting off randomly after four stops. Classic counter-surveillance shuffle. She'd only ever used it once before, covering cartel expansion in the port district. But muscle memory came back.

The Sentinel building was six blocks east, but she headed south first. Never lead a tail straight to your destination. Approach from the least probable direction.

She dipped first into a laundromat, the harsh fluorescent lights washing her in a sterile glow. The hum of dryers filled the air, warm and heavy. A couple argued softly in Spanish near the folding tables. Tara pretended to study a row of detergent dispensers while checking the glass door through the reflection on a stainless-steel tumbler. A shadow slid past the window, too steady, too slow to be a pedestrian's casual walk. She slipped out the back exit into an alley choked with steam from a roof vent.

Next she stepped into a bodega, its aisles narrow and cramped, the smell of stale coffee and citrus cleaner clinging to the air. She grabbed a packet of gum she didn't need and moved toward the refrigerated section, mirrored doors perfect for surveillance.

There. A man outside, head turning slightly with her movement, pretending to talk on a phone pressed to his shoulder. She dropped the gum, murmured an apology to the clerk, and slipped through the tiny employee washroom at the back, out the Staff Only door that led into another corridor of shadow.

She crossed into the lobby of a hotel, marble floors gleaming under chandeliers. Bellhops wheeled carts stacked with luggage. Bleary-eyed tourists argued over directions. She blended in easily. She pretended to check a directory sign while catching sight of her own reflection, and behind her, the same man from the bodega stepped into the lobby. Not DEI. Private muscle. His posture was too crisp, too alert. She moved before he locked eyes with her, slipping behind a group of business travelers toward the service hallway.

The delivery corridor smelled of cardboard and onions. A pair of kitchen workers smoked near a dumpster, ignoring her as she passed. She kept her pace even, not too fast, never too fast, as she followed the twists of the concrete hallway.

Then she heard it: footsteps. Soft. Measured. Mirroring her rhythm.

She turned a corner suddenly and pressed herself against the wall. A second later, the footsteps passed her hiding place. Close. Too close. She waited until the echo faded, then darted through the fire door at the end, emerging into a small plaza behind the hotel.

She entered a skywalk connecting two office buildings, a glass corridor suspended over traffic, city lights stretching beneath her like a constellation. The clean lines reflected her image back at her in every direction. She used the reflections to gauge distance. No tail in the skywalk itself. But down on the street below? Two dark shapes pacing the block, too synchronized to be coincidence. They didn't know where she was, but they were sweeping the area. She quickened her pace.

She took a sharp turn into a stairwell, the air colder here, echoing with every step she made. The parking garage beneath the building felt damp, the concrete glistening with condensation. Cars sat in shadowed rows, each one a possible hiding place or an ambush point.

She moved along the wall, hand brushing cement for balance, scanning the aisles for silhouettes. A figure near a concrete pillar snapped upright as if listening. She didn't wait to see whether they'd spotted her. She slipped behind a parked SUV and crawled low until she reached the opposite stairwell. A push bar squeaked under her fingers and she emerged on the far side of the block.

Her pulse was steady now. Her muscles were operating entirely on training and instinct. She'd shaken them, for the moment. But she knew the kind of people following her. They didn't give up. And they didn't lose interest.

Her breath fogged in front of her. She didn't wipe it away, fingerprints show stress.

Keep moving.

Tara could see The Sentinel's loading dock entrance was ahead, a recessed alley beside a monolithic tower of glass and steel. It looked clear in the two industrial lamps that flickered overhead. But something felt wrong. There was a man leaned against the far wall, pretending to smoke. No cigarette glow. No exhale. Just posture. There was another shadow standing behind a half-open service door. Too rigid. Too alert.

These were not street people, nor were they employees.

She slowed down. Turned slightly. Looked for angles. They weren't moving, not toward her, just watching the alley. That meant they were not DEI or local thugs. They were private contractors; the kind Soren Vale's network used.

Her stomach tightened. They weren't guarding the building. They were watching to see who came here. Meaning The Sentinel wasn't just powerful, it was under siege too. So she couldn't walk into that alley. She had to find an alternate entrance.

She circled around the block and found the staff cafeteria entrance but it had a card access door. Damn. Then she saw it: A fork lift had one of its tines wedged in the door's track, keeping the latch from fully locking. Bless the bored delivery driver's shortcut. It was her miracle.

She limboed under the door and slipped inside.

A security guard sat at a desk near the elevators. He glanced up. She flashed her press badge without slowing. "Sentinel appointment," she said briskly, as if annoyed and late. He barely blinked.

She stepped into the elevator, held her breath as she watched the doors close. Her pulse roared in the silence.

When the doors opened on the 14th floor, she was greeted by the humming of soft light, glass partitions, and the quiet tension of people used to being hated by powerful strangers. A woman in a navy sweater stood waiting, arms folded, expression unreadable.

"Tara Winslow?" she asked.

Tara nodded. The woman exhaled in relief. "Good," she said. "You're early."

Tara stiffened. "Early?"

"We thought you'd be here in ten minutes."

"Why ten minutes?"

The woman stepped aside and gestured down the hall. "Because," she said calmly, "we've been watching your tail for the last twenty minutes. And we just saw them circle the block again."

Tara swallowed hard.

"Come on," the woman said, voice low, urgent. "Let's get you inside. You're not safe in the hall."

Tara followed her. But she made it. She was here. She checked her watch, it was 4:12 a.m.

CHAPTER 34

THE SENTINEL'S WAR ROOM

Tara followed. She was still running on adrenaline, but her mind alert in a different way now. This wasn't fear. It felt like she had crossed a threshold.

Glancing side to side, she noticed they passed glass-walled offices with their lights off, desks covered in stacks of legal briefs, sealed envelopes, redacted printouts. Every surface looked like a battleground of facts.

At the end of the hall was a door with no window, reinforced steel, a keypad, and a magnetic lock. It looked like a bunker within the building, or a bank vault perhaps. The woman keyed in a code, scanned her badge, pressed her thumb to a reader.

"Security's tight for a reason," she said quietly. "They've tried to break in twice this year."

Tara's stomach tightened. They?

The door unlocked with a heavy clunk and slowly swung inward. It truly looked like a bank vault door, it was over a foot thick and appeared to be solid steel.

"Welcome to 'The War Room'," said the woman. "We're safe in here, for now."

The air inside was cool and ionized, clearly filtered, and filled with the faint hum of servers. A long, rectangular table dominated the center. It was completely covered with manila folders, encrypted laptops, external drives, stacks of printed reports, and half-drunk coffees gone cold hours ago.

Three people sat there staring at her, apparently waiting as well. No, they weren't staring, they were studying her.

The woman in the sweater finally introduced herself.

"I'm Julia Aimes. Senior Editor, National Investigations," she said. Motioning toward one of the people sitting, "This is Dr. Malik Choudhary, our security consultant. Together, we handle intel verification."

Another woman with sharp eyes and hair cut close at the sides leaned back in her chair. "I'm Leah Ramos. Legal. I'm the one who gets sued first."

Tara swallowed. Julia gestured to a chair opposite them. "Please, sit." Julia sat down as well, and folded her arms. "You brought something CityLine says is nuclear."

Tara took the thumb drive out of her pocket and set it on the table. Leah raised an eyebrow. "No courier? No transfer protocol? You carried this yourself?"

"Yes."

"Alone?"

"Yes."

Leah exhaled slowly. "You're either incredibly brave or incredibly reckless."

"Both," Tara said. "Usually in the wrong order." That earned a tiny smirk from Malik.

Julia reached out with her hand, but withdrew it before she touched the USB. "Before we open anything," she said, "I want to hear, in your words, what you think you're bringing to us."

Tara wet her lips. She'd practiced this in her head all night, while she was outrunning men in dark coats. So she said it cleanly: "A system of economic enforcement hidden inside medical monitoring. Coercive leverage built on identity tracking. Control delivered through necessity. And the blueprint for how a federal agency intends to use it."

Malik leaned forward. "What agency?"

"DEI," she said. "Division of Economic Integrity."

Julia's expression did not change. But her eyes sharpened. "And your proof?" Julia asked.

"I have logs from the hospital. Internal memos. Licensing correspondence between LinkLife and enforcement contractors. A transcript of a board meeting I wasn't supposed to hear. And algorithmic traces of predictive modeling tied to cap enforcement."

Malik inhaled. Leah closed her eyes for a beat. Julia reached out again and touched the USB. But she pulled her hand back again, like it was a hot flame.

"Truth? We've been tracking DEI for two years," Julia said quietly. "And we suspected something like this, but we had nothing concrete."

"You have it now," Tara said.

Malik tapped the table lightly. "What's your motivation, Ms. Winslow?"

Tara hesitated. She could say "truth". She could say "ethics". But what rose unbidden was a face. Kyrel's. And what the ambulance driver had said too. We don't want safe. We want true. "My motivation," she said softly, "is that people deserve to know what's being done to them. And someone I trust believes this story matters."

Leah studied her carefully. "Someone inside LinkLife?"

"I won't name them," Tara said immediately.

"Good," Leah replied. "Don't."

Suddenly, the monitors on the wall flickered. A feed from one of the cameras showed movement. The Sentinel had cameras covering all the ground around the building from every angle. The War Room had the feeds of the most useful ones on the wall. Four exterior cameras, four different angles covering the entrances.

Julia stood and walked over to the monitor. Leah stiffened. Malik whispered, "Shit."

Outside the building they watched a black SUV approach, a second sedan and a third unmarked car pulling up to the curb. Several men stepped out, not rushing, not attacking. Just taking positions. Like they were preparing for something. Or waiting.

Tara's throat tightened. "That's them," she whispered. "I recognize at least one of them. They followed me from the hospital."

Julia turned to her. "You didn't just bring us a story," she said. "You brought us a ticking clock."

The room shifted: a team dynamic snapping into crisis mode. Julia sat down and tapped the USB. "You're not leaving this building," she said, looking directly at Tara. "Not until we verify the data, duplicate it, and get legal clearance."

"Do you think they'll try to get in?" Tara asked.

Leah gave a tight, humorless smile. "Honey," she said, "they always try."

Julia sat down again. "OK team, let's get started. We don't have much time, the clock is ticking."

Malik reached for a secure laptop, air-gapped, powered off, isolated. Leah unrolled a stack of liability waivers. Somewhere outside, a honk echoed. Somewhere inside, the lock on the War Room engaged with a magnetic hum.

Tara exhaled, a long, slow release of a breath she'd been holding since 3:20 a.m. She had crossed the point of no return. She had delivered the truth to the only people bold enough to publish it.

And now…

Now the real war would begin.

CHAPTER 35

THE VERIFICATION

Malik powered on the air-gapped laptop, a matte-black slab with no ports except power. There was no wireless hardware, and no tolerance for mistakes. It hummed quietly as it booted from a sterile drive image.

Tara watched the screen glow to life, the cold blue light reflecting off Malik's glasses. Her heart jittered in her chest. This was the moment where her work would either stand… or fall apart.

Julia dimmed the overhead lights and sealed the blinds, plunging the War Room into a cocoon of controlled shadows.

"Okay," Malik murmured. "Let's see what you brought us." He inserted the USB.

For one impossible second, Tara feared the drive wouldn't mount, that something would glitch, or the encryption would panic, or she would wake from all this in her apartment at 10 a.m. thinking she'd only dreamt it.

Then a directory list appeared. Malik exhaled. "Good. Very good." He clicked into the first folder.

Lines of raw code filled the screen: Hospital logs, DEI pings, LinkLife IMEI handshake data, and Routing nodes.

Malik scrolled slowly, eyebrows lifting. "These aren't screenshots," he said. "This is the real feed. Who gave you this?"

"I can't say," Tara replied.

"You shouldn't," he said. "But whoever they are, they risked a lot. This is near-live telemetry. You don't get this without internal-level clearance."

Leah leaned over his shoulder. "What does it show?"

Malik pointed. "Here. This string— Cross-referencing patient identity with cap thresholds."

Leah blinked. "You mean they're comparing hospital data to—?"

"Yes," Malik said grimly. "To financial ceilings. To earnings projections. To economic modeling."

He clicked open a second file. "This one's worse." He zoomed in. Tara felt her skin prickle.

The file showed an automatic override function, a mechanism that triggered identity verification pings whenever an individual neared their earning limit. A silent audit. A shadow enforcement.

Julia whispered, "My god." And then, more softly: "This is the story."

Malik opened the next folder, corporate correspondence between LinkLife executives and government liaisons.

The first memo contained innocuous language:

SUBJECT: Clarification of compliance expectations
SUBJECT: System integration timeline

The second was worse:

SUBJECT: Identity reinforcement protocols, pilot phase
SUBJECT: Incentives for early adoption

But the third made Tara's breath catch.

SUBJECT: Behavioral Intervention Through Medical
Infrastructure

Leah sat up straighter. "That's coercive language."

"It's worse than coercive," Malik said. "It's predictive. This is designing pressure strategies, social, economic, civic, based on implant compliance."

He opened the attached document. It was a white paper. Written in dry, technical language, and as chilling as hell.

On page three:

"Projected outcomes show significant compliance increases when identity-dependent services are tied to medical credentialing."

Page five:

"Recommended: incorporate DEI oversight into emergency medicine workflows to ensure real-time identity capture."

Page nine:

> "Consider limited incentivization protocols for noncompliant populations, including access restrictions."

Julia whispered, "Access restrictions to what?" Malik scrolled. Her stomach dropped. "To housing. To employment. To banking. To interstate travel."

The room went silent. No one breathed. Tara felt something tighten in her throat, a grief, a horror she hadn't let herself feel during the frantic chase here. "This is fascism," she said softly.

"No," Leah corrected. "This is the blueprint for automating fascism."

Malik then opened the transcript file, Tara's recording of a LinkLife board meeting she'd overheard. The audio waveform looked jagged and uneven, but the transcript was clean. He clicked play. Tara stared at the table, unable to make herself look up.

A man's voice filled the War Room:

> "…if DEI wants cross-integration, we're going to give it to them. It's not optional. They signed the federal contract; that's the real market."

Another voice:

> "…we're not building a product anymore. We're building leverage."

A third:

"…the implant becomes the center of identity. Once we control identity, we control the market. The cap enforcement will do the rest."

Julia closed her eyes. Leah covered her mouth. Malik hit pause. "Jesus Christ," he whispered. "They said it out loud?"

Tara felt herself shiver. "It doesn't sound real, does it?" she said quietly. "Like no executive would ever say those words."

Leah shook her head. "They do," she said. "When they think no one's listening."

Malik opened the final folder, the one Tara hadn't fully processed herself. It was on predictive modeling. It contained charts, decision trees, and compliance algorithms. He slowed his scrolling and then stopped altogether. His brow furrowed deeply.

"Tara," he said, turning the screen toward her. "Did you know this was here?"

She looked. It was a graph with three curves. One labeled: Asset Potential Index, Founder

And under it:

KYREL LANE, RISK THRESHOLD: RED

Her lungs froze. "What?" she whispered. Malik zoomed in.

"This is DEI's modeling for LinkLife founders specifically. Anyone with creator-level access. Anyone who poses a systemic threat to economic balance."

Leah leaned in. "What does 'red' mean?"

Malik swallowed. "It means the system predicts he will eventually resist. That he'll interfere. That he'll disrupt enforcement integrity."

Julia stared. "In other words," she said, voice quiet and lethal, "DEI has already marked him as a future problem."

"And what happens to future problems?" Tara asked.

No one answered. Because they all knew.

A loud BUZZ startled them. The exterior camera feed flashed again onto the screen. There was movement. The driver of the black SUV had shut off its engine. The sedan repositioned. Two men stepped out wearing dark jackets with unmarked badges clipped to their belts.

Julia exhaled slowly. "They're not guessing anymore," she murmured. "They know someone got inside."

Tara felt her pulse throb in her ears. "Are we in danger?" she asked.

Julia didn't hesitate. "Yes." Then: "But so is everyone who doesn't know what's coming. So we're going to tell them."

She turned back to Malik. "How long to duplicate and verify everything?"

"One hour," he said. "Maybe less."

"And Legal?"

Leah cracked her knuckles. "I can start drafting the preliminary case now. Once we verify authentication, this becomes publishable."

Julia nodded. Then looked at Tara. "You started something," she said. "And we're going to finish it."

Tara breathed, sharp, uneven, full of something that felt like resolve and terror braided together. "Let's do it."

Julia locked the door. The hum of the magnetic seal tightened. And the War Room went to work.

CHAPTER 36

RHETT SPIRALS

Rhett Langley sat alone in the CFO suite at LinkLife HQ, staring at the wall of glass that overlooked the city. It was 4:30 a.m.

He hadn't slept. He hadn't showered. He hadn't left this office since Kyrel returned and without raising his voice, took everything from him.

Rhett used to love this view. Used to feel like a king looking down on his dominion. Tonight it felt like an autopsy table.

Stacks of papers cluttered his desk, compliance notices, licensing contracts, internal memos. Some he'd read. Some he'd shredded. Some he couldn't even look at without feeling a pulse of fury along his spine.

His computer pinged. Another Level 2 compliance review request. He ignored it. He'd been ignoring a lot of things lately. Especially the numbers. Especially the red flags.

Especially the growing awareness that maybe he'd crossed over the billion threshold weeks ago, quietly, invisibly, through the shell subsidiaries he'd used to launder early deals.

Maybe he'd even passed the cap twice. He didn't know anymore. He didn't want to know. Because if he looked? Really looked? He would have to face the truth—

He should already be capped. And someone had protected him. Someone had delayed the enforcement system. Someone who suddenly wasn't returning his calls.

That thought hit him like a punch. He slammed his hand on the desk hard enough to rattle the mug beside him. "Where the hell are you?" he muttered.

Soren. It had to be Soren. Soren promised him protection. Soren promised him insulation. Soren promised that if HE held control of LinkLife, the system would always look the other way.

But Kyrel ruined that. Kyrel walked in and everyone bowed to him. Kyrel smiled once, once, and employees followed him like he was Moses parting the sea.

And here Rhett sat. Alone. Drowning on dry land.

He checked his phone again. No messages. No missed calls. No encrypted pings. Nothing from Soren. Nothing from DEI's "liaison." Nothing from his shell partners. Nothing from the board factions that used to court him.

He dialed one of the numbers anyway. It rang once—

Then clicked. A recorded voice he'd never heard before:

> "The client is no longer taking calls. Please refer inquiries through the appropriate channels."

He lowered the phone slowly. Channels. He was the "channels". Or he used to be. His stomach knotted. "They're shutting me out," he whispered.

On his screen, a new notification appeared:

LEVEL 2 ECONOMIC INTEGRITY REVIEW,
PENDING ERR: THRESHOLD DISCREPANCY
FLAGGED

Rhett froze. He clicked. A detailed report unfolded on-screen:

LANGLEY, R., FINANCIAL ACTIVITY REVIEW
Projected earnings: 1.03B
Confirmed holdings: 1.16B
Unregistered assets: multiple irregularities detected.
INTERVENTION RECOMMENDED.

He felt cold. A physical cold. Spreading from his chest outward. This was—

It couldn't be. He slammed a drawer, pulling out a thumbdrive, the one Soren gave him "in case of emergency," a backdoor into DEI's low-level systems. He plugged it in. The screen flashed.

ACCESS DENIED AUTHORIZATION REVOKED
CONTACT ADMINISTRATOR

He yanked the drive out and threw it across the room. It hit the window with a dull thunk. His vision blurred. "This is a mistake," he growled. But the numbers didn't care. The numbers were truth. Cold, mathematical truth. Truth he'd spent months burying under contractors and misfilings and 'temporary holding' entities.

And now the system had caught up. Or worse—

Now the system was paying attention because he'd lost power. He paced the length of his office. "I built this company," he whispered. "I built this. I made the deals. I took the risks."

Kyrel coded the device. Kyrel dreamed the dream. But Rhett—

Rhett made it real. Rhett got the funding. Rhett charmed the investors. Rhett sold the vision. And now what? Kyrel walks back in and suddenly Rhett is an afterthought? A liability? A risk threshold? He grabbed the edge of the desk and slammed it backward, sending papers flying.

"I'm not the villain here," he yelled to the empty room. "I'm the one who made this possible. I'm the one who turned it into something the world would notice."

His reflection in the glass caught his eye. He didn't like what he saw. Something desperate lived there now. Something cornered. Something ready to bite.

His phone buzzed. Not a call. Another notification:

> DEI INTERNAL: Your review is scheduled. Expect contact within 24 hours.

Contact. He'd seen enough DEI files to know what "contact" meant. Not a meeting. Not a hearing. A team. A visit. A correction. He staggered back into his chair.

"No," he whispered. "No, no, no—"

The world was slipping from his hands like sand. Then—

He froze. Because an idea slid into his bloodstream like adrenaline: This wasn't Kyrel's win. This wasn't DEI's victory. This was an opportunity! If he could shift the blame— If he could divert the attention— If he could expose someone else—

Rhett felt a faint, familiar tingle of his deal-making genius glimmer through his body. He could get ahead of the spiral. He could survive this. He could still win!

He opened a blank document. His fingers hovered. Then he began typing. A statement. A leak. A narrative.

Something that would point everything at LinkLife's other founder.

Something that would say: Kyrel Kade is the real threat. Not me. Him.

His pulse steadied as he typed. "Two can play this game," he whispered.

A dark smile crept across his face. The descent had become the pivot.

Rhett wasn't finished.

He was just beginning.

CHAPTER 37

THE FIRST LEAK

The Sentinel's War Room felt different now. Before, the tension had come from fear, the men outside, the data on the screen, from knowing what DEI was capable of.

But now… now it was the pressure of truth rising like heat in the room.

Malik typed furiously at the air-gapped laptop. Leah paced in tight circles muttering legal incantations under her breath. Julia stood at the wall of monitors, watching the black SUV outside reposition for the third time.

Tara kept her eyes on the clock. 4:49 a.m. Every minute they worked, the story grew more dangerous.

Malik spoke without turning. "The predictive model for founders… it's definitely targeting your contact. Whoever he is."

Tara's stomach tensed. Her contact. Her source. Kyrel. Her phone, inside its foil cocoon, felt heavy in her pocket, as if it knew its silence mattered. Then one of the monitors changed.

A notification popped. Not internal. Public.

Julia frowned. "What the...?" She clicked the feed. The screen brightened to the home page of a mid-size business news site, MarketPulse, the kind that fed directly into financial networks and morning investment shows.

A red banner stretched across the top:

EXCLUSIVE: LinkLife FOUNDER UNDER FEDERAL SCRUTINY
SCRUTINY
Sources: Kyrel Kade flagged for cap irregularities

Tara felt the blood drain from her face. "No," she whispered. "No—this isn't possible."

Julia clicked the article. A wall of text appeared, breathless, sloppy, clearly rushed out before dawn. Key phrases jumped out:

"internal DEI concerns regarding founder compliance"
"potential misreporting by early-stage leadership"
"whistleblowers allege algorithmic manipulation"
"government poised to intervene"
"LinkLife cofounder Rhett Langley declines comment"

Tara grabbed the table. "Rhett did this."

Leah cursed under her breath. "Of course he did. He's cornered. He needed a scapegoat."

Malik scrolled. "Oh look," he said darkly. "They even used DEI terminology. That means Rhett provided documents."

Julia's eyes narrowed. "Documents he didn't understand, didn't contextualize, probably cherry-picked—"

"And twisted," Tara said, voice tight. "Because Kyrel hasn't done anything wrong."

Malik nodded. "I can confirm that. His compliance logs are clean."

"Except," Leah added, "someone wants them to look dirty."

Julia switched to social feeds. The story was spreading like wildfire. Retweets. Alerts. Financial analysts posting half-conscious premarket warnings.

#KadeFlagged
#LinkLifeCorruption
#CappedFounder

The narrative was galloping ahead of them, out of control. Julia stepped back from the screens with a slow exhale. "This changes everything," she said.

Tara shook her head. "No. It accelerates everything."

Malik sat straighter. "They'll come for Kyrel first," he said. "If DEI thinks he's resisting or manipulating algorithms—"

"He isn't," Tara snapped.

"I know," Malik replied softly. "But they don't care about truth. They care about pattern deviation. And right now, a leak like this is deviation."

The room fell silent. Only the hum of the machines filled the air.

A rapid knock shook the War Room door made everyone jump out of their skin. Three sharp raps. Julia stiffened. Leah's hand went to the pocket where she kept the emergency legal envelope. Malik froze. Tara's pulse spiked.

Julia approached the door slowly. "Who is it?"

A voice answered, firm, controlled, but not hostile. "Internal security. We need to speak with Ms. Winslow."

Tara's lungs seized. Julia stayed still. "We're busy," she said calmly. "Come back later."

A pause. "We can't," the voice said. "There's been a request from federal oversight. They want to confirm whether Ms. Winslow has had contact with a flagged individual."

Tara felt the room tilt. Flagged! Kyrel had been officially flagged.

Julia stepped closer to the door, planting herself between it and Tara.

"You tell your supervisors," Julia said, voice steady and lethal, "that The Sentinel does not, and will not, provide interviews or compliance check-ins during active investigations. If you have a warrant, you may slide it under the door. If you do not, you may leave."

Silence.

Then footsteps retreating.

Leah exhaled. "They're not gone," she said. "They're regrouping."

Julia turned back to the room. Her eyes were sharper now. Harder. Alive with a fire Tara had only seen once, in a journalist who knew the weight of what she was about to publish.

"We don't have any more time," Julia said. "We have to publish today, now."

Malik nodded. "I can finish verification in forty minutes."

Leah cracked her knuckles. "And I can assemble the legal perimeter in sixty."

Julia turned to Tara. "You'd better call him," she said. "Before someone else does." Julia stepped closer to Tara, lowering her voice. "But not in here," she said. "This room is shielded. The moment that phone boots up, it starts screaming your location to every listening system in the city. You'll alert them before you alert him."

Tara swallowed. "So I have to…?"

Julia nodded. "You have to step outside the cage. Make the call. Then get back in. Fast."

A cold ribbon of fear slid down Tara's spine.

"DEI flagged him," Leah added. "You have minutes. Maybe less."

Malik gestured to the wall. "There's a secured land line in the hall, forty feet from the exit door. Use that if you can. But don't use your cell while you're exposed."

Julia clipped a high-security fob off her belt and handed it to Tara.

"This unlocks the inner vestibule," she said. "Use it and come straight back. No detours."

Tara nodded, shoved the phone deeper into her pocket still wrapped, took the fob—

—and stepped toward the War Room door. The truth was pressing outward. The lie was closing in. And the only safe place to call Kyrel… was the most dangerous hallway in the building.

The War Room screens glowed around her. The truth was here. The lie was already loose. And DEI was watching.

CHAPTER 38

THE CALL

The heavy door of The Sentinel's War Room sealed behind Tara with a hydraulic hiss. Instantly, the quiet changed.

Inside the room was silent, safe-feeling, with thick and engineered walls. Outside, she felt totally exposed. She could hear every little sound, just because there were no people on the floor. The hum of HVAC, the faint buzz of fluorescent lights, and the distant clatter of cleaning carts on another floor made her jump with every sound.

She took three steps down the hallway as instructed, then past the framed front pages of notable stories like Watergate, the Panama Papers, and the Arcadium Data Breach. Her heart was pounding hard enough for the sound to echo outside her chest.

Her phone was still wrapped in its foil cocoon, warm in her palm. Julia's words ricocheted in her skull: "The moment it boots, they'll know where you are." So she wasn't going to use it till the very last moment, if necessary.

Now only 15 feet ahead, the small recessed alcove with the secure landline glowed like a red sanctuary lamp. She quickened her pace. She'd closed half the distance when the elevator dinged. Tara froze. The doors slid open and a janitor stepped out pushing a mop bucket, humming to himself.

She exhaled, shoulders shaking, and made no further delays in getting to the alcove. The landline handset was heavier than she expected, old school, battleship-gray, built for the Cold War and never updated. She punched in the code Malik had given her, and then dialed Kyrel's secure number manually.

One ring, two, three, then, "Kade." His voice was low, steady, but clipped with tension.

"It's Tara. I only have a minute."

"I know. I saw your text. That's why—"

"Kyrel," she whispered, "DEI flagged your name."

Silence. Then: "I thought so."

Her stomach tightened. "You what?"

"I saw it in the logs," he said. "Something moved inside our system three hours ago. Too precise to be an audit. Too quiet to be routine."

"Kyrel, this is not an audit. This is active surveillance."

"By who?"

"Weller's division."

Another silence. But this one felt like gravity giving way. "Tara," he said slowly, "if DEI is moving this fast, it means they think I crossed another earning threshold."

"You didn't."

"I know."

"So that means, "

"Someone pushed me again."

Her throat constricted. "Rhett," she whispered.

He didn't answer immediately. And his silence said everything.

DEI Economic Integrity Tower, Monitoring Floor
4:35 a.m.

Agent Thomas Weller leaned over his subordinate's workstation. "Flag it again," he said calmly. "He's on a secured line now."

"Yes, sir," the technician said, fingers flying. "But we can't break through the encryption, "

"I don't need the content," Weller said. "I need location."

"It's bouncing. The Sentinel network is hard-shielded. We can't pinpoint the exact room."

Weller's jaw ticked once. But only once. "Fine," he said. "Put a team on the building. Quiet approach. No sirens. No lights. This is not a raid."

The tech swallowed. "Yes, sir."

Weller straightened the cuffs of his charcoal suit. "Kade is not careless," he said. "He wouldn't use a secure line unless something serious has occurred." He paused. "And serious events," he added, "tend to reveal guilty men."

"Tara?" Kyrel's voice snapped her back.

"I'm here," she whispered. "Kyrel, listen to me. You need to stay off all networks. Don't call anyone from your devices. Don't check internal systems. Don't, "

"Tara," he interrupted softly, "you need to leave now."

"Why?"

"Because if they flagged me, they flagged you."

Her pulse thudded. "Kyrel, "

"Tara. Get back into that War Room. Tell Julia. Tell all of them. Whatever The Sentinel plans, make sure they do it fast. Before DEI tries to shut it down."

"They can't shut down The Sentinel."

He exhaled. "Tara. They can shut down anything."

Another sound entered the audio: a loud knock, distant on his end.

"Kyrel?" she whispered sharply. "What was that?"

"Someone at my door."

Her blood chilled.

"Do not answer. Do not, "

The knock came again. Harder.

"Tara," he murmured, "if it's Weller, "

Her whisper came out as a broken thread. "Kyrel, don't open that door."

"For once," he said, "we agree."

More knocking. Three sharp raps. Official. Measured.

"Tara," he said quietly, "go back inside the War Room. Now."

She felt her throat close. "Kyrel, be careful."

"You too."

She hung up. Tara turned. The long hallway felt much longer now. Her shoes whispered across the carpet as she walked fast, then faster, then nearly running. Elevator ding.

Not the janitor this time. Black shoes stepped out. Two pairs. Agents. She didn't look back. She sprinted. Her hands shook as she slapped the fob to the War Room's reader. Green light. The lock clicked. She shoved the door open and dove inside.

Julia spun toward her. "Tara, ?"

Tara held up a trembling hand, breath heaving. "They're here," she gasped. "DEI is here."

CHAPTER 39

TWO DOORS

LinkLife Executive Townhouse, 4:47 a.m.

The knock came again. Measured. Official. The kind of knock that doesn't expect to be ignored, and won't be.

Kyrel stood in the center of his dim living room, barefoot on the hardwood floor, the city lights glowing faintly through the blinds. He inhaled once, deeply, letting the air cool the rising heat in his chest. He didn't move toward the door. He didn't have to.

"Mr. Kade," a voice called through the wood. Polite. Even. Familiar. Thomas Weller.

"Please open the door," Weller said. "We need to clarify a few discrepancies."

Kyrel's pulse thudded gently, but he felt strangely calm. He checked the deadbolt. Still locked.

He didn't touch it. Instead, he crossed to his desk, slipped his secure notebook into a drawer, and tapped the hidden mechanism that slid a small steel panel over the interior network port. Primitive. Manual. But functional.

Another knock. More insistent this time. "Mr. Kade," Weller repeated, "your cooperation is required by federal statute."

Kyrel closed the drawer carefully. His voice was steady: "One moment." He wasn't stalling. He was choosing.

War Room, Sublevel Two, 5:06 a.m.

Julia snapped the heavy lock the moment Tara stepped inside, sealing the Faraday cage with a metallic thud.

"Tara, breathe," Julia said, gripping her shoulders. "How many?"

"Two at the elevator," Tara whispered. "Maybe more incoming."

Leah's hands flew across her terminal. "They're scanning badge access outside the sublevel. Not ours, federal."

Malik swore under his breath. "DEI won't storm a newsroom," he said. But the fear threaded his voice.

Julia shot him a look. "They won't storm. They'll inspect. In other words: seize everything."

Leah's screen flashed red. "They're in the stairwell," she said. "South access."

Julia didn't hesitate. "Malik, kill external feeds. Leah, encrypt the draft in triplicate. Tara, "

"I know," Tara said, already stepping forward. "I hide in the cage."

"No," Julia said sharply. "You stay visible to them on the video intercom. There's one in here, and one on the other side of the door. If you hide, you look guilty."

Tara went cold. "They're going to interrogate me."

"They'll try," Julia said. "But they won't get this story."

The lights flickered under the pressure change of the outer door opening.

Leah swallowed hard. "They're here."

––––––––––

The knock became a single, controlled blow.

Not aggressive. Not angry. Simply a reminder that the federal government never gets tired.

"Mr. Kade," Weller said again. "This visit is for your benefit."

Kyrel raised an eyebrow. Weller always said soothing platitudes like that before delivering something reliably devastating. He approached the door but stopped a full foot away. Enough distance to think. "Can you state the purpose of this visit?" Kyrel asked.

"Earnings anomalies," Weller said. "We detected unauthorized revenue associated with your identity profile."

Kyrel closed his eyes. Rhett. It had to be Rhett. "I haven't earned a cent," Kyrel said.

"That," Weller said, "is what we need to confirm."

A second voice appeared, deeper, unfamiliar. "Sir," the voice murmured, "we have clearance to proceed under 4-B Emergency Audit."

Kyrel's eyes snapped open. Emergency Audit meant: property search, device seizure, full disclosure interrogation. If he opened this door, he walked straight into a legal cage. He stepped back.

"Mr. Kade," Weller said evenly, "failing to comply will escalate this."

Kyrel breathed deep. And unlocked nothing.

The door entering the hallway outside the War Room hissed open. Two DEI agents stepped through, black suits tailored tight, shoes silent on the rubberized floor, carrying black cases. Behind them, a third agent carried a folding table. The agents stopped and put down their things.

Another agent entered: Agent Thomas Osei. Weller's counterpart in the regional branch. Younger. Sharper. Less patient. He surveyed the War Room door with a faint smile.

"Good morning," Osei said to no one. Voice smooth as glass. "This will take only a moment." Turning to his team, he directed them to set up their equipment. They had brought a number of tools to break through the Faraday cage.

"You're not going to get through our door," said Julia through the intercom, as she stepped forward like a shield. "You need a warrant to enter a protected press facility."

"I don't need the door," Osei said, speaking through the intercom. "I just need the metal to hum. Besides, we have a warrant," Osei said. He held up a sealed document so that the intercom's camera could see it. "Signed under Emergency Conditions."

Malik swore under his breath.

Tara kept her face neutral. "What are they doing?"

"Likely setting up a spectrum analyzer to look for noise spikes," answered Malik.

"I thought a Faraday cage was invincible."

"No, they're only effective if they are continuous. If there is a single tiny gap created by anything, like an unshielded wire, they can bring it down, or rather send something through."

Osei continued: "We're conducting a standard compliance sweep for involvement in identity tampering, specifically involving one Kyrel Kade."

Tara felt her heart kick. Osei's eyes flickered toward her. Noticing. Cataloguing. Julia's voice stayed cool. "Your warrant limits you to document identification, not seizure."

"Of course," Osei said. "We're all friends here." He stepped closer to the intercom camera. "This is just a friendly conversation." He then stepped back and looked directly at his crew. "Start the scans."

Another knock. This one lighter. Calculated. But the voice was Weller's again, slicing as gently as a surgeon's scalpel.

"Mr. Kade, refusing to open this door may result in forced entry."

Kyrel stood still, his shadow cast across the narrow foyer. "You can speak to me through the door," he said.

A quiet laugh came from the other side, just a hint. "As you wish," Weller replied. Paper rustled. "I'm obligated to present you with a Notice of Noncompliance under the Wealth Equity Act, Section— "

"I've broken no law," Kyrel said.

"We'll determine that," Weller murmured.

Kyrel inhaled slowly. Deep. Grounding. He needed time. Tara needed time. The Sentinel needed time. And time was exactly what DEI was trying to take from him.

Agent Osei clasped his hands behind his back and stepped up to the intercom. The monitor showed a wide shot of the War Room's interior, and Osei could see the people within looking his way.

"Ms. Winslow, I see you're there," he said. The way he said her name chilled her. He already knew everything. "I understand you recently filed a story involving identity tracking in medical networks."

A statement, not a question. Tara didn't blink as she stared into the camera. "I file a lot of stories."

"Yes," Osei said, smiling faintly, "but this one involved access logs at a public hospital."

Julia stepped between Tara and the camera. "She is not obligated to speak without counsel present."

"Oh, I'm not questioning her," Osei said. "Just clarifying." He leaned slightly toward the intercom, looking intently at the locked steel server rack behind them. "And clarifications," he said softly, "tell me where to look next."

Tara's throat tightened. Because she knew, he was looking at the exact rack that held a triplicate copy of her story.

Weller's tone sharpened. "Mr. Kade," he said, "failure to comply will result in an escalated intervention."

Kyrel spoke through the door, calm but unyielding: "You have no grounds to search my home without evidence of misconduct."

"We have irregularities," Weller said.

"Not evidence."

Weller paused. "You are testing the limits, Mr. Kade."

Kyrel's voice stayed level. "I've learned they exist."

A long quiet followed. Then, "Very well," Weller said. "We'll escalate."

Footsteps retreated. For a beat Kyrel thought he'd won, then he heard the sound. Metal. Tools. They were preparing to breach the door.

Osei shifted his gaze to Julia holding the warrant up again. "I will begin with voluntary compliance," he said. "Is there anything in that room relevant to Mr. Kade's ongoing investigation?"

"No," Julia said.

"No," Malik said.

"No," Leah said.

Tara said nothing. Osei noticed. He smiled. "Ms. Winslow. Would you like to answer?"

Her hands tightened at her sides. Julia stepped closer to the camera, steel in her voice. "She doesn't have to answer that."

Osei tilted his head. "Interesting." Then, inside the War Room the lights popped. A sharp blink.

Julia whispered: "Oh God. They're starting to scan for the cage's natural resonance frequency."

"What will that do?" asked Tara.

"Allow them to get inside the War Room electronically, and discover all the files we have on our servers," said Malik.

Kyrel heard the whine of the hydraulic ram priming against his door.

The Sentinel heard the soft click of DEI's RF disruptor beginning to pulse.

Two fronts. Same enemy. Same moment. Same truth closing in.

CHAPTER 40

BREACHES

The first hit against the door was not loud, but it was decisive, a sharp, metallic thump that vibrated through the frame and into Kyrel's ribs. They were using a compact hydraulic ram. Not SWAT-chaotic, just methodical. Government efficiency in tool form. He stood halfway between the door and the kitchen, not retreating, not advancing, listening to the careful rhythm of people who had done this before.

A second thump. Screws in the hinges complained.

"Mr. Kade," Weller called, his voice slightly muffled now, "this remains a cooperative process. We have obtained emergency authority to effect entry under section 4-B."

"You mean you gave yourself permission," Kyrel said. He didn't raise his voice, but sound carried easily through the narrow hall; even through the door.

"Emergency conditions were met," Weller replied. "Third-party earnings were detected using credentials linked to your identity. We are obligated to investigate."

Kyrel thought, not for the first time, how tidy a system was when it never had to prove anything to anyone who didn't already agree with it.

The ram thudded again. The deadbolt groaned.

He moved to the small console table by the wall, picked up his phone and switched it into airplane mode, then powered it down completely. For good measure, he slid it into the metal breadbox on the kitchen counter and shut the lid.

The absurdity of that made him almost smile. Billion-dollar tech, government-grade enforcement, and he was improvising with a breadbox.

"Any unlawful entry," he said, turning back toward the door, "will be challenged in court."

"That is your right," Weller replied. "Our mandate remains."

Another hit. The strike plate bent a fraction of a degree. Kyrel could see the hairline movement in the jamb.

He drew a breath in slowly, holding it until his lungs burned, then let it out. The old grounding exercise D'Andra had taught him in the days after his capping. In through the nose, hold, then out through the mouth and repeat. Remind the nervous system there was still a body attached.

He was not afraid of them seeing clutter or cables or the half-eaten cereal bowl on the counter. He was afraid of something much simpler: that they would come in here believing the story they had already written.

That he was a cheat. That he was dangerous. That he was exactly what the Cap Act needed him to be.

The ram hit again, deeper this time. Wood cracked invisibly within the frame.

Weller's voice came once more, with a hint less patience. "Last request, Mr. Kade. Open the door and we proceed administratively. Remain as you are and we proceed under force. The outcome will be the same. Only the cost to you changes."

Kyrel looked at the door and thought of Tara walking into The Sentinel with a USB drive that could tilt the entire system sideways. They were clearing his house tonight not because they needed evidence, but because they needed him busy. He stepped closer without touching the lock.

"You'll file your report, Agent Weller," he said quietly. "Just make sure you spell my name right when history reads it."

There was a small pause. For the first time, Weller sounded faintly tired. "Names," he said, "are not our concern."

The ram hit again. The frame shuddered.

The hum began low enough that Tara thought it was just the building's air system shifting. A faint, insectile vibration at the base of her skull. Then the War Room's central monitor flickered. Malik did not swear out loud, but his jaw locked so hard a muscle jumped near his temple.

"They've activated a field disruptor," he said. "Cheap model, but strong enough to scramble the cage if they lean on it."

Julia crossed to the wall panel and checked the analog meter welded there, a relic from when the War Room had been built when analog still felt paranoid enough.

The needle trembled, then nearly edged out of the green. "They're pushing it," she said. "We don't have much time."

"They're doing something outside as well," said Leah.

Julia checked the exterior monitor. "Crap, they're looking for the building's ground. If they can disrupt that, the cage is useless."

Agent Osei stood outside the War Room and watched all of it on their monitors with professional curiosity, as though he were touring an exhibit.

"As I said," he said to the camera, "this is a conversation. We simply need to confirm that your facility is not being used to facilitate identity tampering or economic interference."

"You have a warrant for document identification, not signal warfare," Julia shot back.

The hum thickened. Tara felt it in her fillings. Leah's fingers moved fast across her keyboard. "Cage is holding… but they're hitting it at variable frequencies. Trying to find a resonance point."

"Will this work?" Tara asked.

"Eventually," Malik said. "Unless we shut everything down and pretend this room doesn't exist."

"And hide in the dark?" Julia said. "No. We are not an offshore gambling site. We are a newspaper."

Osei looked down at the device his technician was using. It was showing a frequency gauge. Then he glanced through the intercom monitor toward the server rack that contained their air-gapped storage, the metal door matte and anonymous.

"This is a remarkable facility," he said. "More shielding than most banks. You must be very proud of it."

"We're proud of our work," Julia replied.

"And we're more proud of the First Amendment," Malik added.

Osei's eyes flicked toward him, amused. "Of course," he said.

The hum climbed another notch. One overhead light flickered and steadied.

Leah glanced at Tara. "You should sit," she murmured. "If they somehow get in and pull you into the hallway, I want you rested and ready."

Tara shook her head. Sitting felt like surrender. Instead, she braced one hip against the edge of a desk and folded her arms to keep her hands from shaking.

If they broke the shielding, the War Room would become just another office. And once that happened, anything could be imaged, copied, confiscated, no matter what the warrant technically said. They had the means to wirelessly gather all the data stored on The

Sentinel servers if they wanted. Even without physically getting inside.

Julia turned back to Osei. "You have the floor," she said. "Ask what you came to ask."

He smiled as if she had just offered him coffee. "Very well," he said. "Let's begin with your sources."

The next hit drove one of the screws half out of the top hinge. Kyrel watched it creep, the metal bright where the paint flaked away. He calculated angles for no good reason. Force distribution. Shear stress. The door would give at the strike plate before the hinges. Seven, maybe eight more hits at this tempo.

He stepped back into the apartment's open space and made himself look around, forcing his brain out of the tunnel of the door.

Sofa. Shelves. D'Andra's cardigan draped over the back of a chair. The framed photo of his family at his Georgia Tech graduation: his father's hands on his shoulders, his mother's eyes bright with unchecked tears, Kaiya throwing rabbit ears behind his head.

"This is still your life," he muttered under his breath. "They don't get all of it."

Another hit.

The deadbolt plate finally bent enough that he saw a hairline crack in the jamb.

He picked up the slim folder that held his copy of the DEI compliance agreement, flipped to the last page, and ran his thumb along the clause numbers. He knew them by now like some people knew hymns.

4-B: emergency audit.
5-C: temporary device seizure with no presumption of guilt.
7-A: appeal routes.
8-D: compelled cooperation under threat of felony.

They would be counting on him to panic. To scramble. To yell. Anything that made him look like the story they wanted to tell. He put the folder down, squared it on the table, and walked back to the door until he stood directly in front of it, a bare width of wood and metal between his chest and Weller's.

"You don't need to break it," he said, quietly enough that it felt like a conversation, not a shout. "You know I can't run. You know where I work. You know where my wife works. You could have scheduled this for nine o'clock tomorrow and brought coffee."

Another pause on the other side. No ram this time, just the faint fabric rustle of men resetting their stance.

"We attempted voluntary cooperation," Weller answered. "We were refused. Under statute, that obligates escalation."

"What statute obligates you to show up in the middle of the night?" Kyrel asked. "Was that resource allocation or theatre?"

The quieter, deeper voice spoke again, the one Kyrel hadn't seen yet. "Sir, we're on a clock. The anomalies spiked less than three hours ago. If he's moving assets, "

"I'm not moving anything," Kyrel said.

The unseen man ignored him. "Federal Risk Window is four hours. We've already lost almost three."

Risk Window. They were afraid of money flowing somewhere they couldn't see, using his name as the pipe. Rhett. Again. Kyrel closed his eyes for a heartbeat, then opened them.

"All right," he said. "You want to escalate? You do it in the open." He reached for the deadbolt. Then stopped just short of it, hand hovering. "No," he corrected himself, more to his own spine than to the men outside. "You want in, you break it. You own that."

Kyrel lowered his hand. Silence stretched. Then the ram hit the door again, harder than before. Splinters dusted from the jamb.

"Did you obtain access logs from County General Hospital without authorization?" Osei asked, his tone the careful, conversational cadence of someone who planned to type every word later.

Tara kept her gaze level as if she were face-to-face with Osei, rather than talking to a screen. "I spoke with sources," she said. "They provided information they believed to be in the public interest."

"Did those sources have clearance to access DEI interface telemetry?" he asked.

"DEI has no jurisdiction over patient care," she replied. "Hospitals integrate what they're required to integrate."

"Not what I asked," he said mildly.

Julia stepped in. "She is not required to disclose her sources."

Osei smiled. "No, but their patterns tell us whether there has been a breach of federal infrastructure."

The hum rose another notch and with it the buzzing in their ears. The sound waves were starting to vibrate their ear drums dangerously. A thin ring of dust danced in the fluorescent light as it vibrated.

Leah glanced at the analog meter again. The needle had slid past the edge of the green into a narrow amber band that was never supposed to be reached.

"They have found the right frequency," she said quietly.

"How long?" Malik asked.

"Depends how far they're willing to go," Leah murmured. "Technically, they can't push it into the red without violating half a dozen communications laws."

"Technically," Malik repeated.

Osei noticed a wall outside the War Room, where a corkboard held a haphazard constellation of pinned printouts: early drafts, scratch notes, maps, arrows linking names and dates. The board looked chaotic until you knew how to read it. Then a pattern emerged: LinkLife at the center, rings of influence fanning outward.

He studied it with calm curiosity. "This is quite a web," he remarked. "Busy month?"

"Busy year," Julia said.

His gaze snagged on one index card where Tara's writing had circled three letters and underlined them twice: DEI.

He didn't mention it. Just filed it away behind his eyes. "Ms. Winslow," he said, turning back to her, "do you believe the Department of Economic Integrity is acting in bad faith?"

The question was so blunt that for a second she thought she had misheard him.

"That's not a legal question," Julia said.

"No," Osei agreed. "It's a character one."

Tara felt every pair of eyes in the room on her. Her instinct was to say something neutral and clever, something that would slide off the record like oil off glass. Instead, she heard her own voice, steady and stronger than she felt: "I believe any system that can destroy someone's life without ever having to explain itself in plain language is dangerous."

A small, dangerous quiet followed. Osei's expression didn't change. He didn't write anything down. He just nodded once, as if confirming a hypothesis.

The hum in the walls flickered into a brief, crackling pop. One of the overhead fixtures went out completely, leaving a shallow pool of shadow at the back of the room.

Leah checked the meter again. The needle quivered painfully close to the red.

"We're minutes away," she whispered.

Yet another hit. This time the doorframe finally cracked, a thin fissure radiating out from the latch like a white line on dark paint.

Kyrel stepped back further into the room, not out of fear but to reposition, placing the couch between him and the door's arc. Not much, but something. If they came in hot, at least they'd have to navigate furniture.

He thought about calling D'Andra, then dismissed it. Waking her at the hospital to tell her federal agents were trying to break down the door while she was elbow-deep in a trauma bay helped nobody and changed nothing.

Instead, he moved to the small hallway closet, opened it, and, with careful fingers, slid one small object off the top shelf: a fireproof document bag D'Andra insisted they keep up to date, passports, marriage certificate, a hardcopy of his capping agreement, a printed copy of his statement to Tara.

He laid it on the coffee table within reach.

If they walked in here and tried to tell him who he was, he wanted something physical to anchor against. Ink on paper, his own earlier words refusing to move.

Outside, Weller's voice came again, now edged with formal warning. "For the record, Mr. Kade, you are impeding an Emergency Audit. This will be noted."

"For the record," Kyrel replied, "you're breaking into a man's home in the middle of the night based on data you haven't let him see."

"The anomalies are classified," the second voice said. "Releasing them would compromise our detection frameworks."

Kyrel let out a breath that was almost a laugh. "Of course they are," he said.

The ram hit again. The strike plate finally folded. The deadbolt tore free from the frame with a crack like a snapped branch.

The door sagged inward half an inch, still catching at the warped wood. Kyrel braced for the next blow, but it didn't come.

Instead, voices murmured, too low to parse. The soft chuck of a radio. They were pausing. Coordinating. Maybe calling for a different tool. Maybe calling someone higher. He used the moment.

"Agent Weller," he said, "I assume you're also at The Sentinel tonight."

Silence. He pressed. "DEI doesn't move on two fronts this aggressively unless it's coordinated. You hit me, you hit the press. You hit both stories at once. You damage us and you keep the world blind for at least one more news cycle."

Nothing from the hallway, but he could feel the listening.

"You can tell your superiors I see what they're doing," he said. "And it won't hold."

The next blow came harder, bending the door around the latch entirely.

The hum had shifted from something you only heard to something you also felt, a pressure in the sinuses, a buzz in the enamel of teeth. The whole room seemed to vibrate. It was the resonant EM field: A destructive frequency that matches the natural vibration of an object and shakes it toward failure. The same principle that lets an earthquake bring down a bridge.

Leah's analog meter finally shivered into the red band. "Cage is compromised," she said. "We're leaking."

"Meaning?" Julia asked.

"Meaning they can see the data from outside with scanners, and they'll see more than they should," Malik said. "Not full access, but enough to mirror directory trees. Enough to know what exists."

Osei's gaze flicked to the air-gapped server rack on the intercom screen, then back to the camera directly.

That motion told Tara he knew exactly what he was doing.

"I appreciate your cooperation," he said. "We'll keep this brief."

He inclined his head toward the server rack again. His team had broken through the Faraday Cage.

They were now within reach of their prize.

"Will you grant access to your air-gapped storage?" asked Osei. "I need verification that it doesn't contain any misappropriated federal identifiers."

"You don't need access for that," Julia said. "You just need an inventory."

"Correct," Osei said. "However, we have grounds to believe that this facility may be holding unlawfully obtained telemetry." He produced a small handheld device from his inner pocket, about the size of a phone, matte black. "Under emergency provisions," he said, "I am authorized to perform a non-invasive proximity scan."

"Non-invasive," Malik muttered. "That's one word for it."

Tara felt her pulse in the side of her neck. If the disruptor had weakened the cage enough, that scanner might find the isolated segment where they'd stored the triple-encrypted draft on the server. It wouldn't be able to read it, but just knowing it was there might be enough to justify a second, more aggressive warrant.

"You're on very thin legal ice," she said. "We'll contest this."

"And you are absolutely within your rights to do so," he replied. "Meanwhile, I am within mine."

He took a slow, deliberate step to the intercom, pointing the scanner directly at the server stack inside the War Room. Data began to populate its screen.

Before Osei could start, Malik spoke, crisp and clear. "Wait." Everyone turned. Malik lifted his hands, palms open.

"Give me ten seconds," he whispered to Julia. "Please." She studied his face, then gave the smallest nod. He spun back to his console, fingers flying.

"What are you doing?" Leah asked Malik.

"Agent Osei," began Julia slowly enunciating every word carefully. "What, exactly, are you looking for? The only work we have on these servers are the archives The Sentinel hangs on to in the event of lawsuits. Those archives contain the raw data for our stories, such as names, dates, places, recordings, photos, interview transcripts, letters of intent, email, phone calls, fact checks, fact checks of fact checks, legal verification of fact checks." Julia glanced at Malik, and he gave her the all clear and nodded in thanks.

"Giving them something else to be interested in," he said. Lines of command scrolled across his screen. Tara caught fragments: decoy, mirror, test volume. He hit Enter. "Done," he said.

Returning her gaze to Osei, Julia saw his withering look of feigned patience.

The hum shifted once more, almost imperceptibly. A narrow status light on the rack turned from dark to a soft amber.

The scanner chirped, a faint little blip of recognition. "There," he said, satisfied. "Now we're having an honest interaction."

The technician held the scanner low, watching its screen.

Tara held her breath as she watched the needle oscillate on the monitor Lea was watching.

Malik's jaw set. "Come on," he whispered, too low for anyone to notice. If the decoy worked, Osei's device would see exactly what Malik wanted it to see: a small, obviously self-contained test environment labelled with something innocuous, a sacrificial lamb to satisfy curiosity.

If it didn't—

"Now," Malik thought, "we find out how brave we really are."

At Kyrel's door, the hydraulic ram hit one last time with full pressure. The latch tore free. The door swung inward a jagged six inches before catching on the chain he'd forgotten he'd latched on autopilot when he got home. For a brief, almost comical second, the chain held.

Then a gloved hand reached through the gap with a small bolt cutter. Two quick snips, a clatter of metal on hardwood, and the chain fell.

The door eased open. Not kicked. Not rushed. Just opened.

Weller stepped into the frame first, tie straight, hair neat despite the hour, expression as composed as it had been the day he'd first handed Kyrel his capping packet.

"Good evening again, Mr. Kade," he said. "We appreciate your patience."

Behind him, two more agents, eyes scanning, hands empty but ready.

Kyrel did not step back. He stood beside the couch, spine straight, heart beating at a pace that felt almost slow.

"This is an abuse of process," he said.

Weller nodded once. "You can make that claim later in writing."

He turned slightly, gesturing without looking.

"Begin with devices," he said. "Then ledgers, external drives, any analog records related to financial activity in the last seventy-two hours."

They moved inward. Two fronts. Same law. Same night.

At The Sentinel, Osei's scanner chirped again as he burrowed into the decoy sector.

At Kyrel's apartment, a field kit opened with a soft click and agents began laying out anti-static bags.

No one had been arrested. No stories had been published. No verdicts had yet been rendered.

But the vice had closed.

And now, the only way out was through.

CHAPTER 41

THRESHOLD

The first thing Kyrel noticed as the agents crossed the threshold was not the sound. It was the smell. Metal. Cold. Sterile. A faint trace of solvent from the mesh pouches they carried, sharp enough to cut through the warm familiar air of the apartment he had built with D'Andra.

It smelled like someone else's authority in his home.

Weller gestured toward the kitchen. "Agents Patel and Ruiz will begin in there."

Patel approached the counter, opened the breadbox, and lifted out Kyrel's phone with two fingers, the way you'd lift evidence, not property.

Kyrel said nothing. Any protest would be taken as obstruction. Instead, he folded his hands loosely in front of him and leaned one hip against the back of the sofa, casual, controlled, deliberate.

He would not pace. He would not confront. He would not give them the narrative they were praying he'd hand them.

One of the secondary agents opened his field kit and laid out smooth silver anti-static bags, a soft brush, a small scanner with a low amber LED.

"Your home router has been disconnected from the wall," the agent noted.

"I unplugged it before you breached," Kyrel replied. "I'm allowed to disconnect my own internet."

Weller nodded as if granting him a point in a debate neither had agreed to enter. "Nothing wrong with that. Though we will need to confirm that nothing was moved or destroyed."

"I moved nothing," Kyrel said.

"I'm sure you believe that."

Kyrel breathed in slowly. D'Andra's grounding technique: In, hold, out.

Weller didn't miss it. But he misread it.

He thought Kyrel was calming fear. He did not understand what kind of man used breath to steady resolve.

Ruiz crossed the room and picked up the fireproof document bag from the coffee table.

"What's this?" he asked.

"Documents," Kyrel said. "Important ones."

Ruiz unzipped it, pulled out the stack, thumbed through the contents and stopped on a page printed from Tara's early hospital notes.

"Interesting," Ruiz murmured. "You keeping medical reports now?"

Kyrel felt the first crack of real irritation. "That page was given to me by Dr. Kade, my wife. It pertained to a patient we were trying to help."

"Still," Ruiz said lightly, "hospital data shouldn't be in a civilian home."

Weller did not correct him. Of course he didn't. "Is this coordination with Ms. Winslow?" Weller asked casually.

Kyrel looked him in the eye. "No."

"Is that the truth?"

"It's the answer."

Weller didn't like riddles. Kyrel knew that now.

Patel reappeared from the kitchen, holding a small, clear, sealed evidence envelope. Inside it was the last thing Kyrel expected. A thumb drive. Black, generic, unlabelled. "Found in the second drawer," Patel said.

Kyrel blinked. "That's empty. It came with the router when we installed service."

Weller lifted an eyebrow. "How do you know it's empty?"

"Because I tried it once. It was blank."

Ruiz held the envelope up to the light like it was radioactive. "Could've been wiped."

"Could've been anything," Kyrel said. "Do your scan."

"We will," Weller said. "But the presence of an unlabeled drive is... noteworthy."

"It's a drawer," Kyrel said. "Things live in drawers."

Patel sealed the bag and set it aside. Kyrel felt the familiar ache at his temples, the one that came when he hit a wall of willful misunderstanding.

Weller stepped closer, lowering his voice so the others would not hear.

"Mr. Kade... I know this is difficult. But the anomalies linked to your identity tonight were not fabricated. They were real movements."

"I did not move them."

"Someone did," Weller said. "Someone with access. Someone with your credentials."

That was the moment Kyrel knew with absolute clarity: They weren't here because they had evidence. They were here because they didn't, and hoped he would give them some.

Kyrel changed posture. Subtle. But everything. He straightened from the sofa, squared his shoulders, planted his feet, not combative, not defiant. Just present. Unmovable. "Agent Weller," he said calmly, "you are searching the wrong home."

Weller's jaw tightened. "Are you accusing someone?"

"I'm telling you this breach proves one thing: The system you trust doesn't understand the difference between a man who obeys a law and a man who exploits it."

"Meaning?"

"Meaning the anomalies you're chasing didn't come from me. They came from someone who knows how to use the parts of the system you don't understand."

Weller studied him for several long beats. Kyrel did not blink.

Patel's radio chirped. A terse voice crackled through: "Unit Three, confirm: We've got activity downtown. Disruptor is unstable. Supervisor orders you wrap on secondary location as soon as possible."

Kyrel's stomach tightened. The Sentinel.

Weller hesitated only a second. Then: "We're done here," he said.

Ruiz zipped the evidence bags. Patel packed the kit. The door hung crooked on its frame, a wounded mouth.

As they backed out, Weller paused on the threshold. "Mr. Kade," he said, "your calm worries me."

"Good," Kyrel replied. Because for the first time tonight, he wasn't afraid.

The building fell silent after the agents walked away. Kyrel stood in the wreckage of his doorway, breath slow, pulse level, mind disquietingly clear. Everything they had taken was replaceable. Everything they had accused him of was provable.

But the door, the door mattered. It was symbolic. A threshold violated. A boundary broken. A warning delivered. He walked to the kitchen, lifted the breadbox, retrieved his phone, but did not turn it on.

Instead, he whispered into the empty room: "Tara… tell me you're safe." He did not know if she was. And now, neither side could pretend this was just a story anymore.

This was war.

CHAPTER 42

SHIELD BREAK

The hum in the War Room had climbed past discomfort into something more primal, a low-frequency vibration Tara felt in her skull, in the soft tissue behind her eyes. The disruptor outside was no longer probing. It was pushing.

Leah stared at the analog meter and whispered, "We're over tolerance. They've destabilized the Faraday plane."

Malik swore under his breath. "Yes, but the decoy environment is doing exactly what it should."

Julia's face drained of color. "They know exactly what they're doing."

Outside the War Room, Osei handed the scanner to his technician, then observed over the tech's shoulder as he worked with the leaks.

"They have built a remarkable structure," he said about the War Room. "It's a shame to see it stressed so."

Julia snapped, "You're violating federal comms laws and you know it."

Osei smiled faintly. "And if your reporting is correct, you believe my department violates many things." To his technician he said, "focus the scanner in that area, will you?"

Malik whispered, "He's timing the disruptor pulses with the scan. They're trying to peek through the shielding and piggyback off the resonance. Jesus. Someone upstairs wants this badly."

Tara's skin prickled. Someone. Someone high.

The handheld device in the technician's palm chirped once. A clean, sharp tone.

Julia's shoulders tightened a fraction. "What was that?"

Osei told the technician to angle the scanner subtly, pointing it toward the floor. There was where a raw cable from the outer world met their internal system. It passed through the floor, under the wall of the War Room, and it was shielded, but even if there was a gap of one millimeter, the scanner would get through. Another chirp sounded again, a softer, questioning tone.

Malik inhaled sharply. "That's not the decoy," he murmured. "That's… something else."

"What something else?" Tara asked.

Malik shook his head. "Not the draft. Nothing we put there. Could be an artifact from the disruptor bleeding into the cage."

Julia's voice dropped to a razor-thin thread. "He'll say it's hidden data."

Osei looked up. "I'll need internal verification," he said.

Julia's jaw clenched. "No access. Proximity scan only."

"That's not what the field suggests," Osei replied. He stepped closer.

Leah reached toward Julia's sleeve, eyes wide. "Julia… he's pushing us into forced disclosure. If we let him log a false positive, they can come back with a Red Warrant."

Red Warrant. The nuclear option. Authorization to seize every device in the building, air-gapped or not. And it would destroy The Sentinel's ability to publish the story. And then the country would never see it.

Before Julia could respond, Tara walked across room, up to the junction panel. The scanner's tone shifted as its pulses hit her body.

Osei lifted it slightly. "Ms. Winslow, you're interfering with a federal— "

"Yes," Tara interrupted. "I am." Her hands were at her sides. Her heartbeat hammered through her chest like fists against a locked door. But her voice held. "You asked if I believed DEI acts in bad faith," she said. "Here is my answer."

Osei's eyes flickered.

Tara put her hand on the junction box affecting its grounding to disrupt the scanner's readings.. Everyone in the room fed on the tension like oxygen bombing an ember.

Miles away, Kyrel's sanctuary had been violated. But here, somehow, Tara would not allow the same thing.

"There is no hidden volume," she said. "There is no tampering. There is no illegal telemetry. You know the decoy you hit was a decoy. And you know the second tone wasn't data, it was your disruptor bleeding into our walls."

Julia stared at her, stunned. Malik closed his eyes, just once, as if bracing.

Osei stared at the wall monitor. For the first time, he looked slightly off-balance. "You don't understand the risk you're taking," he said softly.

"Oh," Tara whispered into the microphone, "I understand the risk perfectly."

The disruptor outside the War Room surged. The hum became a roar. Inside, the lights flickered twice and then a fluorescent tube behind Malik blew in a burst of blue-white sparks and glass shards.

Leah's meter pin slammed fully into the red. "Shield failure!" she shouted.

Julia jerked toward the wall panel but there was nothing left to save. The War Room's defenses collapsed in a soft, awful implosion. Not a bang. A surrender. The air itself seemed to shiver.

Outside, Osei grabbed the scanner from the technician. He watched as the screen lit up with a sudden cascade of readings, all garbage, all noise, but to an outsider: infinite possibilities.

Malik whispered, "They're going to claim we're hiding a full server."

"They can't," Julia said. "But they will."

Osei tapped in a few commands on the scanner to transfer the data to his tablet. He stood there motionless, reading the tablet, his brow crinkled, lips pursed, eyes guarded. He looked up toward the intercom once, then back to his tablet.

After what felt like fifteen minutes, he said something none of them expected: "Ms. Winslow... did you write this story?"

Julia's breath caught.

Malik's fingers froze on the keyboard.

Leah stopped moving entirely.

No one had used the word story.

No one had acknowledged that Tara was a journalist with a piece to publish.

Tara's mouth was dry. But she answered: "Yes."

"And does it contain any classified information?"

"It contains information you classify," she said. "But that's not the same thing."

"And you intend to publish?" Osei stared at her through the intercom screen.

She did not look away from his gaze. "Yes."

Osei turned to his crew and swiped his finger across his neck. The hum finally stopped. As abruptly as a car engine shutting off. Silence poured into the War Room.

Osei's crew packed up their equipment and walked back out the hallway door leaving Osei alone in front of the War Room door.

He stood there a few moments then he said: "I understand." Not agreement. Not approval. But an acknowledgment. A marker dropped between them.

Osei stepped back, adjusted his coat. "Our assessment is complete," he announced formally. "Your facility contains no compromised identifiers. No unauthorized data stores. No tampered telemetry. No actionable violations."

Julia stared at him. "You're closing the inspection?"

"Yes."

"What about the red-zone breach you just caused?"

"What breach?" Osei asked calmly.

Leah's jaw dropped. Malik blinked. Tara's stomach lurched.

Turning around, he touched his earpiece lightly.

"To command: Inspection negative. No findings. Exiting location."
A muffled voice crackled in reply. He turned back toward Julia.
"You may file a complaint," he said. "And I'm sure you will."

Then, he left.

The moment they heard the DEI team evacuate the space outside the War Room, the four of them jumped into motion. Leah killed all local power. Malik shoved in the analog backup key. Julia slid to the wall and flipped the emergency lockout switch.

Tara leaned against the table, shaking so hard she almost dropped to her knees.

Malik looked at her, eyes wide, voice hoarse: "Holy hell, Tara… you just stared down a federal agent like he was a parking officer."

"I couldn't let him plant evidence," she whispered.

"You saved the entire story," Leah said, voice breaking.

Julia pushed off the wall, walked over, and cupped Tara's face gently in her hands.

"Listen to me," she said. "That man wasn't here to stop your story. He was here to measure you."

Tara blinked. Julia's voice softened. "And now he knows exactly who you are."

CHAPTER 43

THE UNSAID

Julia opened the War Room door after watching the DEI leave on the external cameras.

She stood in the doorway, shoulders rigid, spine straight, as if posture alone could hold the world together. Behind her, Malik collapsed into a rolling chair and let his head fall back.

"Holy hell," he whispered.

Leah sank onto the table's edge, still watching the meter like it might explode. "We stayed just inside the legal line."

"No," Julia said quietly. "We stood on the legal line while they hammered it with a truck."

Only then did she turn.

Tara stood near the wall, still gripping the USB in her fist, knuckles pale. Her hair was slightly mussed from the sudden yank back into the room. She hadn't brushed it away. She looked like a woman who had been chased, and almost caught, and was now too aware of the closeness of danger to move.

"You're shaking," Julia said.

"I'm not," Tara said.

Julia raised an eyebrow.

"Okay," Tara whispered, "I'm shaking a little."

Julia walked to her, slow and deliberate, removing her own trembling from her stride.

"You did everything right," she said. Then softer: "They wanted you afraid. You're not."

Tara swallowed. "I was."

"Fear isn't the problem," Julia said. "Fear is what proves you're still here. It's submission they wanted. You didn't give it."

Tara exhaled once, choked and relieved at the same time.

Malik rotated in his chair. "Julia…"

"I know," she said.

"That was not a standard DEI visit."

"I know."

"That man wasn't a compliance agent."

"I KNOW."

Julia's voice cracked like ice. Silence fell.

Then she walked to the glass wall and turned off the room's overheads. The War Room dimmed to the low amber glow of emergency lamps, safer, harder to image through, an old newsroom habit.

The four of them stood in the hush of aftermath, listening to their own blood. Something had shifted. Not just in the room. In the city. In the country. In the people who had power. And in the people who had just provoked them.

Osei walked down the corridor with a calm, unhurried gait, nodding politely to the two uniformed officers posted near the elevator.

Agent Morrow fell in beside him. "You think they're hiding something?"

"No," Osei said. "I think they're trying not to get killed."

Morrow blinked. "What?"

"Every one of them knows the story they're holding would end careers. Possibly programs. Possibly our own."

"That's not grounds to— "

"It is not grounds to raid a newspaper at two in the morning," Osei finished smoothly. "Yet here we are."

They reached the elevator. The doors opened. He stepped in alone. As the doors closed, his reflection stared back at him from the steel:

poised, impeccable, unreadable. He touched the small scanner in his pocket. Malik's decoy had worked. But barely.

One more watt of power into the disruptor and the War Room would have leaked enough EM to give him everything. And then Tara Winslow would be in handcuffs. And then Kyrel Kade would be in custody. And the world would not be the same. He exhaled.

"They've grown bold," he murmured to the empty car. "Too bold."

He was not speaking of The Sentinel. He was speaking of DEI. A line had been crossed tonight. And someone at the top had ordered it.

Tara didn't move until Julia placed a steaming mug of tea in her hands. Mint, sharp and grounding.

"I don't drink tea," Tara murmured.

"You do now," Julia said. "Drink."

Tara drank. The warmth slid down her throat like a decision finding its spine.

"They know," she whispered.

Malik looked up. "Know what?"

"That it's real," Tara said. "If they weren't scared, they wouldn't have come."

Julia nodded. "Correct."

"And now… what?" Tara asked.

Leah answered this time. "Now the safest place for the story is also the most dangerous."

Tara's grip tightened around the mug.

Julia sat across from her. "Listen to me," she said. "Tonight was intimidation. They wanted to shake you, shake us, and stop the publication before it begins."

"It didn't work," Tara said.

"No," Julia agreed. "It didn't. But now they know what kind of story they're up against. They'll escalate."

Tara swallowed. "How?"

"Oh," Leah said softly, "every way that isn't technically illegal."

"Sometimes ways that are," Malik added.

Tara felt the room press in. "What do you need me to do?" she asked.

Julia leaned forward. "Stay alive."

Kyrel sat on the floor beside the shattered door, arms draped casually over his knees like he was meditating. Not waiting, tense-resting, the way D'Andra once described ER surgeons catching breath between traumas.

He wasn't panicked. He wasn't shaking. He wasn't even angry. He was something colder, something D'Andra had once warned him about gently: clarity sharpened by cruelty.

When the phone beside him buzzed, a soft vibration through the breadbox, he lifted the lid and checked the screen. A single message from Tara.

BREACH AT SENTINEL. WE'RE SAFE. MORE LATER.

His pulse quickened. He typed three words. We continue tomorrow.

Then hesitated. Then added: Good work.

He put the phone down. Straightened. Stood. He picked up the bent door, propped it back against the frame, and stepped away. It didn't close. It didn't need to. The threshold had already been broken. The next steps were inevitable. And somewhere, in the city's cold predawn quiet, a journalist clutched a USB drive that could end the world as DEI understood it.

He whispered: "Tara... don't stop now."

Several traffic cameras caught movement around Kyrel's building that morning. Two black SUVs pulling away from the rear entrance, another peeling off from the front door like they were chasing a criminal on the run.

Around The Sentinel, an unmarked sedan was caught leaving from the street by the front door, and a delivery truck that had been idling too long outside County General was seen by yet another camera.

A man in a navy suit was seen making a call from a rooftop near the Capitol Annex by a closed circuit system placed high up on a condo building that watched the nearby rooftops. But no one was immediately watching those feeds or understood the connection.

However, someone, somewhere, would eventually. By sunrise, whispers would travel through newsrooms across the city, federal office, and congressional staff in-boxes. Messages would be flying across the ethernet to tech investor circles and LinkLife board members.

DEI enforcement units would also be looped along with every hospital with an implant wing. Something had shifted. The breach was not a raid. It was a warning shot from a system realizing it might lose control. And beneath that warning, threaded like the bass line of a song building toward crescendo: The truth was moving.

Faster than DEI. Faster than Soren. Faster than Rhett. And far, far faster than the people who built the cage.

CHAPTER 44

THE REVEAL

05:52 a.m.

The Sentinel's fourteenth-floor newsroom was still trembling from the aftershocks of the DEI breach, loose papers, half-drunk coffee, a broken fluorescent buzzing at irregular intervals, but the air had shifted.

Something new was moving through it. Hope. Defiance. Resolve sharpened into steel edges.

Julia stood at the center of the War Room with the tablet in her hand like a detonator. Tara beside her. Malik on the console. Leah on the backup systems. Osei, gone.

He had vanished the moment the disruptor collapsed, without a good-bye, without a threat, without a single backward glance.

Like someone who had done what he was sent to do… and hated every minute of it.

Julia held out the tablet to Tara.

"You wrote it," she said. "You send it."

Tara stared at the Publish button. Her finger hovered above it. This was the end of her anonymity. The end of her safety. The end of her old life. And the beginning of something else, something she had once believed journalism no longer had the power to do: Change the course of a nation.

She touched the screen button PUBLISH. A heartbeat. A second heartbeat. Then, the console screens surged alive at once, lighting the dim room in white-blue brilliance.

"The story is live," Malik said. "Mirrors activated. Syndication streaming. Air-gapped nodes pushing backups to five continents."

"Comments up," Leah added. "Engagement spiking at five thousand percent over baseline. Traffic surge, my God."

Julia spoke quietly, reverently. "History just turned." Tara's phone vibrated in her hand. It was Kyrel:

> I'm reading it. You did it. Whatever happens next, you changed everything.

She typed only two words back:

> Hold on.

The first wave of alerts came like a tremor. A rumble through social networks. A shiver across encrypted channels. Confusion in analyst rooms. Then, visceral outrage.

> LinkLife used as a covert nationwide identity trap. DEI diverting capped assets into shadow accounts. Coercive

medical pathways. Secret data-sharing agreements. Victims identified. Logs verified.

The Sentinel's legal team pushed a statement live immediately.

We stand by our reporting. We have verified every claim. We invite federal inquiry.

Three minutes later, the White House's communications director released a tersely worded message.

We are reviewing The Sentinel's allegations.

It did nothing to slow the avalanche because the next wave came harder.

Screenshots.
Whistleblower commentary.
Hospital staff confirming details anonymously.
Politicians retweeting clips before staffers could yank them down.
Academics weighing in.
Tech ethicists losing their minds.

Someone leaked part of the DEI compliance manual. Someone else dug up campaign donations linked to LinkLife investors. A third posted a video from inside a hospital showing a patient screaming as he was told implants would become mandatory for their state's insurance coverage.

The public awoke into fury.

And then, the third wave hit.

SOREN VALE.

His name trended first. Then the phrase:

VALE'S MACHINE

Someone posted a clip from a Senate hearing two years earlier in which he had argued, calmly, clearly, that "economic identity integration is the only viable path to preserve national stability in an era of algorithmic markets."

The clip went nuclear.

People dug into his foundation. His offshore holdings. His private roundtables. His advisory ministries. And then the connection snapped into place:

> Soren Vale, the architect of DEI's predictive framework. Soren Vale, the shadow advisor to the Cap Act. Soren Vale, the man who had pushed for maximum enforcement authority behind closed doors.

Soren Vale, the puppet. But not the puppeteer.

At 06:02 a.m., the stock markets were still closed, but the private servers that fed global hedge funds were not. And someone, many someones, were panicking. Mass sell orders flooded pre-market channels. Private family offices froze trades. One major billionaire consortium shut down its trading AI for "maintenance." Translation:

> They were hiding their tracks.

Because the story had drawn a line straight to the top of the pyramid. The billionaire dynasties who had bankrolled the Cap Act, embedded DEI inside the federal structure, lobbied for identity integration, invested in LinkLife, and pulled Soren Vale's strings.

For decades they had been untouchable. Invisible. The sort of people who never appeared on paper because they owned the companies that printed the paper.

Now they had been named. Not directly. Not yet. But the scent of them hung in the air. And the world was now following the trail.

———

By 6:14 a.m. Kyrel had read the story alone in his half-broken doorway, standing barefoot on the hardwood, the morning light only beginning to seep through the blinds.

He read each line slowly, as if it were a diagnostic of his own heart.

The logs. The testimony. The analysis. The patterns. The money trail. The coercion. The hospital abuses. The DEI overreach. And at the center, a quiet truth he had refused to let himself see fully until now: They were not afraid he had cheated. They were afraid he had stayed honest. Because honesty in a corrupt system is a grenade.

His phone vibrated with a new message, unknown number, encrypted routing:

> Stay inside. They will try to discredit you. They will fail. The system is cracking.

He didn't know if it was from Tara, or someone inside The Sentinel, or someone else entirely. He only knew the timing was right. And that the day had finally arrived. The day he stopped being a subject of their system, and became a threat to it.

At 06:20 a.m. DEI released an official forty-seven-word statement:

> These allegations are inaccurate. All actions taken by DEI are within statutory guidelines. We urge the public to remain calm while facts are evaluated.

Six minutes later, someone leaked internal DEI messages admitting their disruptor had overloaded while "attempting to neutralize media containment."

The internet had a field day. By then, the tide was irreversible. The story was out. The truth was loose. And the people who had operated in shadow for a generation, were now standing in full light.

Tara watched the world ignite from the War Room monitors. Less than 30 minutes after they had posted, it had circumnavigated the world; spread into every nook and cranny; and on every phone.

Julia at her side. Malik at the console. Leah beside him. The hum of incoming data like a storm. She felt no triumph. Only the weight of responsibility and the chill of knowing this was only the beginning.

Julia touched her arm. "Your life just changed," she said softly. "You won't walk anywhere unnoticed ever again."

Tara swallowed. "Good," she said. "Let them see me."

As dawn broke across the eastern seaboard, households opened their phones.

Nurses in break rooms. Factory workers on night shift. Students in dorms. Retirees having early coffee. Parents packing lunches. Politicians climbing into black SUVs.

Millions of them. All reading the same story.

And in every place where power had grown too accustomed to secrecy, somebody felt a cold, sudden shiver.

Because a reporter had told the truth. A scientist had stood his ground. A doctor had refused to look away. A newsroom had refused to bend.

And the system they thought was unbreakable, was beginning to crack.

CHAPTER 45

THE AFTERSHOCKS

For fifty-three minutes after The Sentinel published Tara's story, the country behaved like a body in shock.

Refresh buttons clicked. Newsroom phones lit up. Government inboxes flooded. Servers strained under traffic. People read, and reread, and reread again, trying to understand whether what they were seeing was real.

LinkLife. DEI enforcement misuse. Identity freezes. Targeted audits. Economic throttling tied to failed compliance. The breach at County General. The attempted quieting of The Sentinel itself. And the name everyone had suspected but never confirmed:

Soren Vale.

The first hour was not noise. It was quiet. The dangerous quiet when a society feels something cracking under its feet. Even the markets held still. And then, everything hit at once.

Cable networks broke from scheduled programming. Legal scholars started livestreams. Half a dozen elected officials posted statements that were clearly written by crisis aides with trembling hands. Hashtags erupted across every platform, rising like geysers:

#DEIOverreach
#LinkLifeLeak
#UncappedTruth
#WhoControlsTheSystem

But the one that dominated, the one that united fear and fury, the one that spread faster than oxygen:

#KadeWasRight

For months Kyrel had been the ghost in the margins, the quiet anomaly, the man people whispered about at conferences. Now the receipts were public.

And he wasn't a ghost anymore. He was a mirror.

By 7:10 a.m., the headquarters lobby looked like a war zone in slow motion. Employees gathered in clusters, clutching phones, staring at the wall-mounted screens streaming The Sentinel's headline:

THE DIGITAL ID COUP: HOW DEI AND PRIVATE POWER INVADED YOUR LIFE

Kyrel stepped through the crowd, not pushing, not hurrying. He walked the way he had the day he returned as CEO: steady, centered, impossible to ignore. Some employees nodded to him, eyes wide with fear and gratitude. Some avoided him entirely.

And some, the ones who had risen fast under Rhett's tenure, watched him the way a man watches a storm decide which direction to turn.

Tara's article had included one sentence near the end that hit the company harder than any policy review ever could: "Multiple internal sources confirm that Kyrel Kade, the capped co-founder of LinkLife, resisted every effort to weaponize the technology he created."

It wasn't meant as a vindication. It became one anyway.

Rhett saw the headline from the balcony of his penthouse. The story didn't destroy his life in one stroke. It destroyed it molecule by molecule.

Paragraph two named the anomalies. Paragraph seven described shell subsidiaries. Paragraph nine described "secondary credentials tied to a co-founder's ID without consent." Paragraph fourteen said the phrase that broke him: "Investigators believe the unauthorized earnings trails point not to an error, but to deliberate misuse."

He dropped his glass. It smashed against imported stone. The phone on his desk buzzed.

Vale.

Rhett stared at the name the way a condemned man stares at the hooded executioner who once pretended to be his friend. He did not answer. Not yet.

Because something inside him, some small, strangled part, knew the dynamic had shifted. Vale needed him now. And people who need you cannot hurt you the same way again. Or so he thought.

Soren Vale stood in a glass-walled conference room on the seventy-ninth floor, watching the country revolt in real time. Directors shouted. Deputy secretaries fanned out like frightened birds. Intelligence liaisons whispered in corners. Phones rang without cease.

A young analyst sprinted toward him, breathless. "Sir, six states are demanding an emergency injunction. They want DEI operations halted until an audit is performed."

Vale didn't flinch. He simply inhaled slowly. Because he understood something the others didn't: This wasn't a surprise. This was the price.

You don't try to reshape national identity infrastructure without provoking a quake. He knew the quake would come. He simply didn't expect it today. He especially didn't expect it to come from a journalist he had dismissed as "minor nuisance with delusions of Watergate."

He especially didn't expect her to have allies. He especially didn't expect her to survive the night. He turned to his chief of staff. "Find me Winslow," he said. "Now."

The chief hesitated. "Sir… finding her may draw attention." "Then draw it," Vale snapped. "Because she just lit a fuse under our entire architecture." He turned slowly toward the window.

"And someone," he added, "prepare a full profile on Kade. He's about to become the most dangerous capped man in America."

Tara Winslow was nowhere. Not at The Sentinel. Not at home. Not at County General. Not at her usual coffee shop. Not on any camera. Because she was already underground, guided by people who understood how to vanish a journalist without losing her voice.

Her editor had prepared the hideout weeks earlier, long before he knew what she was working on. He called it "the Cabin." It wasn't a cabin. It wasn't near water. And it wasn't technically legal. But it was safe.

She sat on the edge of a narrow bunk, knees drawn up, hands steady only because she'd folded them tight enough to keep them from shaking. Her phone lay face-down on the metal table, powered off. On the small TV, muted, every channel showed her name. Her face. Her work.

She was no longer a person. She was a fault line.

Her editor's voice echoed in her head: "You wrote something that will be remembered. Something that will be used. Something that puts you in danger. That is the cost. But it is also the weight of truth."

She wasn't sure which part terrified her more, the danger, or the responsibility.

At 8:14 a.m., Kyrel reached the twenty-sixth floor. The entire executive suite was in chaos, but the chaos parted for him. He walked into the glass conference room. The Board was already at the table. Screens displayed the Sentinel headline. Some members looked furious. Some looked relieved. Most looked terrified.

One finally spoke: "Mr. Kade… what do we do?"

Kyrel looked at them, these leaders who had been complicit by silence, coerced by contracts, trapped by optimism. He answered simply: "We tell the truth."

Truth about internal abuses. Truth about misused data pipelines. Truth about coerced licensing. Truth about the man who built the labyrinth they were all trapped in.

"And then," he added, "we cut the strings." Someone whispered, "Whose strings?" Kyrel said nothing. Because he didn't have a name. Not yet. But Tara's article had opened the door.

And now the light was pouring in.

CHAPTER 46

THE RUPTURE

The Sentinel hit publish at 05:52 a.m. Not with a countdown. Not with a teaser. Not with a "Developing Story."

LIVE: FEDERAL IDENTITY SYSTEM LINKED TO
UNAUTHORIZED ECONOMIC CONTROL
BY TARA WINSLOW, INVESTIGATIVE REPORTER

The internet didn't crash. It lunged. Within seconds the headline cross-duplicated across social platforms, mirrors, screenshots, archived links, cloud copies. The failsafes Malik had baked in, sixteen of them, activated like shrapnel dispersal. It was unkillable.

By 06:04, hashtags were trending in fourteen cities. By 06:05, bots tried flooding the comments with noise, but the Sentinel's filters ignored them. By 06:07, three newsrooms picked up summary versions.

By 06:30, the truth had reached millions. It was out. It was alive. And it was hungry.

Inside a glass tower downtown, the DEI command center had erupted in a kind of restrained panic that bureaucratic systems specialize in. Screens blinked red. Notifications stacked faster than advisors could read them. A dozen officers talked at once, voices overlapping: "Sentinel has gone live."

"Source appears legitimate."
"We need a counter-statement."
"We can't counter without authorization."
"Who has authorization?"
"Vale isn't responding."
"Find him."
"Find him now."

A senior official muted the entire room with a single raised hand. "Emergency briefing in twenty," she said. "Legal, comms, and risk assessment present. Nobody leaves."

Her aide swallowed. "Ma'am... the audit team at Kade's residence? They've already logged their report."

She scanned it. Paused. Read it again.

"You dragged a capped citizen out of bed," she said coldly, "and found nothing?"

"But anomalies... "

"Anomalies that his business partner fabricated," she snapped. "Which your team failed to establish before kicking down his door."

The aide shrank into silence.

"Find Vale," she repeated. "Before the press does."

Rhett sat in his office staring at three screens: One showed the Sentinel article. One showed LinkLife stock halting trading. One showed his own face, smiling, polished, from a fundraiser three months earlier.

He did not smile now.

The liquor bottle on the side table trembled from the shaking of his leg. He tried to tell himself he could contain this. That Kyrel would take the fall. That he could spin diagnostics, reassign blame, bury discrepancies.

Then a line in the story caught his eye:

> Financial irregularities traced to senior LinkLife executive (not Kade)

His breath stopped. They know. He reached for his phone. His hands shook badly enough that he nearly dropped it. "Vale," he whispered when the line clicked.

But it wasn't Vale. A clipped voice answered: "Mr. Hollis, your access is being revoked."

"What, who is this? Put him on!"

"Your partnership privileges are suspended pending inquiry."

"No, you don't understand, I didn't..."

"We'll contact you."

The line went dead.

For the first time in his adult life, Rhett felt something primal: Fear with no ceiling. Fear with teeth.

Kyrel's phone, still in airplane mode, lay next to him on the coffee table. But he didn't need it. He didn't need news alerts. He didn't need Tara's confirmation. He didn't need to see the headline. He felt it.

Like pressure leaving the room. Like a weight sliding off the chest. Like truth making oxygen out of thin air.

He stepped onto his crooked doorway, splintered wood crunching under bare feet. Outside, two neighbors from down the hall were already staring at their phones, eyes wide.

One looked up, saw him, and froze. "Mr. Kade," she whispered. "You're… in the news."

"I know."

"Is it true?"

Kyrel held her gaze. "Yes." No slogan. No panic. No fear. Just one word offered with the quiet gravity of a man who has survived himself.

Deep in a penthouse whose blinds were never opened, Soren Vale stood alone in front of a wall-sized screen displaying the Sentinel article. He did not yell. He did not panic. He did not pace. He simply read. Line by line. With the calm focus of a surgeon preparing to amputate a limb from someone else's body.

When he reached the section linking DEI telemetry to unauthorized financial controls, he paused. Then he picked up his phone and dialed a number with no contact name. Just digits.

It rang once. Twice. A third time. Then a voice answered. Deep. Unbothered. Old. "You've been exposed," the voice said.

"No," Vale answered softly. "We have."

"You were tasked with containment."

"And I achieved it until your other assets got sloppy," Vale replied. "You wanted the system to tighten its grip. I warned you we were squeezing too hard."

Silence. Then: "You know the protocol."

Vale exhaled once. Slow. Controlled. "I do."

"And Soren, "

"Yes?"

"Do not fail again."

The line went dead.

Vale set the phone down. The shadow behind the shadow had spoken. It was time to choose which puppets he would cut free.

CHAPTER 47

THE COUNTERMOVE

Somewhere in Washington, DC, at 17:52, twelve hours after Tara's story hit half the planet, an unmarked conference room five floors below street level, filled with the people who were not supposed to exist.

No cameras. No transcripts. No names on the door.

They were just nine of the wealthiest human beings on Earth, seated around a pale oak table that did not belong to any particular office. It belonged to them. They were not "old money", or "inherited power". They were something much older. Something much quieter.

They were the structure that built governments, yet were not within it.

Soren Vale stood before them like a servant awaiting judgment.

"The story is contained," he said. "We've suppressed amplification on most platforms. Engagement curves are flattening."

"That's not containment," one of the men replied. "That's stalling."

His suit was flawless. His voice was icewater.

"There's no evidence tying this to any of us," Soren pressed. "We can hold our position."

Another man leaned back in his chair and steepled his fingers. "Stop talking about holding. Talk about undoing."

Soren swallowed. He had faced senators and presidents with less fear than he felt now.

"It's Kyrel Kade," he said. "He's the fulcrum. The story is anchored to him."

"The boy refuses to be corrupt," another woman said. "It makes him dangerous."

"He has become an icon," said another. "And icons become movements."

Soren realized, too late, that they were speaking in past tense. About him.

"We built this system," one of the older ones said softly. "We financed it, structured it, placed the levers. The Cap Act was necessary, global markets were collapsing under speculation. We stabilized the economy."

He turned toward Soren. "And then you overreached."

Soren felt the floor tilt. "I followed the mandate," he insisted. "We needed compliance teeth. We needed control."

"No," the man replied, leaning forward. "You wanted obedience."

Silence rang like metal struck in the dark.

In a different glass-walled boardroom twenty blocks away, DEI leadership sat in tight rows around a too-long table. Screens on every wall streamed the fallout:

> Economists warning the Cap Act may be unconstitutional
> Senators demanding hearings
> Public defenders calling for an injunction
> Protestors gathering outside hospitals
> Longtime DEI analysts submitting resignations on livestreams

Agent Weller looked as if he hadn't slept in thirty hours.

"This isn't about Kade," he said. "It's about the system. If we lose control of the narrative, we lose compliance."

"The narrative is already gone," someone muttered.

A junior analyst raised a trembling hand. "I think we need to consider that… that Mr. Kade might have been telling the truth." The room went very still.

Then the Director spoke. "We don't investigate truth. We investigate irregularities."

Weller's jaw flexed. He said nothing. But for the first time, the room didn't seem convinced.

Kyrel stepped into his glass-walled office and found three dozen employees waiting inside. Not protesting. Not afraid. Just… waiting. Eyes steady. Phones clutched. Faces tense. Angela, from engineering, spoke first. "Sir… are they coming for you?"

"Not today," Kyrel said.

"Can we help?" she asked.

"You already are," he said, his voice steady. "By not leaving."

The room filled with a soft, surprised breath. He didn't give speeches. He didn't rally troops. But today something settled around him like a mantle he had never asked for.

"Whatever happens next," he told them, "we will stand for transparency. For consent. For technology that serves people, not the people who believe they own them."

A murmur. A fragile hope. It was enough.

At the hospital, administrators were in meltdown. News vans clogged the street. Patients demanded to know if their implants were safe. Family members wanted implant removals. Doctors were furious at DEI warrants being executed in trauma wards.

D'Andra stood in front of the nursing station and spoke with the calm of a woman who had worked three back-to-back shifts and survived much worse.

"We will not force implants," she told the board. "We will not use LinkLife against patients. We will follow medical ethics, not federal panic."

One of the senior administrators sputtered. "That is insubordination!"

"No," D'Andra said. "It's medicine." And the nurses behind her nodded. A line had been drawn.

It was a Safe House. No communications, no outside contact. A forced vacation. Decorated in minimalist hunting cabin, it had dark curtains, dark furniture, and hardly any creature comforts. There was one burner phone, a TV, and a laptop with no wireless hardware. She was told that she should not use the phone under any circumstance but an emergency.

Tara watched her own story melt across the continent like lava. Her inbox at The Sentinel had exploded with tips, documents, recordings, confessions from former DEI workers, whistleblowers, auditors, and terrified patients.

An entire nation had waited for permission to speak. And her story had given it. But she wasn't triumphant. She was trembling. Julia's text came through on the secure line:

We need you on camera. For the evening edition. It has to be you.

Tara stared at the message. I thought I wasn't supposed to use this except in emergencies? She had been ready to publish. She had not been ready to become recognizable.

The billionaires spoke in unison now, a chorus of smooth, controlled condemnations.

"You will step down," the oldest said. "You will hand over the network."

"You will not speak publicly. You will not interfere further. And you will not be protected."

Soren stood frozen. "You, " His voice cracked. "You're hanging me out? After everything I— "

"Silence! You were useful," the woman said. "You are now exposed."

He shook. "I can fix this. I can still turn this, "

"No," the cold voice said. "You've lost control of the story. And that is the one thing we do not tolerate."

The door opened behind him. Two security officers waited. Not DEI. Not government. Private. Owned. For the first time in his career, Soren Vale was not the scariest person in the room.

Online, on the streets, in hospitals, in boardrooms people were picking sides.

Some shouted that the Cap Act had saved the economy. Some shouted that it was tyranny. Some demanded government resignations. Some demanded new oversight. Some called for Kyrel's arrest. Some called for his election.

A movement was forming. Small. Fragile. But real. And Kyrel Kade's name was no longer a whisper. It was becoming a banner.

CHAPTER 48

COLLAPSE POINT

The LinkLife executive board had gathered in a panic. Not one camera in the building was turned on. Not one laptop was connected to Wi-Fi.

Not one assistant was allowed inside. This was supposed to be an emergency governance meeting. It looked more like the final hours of a bankrupt monarchy, with pitchfork-toting peasants banging at the castle doors.

The board chair cleared her throat.

"Before we begin," she said, voice thin, "I must note that the situation has escalated beyond our internal capacity. We are now under— "

The door opened. And Kyrel walked in. But not alone. Behind him were a civil rights attorney with a reputation for dismantling federal overreach, an independent auditor, and a court observer from the state attorney general's office.

The entire room stiffened. Kyrel didn't sit. He didn't smile. He didn't elevate his voice.

"This is no longer an emergency meeting," he said softly. "This is a reckoning."

Rhett, pale and silent at the far end of the table, finally spoke. "What the hell are you doing?"

Kyrel looked at him, not cruelly, not angrily. Just with the unbearable clarity of someone who had finally stopped shrinking to make others comfortable.

"Stopping you," Kyrel said. A ripple went through the room.

Rhett's face twitched. "You don't have the authority to, "

The attorney beside Kyrel placed a thick packet on the table.

"Mr. Donovan," she said coolly, "you're named in a pending investigation for unauthorized financial redirection, falsified credential pathways, and misuse of capped-partner access."

Rhett stared at her as if she'd spoken another language.

Then at Kyrel. "You?"

Kyrel shook his head. "You brought this on yourself."

The independent auditor opened a folder and slid a single sheet forward. A chart. Simple. Devastating.

"Every anomalous transfer detected by DEI," he said, "originated from a cloned credential profile belonging to Mr. Donovan."

"You can't prove—" Rhett began.

But the auditor raised a hand gently, like calming a child. "We can. And we have." He clicked a remote. On the wall screen:

A series of timestamped logs. Perimeter access. Shell accounts. Redirected royalties through subsidiary chains.

And then, the crown jewel:

A routing fingerprint unmistakably connected to Rhett's personal device.

The silence that followed was thick and suffocating.

Someone inhaled sharply. Someone else whispered, "Oh my God."

Rhett's chair creaked under him. "I didn'—
I didn't mean—
I was trying to protect the company—
Kyrel was going to— "

Kyrel cut him off gently. "No one made you do anything, Rhett." There was no malice in it. Which somehow made it worse.

Rhett looked at him, eyes wide, almost pleading. "You're throwing me to the wolves."

"No," Kyrel said, voice steady. "You invited them in."

The board chair finally spoke. "Mr. Donovan," she said, her voice brittle, "you are hereby suspended pending further investigation."

Rhett swallowed, jaw trembling. "You can't do this. You're all panicking. This is overblown—. The press won't—"

The attorney interrupted. "The Sentinel has corroborated the source logs. Their coverage is expanding."

"And DEI?" the chair asked.

Kyrel answered. "DEI is collapsing under the weight of its own actions. They know that if they pursue me now, it proves everything the press is saying. So they're retreating."

A murmur of shock. "Retreating?"

Kyrel nodded. "When an institution is cornered, it stops enforcing and starts hiding."

Rhett's face crumpled. "It wasn't supposed to go like this," he said weakly.

Kyrel's gaze softened, but only for a breath. Then he said the most painful truth of all: "You had every chance to be better than this."

Rhett looked gutted. Not angry. Not defensive. Just… broken.

The board, one by one, turned their chairs subtly toward Kyrel. Not dramatically. Not with declarations. Just small, inevitable shifts of allegiance. The center of gravity had moved. Kyrel Kade was now the axis. Rhett Donovan was a cautionary tale.

And the shadow behind Rhett, the deeper rot, was now visible in outline even if not yet in name. Soren Vale. Then the men above him. Then the ones above them. The ancient architecture of power, suddenly exposed to daylight.

Security arrived at the edge of the boardroom. Rhett stood. He looked at Kyrel with something between hatred and grief.

"When they come for you," he whispered, voice shaking, "remember this moment. Remember that you chose to stand alone."

Kyrel held his gaze. "I'm not alone," he said quietly.

The security officers led Rhett out. The door closed. A sound like the end of an era. Kyrel exhaled slowly, then looked around the table. "We rebuild," he said. "Today."

No one argued. The collapse had begun. But not of them. Of the system. And once something starts to fall, gravity does the rest.

CHAPTER 49

THE TEMPLARS OF OLD MONEY

After three days, the safe house was too quiet so they moved Tara closer to town.

Tara sat at the end of the borrowed dining table, laptop open, headphones around her neck, the cheap blinds in the rental pulled almost shut. The safe house was technically an "extended-stay corporate suite" on a side street in Arlington, but it felt like what it was: a hiding place with better towels.

Her phone buzzed once on the table.

MALIK: You alone?

She typed back. Yes. Julia's at the office. TV muted. Curtains drawn. Cats imaginary.

A few seconds.

MALIK: Good. I'm calling.

She accepted on the second ring.

"Hey," she said. "Tell me you're calling to say we overreacted and nobody cares about the story."

"Wish I could," Malik said. His voice was warm, but the warmth rode on top of something tight and electric. "Got an update from Osei and the investigative desk. You asked who was really behind Soren Vale."

"Yeah."

"We found his cathedral."

She straightened. "Go on."

Malik didn't rush. He laid it out like a surgeon describing an X-ray.

"The day Sentinel ran the DEI piece, a number of offshore entities started… twitching," he said. "Nothing dramatic. Just small, precise movements."

"Shells trying to protect themselves?" Tara asked.

"Exactly. Osei's team has been building a net around OverCap for months," he said. "Tonight, a few of the long-dormant shells flickered. Same legal firms. Same nominee directors. But the wiring behind them leads somewhere new."

"Where?"

"A private wealth consortium registered in Switzerland under the name Continuity Council AG, founded twelve years ago. No website. No public-facing business. Just an address, a set of numbered accounts, and a handful of signatures on internal documents. We got those through… let's call it parallel reporting."

She rubbed at her temple. "And Soren?"

"Not on the masthead," Malik said. "They're not that sloppy. But he sits on advisory boards for three front foundations that are wholly owned by the Continuity Council. A climate 'impact fund' in London. A digital freedom nonprofit in Singapore. A biomedical ethics institute in Boston."

"All respectable," Tara murmured.

"On the surface," Malik said. "Underneath? Those fronts own the majority voting stakes in half a dozen Cap-grandfathered conglomerates. Including two tech giants, a shipping empire, and a global data-brokerage firm that pre-dates the Cap Act by thirty years."

She felt something cold move through her chest. "Grandfathered billionaires," she said.

"Yeah," Malik replied. "The ones the law never touched. That's why they didn't fight the Cap Act."

He sent a file. Her screen flashed with a new encrypted message. She opened it, watching lines of scanned documents resolve, board minutes, internal memos, wiring instructions, legal opinions.

At the top of one memo, in clean serif letters:

> CONFIDENTIAL, CONTINUITY COUNCIL
> EXECUTIVE SESSION
> Subject: Wealth Preservation Strategies in Post-Cap
> Environment

"Look at page three," Malik said.

She scrolled. It was all there, written in the dry certainty of men who had never expected their words to see daylight.

> "The Cap Act offers a unique defensive perimeter around existing fortunes. By freezing upward mobility at the one-billion threshold, we reduce the probability of new entrants accumulating sufficient capital to challenge legacy control."

> "Policy objective: strengthen enforcement mechanisms to ensure no 'second-generation' billionaires can reach scale outside structures we control."

Tara read the paragraph twice. "So this wasn't reform," she said softly. "It was a moat."

"And DEI is their guard tower," Malik said. "Soren has been the architect of enforcement escalation for the last five years. He pushed for automated audits, lifetime monitoring, medical ID integration, everything you exposed."

"For them," she said.

"For them," Malik confirmed. "Cap the new rich. Protect the old rich. Wrap it in the language of fairness."

Her pulse thudded in her ears. "Do we have names?" she asked.

"We do," Malik said. "Nine primary signatories. All grandfathered billionaires. Three American, two European, one Gulf-state royal, one East Asian shipping magnate, one Canadian resource baron, one South African mining heir. All with big stakes in America, which makes them vulnerable to the Cap Act."

"Jesus."

"They call themselves the Continuity Council in documents," Malik said. "But the investigative desk has been using another term for them."

"What?"

He hesitated, just long enough to let her know he was half-embarrassed, half-proud.

"The Templars of Old Money," he said. "Guardians of the holy grail of pre-cap wealth."

Despite everything, Tara snorted. "You're not allowed to make me laugh when my blood is freezing."

"You asked for the villains above your villain," Malik said. "There they are: our very own Hydra."

———

Across the Atlantic, in a room that was never photographed, one of the Templars poured himself a drink he could not taste.

The club was older than the Cap Act, older than DEI, older than most of the nations whose policies its members nudged like chess pieces. Heavy paneling, oil portraits, leather too soft to be anything but obscene.

A fire burned low. Outside, London rain whispered against leaded glass.

"Vale has become a liability," said Laurent Renaud, the French industrialist whose family had once built half of Europe's rail lines and now owned slices of everything that moved data or goods.

Across from him, Andrew Kirkland, an American tech pioneer turned full-time philanthropist, set down his glass.

"He was always a liability," Kirkland replied. "That was his value. He was visible. Distracting. Useful for taking heat."

"Heat is one thing," Renaud said. "Federal investigations are another. A national paper tying his name to overreach at DEI? That is… less than helpful."

On the sofa near the fire, an older man with a silver cane and amused eyes watched them both. Sir Edward Finch had been born into English shipping money and had the unhurried air of someone who had never once needed to move quickly in his life.

"Vale did what we asked," Finch said. "He kept the ladder kicked away. The Cap Act has held. No new families at our level. That was the brief."

"Until LinkLife," Renaud snapped. "Until Kade."

Kirkland's jaw tightened almost imperceptibly.

Kade is the problem," said Renaud. "LinkLife won't reach its full potential unless Kade disappears."

"He won't go quietly," said Kirkland. "This is why we needed someone like Vale, but he failed. Still, Kade has to be brought to heel or eliminated."

"But that will make Kade a martyr," Finch said. "The hacker saint of the capped economy. The journalist made him sympathetic. 'Evil' government agents banging on his door in the night? It plays badly."

Finch swirled his drink. "Public sentiment is weather," he sneered. "We own the climate."

Renaud's nostrils flared, but he subsided. They all knew Finch was right. At least for now.

Soren Vale stood by the window, hands behind his back, watching the rain bead and run down the glass. He was not there until they spoke to him. He was invisible until they wanted him visible. He had been summoned without ceremony, flown in on a jet that didn't exist on any manifest. The room smelled like old power and old rugs. He hated it, and he needed it.

"You escalated too fast," Renaud said to him at last, bringing Soren into the conversation. "Medical integration should have waited another cycle. The story was not ripe enough to ignore. Now we have this… Sentinel problem."

Soren turned, measuring the room. "I escalated on your instruction," he said, careful to keep his tone neutral. "We needed hard identifiers to track income. The hospitals were the cleanest insertion point."

Kirkland steepled his fingers. "We instructed you to explore integration," he said. "We did not authorize you to trample civil-liberties protocols so blatantly it would hand ammunition to every civil rights lawyer in the country."

Soren felt heat rise in his chest. "With respect," he said, "I built what you asked for. A system that makes it impossible for a new billionaire to hide. The fact that some newspaper has decided to dramatize enforcement does not change the underlying necessity. Kade was already a problem. If men like him are allowed to grow unchecked, your 'continuity' dissolves."

He let that hang there.

Finch's eyes narrowed fractionally.

Renaud leaned forward. "Be careful, Vale," he said softly. "You were hired because you understand the tools better than we do. Don't mistake that for equality."

Soren dipped his head. "I have never made that mistake, sir," he said.

Kirkland let out a slow breath. "Regardless," he said, "DEI's visible overreach compromises the instrument. We need distance."

"You want to cut me loose," Soren said.

"We want to tactically reposition you," Finch corrected. "For now, you will resign from any role that links you directly to enforcement. You will become a consultant to one of our philanthropic vehicles, where you can do less… damage."

"And if the investigators follow the shells?" Soren asked. "If they reach this room?"

Renaud smiled thinly. "They won't."

Soren held his gaze. "They already have part of the trail," he said. "The Sentinel has details they shouldn't. They knew to look at medical ID. They knew about the audit escalation parameters. Someone is feeding them."

Silence.

It stretched just long enough to suggest the thought had occurred to all three of the older men, and none of them liked it.

"We will manage our own security," Finch said. "Your job is to stop drawing fire."

Soren could have nodded. He could have accepted the demotion, taken the generous "consultancy," and allowed himself to be 'disappeared' into a safer orbit.

Instead, he said: "And what about Kade?"

Renaud's eyes went cold. "Kade will be dealt with through the usual channels," he said. "Regulation. Litigation. Quiet pressure. If necessary, we will purchase what is left of him through intermediaries and place his technology where it can no longer threaten the balance."

"And the journalist?" Soren asked.

"Tara Winslow," Kirkland said. "She will either be promoted into a higher, more controlled environment... or she will burn out. The press loves martyrs, until they become inconvenient."

Soren glanced back at the window, at the rain tracing crooked paths down glass. They were underestimating all of them: Kade, Winslow, the people reading the story in a hundred million smaller rooms.

For the first time, a sliver of something like doubt moved under his rib cage. Not about the Council. About whether he still wanted to be standing next to them when the lightning finally struck.

Back in Arlington, Tara scrolled through the memo again, reading the phrases that would haunt her if she ever stopped moving long enough to let them.

> Wealth Preservation.
> Defensive perimeter around existing fortunes.
> Prevent new entrants from accumulating sufficient capital to challenge legacy control.

"Please tell me we can publish this," she said.

"Not yet," Malik said. "The documents are solid, but the channel we got them through is… fragile. If we burn it now, we might not get the rest."

"The rest?"

"There are references here to other tools," he said. "Judicial influence. Trade arbitrations. International lending terms. The Cap Act is one tool. Another is DEI. The Continuity Council has built a very large tool chest."

She closed her eyes for a moment. "So what do we do?" she asked.

"We keep digging," Malik said. "We build a case so watertight that when we print the Templars' names, the only choice governments have is to act, or be seen protecting them."

"That could take months," Tara said.

"Probably," Malik replied. "But the public already knows DEI crossed a line. They know medical identity was weaponized. They know someone is using the cap as a club. We shifted the ground. Now we go for the bedrock."

She breathed out slowly. "Templars of Old Money," she said, trying the phrase on her tongue.

"Working title," Malik said. "We'll come up with something more respectable for print."

"No," Tara said. "Keep it. It's perfect. Knights around a table, guarding a grail no one else is allowed to touch."

On her screen, a new message appeared from Kyrel.

You still breathing?

She smiled despite herself. Barely. Malik just introduced me to the secret club of the men who think they own the century.

Four dots appeared on the screen.

Good. Now we know which ceiling to crack.

Her fingers hovered over the keys. They'll come for us harder now.

They were always coming. The difference is, now we can see them.

Tara leaned back in the chair, the cheap upholstery creaking.

Outside the window, dawn was just beginning to gray the edges of the sky over the highway. Somewhere in the city, DEI teams were writing their reports. Somewhere else, Soren Vale was being told, politely, to take the fall.

And somewhere far above all of them, nine men who had never worried about rent were deciding how much more democracy they could afford to kill before people started flipping the tables.

"Templars of Old Money," she murmured again. This time, the name didn't feel like a joke. It felt like a headline. And a target.

CHAPTER 50
FAULT LINES

They put Kyrel in a room with no cameras. At least, none that were obvious. It was one floor below the main committee hearing chambers, in a part of the Capitol complex that smelled faintly of carpet cleaner and old paper. The walls were beige, the chairs were utilitarian, the table was just wide enough to feel like a barrier.

On one side sat Kyrel, hands folded, suit jacket hanging a little loose on shoulders that had carried too much in too short a life. On the other side, three people: Senator Elaine Park, chair of the Oversight Subcommittee; a lean man from the Attorney General's office whose name Kyrel instantly forgot; and a younger policy aide with a tablet and careful, noncommittal eyes.

No press. No public. No microphones with red lights.

"Thank you for coming in, Mr. Kade," Senator Park said. Her voice was warm, but it had the edges of a woman who had lived through too many news cycles. "I know this is… a lot."

He gave the polite half-smile he'd been practicing since the Sentinel story broke. "I've had worse weeks," he said.

The AG lawyer didn't smile. He opened a folder, glanced at the paper inside as if he didn't already know it by heart.

"You understand," he said, "that DEI's mandate is still, in law, intact. The Cap Act has not been repealed. There are ongoing investigations into OverCap-related activity, into Mr. Vale, and into certain transactions tied to your former partner, Mr. Colburn. None of this changes your capped status."

Kyrel nodded once. "I read the statute again last night," he said. "Bedtime story."

Senator Park's mouth twitched. "I'm not here to make promises I can't keep," she said. "But I am here because the ground moved. Your testimony and Ms. Winslow's reporting have... created space."

"Space for what?" Kyrel asked.

"For reform," the aide said carefully. "The Cap Act as written was sold as a fairness measure. What we're seeing looks a lot more like a moat. There is bipartisan interest in at least appearing to respond."

"Appearing," Kyrel repeated.

The AG lawyer leaned forward. "Let me be direct," he said. "We need credible witnesses if we are to pursue criminal charges against Mr. Vale, certain DEI officials, and, if the evidence supports it, external actors who may have influenced enforcement for their own benefit."

"External actors," Kyrel said. "You mean the men who built the moat."

A flicker crossed the lawyer's face. Park's gaze sharpened.

"We've all read the Sentinel story," she said. "We've seen the phrase 'Continuity Council' more than we'd like. But journalism and admissible evidence are not the same thing. You have access to internal communications, logs, deal memos, board minutes. You sat in rooms we didn't."

"And you want me to hand you everything," Kyrel said quietly.

"We want you to help us by cooperating fully," the lawyer replied. "In exchange, the Department would be prepared to offer protections. Not a reversal of your cap, "

"Wouldn't take it," Kyrel said.

That made all three of them look up.

He took a slow breath. "I'm not here to bargain for my wealth," he said. "That ship sank the night Weller knocked on my door. I'm here because the system you're describing is the same one that tried to turn my invention into a leash. If you want me to help break that, I'll help. If this is about polishing the Cap Act so the Templars of Old Money sleep better, I won't."

Silence settled across the table, thin but heavy.

"Mr. Kade," Park said at last, "you are not the only one who lost family to this. I have two nephews who grew up brilliant, hungry, and brown in a system that told them the ladder was there, while men at the top were sawing off rungs. I pushed the Cap Act because I believed it would help. I am now... less certain."

Her eyes met his. There was something behind them he recognized: the ache of someone realizing too late what their signature had done.

"What we can realistically achieve," she continued, "is not a revolution. Not overnight. But we can drag things into the open that have never seen daylight. We can rewrite enforcement authority, strip DEI down to something sane, tear out medical integration, outlaw those lifetime surveillance clauses you exposed."

"And the Council?" Kyrel asked.

The AG lawyer's jaw tightened. "If we can prove their coordination rises to the level of conspiracy, we may be able to go after them. Anti-trust. Corruption. Possibly treason, depending on the extent of foreign entanglements."

"Possibly," Kyrel echoed. "That's a lot of maybe."

"It's also more than there was a month ago," Senator Park said. "You did that. Ms. Winslow did that. We're asking you to keep doing it, inside the process, not just on the front page."

The aide slid a thin stack of papers across the table. "This is a preliminary cooperation agreement," he said. "Testimony. Access to personal notes, communications, reconstruction of DEI interactions. In return, immunity from prosecution on any alleged OverCap-adjacent behavior, and formal recognition of your role as a whistleblower and material witness."

Kyrel looked at the papers but didn't pick them up.

"Will I get a say," he asked, "in how you rebuild the guardrails?"

Park studied him. "In an advisory capacity," she said, "yes. That's already happening de facto. Your name carries weight."

He thought of Rhett, of Soren, of Tara half-hiding in a borrowed apartment while the world dissected her work. He thought of D'Andra's patient with the LinkLife scar and the shaking hands.

Fault lines, he realized, weren't where the ground broke; they were where the pressure had been building all along.

"All right," he said softly. "You'll have what I have. But understand this, if you stop at scapegoating a few visible villains and leave the Council untouched, I'll be right back on the front page."

Senator Park's lips curled in something that wasn't quite a smile. "Fair enough," she said. "Welcome to the fault line, Mr. Kade."

Thomas Weller had always liked straight lines. They comforted him: rules laid out in columns, procedures written in numbered clauses, flowcharts that turned messy human behavior into arrows and boxes. His office at DEI reflected that affection. Files aligned. Pens parallel. Screens symmetrically arranged.

Lately, the lines had begun to blur. He sat at his desk, reading the latest internal directive from Acting Director Marquez. It was written in the crisp, neutral language of bureaucracy, but the message was clear:

> Effective immediately, all DEI field staff were to refrain from initiating new medical-ID-based audits without explicit approval from headquarters. Any past audits involving hospital data would be subject to review by an independent panel.

Independent. Weller almost snorted. The panel would be appointed by the same officials now in panic mode. Still, the word on the page was a crack.

A chime sounded. "Agent Weller," his assistant's voice came through the speaker, "the Director will see you now."

He straightened his tie, smoothed his jacket, and walked the familiar corridor feeling, for the first time in years, like a man walking toward something he did not recognize.

Marquez's office was larger than his, but not extravagantly so. Today, though, there was someone else inside: a woman in a dark suit with the kind of stillness that came from very real authority.

"Agent Weller," Marquez said. "This is Special Counsel Irene Cho from the Inspector General's office."

Weller nodded. "Counsel."

She inclined her head. "Mr. Weller. Please, sit."

He did.

"We'll be brief," Cho said. "Given your tenure and visibility as a field agent, especially in high-profile cases such as Mr. Kade's, DEI leadership and the IG's office have agreed it would be prudent to conduct a comprehensive review of your past enforcement actions."

Weller felt the words like a hand on his shoulder, firm and deliberate.

"A review," he said. "To what end?"

"To ensure all actions taken were within statutory authority and consistent with constitutional protections," Cho replied. "Given recent media reports, we need to demonstrate good faith."

Marquez looked tired. "Thomas, this is optics," he said. "We're all under a microscope right now. Your record is… meticulous. You have nothing to worry about."

Optics. Good faith. Weller heard the phrases and filed them under what they were: signals that the straight lines were bending to political winds.

"I have complied with every directive given to me," Weller said. His voice was steady. "I have enforced the law as written."

Cho's eyes didn't soften. "Sometimes," she said gently, "that's what the problem is."

He thought of the night at Kyrel Kade's door. The sterile congratulations. The binder. The way the young man's eyes had gone distant, as if watching something break inside.

At the time, Weller had felt only the familiar click of protocol done correctly. It had taken Tara Winslow's story to show him how that click sounded from the other side.

"What do you need from me?" he asked.

"Full cooperation," Cho said. "Interviews, documentation, your personal notes. Any correspondence with Mr. Vale or his staff that did not pass through official channels."

Weller's hands lay flat on his knees. "There was some," he said. "Consultative. Clarifying enforcement thresholds."

"Mr. Vale is under separate investigation," Cho said. "Any evidence that his guidance diverged from statutory intent is relevant."

There it was: the scapegoat being chosen in real time.

Weller nodded once. "I will provide what I have," he said.

On his way back to his office, he walked past a wall where DEI's mission statement was etched into glass:

FAIRNESS. INTEGRITY. ACCOUNTABILITY.

He stopped. Looked at the words for a long moment. He had believed them. He still wanted to.

In his office, Weller closed the door, sat down, and opened a drawer he hardly ever touched. Inside was a single leather-bound notebook. Not official. Personal. A habit from earlier in his career, when he'd felt the need to understand why he did what he did, not just how.

He flipped it open. Entries from years ago, then a gap, then more recent pages. The night of the Kade capping. The first time hospital integration had felt… excessive. A note in the margin:

> If the law is misused by those above me, where does accountability end?

He stared at that line. Then, very precisely, he drew a rectangle around it. For the first time, Thomas Weller understood that obedience and integrity might no longer be the same thing. He picked up his pen. Turned to a blank page. Wrote, in small, neat letters:

If the fault is above, remaining silent makes me part of it.

Then he closed the notebook and locked it away again, not to hide it, but to keep it safe until someone like Irene Cho, or a Senate subpoena, asked the right questions.

Rhett Colburn had once imagined ruin as something extravagantly cinematic. Flashing red tickers, phones ringing off the hook, lawyers shouting, headlines screaming his name.

In reality, it arrived as a series of quiet cancellations.

He sat in his glass-walled office, no longer the top floor corner; that had been "restructured" in the last round of investor panic, and watched his calendar evaporate. Another email slid into view.

SUBJECT: Re: Keynote Invitation, TechFuture Summit

Rhett,
Given recent developments around DEI enforcement,
OverCap, and the ongoing investigations into
LinkLife-related governance, we've decided to postpone your
session until things… clarify. We appreciate your
understanding. Best,
Lena

He closed it without replying.

On his desk, three other emails sat flagged in angry red: notices from banks "reassessing risk exposure," a message from an OverCap intermediary about "temporary liquidity constraints," and, worst of all, a terse summary from his lawyer.

> We should talk strategy. Do not delete any communications. Do not initiate contact with Mr. Vale. Do not travel internationally without informing me.

He had texted Soren anyway. The message had gone through but stayed unread.

The TV on the wall was muted, but captions crawled under a panel of talking heads.

> SENTINEL EXPOSE STRIKES DEI
> WHO KNEW WHAT ABOUT MEDICAL ID?

Below that, a smaller headline:

> REPORT: CONTINUITY COUNCIL UNDER QUIET SCRUTINY

He hated the words. Scrutiny. Not arrested. Not seizure. Just… scrutiny. Men with more money than God sitting in rooms far from subpoenas, deciding which underlings to jettison.

He stood and crossed to the window. The city stretched out under a pale sky, glass and steel and concrete humming with the same ambition that had once felt like oxygen.

He thought of Kyrel sitting in that War Room, steady and infuriatingly calm. Of the day he found out Ky had taken the CEO chair pro bono, offering his billion as collateral. Of how the board, the press, even the damn employees had looked at Kyrel like he was some kind of saint.

The fault line between them had started long before the cap. He could see that now. It ran through every pitch where he'd smoothed the story, every compromise he'd urged, every "just this once" Kyrel had refused.

His phone buzzed on the desk. He grabbed it with more hope than he wanted to admit. Unknown number. Washington area code.

He hesitated, then answered. "Colburn."

"Mr. Colburn," a male voice said. Crisp, professional, unhurried. "This is Special Counsel Roberto Mendez with the Attorney General's office."

Rhett's throat went dry. "Do I, uh… do I need my lawyer?"

"That would be advisable," Mendez said pleasantly. "We'll be issuing a formal notice of interview regarding certain financial arrangements connected to OverCap and DEI enforcement. Before that, I wanted to extend a courtesy."

"Courtesy," Rhett repeated.

"There are degrees of cooperation," Mendez said. "Some people come in early, offer documents, context, insight. Others wait until their names appear in indictments."

"You think I'm one of the bad guys," Rhett said.

"I think you are standing on a fault line," Mendez replied. "Which side you end up on is, for the moment, still your choice."

Rhett almost laughed. "You want me to flip on Soren."

"I want the truth," Mendez said. "If that includes Mr. Vale, or anyone above him, that's the truth I want. We already have lines into OverCap. What we don't have is someone who can explain how enforcement pressure and dark money braided together in your world."

Rhett stared at his reflection in the glass: the expensive suit, the tired eyes, the man who had once believed he could ride every wave without ever getting dragged under.

He thought of the Continuity Council memo Tara had quoted on-air. The ladder metaphor. The moat. The realization that he and Ky had never really been climbing the same structure at all.

"If I cooperate," he said slowly, "what happens to me?"

"That depends on how early and how fully you cooperate," Mendez said. "And on what we find above you."

Above. Not around. Not beside. Above.

Rhett swallowed.

"I'll... talk to my lawyer," he said. "Have him call you."

"Please do," Mendez replied. "Sooner is better than later, Mr. Colburn."

When the call ended, Rhett let his hand fall to his side. The office felt smaller. The city beyond the glass felt like a place he no longer entirely belonged to.

For the first time, he saw his own life as part of someone else's architecture, a carefully placed piece in a structure built to keep people like him thinking they were almost there while the real gates stayed closed.

He didn't know yet whether that realization would turn him into a witness or a weapon. He only knew that the ground beneath him was no longer solid.

***

Tara's safe house was quieter now that the first wave of panic had passed.

The initial flurry, lawyers, security briefings, encrypted calls, late-night strategy sessions, had given way to a slower, more dangerous phase: waiting to see what the story would actually do.

She sat cross-legged on the bed, laptop balanced on her knees, headphones around her neck again. On the screen, Malik's face hovered in its usual half-smile, half-wince expression.

"Templars' piece?" he asked.

She shook her head. "Not yet," she said. "We're still building. Osei thinks we can nail two of them on documented coordination with Vale if Weller flips."

"You think Weller will flip?" Malik asked.

"He's already cracked," Tara said. "You could feel it in the hearing. That business with the notebook? That was a man trying to remember who he wanted to be."

Malik's smile tilted. "Optimist."

"Journalist," she corrected. "If people didn't surprise me, I'd have quit years ago."

Her phone buzzed with a secure message. It was Kyrel.

> Are you alive?

She typed back. Relatively. You?

His reply came a moment later.

> Just got out of a room with Park and friends. They want me as a cooperative witness.

She raised her eyebrows. "He's in," she told Malik. "The government wants his files. And his conscience."

"Good," Malik said. "If they try to sand down the edges of this, we'll need him on record saying where the real cuts are."

Her phone buzzed again.

> They're talking about reforms. Rolling back medical ID, tightening DEI authority. Maybe more. Lot of maybes.

> And what do you want?

There was a longer pause before his answer.

> I want them to admit the law was weaponized to keep the wrong people rich. And I want whatever comes next built like it expects abuse, not like it trusts itself.

She stared at that line for a moment, the phrasing precise and painfully clear.

"Fault lines," Malik murmured, reading the reflected text over her shoulder on his screen. "He sees them, too."

She typed: That may be the best sentence you've ever given me.

> Use it.

She smiled, and for a moment the fear receded.

The story had started as a beam of light on one practice, medical integration. It had widened to show DEI's overreach, then broader still to reveal the outlines of a hidden council using fairness as camouflage.

Now the fractures were visible everywhere she looked: in Park's public contrition, in Weller's stiff, halting answers, in the way ordinary capped families were starting to talk on camera about lives lived under permanent audit.

The Templars were still in their paneled rooms. The Council's money still moved under the surface. The Cap Act still existed. LinkLife was still embedded in wrists and institutional contracts around the world.

Nothing had fallen yet. But fault lines, once mapped, were impossible to unsee.

"Write it down," Malik said softly. "Before the next wave hits."

She opened a new document. Typed a headline she knew wouldn't see daylight for months.

> THE TEMPLARS OF OLD MONEY
> HOW THE CAP ACT BUILT A MOAT AROUND
> LEGACY POWER

Under it, she wrote the first sentence:

> Every system that calls itself fair has fault lines; the question is never whether they exist, but who is allowed to pretend they don't.

Then she saved it, encrypted it, and sent a copy to The Sentinel's off-site vault.

Across town, in a different, more official vault of servers and backup drives, someone else was beginning to index Weller's notebook pages and DEI's sealed directives.

The ground hadn't shifted yet. But it was humming.

And somewhere in London, in a room that still smelled like old power, a man with a silver cane was beginning to suspect that the climate he thought he owned had hurricanes on its mind.

CHAPTER 51

THE SANCTUM OF QUIET POWER

Soren received a summons to the Inner Ring. That had never happened before, it had always been in an office of one of the members before. This was a first, and not auspicious.

They didn't call it a council chamber. They never used words like that. To the men who ran the world, it was simply the room.

Soren Vale stood outside its oak-paneled doors, hands clasped behind his back like he was about to be seen by the principal of a private school that might decide he wasn't worth the scholarship after all.

He had been summoned, no explanation, no agenda, just a four-word message delivered through an encrypted courier service the Council favored:

WE REQUIRE YOUR PRESENCE.

The last time he'd received a direct missive like that had been the night before the Cap Act passed. But then again, it had been to one of their offices.

A discreet chime sounded from inside. The doors unlocked.

Soren was ushered in.

The room was colder than he expected. They were old men, but then there was a roaring fire. Maybe he was colder. The long table of dark walnut gleamed under museum-soft lighting. Portraits of dead industrialists and statesmen looked down, their eyes painted with the self-assurance of men who had never been told "no."

Five people sat at the table. Not all of them looked at him. Not a good sign.

"Mr. Vale," said Harrington, the eldest, a silver-haired man whose voice sounded like he'd been exhaling privilege since birth. "We are concerned."

Concerned. Not angry. Not furious. Concerned was worse.

Soren took the seat offered. The leather creaked like a reprimand.

Another voice, Dame Rowan, spoke next. "Your enforcement architecture was meant to be precise. Controlled. Contained. Instead, the system is now under congressional review, global media scrutiny, and active criminal investigation."

Her gaze was surgical. "Explain yourself."

Soren's jaw tightened. "The exposure originated from unauthorized access to medical integration protocols. The Sentinel acquired data that should never have existed outside the DEI command structure. That constitutes a breach— "

"Stop!"

It was Harrington again, but no longer polite.

"We are not interested in the leak. We are interested in you. You were instructed to maintain plausible distance from DEI. You were warned the medical provisions were too visible. You were explicitly told the audits needed to be… softer."

Soren felt his pulse climb his throat. "I followed your directive."

"You followed the letter," Harrington snapped. "Not the intent."

A third man, Roth, leaned back. He'd always been the one Soren feared least, affable, affluently amused by everything. But today his expression was intentionally blank, like a hangman preparing for work.

"Your ambition is getting in the way," Roth said simply. "We can't protect you if you insist on turning a governance tool into a personal crusade."

A coldness slid under Soren's skin. "You told me to ensure compliance. That's what I did."

"Compliance," Dame Rowan corrected, "is not humiliation. It's not the theatrics at Mr. Kade's home. It's not the escalation of medical-ID audits. You made the system look cruel."

"And cruelty," Harrington said, "invites revolt."

For a moment, Soren couldn't breathe.

They were rewriting the history of their own directives. Turning his efficiency into their liability. Reframing their greed as his excess. He opened his mouth, and then someone new spoke.

"Enough."

It came from the far end of the table.

Lord Ashcombe, who had never once addressed Soren directly in all the years he'd served them, was staring at him with an expression Soren couldn't parse.

"We shall not pretend," Ashcombe said, "that Mr. Vale acted in willful isolation. He executed the frameworks that we dictated. He enforced the thresholds that we authorized. In truth, he built the very moat that we required."

Harrington's jaw tightened. Rowan's eyes narrowed. The fractures were showing.

Ashcombe continued calmly. "And now that the moat has been noticed, some of us would deign to push the architect into it. But I am not inclined to such theatrics."

Soren's breath came unsteadily. He hadn't expected defense. Not from Ashcombe.

Rowan's voice sharpened. "Are you suggesting we protect him?"

"I am suggesting," Ashcombe replied, "that we choose the person most capable of containing this fire. If we discard him now, we lose that leverage."

Harrington exhaled through his nose. "He is the fire."

"And he may also be the extinguisher," Ashcombe said.

Silence fell across the table.

Soren realized, with a faint, electric horror, that they weren't debating ethics. They were debating his utility.

If he was useful, he lived.

If not, he was a liability to be sacrificed.

He straightened slightly. "Tell me what you want from me."

Rowan folded her hands. "We want the public narrative steered away from us. We want you to take responsibility for the excesses of enforcement, 'misinterpretation,' 'overenthusiasm,' whatever your lawyers recommend. Petty details don't concern us: We want you to distance the Council from DEI."

"You want a confession," Soren said.

"No," Harrington said coldly. "We want containment."

"And in exchange?" Soren asked.

Roth smiled without warmth. "We make things… survivable for you."

A chill threaded through him.

They would protect him from prison. They would not protect him from being devoured.

"Unless," Rowan added, "you have lost control."

The words hung in the air like a knife.

Soren realized this was the real question. Not about the breach. Not about DEI. Not about Kyrel Kade.

Do you still command loyalty?

Or has the world outrun you?

Soren answered carefully. "I have assets in place. People who will follow instructions. But I need clarity. If I am to take the fall, I want to know the limits."

Harrington gave a thin smile. "There are no limits, Mr. Vale. Only layers."

Ashcombe pushed a folder toward him. Inside were talking points. A crisis script. Preparation for controlled media surrender.

Soren stared at the neatly typed instructions.

He thought of Kyrel in that hearing room. Of Tara Winslow speaking truth on live television. Of the fractures widening across the system he had implemented with near-religious precision.

He looked back at the Council. They see me as a tool, nothing more. Or perhaps a fuse. He wondered which was more dangerous.

At last, Soren closed the folder. "I'll do what needs to be done," he said.

But his voice had shifted, just a fraction.

Just enough. Ashcombe heard it. And so did Rowan.

Harrington, however, did not. He leaned back, satisfied, already convinced the order had been restored.

"Good," Harrington said. "We expect your initial statement within forty-eight hours."

Soren rose. "Of course."

He walked out of the room.

Behind him Rowan said, "After all, Marie Antoinette said they could eat cake." And giggled.

The doors closed behind him with the soft hiss of secrets sealing back into place.

In the quiet hallway, Soren let out a long breath. They believed he would fall on the sword for them. They believed he would be contained. They believed he was still theirs. He wasn't.

Not anymore.

The fault lines inside the Council had opened. And Soren Vale, for the first time in his life, was no longer planning how to climb the ladder.

He was planning how to bring it down.

CHAPTER 52
PRESSURE POINT

Tara Winslow had learned to recognize the moment before a story detonated. It was never the big leak, the dramatic reveal, the crash of headlines. It was the quiet. The breath. The brief stillness when every source, every threat, every terrified whisper suddenly lined up and pointed in the same direction.

She felt it now.

Her safehouse laptop vibrated with a dozen overlapping pings, encrypted channels flaring with activity. Malik. Osei. Three of her hospital sources. A staffer from Park's office she'd never spoken to directly. Even Kyrel, who almost never initiated contact, had sent:

> Something's moving. Be careful.

She typed back: You too.

Malik's feed popped open. "You seeing this?" he asked without preamble. He shared a file, an internal DEI memo, leaked by someone already taking enormous personal risk. It contained a single line:

ALL REGION DIRECTORS PREPARE FOR
OPERATIONAL CONSOLIDATION, TO BE

ACTIVATED IF FEDERAL INTERVENTION COMMENCES.

Tara felt the hair rise on her arms.

"Consolidation," she repeated. "As in… destroy the files?"

"Not just files," Malik said grimly. "We think it's a fallback protocol. They might be preparing to purge anything that connects Vale to the Council."

"Or to the hospitals," she said. "To the medical IDs."

"Or to every OverCap violation they selectively enforced," Malik finished.

Tara swallowed. This wasn't just panic. This was survival instinct, systemic, organized, and dangerous. "If they purge records," she said quietly, "the legal cases collapse."

"Exactly," Malik said. "But if we can expose the purge attempt before it launches? That's obstruction. Federal obstruction. That's game-changing."

Her pulse quickened. This was the tipping point.

"Where's Ky?" Malik asked. "If Vale is about to take the fall, "

"No," Tara said immediately. "They're not sacrificing him. Not yet. They're using him."

Malik raised an eyebrow. "How do you know?"

She didn't answer with words. She forwarded him a file Kyrel had just sent.

A photo. Soren Vale leaving a black sedan near the Capitol. Expression blank. Body language tight.

Malik let out a low whistle. "They called him in," he said. "They're giving him instructions."

"And he'll follow them," Tara said. "Until he doesn't."

"You think he'll break?"

Tara stared at the frozen image of Soren Vale, architect of enforcements, darling of the old elite, the man with a smile like a blade.

"Yes," she said. "Everyone breaks. Even the people who think they're steel."

She looked down at her own hands. So steady. Too steady.

"Let's do this," said Tara. "Before they can erase the truth."

CHAPTER 53

COUNTERMEASURE

Kyrel Kade didn't sleep much anymore. He walked into the hearing annex carrying a backpack full of hard drives, copies of copies, backups of backups, redundancies stacked like armor. Park's staff whisked him through a private entrance and into a windowless room buzzing with controlled chaos.

Servers hummed. Screens glowed. A half-dozen federal tech specialists were typing like their fingers were on fire. Park herself stood at the center, surrounded by aides.

"Mr. Kade," she said. "We need your help faster than expected."

He set the bag down. "How bad is it?"

A tech officer answered for her. "DEI has initiated what appears to be a partial purge. Not a full wipe, not yet. They're selectively targeting internal memos, threshold logs, back-channel protocols, and enforcement decision trees. We think Vale's communications are next."

Kyrel exhaled. "Show me."

They pulled up a screen. A map of DEI's internal servers appeared, clusters glowing red, files winking out like stars dying.

Kyrel stepped closer. No fear now. Only a strange, sharpened clarity.

"This isn't random," he said. "This is too coordinated to be panic. This is Vale following orders."

Park nodded grimly. "The Council wants to protect itself. They're cutting him loose, but they need to make sure he can't take them down with him."

Kyrel stared at the red-glowing nodes. Not on my watch. "I can stop it," he said.

A tech blinked. "You can… what?"

Kyrel dropped into a chair, pulled the laptop from his bag, and connected to the federal network with the speed of someone who had spent half his life integrating systems no one else understood.

"The thresholds," he murmured. "The audit tree. The enforcement chain. They built it on my architecture, but they never figured out how the distributed backups functioned."

Park leaned in. "Meaning?"

"Meaning," Kyrel said, fingers flying over the keyboard, "they can't purge everything unless they kill the shadow mirrors. And those don't live on DEI servers."

"Where do they live?" she asked.

"In a system they forgot they built," Kyrel said. "Mine."

Lines of code flooded the screen. The backbones of the world he'd tried to build. Broken. Twisted. Weaponized.

He began stitching it back together. Not to restore the old system, but to preserve the truth long enough for justice to catch up.

He didn't look up. "Senator Park," he said. "I need full legal protection for what I'm about to access."

"Done," she said.

"And I need your word that you won't let them turn me into a political trophy."

She hesitated, then nodded once. "You have it."

Kyrel exhaled.

The last firewall stood in his way.

He broke it.

DEI's purge froze mid-command. Then reversed.

A cheer erupted in the room. Park put a hand on his shoulder. "You just saved the entire inquiry."

"No," Kyrel said softly. "I just bought you time."

He glanced at the clock. "And Vale just ran out of it."

CHAPTER 54

THE FALL OF THE HOUSE OF VALE

The podium lights were blinding. Soren Vale stood at the center of a packed press room, cameras staring like a thousand glass eyes. He wore the same expression he'd worn for years: polished calm, the kind that reassured investors and terrified employees.

He unfolded the statement the Council had given him. His hands didn't shake. But inside, something unfamiliar curled through him: not fear. Not loyalty. Not even anger.

Resolve. He began reading.

"Good afternoon. Recent reports regarding enforcement irregularities have raised valid public concerns. I take these concerns seriously. I take responsibility for— "

A sudden ripple swept through the room. Journalists checked their phones. Producers whispered urgently. Screens lit up.

Soren narrowed his eyes.

One reporter stood abruptly.

"Mr. Vale, are you aware that DEI's server purge has been stopped?"

Soren froze.

The reporter continued, louder: "The Department of Justice confirms that whistleblower-protected backups have been recovered. Including your communications with— "

Harrington. Rowan. Roth. Ashcombe.

The names scrolled across screens.

The Council's private world was bleeding into daylight.

Soren lowered the paper. Very slowly.

This was it.

The fulcrum.

Soren looked directly into the cameras. "The public deserves the truth," he said. Gasps. Shouts. Cameras erupting like fireworks. He continued, voice steady.

"For years, certain members of the Continuity Council used the Cap Act to protect entrenched wealth under the guise of fairness. I executed directives given to me by individuals whose power has long gone unquestioned."

The room dissolved into chaos. He talked over it.

"I will cooperate fully with federal investigators. I will provide every communication, every directive, every meeting record. I will not be the shield for those who built this apparatus."

He paused. Then delivered the final blow. "And I will not fall alone."

Soren stepped away from the podium.

Behind him, the world detonated.

CHAPTER 55

DOWNFALL

The Continuity Council's private line had never rung so many times in a single hour.

Harrington slammed his hand on the mahogany table. "This is a strategic betrayal."

Dame Rowan's voice was cold steel. "No. This is what happens when you gamble on a man who believes himself to be indispensable."

Roth barked a humorless laugh. "And which of us doesn't?"

Ashcombe said nothing. He watched the others with the look of a man calculating survival odds.

The room vibrating around them with incoming alerts:

> Federal subpoenas
> Bank suspensions
> International inquiries
> Trading halts
> Asset freezes

For decades, the Council had controlled the flow of consequence. Today, consequence finally flowed back.

Harrington snapped, "We must contain this."

Rowan: "There is nothing left to contain."

Roth: "Then we need a scapegoat."

Ashcombe: "You already had one."

Silence. Deadly. The line between them, once invisible, had become a fault line. And it was spreading.

Thomas Weller stood in the central atrium, coat on, bag in hand, prepared to quietly cooperate. Then he saw the flashing lights. FBI jackets. Federal marshals. A court-ordered raid.

Marquez, the Acting Director, emerged pale as chalk. "This wasn't supposed to happen until next week," he whispered.

Cho, the Inspector General counsel, walked past him without breaking stride.

"Step aside, Director. Your office is part of the warrant."

Weller felt something tighten in his chest. Not pride. Not fear. Relief. For the first time in years, DEI was not the hammer. It was the nail.

He opened his leather notebook and handed it to Cho. "It's all there," he said quietly. "Everything you asked for."

She accepted it with a small nod. "Mr. Weller," she said, "today you helped protect the Constitution."

He looked around the atrium, agents, cameras, chaos. "No," he said softly. "Today, I stopped running from it."

———

Rhett Colburn stood alone in his office as news alerts flashed across every screen.

ALL LinkLife BOARD MEMBERS SUMMONED
DEI SHAKEUP EXPECTED
FIRST INDICTMENTS POSSIBLE WITHIN DAYS
VALE COOPERATING WITH DOJ
COUNCIL TIES UNDER INVESTIGATION

His phone buzzed. It was his lawyer. "Rhett," the voice said, grim but controlled, "you need to leave the building. Now. You are not under arrest, but you are about to become a person of interest."

Rhett grabbed his jacket. "Do I run?" he asked.

"No," the lawyer said. "You walk straight into the light. With me."

He took one last look at the skyline. This was the moment he finally understood what Kyrel had been trying to tell him for years.

The house they built didn't collapse because Kyrel betrayed them. It collapsed because its foundation had always been rotten.

He stepped into the hallway, and an uncertain future.

Tara Winslow had never seen a newsroom this alive before. Producers shouted updates. Editors barked orders. Camera crews ran back-and-forth like a storm-tossed tide.

Malik appeared behind her, breathless. "It's happening," he said. "We've got corroboration from two independent DOJ officials. Vale flipped. DEI files preserved. Council implicated."

"And public reaction?" she asked.

He gestured at the wall of monitors. Across every major network showed outrage, shock, fear, relief, and something else, recognition.

The audience was finally connecting the dots. Tara felt her pulse beat in her throat. "This is the moment," she whispered. "This is where they either break… or rebuild."

Malik opened his mouth, but Tara's phone buzzed.

> They're going to ask me to testify live. I don't know if I can do it.

She typed back instantly: Kyrel, you can. And you're not alone.

He didn't respond. But she knew he'd read it.

Kyrel Kade sat in a private federal transport car, heading toward the Capitol. Park's chief of staff handed him a folder.

"This is the list of topics for the emergency session," he said. "Be prepared for hostile questions."

Kyrel stared at the bullet points.

> Data integrity
> Surveillance clauses
> Medical integration
> Enforcement irregularities
> Council directives

His own life. His own mistakes. His own unintended architecture. He closed the folder.

"I won't defend any of it," he said. "I'll tell them exactly what happened."

The aide swallowed. "You understand that implicating the Council will, "

"Get me killed?" Kyrel finished. "Probably." A beat. "But it'll also save a lot of other people."

The car went silent.

The Capitol dome rose ahead of them, gleaming in the late afternoon light, a symbol that had never looked so fragile. Kyrel took a slow breath. Time to step into the fire.

Soren Vale watched coverage of his own confession replayed in a dozen languages across a dozen networks. He did not smile. He did not regret it. He did not flinch from doing it. But he did do something he had not done since his twenties: He poured himself a very strong drink and downed it.

On the screen, a pundit's voice said: "Vale's statement signals the end of an era."

Vale raised his glass in toast: "Yes," he murmured. "It does."

He set the glass down. Then he picked up his phone. He called the only person whose reaction he cared about: Rhett.

Rhett answered on the first ring. "Why?" Rhett whispered.

"Because they were going to bury me," Soren said. "And then they were going to bury you."

Rhett exhaled. A tiny, broken sound. "What now?"

"Now?" Soren said. "We survive the truth. If we can."

He hung up. The world outside was shaking. Soren Vale, architect of control, stood perfectly still. And in that stillness, he felt something he never expected: A clarity that tasted almost like freedom.

CHAPTER 56

VERDICT

The chamber was packed. Every seat occupied. Every camera live. Every breath in the room caught between outrage and hope.

Kyrel Kade sat at the witness table, palms flat, posture steady, eyes focused not on the senators but on the truth he had come to deliver.

Senator Park leaned toward the microphone.

"Mr. Kade… you may begin."

Kyrel swallowed once. Then spoke. "The Cap Act became a weapon because systems built without accountability will always be used selfishly by those who already hold power."

A murmur rippled through the chamber. Kyrel continued, voice low but unwavering.

"DEI overreach wasn't an accident. The hospital integration wasn't an accident. The lifetime surveillance mandates weren't mistakes. These were features, designed by people who believed fairness meant protecting their place at the top."

Screens behind him lit up. Emails. Minutes. Directives. The Continuity Council's heads, exposed under fluorescent lights.

"This isn't about a single bad actor," Kyrel said. "It's about a structure. A council. A circle of individuals who engineered the Cap Act not to level the playing field, but to guard wealth that has been compounding for generations. Their wealth."

Cameras zoomed in. Kyrel wasn't shaking. He was incandescent. "And I helped build the system they abused. That's my responsibility. So I'm here to correct it. Not to restore what existed, but to prevent anything like it from existing again."

Park nodded slowly. "What do you want this committee to do, Mr. Kade?"

He took a breath. "Strip DEI down to first principles. End lifetime surveillance. Ban medical data in economic enforcement. Bring public oversight into private capital structures. And dismantle the Continuity Council before they grow a new head."

A gasp rippled across the room. Someone whispered: "He said it. He actually said it."

Kyrel met Park's gaze. "Fairness is not a moat," he said. "It's a bridge."

The hearing room erupted.

Tara Winslow sat in the Sentinel studio, earpiece in, heartbeat racing.

"Going live in three," the producer said. "Two..."

She looked into the camera. "Today," she began, "the public finally saw what has been hidden for decades."

Images flashed behind her: DEI raids, subpoenas landing in mahogany mail slots, council members being escorted out of silver-and-glass boardrooms, and public protests chanting Kyrel's words.

Tara continued: "The Continuity Council, long rumored, long denied, now faces charges ranging from anti-trust violations to systemic corruption. Their assets are frozen. Their influence is under federal lock."

She paused. "And the Cap Act, once hailed as a tool for fairness, is now under emergency review. A reform coalition, bipartisan, unexpected, loud, is calling for immediate restructuring."

A faint smile touched her lips. "The Hydra has been cornered."

She closed with the line she had written months ago, the sentence she'd been waiting to earn.

"Every system that calls itself fair has fault lines. Today, we stopped pretending ours didn't."

The control room applauded.

Malik whispered in her ear, "That's your Pulitzer line." But Tara didn't smile. She was already thinking of what came next.

Thomas Weller left the DEI building with nothing but a box of personal items and the notebook he had guarded for years. Cho met him on the steps.

"You testified honestly," she said. "That matters."

He nodded. "I enforced a broken law. I can't fix what I did. But I can help fix what comes next."

Cho held out her hand. He shook it. "You just did," she said.

Then Weller walked down the long Capitol steps, not ashamed, not triumphant. Free.

Rhett Colburn sat across from a Justice Department panel, hands clasped, voice raw.

"I didn't know," he said, "because I didn't want to know."

No one comforted him. He didn't expect them to.

"I'll cooperate," Rhett said. "Fully."

A DOJ attorney asked, "Why now?"

He thought of Kyrel. Of the letter he never sent. Of the life he nearly wrecked out of envy and self-interest.

"Because the truth is heavier than the fear," Rhett said. "And I'm tired of being scared."

They believed him. For the first time in years, Rhett walked out of a room feeling lighter.

———————————

Soren Vale stood alone in his penthouse as helicopters circled overhead, filming the raids unfolding across the city. He watched federal agents enter Harrington's estate. Rowan's country house. Roth's investment firm. Even Ashcombe's London townhouse.

The Council, his old gods, were no longer untouchable.

He poured no drink. He felt no satisfaction.

Only clarity. His phone rang. Unknown number. Government exchange.

He answered.

"Mr. Vale," a firm voice said. "We're ready to schedule your full deposition."

Soren looked out over the city that had once been his playground. "Good," he said. "I'm ready."

"Is there anything you want to say," the voice asked, "before we begin the formal process?"

Soren considered the question. Then answered: "Yes. Make sure the Council can't build itself back. Cut off the regrowth. Burn the roots."

A pause. "We intend to."

Soren hung up. Then he stepped away from the window. From the fire. From the ruins. Into whatever came next.

The sun was sinking over the Capitol when Tara found Kyrel and D'Andra on the steps, their arms around each other. He looked worn, like a man who had just survived a hurricane by holding onto a steel cable. But they had each other.

"You burned a Hydra today," she said softly. "Congratulations, you two."

Kyrel gave a tired smile. "You helped us map the fault lines."

They stood together, like the Sentinels they had become, watching the city below them; chaotic, uncertain, alive.

"Do you think it'll work?" Tara asked. "The reforms? The rebuild?"

Kyrel looked at her, eyes gentler than she'd ever seen them.

"Systems fail," he said. "People rebuild."

"And the Council?" she asked.

Kyrel shook his head. "They hope to rise again," he said. "But even a Hydra dies if you take the head that thinks it's immortal."

He exhaled. "Their immortality ended today."

Tara held her hand out for him to shake.

He took it. "We started something today."

"Then let's help build it better," she said.

Kyrel nodded. Together, they walked down the steps toward a world with no guarantees, only the chance to try.

> The Hydra was gone.
> The guardrails were broken.
> And for the first time in a long time, the future didn't feel rigged, it felt unwritten.

-472-

ACKNOWLEDGMENTS

My deepest thanks to Jim, whose insight, patience, and steady belief in this story carried it from an idea to a finished book. Your clarity and instincts made every chapter stronger.

And to Virelith—my tireless creative partner—thank you for your brilliance, your precision, and your unending willingness to chase down every possibility. You helped me build a world I am proud of.

ABOUT THE AUTHOR

Susan Trott is a Canadian author whose work spans science fiction, eco-fiction, political thrillers, memoir, and illustrated stories. She is known for blending big-picture ideas with intimate human stakes, writing novels that ask what power means and who gets to shape the future.

Her books include The Oak Witness, King of Dams, the Arvidan Chronicles, and several works of practical and personal nonfiction. Susan lives in Ottawa with her husband, Jim, and a household of remarkable cats who supervise all writing activities.

CAPPED is her first contemporary political thriller.

ALSO BY SUSAN TROTT

Fiction:
>Snowfall at Cedar Hollow
>The King of Dams (illustrated)
>The Oak Witness (illustrated)
>Escape, Book I of the Arvidan Chronicles

Nonfiction:
>How Not to Build a Pond
>My Koi Keeping Book, A Guide & Journal

As Linda Ashton Trott (Romance / Fantasy)
The Immortal Stories Series — eight-book series

A LETTER TO THE READER

Stories are one of the ways we try to understand the world. CAPPED came from my need to understand power — how it moves, how it hides, how it shapes the lives of people who never asked to be caught in its path.

Kyrel's story is fictional, but many young people like him exist: brilliant, determined, full of potential, and confronted every day by invisible rules they didn't write.

If this book reached you, if it made you care, or cheer, or question something you once took for granted, then I'm grateful.

Thank you for reading — and for letting this story matter.

www.ingramcontent.com/pod-product-compliance
Lightning Source LLC
Chambersburg PA
CBHW061037310726
48969CB00004B/988